Jubilate

'I was amazed at how emotional this book is … The shrine, the landscape, the trinket shops, the vile hostels and the pilgrims themselves are all meticulously – and mercilessly – observed. What makes the book so poignant, and so urgent, is that the ethics of choice, and how we care for one another, are made to matter, not just to the characters but also to the readers'

Patricia Duncker, *Literary Review*

'*Jubilate* demonstrates once again Arditti's considerable strengths. Set against the backdrop of the French shrine of Lourdes (it is hard to think of another novelist who might consider the place worthy of attention), it is about an unexpected, unsought-after, almost fated love affair between Gillian, a dutiful Catholic wife approaching middle age, as she accompanies her brain-damaged husband, Richard on a pilgrimage, and Vincent, a lapsed Catholic documentary film-maker, whose avowed intent is to explode the myth that this is a place of miracle cures. They are an unlikely couple, but Arditti's tale of their falling in love is beautifully told'

Peter Stanford, *Guardian*

'An exhilarating read, reminding us how much in real life we glean from shreds and patches as well as from moments of sudden revelation. Arditti poses leading questions about God, religion and moral values. At the same time, a wonderful humour sparkles from these pages like sunlight on water'

James Roose-Evans, *Ham & High*

'Re-evaluating notions of love, health, sacrifice and modern-day miracles. You'll laugh, you'll cry, you'll think'

Easy Living

'Skippering love boats through religious waters is an Arditti speciality. His moral clear-sightedness through such turbulence is a rare find. With compassion as a compass, Arditti shows how two vulnerable people can help each other move on from difficult pasts … As a writer, Arditti excels in exposing the frailty in us all'

Laura Silverman, *Daily Mail*

'A hint of Greene in the way faith provides both alibi and motive threads through an unlikely love story set against a recreation of a place that is half Disneyland and half genuinely mysterious'

Charlotte Vowden, *Daily Express*

'Arditti is one of the few novelists to write about religion as if it mattered. The consciences of the characters are as carefully described as their hormonal surges. A sublime (literally) romance, beautifully told'

Kate Saunders, *Saga*

'Arditti compresses a great deal of humour, argument, sympathy and insight into his five-day storyline, elegantly structuring his book so that the reader moves backwards and forwards in time, learning about the relationship from different angles and different perspectives. Like all good novels, this one does not preach; it shows, with perception and finesse, the crooked timber of human love and the hope and healing that (might) flow from it; sadness and jubilation in equal measure'

Charlie Hegarty, *Catholic Herald*

'Few contemporary novelists are able to engage with both a secular and a religious view of the world in such a way as to feel the pull of both. Michael Arditti is someone who does this, and the theme of his fine new novel is ideally suited to his gifts … Another of Michael Arditti's gifts is to combine high seriousness with laughter and occasional comic absurdity, and again he does this to great effect in *Jubilate*'

Richard Harries, former Bishop of Oxford, *Church Times*

'*Jubilate* is a passionate, provocative account of an affair between the wife of a brain-damaged man and a documentary film-maker that challenges accepted notions of duty and sacrifice'

Will Davis, *Attitude*

'Michael Arditti has continually proved his versatility with settings as diverse as prisons, seminaries, film-sets and a refugee cruise ship. The extent of his research is subtly evident in every sentence. His humour ranges from deep-bellied out-loud fun to the kind of laughter one can't help expelling at a funeral. Closing this novel after reading the last page, one briefly believes in miracles, at least of the human redemptive kind'

Rivka Isaacson, *Independent on Sunday*

'The relationship between Gillian and Vincent is the touchstone of the book. Their courtship is set against the backdrop of the other pilgrims. Arditti paints this in wonderfully. He also manages to inject a large dose of humour'

Philip Womack, *Daily Telegraph*

'A company of characters as varied as Chaucer's pilgrims. It is heartbreaking, often funny, certainly unlike any other love story'

Ruth Gorb, *Camden New Journal*

'A rich, stimulating and involving novel. Arditti displays an admirable lightness of touch'

Stephanie Cross, *The Lady*

'*Jubilate* is a wily and accomplished novel that explores the contested ground between human and divine love. Arditti expertly switches the narrative voice between Gillian and Vincent, shuffles the time lines backwards and forwards, and proffers and withholds just enough information to move the story along, while keeping the reader's tongue wagging'

Brendan Walsh, *The Tablet*

'It is a brave writer who starts a novel with an X-rated scene in Lourdes. But Arditti has never lacked the courage of his convictions. *Jubilate* is a typically intelligent piece, examining the moral implications of a love affair between an agnostic investigative journalist and a devout Catholic woman with a disabled husband. Arditti addresses serious moral questions in a frank way'

Max Davidson, *Mail on Sunday*

'*Jubilate* is as uplifting a novel as its name hints at. Aside from the deeply complex love story and the religious overtones, there are some hilarious sections … Full of dark humour and deeply believable reactions in the strangest of situations, if anything, *Jubilate* reminds one of how the strength of the human spirit can sometimes win through'

Shelley Marsden, *Irish World*

'Will faith survive? Will it find new believers? Are miracles possible? These are just some of the issues raised by Arditti. A page-turner, *Jubilate* challenges concepts of disability and health, duty and sacrifice and the nature of miracles'

Emmanuel Cooper, *Tribune*

'A wonderful exploration of love, loss, faith and the many forms it can take … one of those beautifully written stories that takes you deep inside a character – it reminded me of *The End of the Affair*'

Nick Ahad, *Yorkshire Post*

MICHAEL ARDITTI

Jubilate

ARCADIA BOOKS

Arcadia Books Ltd

www.arcadiabooks.co.uk

First published by Arcadia Books 2011

This B format edition published 2012

A catalogue record for this book is available from the British Library.

ISBN 978-1-908129-40-6

Typeset in Minion by MacGuru Ltd
Printed and bound in Great Britain by the CPI Group (UK) Ltd, Croydon, CRO 4YY

Arcadia Books gratefully acknowledges the financial support of Arts Council England.

Arcadia Books supports English PEN, the fellowship of writers who work together to promote literature and its understanding. English PEN upholds writers' freedoms in Britain and around the world, challenging political and cultural limits on free expression. To find out more, visit www.englishpen.org or contact English PEN, 6–8 Amwell Street, London EC1R 1UQ

Arcadia Books distributors are as follows:

in the UK and elsewhere in Europe:
Macmillan
Brunel Road
Houndmills
Basingstoke
Hants RG21 6XS

in the US and Canada:
Dufour Editions
PO Box 7
Chester Springs
PA, 19425

in Australia/New Zealand:
The GHR Press
PO Box 7109
McMahons Point
Sydney 2060

in South Africa:
Jacana Media (Pty) Ltd
PO Box 291784
Melville 2109
Johannesburg

Arcadia Books is the *Sunday Times* Small Publisher of the Year

For Cassandra Jardine

'*The conflict of faith and scepticism remains the proper, the only, the deepest theme of the history of the world and mankind to which all others are subordinate.*'

Johan Wolfgang von Goethe

'*He carried out the gestures and by doing this he found faith.*'

Blaise Pascal

'*To Conscience first, and to the Pope afterwards.*'

Cardinal Newman

'*Love is lovelier the second time around.*'

Sammy Cahn

GILLIAN

Friday June 20

It's his breath that wakes me. Hot, heavy breath on the nape of my neck. Breath that for a moment I mistake for his kiss. The breath of a man sated with passion: the breath of a man sated with me. I turn my face towards his, drinking in the sweetness of his breath. Even the faint fumes of alcohol exude no hint of decay. They are as fresh as the wine at Cana.

I slip my hands behind my back to prevent their straying. Like the mother of a newborn child, I long to run my fingers all over his skin, exulting in his sheer existence. Like a girl with her first love, I long to arouse him with a single touch, marvelling at his maleness. But most of all I long to preserve the moment, extending it beyond the clock, fixing him forever in a world where only I know that he is alive, one where he is alive only for me.

The basilica bells ring out to thwart me. The jangling melody of the Ave Maria that reminds me of the purpose of my visit is followed by seven stark chimes that warn me I have lingered in bed too long. My mutinous mind replays the chimes as six and I sink back on the pillow, but a casual glance at my watch robs me of hope. It is seven o'clock and all over town bleary-eyed young men and women will be making their way to the Acceuil. Young men and women, harried by hormones, will be setting about their duties, while I, twenty years their senior, seek any excuse to shirk mine. I am ashamed.

Would anyone miss me if I went away, took a gap year at the age of thirty-nine, a career break from a life of leisure? I except Richard; I always except Richard. I see him now, waking up at the Acceuil, confused by the emptiness in the second bed, searching for the mother who was once his wife. I see a pair of young men holding him under the shower and pray that he does nothing to offend them (I have discovered the modesty of schoolboys twenty years too late). I see them leading him to the basin and handing him a toothbrush. 'But why do I have to clean my teeth,' he asks, 'when I've not eaten anything since bedtime?' Will they come up with a credible answer or will they take his point, a point that gains force as I lower my head towards Vincent's? I pull away. What if Richard has been awake all night, plagued by the phantoms in his blood-damaged brain? What if the nurses ignored the notes and halved the double dose of pills that he is prescribed in an emergency. And this was an emergency. Oh God, are there no depths to which I will not sink?

Vincent scratches his chest. I revel in my privileged perspective. There is none of the awkwardness that I feel with Richard, whose every involuntary movement is directed towards his groin. I have an absolute right to watch him. He is my love, my lover, the object – no, subject – of my affections. I study him like a mail-order bride preparing to face the authorities (I must put all thoughts of marriage firmly from my mind). He still has a full head of hair, the boyish curls belied by the greying sideburns. The flaming red may be turning ashen but its pedigree remains clear. 'Bog Irish,' he declared defiantly, in case four generations of Surrey shopkeepers had filled me with proprietary pride. He has sea-green eyes, with a slight cast in the left one which would seem to be a hindrance in his profession, and a scattering of freckles along each cheek which put me in mind of autumn. His nose is straight with surprisingly wide nostrils. But his crowning glory is his set of perfect teeth. When he smiles, as he does in private, I am dazzled.

God forgive me but I love him! I came here looking for a miracle and I've found one. So what if it wasn't the one I expected? Should I spurn it like an ungracious wife whose husband gives her a dress better suited to the salesgirl? Was I that woman? People change.

I lie back on the pillow and my head fills with questions: questions which resound so violently that I am amazed they don't wake Vincent. Must I throw up the chance of happiness? Must I turn my back on love? But I don't need to hear him speak to know his answer. 'Your religion makes it quite clear. Christ charged us to love one another. St Paul taught us that the greatest of all virtues is love.' But for once his smile fails to blind me. If the Eskimos have so many words for snow, why do we have only one for love? Or do we? I am brought short by a rush of synonyms. Tenderness. Devotion. Compassion. Service. Sacrifice. And the one that makes a mockery of them all: Lust.

A hand pulls me out of my reverie. A hand in the small of my back pulls me a few inches across the mattress and into the unknown. I am startled, affronted, delighted, grateful. I open my lips to his kiss and am flooded with peace.

'How long have you been awake?' I ask, with the unease of the observer observed.

'Hours,' he says languidly.

'Liar,' I say, relieved by his shamelessness. 'I've been watching you sleeping.'

'I rest my case. You and I are one and the same. If you're awake, then so am I. Why are you crying?' he asks with alarm.

'I'm not,' I say, surprised by the tear that he wipes off his shoulder and presses to my tongue. 'I should say that it's because I'm happy, but it's far more complicated than that. It's because I'm here. It's because one way or another somebody's going to be hurt. It's because to keep being happy, I'm going to have to choose.'

'Choice is what makes us human,' he says, suddenly alert. 'Unless you think God's some celestial Bill Gates, programming everything in advance.'

A blast of cold air makes me shiver. I gaze at the window but it's closed. He is not just the naked man spread out beside me, stroking my forehead until it feels as if it is made of silk, the man who knows instinctively, mysteriously, the perfect way to pleasure a body he first held a mere two days before. He is a man with a past that chafes him like a shoulder strap; a man with set ways and prejudices; a man who, for all our differences, I see as my second self. If only we had been childhood sweethearts, sharing our hopes and dreams like lunchboxes. If only it had been his office, rather than Richard's, that I had walked into as a girl of nineteen.

'We must get up!' I take us both aback by my abruptness. 'It's half past seven.'

'Half-six. Here! Look at my watch.'

'Only because you were too lazy to adjust it! Next you'll be glued to the Sky sports channel in the hotel bar.'

'I'm trying to be kind to your body clock.' Then he presses his lips to my breast as if in confirmation. My protest dies in my throat. As he inches his tongue down my ribs, I luxuriate in my weakness. I wonder at my perversity, when the prospect of future entanglement only adds to the illicit pleasure of the here and now.

I have never felt so fully in the present. As he laps my stomach in ever-smaller circles, I throw back my head and find myself staring at the ceiling. The cracked cream paint glows as golden as the Rosary Chapel mosaics. I struggle to keep my arms and legs from thrashing about, afraid that my passion will compromise me, showing him that it is no longer a matter of 'if' but of 'how.' He insinuates his tongue inside me. My body and mind are mere adjuncts to my desire. I am fire and water, the perfect balance of opposing elements.

His tongue grows more insistent and then, in an instant, the sensation shifts. I feel not an emptiness but a silence, like the lull between two movements of a symphony. Suddenly, he is all percussion and I sense the crescendo in my flesh. I am at once overpowered and strengthened, pulled apart and made into a perfect whole.

I smile as a picture takes shape in my mind.

'What are you thinking?' He licks the tip of my nose.

'St Bernadette,' I reply too quickly.

'What?' I sense a slackening that threatens us both.

'I was wondering if she knew what she was giving up when she entered the convent.'

'Not every woman's lucky enough to enjoy the Vincent O'Shaughnessy treatment.'

'It's not just you and me,' I say, emboldened by his swagger. 'This is God.'

He replies by redoubling his efforts. He whispers inaudibly in my ear and I thrill to the rush of his breath. He picks me off the sheet and perches me on his thighs, never once loosening his grip. I feel exposed, no longer hidden from the day but brazenly upright. If the walls of the room were to roll away like a stage set, leaving me in full view of Patricia and our fellow pilgrims, I would stand fast. All the opprobrium in the world could not outweigh this. He lies back, pulling me on top of him, and nuzzles my breast. I cradle his head as if he were a child, but a child who is nurturing me. Then he thrusts again so vigorously that I fear I may topple off the bed, but he roots me to him. Next, we are in the air, floating as if on the magic carpet I created from my childhood mattress. It cannot last. The tender expression on his face begins to tauten. Waves of pleasure surge up inside him and crash into me. We cling to each other, desperate to contain the impending ebb. Too soon the inevitable is upon us, as he yelps like an injured dog and struggles to regulate his breathing. I sense that, for my sake, he is fighting his instinct to break free. I know that I ought to release him, giving him my blessing with a gentle kiss, but for the first time I put *me* before *us*. He sinks back, his hands limp on my waist. I clench my thighs to keep him with me, but it is no longer enough.

Reluctantly, I let him go. I shiver as if already stepping into one of the baths. I feel lost and alone and vulnerable. Then he gathers me in his arms and I know that all is safe again. We have a new connection, a daytime connection, a closeness greater than proximity.

Time re-enters the room with a peal of Aves. I shut my ears to the inexorable chimes and heave myself up before he has a chance to protest.

'It's eight o'clock. I have to get back to the Acceuil. For Richard,' I add, more for my own sake than for his. He lifts himself up on his elbows and I am suddenly aware of the shrivelled condom. I don't know whether to laugh or cry.

He peels it off as if reading my mind. 'Another one to get rid of! Any suggestions? It's probably a criminal offence to wear them in this town.'

'No, just a mortal sin,' I say, for once with no trace of contrition. 'Can't you flush it down the loo?'

'You're so gorgeously naïve.' I decide not to ask him to elucidate but watch him wrap it in a wad of tissues. 'I'll chuck it in a rubbish bin outside. I feel like I've regressed to sixteen.'

'You started early.'

'And stopped far too soon,' he replies darkly. I lean across and kiss him, but the shadow remains.

'I'll have a quick shower.'

'I thought you were going to the baths first thing.'

'I am. You're not serious?'

'What? You think St Bernadette might object if you turn up in the rank sweat of an enseamed … whatever?'

'You're a monster,' I say, turning away to hide my smile. I move into the bathroom, surprising myself by neglecting to lock the door. Any hope of a revitalising shower is dashed by the trickle of water. I inspect my vulva, finding no sign of blisters, and swiftly withdraw my hand as Vincent comes in to pee. I feel sure that he is making a point and resolve not to flinch.

'I see you've discovered the state-of-the-art plumbing. I think Madame Basic Jesus would consider a fully functioning shower not just an indulgence but a snare.'

'You mean pilgrims should keep their minds on higher things?'

'And there's an endless supply of incense for when things get rancid.'

I draw back the curtain and step out of the shower, acutely aware of the brutal strip light. 'Of course, the truly devout needn't worry.' I say, both to tease and distract him. 'Remember St Bernadette. When they opened her coffin years later, her body was incorrupt.'

'No kidding?'

'There were independent observers. Not just nuns.'

'I'd rather think of those early hermits who wallowed in their own shit. I once got caned at school for asking how St Simon Stylites went to the toilet on the top of his pillar.'

'I bet you were a vile little boy.'

'But the girls loved me.'

I neatly evade his affirmative lunge and return to the bedroom, where I gaze in dismay at my underwear, wishing that I had thought to pack more alluring pants. There again, if he aims to last the course, he may as well know the whole passion-killing truth.

'I'd kill for a cup of coffee,' I say, buttoning up my shirt.

'You needn't go that far. The dining room's open and the coffee's not half-bad. I know for a fact because I heard some of the Liverpudlians complain.'

'I couldn't! You may be feeling demob-happy. It may even make the perfect end for your film: a shot of the director being drummed out of Lourdes with his flies undone. But you're on your own. I'm not having the waitresses gawp at me as if Mary Magdalene's rolled into town.'

'Suit yourself. Just don't start telling people I don't give breakfast.'

'Pig!' I grab a pillow but cannot bring myself to hit him even in jest, and let it drop feebly. 'Now I must go. I really must. Don't try to stop me.' He holds up his hands, open-palmed. 'If you intend to go to the baths yourself, you'd better get a move on.'

'There's plenty of time. The queues aren't nearly as long for men. Besides, you shouldn't underestimate the power of the camera. Forget the stretchers and wheelchairs; make way for the director and crew.'

'I bet you'd take advantage of it too.'

'You do the penance. I get the perks.'

'I don't know what I ever saw in you.'

'Oh, I think you do.'

He kisses me and I have no choice but to agree. I pick up my bag with my precious new angel and move to the door. 'I expect I'll see you at the Grotto?'

'You will indeed.'

'I'll be with Richard and Patricia.'

'Don't worry. I promise to behave.'

I leave the room without looking back. The atmosphere in the corridor is so different that it feels less like closing a door than crossing a frontier. The cloying mixture of stale air and dust, cooking oil and cleaning products, makes my yearning for coffee more intense than ever and I weigh up whether I have time to slip in to a café on the way to the Domain. The lift is so slow in coming that I suspect a plot to force all but the most disabled guests to take the stairs. At last the doors open, to reveal an elderly man with heavy jowls pushing a withered woman in a wheelchair.

''F out, dear?' she asks, from the corner of her mouth.

'To the baths,' I say, praying that I have answered the right question.

'Yesterday,' she says, indicating her husband with her eyes. ''Ew woman. Old bones … ew woman.' She chuckles. 'God 'ess!' I notice the pennant of the Pope in her frozen fist and feel ashamed.

I take the lift to the ground floor and dodge the piles of luggage in the vestibule. The Liverpool pilgrims are going home. A young girl, wearing a shocking pink shell-suit, sits on a case, fiercely picking off a label, while her older sister, dressed like her twin, reassures a frail old woman that 'me ma and me da are just out fetching a last-minute bottle of holy water.' Having braced myself to outstare the proprietress, I am relieved to find a young man at the desk, his face as trusting as if he had just changed out of his cassock. I greet him with my sunniest *Bonjour* and head for the door, confident that he takes me for a tour rep or an official fresh from a breakfast meeting. To my horror, I walk straight into Madame Basic Jesus herself, carrying a box of plastic saints to the gift shop. I feel more rumpled than ever in the face of the grey cashmere cardigan draped effortlessly around her shoulders, the immaculately ironed white blouse and lemon-and-grey check skirt. She smiles coldly and I quail before the formidable blend of worldly elegance and spiritual authority. Unlike her assistant, she is under no illusions about my visit but, for all that she is Lourdes enough to disapprove, she is French enough to say nothing.

Foolishly, I resolve to speak. '*Bonjour Madame, je viens de visiter un de vos invités, Monsieur O'Shaughnessy. Il faut profiter de notre dernier jour dans votre si belle ville.*'

'I'm sure you'll profit by it, Madame,' she replies.

'*Ce matin, notre pèlerinage va aux bains avant de fêter la messe à la Grotte,*' I add, determined not to give her the linguistic advantage as well as the moral.

'I wish you a safe journey home,' she replies stonily.

Ceding defeat, I hurry out of the hotel. I hesitate outside the adjacent café, but all thoughts of entering vanish at the sight of a table of Czechs wolfing down their early morning *steak frites*. I walk through a shadowy side street, past a young beggar who makes little effort to look the part. Leaning on a bulky rucksack and wearing earphones, he studies a book of Sudoku puzzles, with nothing but the coin-filled cap at his side to indicate his purpose. Ignoring both Vincent's claim that pavement space in Lourdes is controlled by a syndicate and my own resentment at his able-bodied indolence, I toss a couple of euros into the cap. Obliged to conceal my happiness from the world at large, I am eager to share it where I can. Keeping his eyes glued to the book, he emits a small grunt of acknowledgement. I wonder whether his pickings are so rich that he disdains my meagre contribution, or else that he judges my need to give to be greater than his to receive and sees me as the beneficiary of the exchange.

I continue past a lavender-seller setting out heavily perfumed sachets on his cart and down a pavement barely wide enough for pedestrians, let alone the wheelchair that sends me scuttling into the road. I linger outside a photographer's window where a solitary wedding portrait sits among the pictures of current pilgrimages. The Jubilate has its own screen on the far right and I spot myself in the formal group on the basilica steps as well as in a snapshot with Richard, Patricia and Father Dave at the Grotto. I think of all that has happened since they were taken on Tuesday. I examine my face through the blurry glass for any hint of anticipation, any awareness of having agreed to do more than consider giving Vincent an interview, but it is as blank as the one in my passport. Richard beams. Perhaps he has just told a joke? Which would explain Patricia's frown. Or has she seen me with Vincent and understood my feelings more clearly than I did myself?

I move away, resisting the urge to buy a copy, refusing to let a photograph compromise my memories, and reach the main road. I pass a crocodile of African nuns, their white habits and black faces still a novelty to my black-and-white mindset, and enter the Domain through St Joseph's Gate. Even after a week of constant coming-and-going, I thrill to the sight of the grey basilica spire soaring above the treetops and the glimpses of the bronze Stations among the foliage on the hill. I join the steady stream of pilgrims making their way to the Basilica Square. Large groups congregate behind banners in Italian, Portuguese and Dutch and one, to my amazement, in Arabic. Most wear matching sweaters or baseball caps or scarves and I think, with a pang, of the wilful individualism that has limited my use of the Jubilate sweatshirt to the pilgrimage photograph. Smaller groups of family and friends stroll hand-in-hand with an intimacy that warms the heart, until a glance at the vacant eyes and too-trusting smiles of the ageing children and the freakishly unlined skin of the childlike adults reveals this to be from necessity rather than choice.

I pass under the massive stone ramp that leads to the upper basilica and glance at the knot of people by the drinking fountains. Some put their mouths to the taps; others fill bottles and jugs; still others wash their faces and hands. A wiry old man, with tufts of white hair protruding from his grimy vest, cups water in his hands and pours it over his head and shoulders. To his right, an olive-skinned boy struggles to carry a canister which dwarfs him. I allow my gaze to

11

drift towards the Grotto, but the sight of the crowds hurrying to the baths keeps me from dawdling. I step on to the bridge and look up at the Acceuil, its irregular, fan-like structure strangely reflective of its status: half-hospital, half-hostel. I slip in by a side-door and walk down the labyrinthine corridors to the lift. Making way for a stretcher, I brush against a pair of Milanese youths, their *Buon giornos* muted by the rivalry at yesterday's procession. Irritated by their private jokes, I consider disconcerting them with my Linguaphone Italian, but I arrive at my floor too soon.

I enter a hive of activity. Everywhere, nurses and handmaidens are preparing their charges for the final morning of the pilgrimage, anxious not to hasten the moment of departure while at the same time packing up the equipment for the journey home. An end-of-term mood grips some of the young helpers, with one steering his friend, the virtuoso guitarist of last night's concert, around the nurses' station in a rickety wheelchair. He earns the inevitable reprimand from Maggie, as keen to prolong the stay as any of the '*malades*', acutely aware of the authority that will seep away on her return to the small retirement flat in Deal where her only subordinate is her cat.

I break off in dread at the dismal picture. For all I know, she may be the leading light of the local bowls club with a social life that is the envy of the South Coast. I realise that it is not her future so much as my own which frightens me and despair that my happiness should have evaporated so fast. I head for the bedroom and bump into Ken, supervising the brancardiers, while exuding his familiar air of a hunting dog that has been kept too long as a pet.

'Been for a stroll?' he asks, weighed down by the box of groceries he is carrying to the van. Caught off guard, I strain to detect a double meaning. His kindly smile makes me feel twice as guilty. The only duplicity is mine.

'Making the most of it while I can. Now I'd better go and find Richard.'

'No rest for the wicked!'

'None,' I reply, determined to keep from anatomizing every remark.

I approach my bedroom and am intercepted by Fiona, formally

dressed for the trip, her Easter Island face at odds with her Barbie doll hair. As ever she carries her tape measure, which she presses against my legs. I pause as she loops it slowly around my knees before holding it up for my inspection.

'I can't bear to look. Have I put on weight? All this rich food!' Unsure whether it is my jocular tone or her own high spirits that spark off her fit of giggles, I carry on down the corridor where I come across the guitarist and his friend, now gainfully employed hauling boxes of equipment.

'I really enjoyed your playing last night,' I say as we pass. A boyish blush suffuses his pustular cheeks and his friend smirks as though at an innuendo. I speculate on the street meanings of *enjoy* and *play* and recall my first encounter with Kevin who, four days later, still cannot look me in the eye. Talking to teenagers is even more fraught than talking to Fiona.

I enter the empty bedroom to find the floor strewn with clothes, evidence either of Richard's primitive attempts at packing or the brancardiers' struggle to get him dressed. The noise emanating from the dining room suggests that he is still at breakfast and I seize the chance to change my bra and shirt, free from the threat of his prying hands. I am busy folding pyjama bottoms and T-shirts when I hear a knock at the door.

'Come in!' I call, too feeble as ever to emulate Patricia's commanding 'Come!' Louisa enters, her upright bearing and forthright manner a testament to her years in the WRAF. For all her fusty officiousness, I like her. It is as though she once heard one of her subalterns describe her as 'Firm but Fair' and has striven to live up to the label ever since.

'I understand you didn't sleep here last night?' she asks, instantly slipping into Pilgrimage Director mode.

'No,' I say, strangely relieved by her bluntness. 'I went for a drink with some of the kids at the Roi Albert. I knew I'd be late and didn't want to disturb anyone so I stayed with my mother-in-law in the hotel.'

'Yes, Patricia's here,' she says, in one breath blowing my cover. Her eyes fill with disappointment, as though I were a pregnant flight sergeant afraid to trust her. I suddenly feel sick. 'Why do you ask? Has anything happened to Richard?'

'Don't worry; he's fine. Busy having breakfast. The last I saw, he and Nigel were competing with each other as to who could eat the most Weetabix.'

'What it is to be six again!'

'Nigel's been six since the age of twelve,' she replies severely. 'But I'm sorry to say there was an incident last night. Richard went on walkabout. I expect he was looking for the lavatory.' She glances in confusion at the bathroom. 'By a stroke of bad luck, the nurses' station was temporarily unmanned. He muddled the rooms and made for Brenda and Linda's next door.' She rehearses the evidence as though for a military tribunal, while I picture the two women: Brenda, paralysed and solid, her face shadowed by a visor, forever seeking to sell me a cure-all magnetic bracelet for which she is hardly the best advertisement, and Linda, scraggy and wan, with no distinguishing features other than lank hair and foul breath. 'Richard tried to get into Linda's bed. She woke up screaming, which alerted the nurse, but she couldn't get him off. He's very strong.'

'Yes, I know.'

'Fortunately, Father Humphrey and Father Dave were burning the midnight oil. They heard the rumpus and managed to disentangle Richard and take him back to bed.'

'Is Linda all right?'

'Just a few ruffled feathers. We've explained that Richard isn't himself.' I nod politely at a phrase that has made me squirm for the last twelve years. 'But the Pilgrimage has a duty to protect vulnerable people.'

'Richard is vulnerable too.'

'Believe me, I do understand, but we're in a delicate position. Linda could lodge a complaint when she gets home. Some of our hospital pilgrims are funded by their local authorities.'

'Yes, I see. It's my fault. I should have stayed with him. I'm extremely sorry.'

'It's forgotten.' She moves towards me and I fix my grin in anticipation of a squeezed shoulder or, worse, a hug, but she thinks better of it and, with a sunny smile, turns and walks out. I am left to clear up the mess of my marriage and seize gratefully on the more pressing task of clearing up the discarded clothes.

Richard saunters in, stopping dead the moment he sees me. He stands still, putting his hands over his eyes like a child who has yet to learn the laws of perception.

'I've been a naughty boy.' I blench to hear the timeworn words, which used at least to be ironic. He walks towards me with a shy smile. It feels wrong that, after all that has happened, he should still exude such charm. He plants a wet kiss on my cheek and continues across my nose and up to my ear, until I feel devoured by his empty affection. I take him in my arms and stroke his hair, proving yet again that pity is a most overrated virtue.

'I looked for you in the night and you were gone.'

'I told you I was staying at the hotel.'

'You told them you were staying with me.' I look up to see Patricia, her timing worthy of a wider stage, her face a mask on which I project my guilt.

'I'm sorry. I thought it for the best.'

'Who for? I came in at eight o'clock to serve the breakfasts and what do I find?' Richard, responding to the inflection, looks up, but she is not playing the game. 'Whispers and insinuations flying around from people who should know better: people who know nothing at all. Poor Richard muddling the rooms in the dark. It's an easy mistake. But no, you'd think some people had never taken medication! All that screaming and shouting. My darling, you must have had a dreadful shock, and on the last night too! Are you feeling better now?' She moves to kiss him but he burrows his head in my breast and she adroitly switches to stroking his neck, while turning her fire on me. 'I can't believe you'd be so irresponsible. Gallivanting off and leaving him here on his own.'

'One night! One night in twelve years! There are doctors, nurses, priests. How much more responsible could I be?' I hate myself for craving her understanding, even if not her approval.

'They asked me where you were. "Here," I said, not realising. And then I found out that you were supposed to be spending the night with me. I mumbled something about you getting up early to come back to the Acceuil. I think I got away with it. I can't be sure.'

'I didn't mean to drag you into it. I'm very sorry.'

'Me? What do I matter? It's Richard. How can we ask Our Lady for a miracle with you in a state of mortal sin?' I say nothing. 'Oh Gillian ... Gillian.' She takes my hands. Richard slips in and out of our extended arms until he grows bored and sits on the bed in a stupor. 'I know it's not been easy for you. Who knows that better than me? But believe me, this isn't the way. You're worth more.'

'Am I? I thought I was just a money-grubbing nobody who wasn't worth your son's little fingernail.'

'That was nearly twenty years ago! I can't believe you still hold it against me now.' Her air of genuine distress makes me feel even more guilty.

'I don't. We all say things we don't mean. So let's not say any more,' I reply hopefully. 'We should get ready for the baths.'

'Everything happens for a reason. That's what you must cling to. The more confusing it seems to us, the clearer it is to God. I've pondered and prayed and asked myself *why*: what have I done to deserve this? But it's no use. The Lord will explain it in His own good time.' Her voice rings with conviction and I feel a mixture of admiration and envy. 'We all have our crosses to bear.'

'Aren't we allowed to share the load? Even Our Lord had Simon of Cyrene.'

'I hardly think that what you were doing last night – ' her voice quavers as if in response to the darkness – 'counts as sharing.'

'You don't – you can't – understand.'

'No? Richard hasn't been the only sadness in my life.'

'I know.'

For all the placid assurance of her manner, she too has endured much. It is hard to reconcile the elderly woman standing before me with the fresh-faced bride posed on the steps of St Wilfrid's, Burgess Hill. It is not so much that her cheeks have puffed, neck puckered and waist thickened, but that an inner light has been doused. The vision of married life instilled in her by the nuns faded when her husband treated his vows like tax demands, leaving sacrifice as her only satisfaction. Watching her play the widow with more conviction than she ever did the wife, I wonder if adversity has made her strong or simply hard.

'Did you never think of leaving Thomas?' I ask, building on the rare moment of intimacy.

'Never! We were married. In the sight of God.'

'I know you were unhappy.'

'He was the perfect husband.'

'That's not true.'

'You were there, were you?'

'No, of course not. But I've heard from Richard – and Lucy.'

'She never got on with her father.'

'And I worked at the office. I saw how he behaved towards the other girls.'

'Why are you doing this? Isn't it enough to betray your husband? Must you attack mine too?'

Richard starts to whimper. I move to the bed and rub his hands.

'No, of course not. I thought if we could only be honest, just this once.'

'I'm not your priest.'

'No, I know. Forget I mentioned it. Come on, old boy. You need to go to the loo before the baths.' I pull Richard off the bed, anxious to forestall any inadvertent sacrilege.

'Why did you ask?' Patricia refuses to take her cue from me. 'Are you thinking of leaving Richard?'

'No, of course not ... not really ... from time to time. Wouldn't you? Sorry, I know you've already answered that question.' I push Richard into the bathroom. He turns it into a game by pressing back on my hands. 'Thinking, perhaps, in the sense of dreaming, not in the sense of making plans. I dream of so many things that would make life easier.' I catch her eye and know that she takes me to mean Richard's death. 'Like a miracle,' I say brightly, but she is not deceived.

'How much do you know of this cameraman?'

'He's a director.'

'Vincent O'Shaughnessy.' She drags out every offending vowel.

'You were the one who was all over him, angling to feature in his film.'

'That's not true! Did he say that? It's not true!'

'No?' I ask, as Richard bounds back into the room, pointedly drying his hands on his trousers. 'I remember how keen you were for me to talk to him.'

'I thought we should show willing, help him to see the pilgrimage in its best light. I didn't expect you to jump into B-E-D with him.'

'Bed,' Richard shouts out, which makes me wonder how much more he understands.

'Have you never suspected that he might be using you as material for his film?'

'Come on! Surely you see that that's nonsense?'

'Remember Julia Mason at the Holy Redeemer? A reporter from the *Dorking Advertiser* visited her at home. Spent ten minutes complimenting her on her japonica. The next week, her private views on Father Aidan and his housekeeper were splashed all over the front page!'

'Vincent's a serious film-maker not a muckraker.'

'I wouldn't be surprised if he's been given a secret brief to show that pilgrims are all liars and hypocrites, that Lourdes is a seedbed ... a hotbed –' she struggles to find a less compromising word – 'a melting-pot of immorality. The BBC will go to any lengths to undermine the Church.'

'He was brought up Catholic himself.'

'They're the worst.' She changes tack with surprising adroitness. 'Not that anyone would want to keep you here against your will. I'm seventy-one years old, but I'm still in full working order. You remember Mrs Jameson?'

'I'm afraid not.'

'Of course you do. Brian Jameson's mother. Died at a hundred and one. Telegram from the Queen. Kept going for the sake of her other son. Not Brian: I forget his name. He was a little ... well ...' She looks at Richard. 'I don't need to spell it out. Then he went all of a sudden. Pneumonia, I think. Three months later we were at her requiem.'

'Poor woman!'

'Not at all. I've never seen anyone more at peace. I remember speaking to her after ... what was he called? I'm thinking one of those "en" names: Ben, Ken, Len ... no, it's gone. "They say there's nothing worse than to outlive your children," she said. "But not for me. I washed and powdered him when he was born and I laid him out when he died." And, if she can do it, so can I.' My image of Patricia cradling her son shifts imperceptibly to a Pietà and I wonder, not for the first time, whether she sees that as the crown of motherhood. 'Isn't that right, darling? If Gillian wants to go off for a holiday, you can come to me.'

'I don't want you,' he says gruffly.

'Oh really?' she asks, with unconvincing nonchalance. 'So what have I done that's so terrible?'

'I want Gilly.' He cushions his head on my breast and I feel that, for all his protests, I might as well be his mother. 'Don't go away from me!' He clasps me so hard that I almost topple over.

'I'm not going anywhere. We're both going home,' I say, with studied neutrality.

'I know I shouldn't do things, but I can't think in a line. I start off all right, then it twists and turns and I end up in a muddle.'

'I know. It's not your fault. It's just that you look so well we sometimes forget how hard it can be for you.' I think how much easier it would be if he were confined to a wheelchair or had a face as distorted as his brain and hate myself for wishing away his one remaining distinction.

'Have you got any money for me?' He grabs my bag and, before I can stop him, tips its contents on to the rumpled sheets.

'Oh Richard, how many times have I told you not to go through my things?'

'That would be secrets. We shouldn't have any secrets, should we, Mother?' To her credit, Patricia gives him a noncommittal smile. Richard picks up the box containing my crystal angel. 'What's this?'

'Nothing.' He rattles it. 'I mean it's nothing for you. Take care. It's glass; it might break.'

'Finders keepers.'

'It's mine.'

'You can't buy yourself presents.' He pulls off the lid. 'It's an angel.'

'It's the one we saw in the shop,' Patricia says. 'The one I admired.'

'Yes.'

'So you went back to buy it for me!' Her pleasure is so palpable that I nod.

'Yes.'

'What about me? You should have brought something for me.'

19

'I planned to give it to you when we got home. As a thank-you for bringing us here.'

'It's beautiful!' She holds it to the light and examines it from every angle. I pray that Vincent will be more amused than hurt by the recycling of the gift. 'I'm sorry if I spoke harshly. You mustn't think I don't appreciate all the things you do for Richard.'

'I do things for Gilly too.'

'Of course you do, my darling.' She turns back to me. 'It's just that I appreciate them so much that it can be frightening to think what would happen if … if …'

'I know. Don't worry.' What is it about me that makes her censure easier to take than her gratitude? 'Now I must clear up in here and start packing.'

'Let me do that,' Patricia says. 'You're due at the baths.'

'I was, but we're running so late. We have the Grotto mass at eleven thirty.'

'That leaves you more than two hours. You can't come to Lourdes and not go to the baths.'

'I was looking forward to it.'

'The brancadiers will be coming for Richard soon. I'm surprised they're not here already.'

'I don't need a bath. I had a shower.'

'Don't be silly, darling. You know it's not the same.'

'It's still water.'

'You go ahead, Gillian. They won't keep you waiting long. The Jubilate has priority this morning between nine and ten.'

'Thank you, I will.'

'I want to go with you.'

'You can't go to the Ladies,' Patricia says. 'What would people say?' Richard giggles. 'You'll see Gillian at the Grotto.'

'Do we have to go there again?' he asks sulkily.

'Of course. It's where St Bernadette saw Our Blessed Lady.'

'It's boring. You said it'd be like a cave.'

I slip away and out of the building. My mind is more confused than ever and I long for a sign as explicit as Bernadette's. But I can hardly expect the Virgin to manifest herself to an adulteress, especially one whose penitence is provisional.

I make my way over the pedestrian bridge, through the John Paul II Centre and down to the Esplanade, stopping only to rub sun-cream on my face and arms. Two of my fellow pilgrims, clearly identifiable by their sweatshirts, are standing by the statue of the Virgin. I am about to sneak past when I see to my amazement that it is Jenny, hand-in-hand with Matt. I am delighted. After our conversation at Stansted, I was afraid that she would be too shy to make friends even among the girls. Curiosity outweighs discretion, as I seek to learn more about a romance that has run in parallel to my own.

'Hi there!' I shout. Jenny drops Matt's hand as though confronting her mother. He grabs hers back with deliberate defiance. 'It's a beautiful morning. Have you come for a final look round?'

'A final look round,' Jenny echoes.

'We've been out all night,' he says, in what sounds like a challenge. 'We didn't go to bed.'

'Or anywhere else,' Jenny adds quickly.

'But that's wonderful,' I say, eager to move off and put them out of their misery but afraid of appearing to disapprove. 'How long have you been…?' An item; a pair; a couple: I search for a less forbidding word. 'Together?'

'Two days,' he says.

'Since Saint-Savin,' she adds. 'I was struggling to push Mrs Clunes up to the Abbey. Matt came to help.'

'So your eyes met across a crowded wheelchair?' I ask lightly.

'It was fingers first,' Jenny says, prompting Matt to squeeze her hand.

'Well I think it's wonderful,' I say, both touched and troubled by a love that is so much freer than mine. I long to make common cause but am afraid of seeming ridiculous. The spontaneity that is the stuff of youth feels suspect – almost dangerous – in early middle age. 'Any plans for when we get back to England?' I ask, sticking to practicalities. 'How close to each other do you live?'

'I'm from Stoke,' Jenny says. 'But if I get my two As and a B, I'm off to Warwick.'

'And I'm in Solihull.'

'That's not too bad,' I say, alert to their mournful faces, 'it could have been John O'Groats and Land's End.'

'You don't understand,' Jenny says. 'Matt isn't flying home with us; he's in the van with the equipment. It takes them two days to drive through France. I've asked everyone if they'll swap places. I don't care about feeling sick. But they all said they had too much fun on the way down.'

'Two days.' I don't know whether to laugh or cry. 'I had a great aunt who married the day before my uncle went off to fight in North Africa.'

'It's easy for you,' Jenny says. 'If you were our age, you'd understand.'

'Yes, of course, I'm sorry. I'll leave you in peace.'

'No, we have to get back to the Acceuil,' Matt says. 'We only came to say our Hail Marys.'

'What? Oh yes. You were on Father Dave's walk.'

'How about you?' Jenny asks, with affecting credulity. 'Have you said yours?'

'No, not yet. I think I'd rather leave it to fate.'

I walk through the Basilica Square and under the ramp, past the drinking fountains and the Grotto to join the pilgrims on their way to the baths. I pause for a moment by the candle burners, with the forest of flames in various stages of extinction, and picture all the faith, all the hope and all the entreaties that they represent. I want to add some words of my own but fail even to formulate them in my head. It is not just my throat but my entire being that is parched.

The crowds at the women's baths plunge me into panic. Convinced that the wait will be too long, I decide to turn back. All at once I am spotted by Louisa, who lives up to the emblem emblazoned on her chest by bellowing my name.

'Gillian! Over here!' I smile apologetically at the people in front, but the queuing system is so erratic that no one – not even the Italians – seems to blame me for jumping it. 'You sit here,' she says, directing me to a bench next to a trim, well turned-out woman who, if it weren't for the wheelchair beside her, might have been lining up for the summer sales. 'Most of our lot have already gone in. I'm just keeping an eye out for stragglers.' That puts me firmly in my place but, as I glimpse my neighbour's friendly smile, it no longer feels such a lonely place to be.

No sooner has she found me a seat than Louisa moves away. I

settle on the bench and examine the figure in the wheelchair. Both her arms and waist are strapped in position and she wears a woollen cardigan in spite of the heat. Her neck is stretched back on a pillowed ledge, making it hard to determine her age, although I detect the faint outline of a bust beneath the baggy clothes.

I watch as my neighbour stands and, with infinite solicitude, lifts the lifeless head from the pillow and holds a bottle of water to her lips. 'Is this your daughter?' I ask, trusting that I have not confused a wizened mother or a flat-chested friend.

'Yes, my Anna,' she says, in an indeterminate accent.

'Was there … was she in an accident?'

'Birth,' she replies flatly, putting my twelve years of nursing Richard into perspective. However much he may have changed, I at least retain the memory of the man he was. She only has the elusive image of the girl her daughter might have been.

'Is this your first time at the baths?' I ask, taking the shortcut to intimacy that has defined my week in Lourdes.

'No, we come every year. Every year since Anna is three. She is now sixteen years old.' My hopes of the water's miraculous properties begin to founder. 'We come here from Groningen in the Netherlands. Perhaps you know of it?'

'Of course,' I say, eager to offer her what little support I can.

'And you?'

'From Surrey in England. Oh, I see what you mean. Yes, this is my first time. My husband had a brain haemorrhage twelve years ago. In many ways he is like a child.'

'There is no hope?'

'Not for him, no … Do you have any other family?' I lower my voice in case Anna's condition should turn out to be congenital.

'Just Anna and me. She is the first child. The only child. I used to wish that I had other children before, but now I am glad that it is just us. With others there would have been comparing. There would have been too much time with Anna and not enough time with them. There would have been "please do not bring her out when my friends are nearby". No, it is better like this.'

'And your husband?' I ask, trying not to let myself be distracted by the flies circling above Anna's head.

'He is no more. I mean he is no more my husband. He has a new wife and family in Rotterdam. Please do not think he is a bad man for leaving.'

'No, I'm the last person to think that.'

She gives me a searching glance. 'He tried to do his best but he couldn't make a life with Anna. To him there is only one life. He is not like us.' It is unclear whether she is alluding to our faith or our gender. 'He wanted to put Anna in a home, a good home, a home that he would have to pay for … a home that he would find it hard to pay for, but then he wanted it to be hard. I said "no". I wouldn't permit him to shut her away because she was not perfect. My parents grew up in a world like this, a world where not perfect people were thrown out from the rest.' She swats at the flies and I realise that, far from not noticing them, she is sensitive to every detail of her daughter's state.

'Do you have friends? Old friends who are there for you when it all gets too much?'

'One or two, yes. But not so many any more. There are the mothers of the children at the centre where Anna goes three mornings each week. With three of these I play tennis. But with my old friends it is harder … for them as it is for me. They have their lives and I have Anna. How can they talk to me about the things they have wrong in their lives when I have Anna? How can they talk about the things they have right in their lives when I have Anna?'

'Oh yes, I know that syndrome so well. They start by wanting to help and end up blaming you for their failure.'

'It is not their fault. But it is better not to wish for too much.'

'I'm amazed – full of admiration but also puzzled – by the way you can be so accepting of everything. Do you never think of packing a suitcase, running off and not looking back?' I am so desperate for an answer that I no longer worry about giving offence.

'Sometimes, yes.' She seems to be struggling with her inner self. 'But only at night.' She stands and wipes her daughter's face with a damp cloth. 'And you must not feel sorry for me. I have so many happy things in my life. Small things that are no longer small. The sounds Anna makes when I rub her skin with lotion or when I scratch, you know, like a mouse behind her knees. Jörgen, my husband, he said it was just the gas in her stomach: the air in her throat. But I know it is so much more.'

'You're very brave.'

'If you knew me, you would not say that. I am frightened of so many things. But, most of all, I am frightened of my Anna dying. I used to be frightened that I would die before and leave her on her own. But not any more. I know it is selfish. I know I am a bad woman – ' She brushes aside my protests as casually as she did the flies. 'But she is my life; without her, I could not go on.'

'Madame!' The woman starts as an official in a navy sash summons her into the building with a flick of the wrist that cuts through the confusion. She releases the brake on her daughter's chair, ready to wheel it inside. Then, confident that we will never meet again, she leans towards me and whispers: 'Most of all I am frightened of the pills, the pills I give Anna to help her sleep ... that, when she is sleeping for ever, I will take them for me. It is then that I will know that my life is no longer worth living. It is then that I will turn my heart against God.'

She makes her way inside and I resist the urge to ask for an address or a number or even a name that might compromise the essential anonymity of our association. I shuffle up the bench, soaking up its residual warmth, while moving one step closer to my goal. I watch while entrants are selected seemingly at random until, at last, the all-powerful finger beckons me and I walk into a long low room, dominated by a row of green-and-white curtained cubicles, resembling a municipal swimming pool. I take a seat to the right of the door between an albino girl, surrounded by shopping bags, noiselessly saying her rosary, and a gnarled nonagenarian with filmy eyes and a toothless smile. Every few minutes a glowing woman emerges from one of the cubicles and a replacement is ushered in. I strive to empty my mind of worldly concerns but find it filling with more speculation about the men's cubicles than at any time since school. Is Vincent in there filming, his innocent camerawork later to be subverted by a lethal voice-over? Is Richard behaving? I pray that he will be neither prurient nor coy, dipping one toe into the icy water and refusing to venture further, when a woman in a damp T-shirt printed with a portrait of the Virgin leaves the extreme right cubicle and the attendant summons me.

I enter the cramped space to find five women in varying states of undress. In semaphored French, the attendant tells me to strip to my bra and pants and then slips out through a second curtain. I smile encouragingly at my Slavonic-featured neighbour, who sits hugging her chest in a vain attempt to hide the rolls of flab that spill over her knees, but she seems so wretched that I turn away, taking off my jumper and skirt and folding them with studied precision in a bid to delay the moment when I must turn back and face the room.

I am distracted by a delicate young woman who returns from the inner sanctum. She makes straight for the pile of clothes to my left and I watch in awe as the beads of moisture on her neck and shoulders evaporate like water on a hotplate. The force of Vincent's jibes dries up with them. It is clear that we have no need of towels.

'*L'eau était froide*?' With no clues as to her nationality, I choose the courteous option. She fails to respond, and it is not until she puts on her clothes that I realise her plain grey dress is a habit and her mind will be full of God. Twenty years after leaving school, I still expect nuns to be old.

Each of the women takes her turn to go through to the bath until finally it is mine. I shiver so violently at the prospect of the glacial water that they must think I have come to be cured of a tremor. The attendant leads me into a small granite-lined room with a tub like an outsize hip bath at the centre. The air is damp with a metallic tang, and a layer of condensation lines the walls. I am welcomed by two more attendants wearing light plastic aprons.

'English?' one of them asks.

'Yes,' I say, wondering if it is the Marks and Spencer pants that give me away.

She nods at her companion, who tells me in a soft Scottish burr to remove my underwear and place it on the shelf. She then holds up a small piece of wet linen, wrapping it around me like a sarong and tying it loosely at the back. Taking my arm, she guides me into the bath and down its three inner steps. The water is so biting that it feels like treading in a tub of broken glass. With her companion holding my other arm, she instructs me to sit. I lower my bottom gingerly into the arctic depths.

'No, no, bend your knees as if you're on a stool!' I do so, pressing heavily on their arms and leaving my bottom suspended. 'Now you must make your intentions.'

This is the moment of truth: the moment when I am planning to ask St Bernadette to intercede for Richard, to give me back the man I loved, the man I married, or, at the very least, the man. She herself said that the water of Lourdes had no power without faith. Well, mine is a faith that has never faltered even at the bleakest prognosis. This is the chance for it to reap its reward. Or is the clear-cut faith of my catechism irredeemably muddied by desire?

I look into my heart and wish that I saw nothing. I pray for Richard's recovery as intently as ever, but my motives are no longer pure. Should a miracle occur and he regain the forty years he has lost during the last twelve, my Te Deums would ring across the Pyrenees, but I fear that, even then, St Bernadette would find them wanting. Knowing that he no longer depended on me, would I at last be able to leave him with a clear conscience, or would I feel obliged to stay out of gratitude for my deliverance?

The water is still but I feel it swirling around me. The Scots attendant recites the Hail Mary and, fixing my gaze on the statuette of the Virgin directly in front of me, I strive to drain my mind of everything but her compassion. Although she lived more than eighteen hundred years before Bernadette, her experience and understanding feel so much closer. I cannot believe that, having followed her son to Calvary, she would endorse Patricia's 'We all have our crosses to bear,' or that, given Christ's gospel of love, she would condemn my love for Vincent.

Or is that sheer self-deception, more contemptible than ever in this sacred place?

A chill spreads through me from somewhere beyond the water. I realise that I am agonizing over questions that have already been answered. How typical that I should be so fixated on the mystery of the baths that I have ignored the message of the courtyard! How typical that God should speak to me not through the Virgin or St Bernadette but through a nameless Dutch woman in a queue! Her selfless devotion has shown me the true meaning of love. I feel faint and am afraid of sinking, but the attendants have me in their grip. It is clear that I can never leave Richard. It would be hard enough to justify in Bath, let alone in Lourdes. I shall speak to Vincent at once and without apology. If he asks for reasons, I shall cite my original ones for coming. The rest has just been a week-long moment of madness. And I shall refuse to let him portray it as a sacrifice. He must have no grounds for appeal. Nothing has been sacrificed except for my own self-esteem.

I suddenly feel strong and, what's more, I have learnt a lesson which I could never accept from the exemplars at school: true strength lies in self-denial.

The attendants recite the Lord's Prayer, a sign that my allotted time is up. They raise me to face the statuette of the Virgin and I feel a dizzying sense of peace as I kiss her feet. After helping me out of the bath, the Scot unties my wrap and gives me the same scrap of privacy as before while I put on my bra and pants. Decent again – at least in the eyes of the world – I say an inadequate '*Merci*' and return to the cubicle where I quickly slip into the rest of my clothes.

I hurry out into the open. The sun's glare makes me squint and I struggle to read my watch, but, even in the blur, I am sure that I must be due at the Grotto mass. For the first time since the International mass on Tuesday, I feel that I can participate with a pure heart.

'Gillian!' I hear a voice which, after a moment, I identify as Patricia's.

'I wasn't expecting to see you here,' I say. 'Aren't we meeting at the Grotto?'

'Yes, but I need to speak to you. Before you make any decisions you may regret.'

'They're made. But don't worry. I shan't be leaving Richard. Not now, not ever.'

'Oh Gillian!'

'We came looking for a miracle and I've found one. I'm cured of my delusion; I'm ready to resume my life.'

VINCENT

Monday June 16

'W hen I was fourteen, my mother asked me if I'd ever thought of becoming a priest. "No," I replied, "isn't it bad enough being a Catholic?"'

'I bet that had them rolling in the aisles at Television Centre,' Jewel says.

'I see you're setting out with your usual open mind,' Sophie says.

'You've missed your calling, chief,' Jamie says.

'That's what my mother thought.'

'Yeah, you're wasted in broadcasting. You should be wowing them on the club circuit.'

I sit with my crew of three at a lozenge-shaped table in a café at Stansted airport, waiting for the pilgrims to arrive. The stools, which resemble pawns on a giant chess set, have been fixed at such a distance from the table that it is impossible to relax. I have been trying out the opening line of my voice-over on an audience who, I know, will not spare me. We are a close-knit team, sufficiently respectful of each other's talents to be able to mock them, veterans of a day in an asylum centre, a week at *Hello* magazine and a trip with two soap stars to a WaterAid project in Zambia. To my left is Jamie, the cameraman, whose sharp eye belies his burly physique and bluff tone. He has a bristly beard, a ring in each ear and a propensity to sweat that bothers him far more than it does the rest of us. To my right is Jewel, the sound recordist, who with characteristic rigour, has had her childhood nickname ratified by deed poll. Unlike Jamie's beer-and-indolence belly, Jewel's bulk is congenital and, what with her cropped hair, regulation check shirt and jeans, not to mention the Celtic tattoo which first came to my notice in Africa, it would be easy to assume that her desire to be one of the boys went beyond the professional, had not her outrageously raunchy stories in various hotel bars proved otherwise. Completing the group is our newest recruit, Sophie, the assistant producer, a tirelessly efficient media studies graduate who, unlike the rest of us, makes no secret of her longing to work on features. Petite, stylish and as studiedly accessorised as a fashion editor, she currently sports a fitted black satin waistcoat, grey pencil skirt and carmine lipstick, which exactly matches her handbag and shoes.

Sophie's outfit has caught the eyes of a gang of Geordies at the neighbouring table. Having worked out that our quartet is not romantically entwined, one of them approaches. His courage, bolstered by the whoops of his friends, wilts in the face of our expectant smiles. 'Can I get you a coffee, love,' he asks, 'or how about something harder?'

'Ta very much,' she says with a Mockney twang. 'I'd love some. I'm sure my friends would too.'

'That's great then,' he says, taken aback.

'One mocha, two lattes and an espresso. Ta.'

'Great. Well then, I'll go and get them, shall I?'

'That's so kind,' she says dismissively. 'Now where we were? Oh yes, your opening gambit, Vincent.' We watch the chastened suitor slink away and join the queue at the counter.

'The poor lad,' Jewel says. 'We'll have to pay for them.'

'Don't you dare! Make him think twice before trying it on next time,' Sophie says with chilling indifference. Yet, for all my reservations about her manner, I have none about her expertise. She cuts through red tape as effortlessly as her mother cuts the ribbon at a village fete. Ambition and altruism may be uneasy bedfellows but, when we are on a shoot, she allows nothing to distract her from the matter at hand. Like Jamie and Jewel, she has a shrewd understanding of the kind of film I make: passionate, polemical and quirky, where the director is a presence in front of the cameras as well as behind. Nonetheless, I take it as a compliment that, even after hobnobbing with the *Eastenders* in Zambia, I've only been recognised – or at any rate accosted – once, by a boy who asked if I were a weatherman.

I wonder whether our professional shorthand will be as effective this time. If so, they will need to know my mind better than I do myself. I am still perturbed by the strength of my reaction when Miles Redfern, head of Lion's Share, announced that the Beeb was looking for someone to make a film to mark the 150th anniversary of the Virgin Mary's apparitions at Lourdes.

'The so-called Virgin's so-called apparitions,' I insisted.

'Which is why you're the perfect man for the job.'

'It's such an easy target. However cynical Scott's and Sammy Jo's motives may have been for travelling to Zambia, the trip at least ensured that the villagers got their latrines and the great British public was alerted to the problem. What can we possibly find to say that's positive about Lourdes?'

'Challenge yourself along with the viewer. How often have I heard you hold forth on the evils of the Roman Catholic church? The opium of the masses; the absurdity of the mass. Anti-abortion; anti-birth control; pro-life but life-hating. Now's your chance to put it to the test. Spend a week in a place where their faith and your scepticism are at their most pronounced. It's a brilliant opportunity all round. Prime time, not God slot.'

I delayed signing until my long-awaited drama debut fell through, when the BBC hired Douglas Simcox to helm its serialisation of *The Ragged Trousered Philanthropists*. All the class resentment that afforded me an intimate insight into the piece bubbled up when they chose Simcox's public school poise and confidence over my commitment and experience. Alarmed by the lack of alternative offers, I accepted Miles's. He arranged for us to join the Jubilate, an independent pilgrimage about two hundred strong, which, drawing its members from around the country, is less parochial than most. Now that we are finally on our way, I remain at a loss as to the cause of my unease. I have never made any secret of my contempt for the Church, but I am equally exercised by the incarceration of asylum seekers and the cult of celebrity, and I had welcomed the chance to shed light on them.

Then, when the luckless Geordie returns with the coffee and I clasp the steaming cup by the flimsy handle that protrudes like the cardboard wings on a Nativity play angel – an angel played by a perfectly cast five-year-old girl – I realise why my feelings are so intense.

'Shall we play I-spy?' Jamie asks, as the conversational lull slumps into boredom. He takes no offence when no one replies.

'It's not fuel prices or carbon footprints that will ultimately do for mass travel,' I say, 'it's airports.'

'The Japanese have the best idea,' Jewel says. 'They don't bother to actually go anywhere anymore – except to the photographer's, where they have themselves filmed against massive blow-ups of the Eiffel Tower or the Statue of Liberty or whatever. Then they put out the photos for all their friends to admire.'

'But don't their friends piss themselves?' Jamie asks.

'Not at all. They're doing the same thing. It's the accepted practice: the new way to travel in the virtual world.'

The word *virtual* has its usual effect on me and I switch off until I hear Sophie say that it's half past eight and the coaches should be arriving soon.

'All you want are some establishing shots of the guys gathering at the check-in, is that right, chief?' Jamie asks.

'Yes, as colourful as you can. I should be able to pick out our lynchpins. If not, I'll ask one of the organisers for help.'

Louisa, the Pilgrimage Director, with whom I've been in such frequent contact over the past three months that I've bumped her up to Friends and Family on my phone, has given me a list of the pilgrims, along with brief descriptions which at times stretch to a paragraph and at others stop at a word ('teacher', 'goitre', 'Scottish'). Prompted by dim memories of O level English, I envy Chaucer the more compact and flamboyant cast in his Prologue and yearn for someone even half as salty as the Wife of Bath. With nothing but instinct to guide me, I have chosen a representative selection of hospital pilgrims: Brenda, a sixty-year-old with MS; Martin, a teenager with cerebral palsy; Frank, a former chartered surveyor with chronic Lyme disease; Fiona, a six-year-old with Down's Syndrome; and Lester, a middle manager with terminal cancer, a fact which, grossly overestimating our audience, he declared himself willing to share with ten million strangers but none of his fellow pilgrims. I spoke at length on the phone to Lester and his wife, Tess, as well as to Martin's and Fiona's mothers, the latter assuring me that her daughter is 'quite personable', as though I were the scout for a disabled talent show. Brenda's snarled and Frank's slurred speech made sustained conversation impossible but, after a few strained words, I secured the cooperation of both Brenda's girlfriend and the warden of Frank's sheltered housing.

My able-bodied selection is to a large extent dictated by the sick: Lester's wife, Tess; Fiona's parents, Steve and Mary; Martin's mother, Claire; Brenda's girlfriend, Linda (the cynic in me wondered whether Louisa's ease with their relationship had been assumed for my benefit). For human drama I have chosen Lucja and Tadeusz, a young Polish couple with a brain-damaged baby: she a staunch Catholic with an absolute belief in miracles; he a sceptic who only agreed to the trip when his wife's church presented him with a ticket. From the volunteers I have chosen Maggie, a retired midwife, with sixteen pilgrimages under her belt (and three long-service medals above it), and Kevin, who is currently suspended from school and will only be allowed back on proof of good behaviour. Finally, I have chosen two priests: Father Humphrey, the spiritual director, who wants it known that, despite the committee's approval, he has strong reservations about the filming; and Father Dave, a former estate agent who, in his own phrase, 'once sold time-shares and now sells eternity'.

Having run through all the names in my head, I am seized by a momentary panic, convinced that I have forgotten some vital piece of documentation which will prevent my boarding the plane.

'Hey chief,' Jamie asks, 'are you making the sign of the cross or playing with yourself?' Looking down, I realise that I have involuntarily checked for my passport, ticket and wallet in my jacket pockets and coins in my trousers.

'Who should be on the comedy circuit now?' I reply, flustered in spite of myself. Travelling always brings out the child in me: more precisely, the child who was left behind on a school camping trip because his mother had sent him on the coach with a duffel bag, refusing to 'waste good money' on a rucksack. I choke down the bile that has risen in my throat. It can be no accident that a visit to Lourdes should put me in mind of my mother.

Jamie goes to Smith's in search of magazines and Sophie and Jewel to the Body Shop to 'check out the three for twos', leaving me to guard the bags. I struggle to memorise the schedule, but thoughts of my mother distract me. The diocesan pilgrimage to Lourdes was her first ever trip abroad and, despite my offer to pay for the flight, she insisted on taking the coach as if to keep faith with the charabancs of her past. Every August we would spend a week in either Blackpool or Skegness. When my father suggested that one year he might quite fancy Scarborough, she was outraged, less by the break with tradition than by the presumption. 'Dr Supple goes to Scarborough,' she said reverentially, 'with his widowed sister.' In retrospect I suspect that, along with the desire to maintain strict class divisions, which also ensured that even when seated two rows in front she would defer to the doctor at mass, she was anxious to avoid a reciprocal glimpse of his unclad flesh.

My memories of icy seas and heavy downpours, of humiliating changes behind skimpy towels and luncheon-meat suppers served by supercilious landladies have no doubt been embellished, but I realised even at an early age that my mother regarded such ordeals as the price of pleasure. The only holidays she embraced were authentic holy days: the Marian feast days when, along with our fellow parishioners, we would process through the streets of Barnsley behind a statue of the Virgin, while I prayed that none of my school friends caught sight of me in my surplice.

For once, however, I have reason to be glad of my background. 'I presume you're a Catholic, Mr O'Shaughnessy,' Louisa asked, on hearing my name.

'In one respect,' I replied lightly, 'the guilt.'

Jamie returns, munching an Aero and brandishing copies of *Maxim* and *Club*.

'For God's sake, Jamie! This isn't sex tourism in Eastern Europe; it's a pilgrimage to Lourdes.'

Looking hurt, he rolls up the magazines into the pocket of his shoulder bag. We sit in awkward silence until Sophie and Jewel appear, the latter carrying a packet, which she pulls open. 'Smell this, Jamie. It's bliss.' He squeezes some oil on to his palm and presses it to his nose. 'Hey, I said *smell*,' she says, grabbing back the bottle, 'not scratch and sniff.'

She passes the bottle to me, but we are interrupted by the ring of Sophie's mobile. I listen eagerly as she takes a call from Louisa announcing that the London coach has arrived.

'Let battle commence,' I say, leading my troops to the check-in. Jamie sets up his camera, arousing the suspicion of two security guards, whom Sophie deftly placates with the requisite permit. My heart sinks as the first pilgrims appear, immediately identifiable by the lime-green luggage tags which, unlike us, they have obediently tied to hand-baggage and even wheelchair handles. While not expecting the beautiful people of the *Hello* film or the exotic landscape of Zambia, I was hoping for something a little less drab. I wonder whether there is a tenet in canon law that restricts the wearing of primary colours to priests.

Louisa stands to one side, with a quartermaster's clipboard. Giving me a hearty wave, which draws attention to the filming, she heads our way. She greets Sophie and myself and I introduce her to Jewel and Jamie.

'That's some green,' I say of her sweatshirt.

'Easy to spot in a crowd,' she says. 'You need it in Lourdes. Of course it's not so useful when we hold mass in a meadow.' I smile politely.

'What's that?' Jamie asks, pointing to the logo stretched across her impressive bust.

'Oh, it's the Jubilate angel blowing her horn. His horn; her horn: you can't tell with angels.' I find myself warming to her. 'We have one for each of you. It's designed specially for the anniversary. You never know,' she adds with an embarrassed laugh, 'it may turn out to be a collector's item.'

Louisa leads us to the check-in counter, where she introduces us to Sister Anne, whose title is the only sign of her vocation. As I shake hands with the sturdy forty-year-old in sensible shoes and an anorak, wearing a more discreet cross than many of her charges, I think back to all the penguin jokes of my boyhood and wonder how we are supposed to know who's who any more. I picture myself as a McCarthyite commentator in fifties America, warning the honest citizen of the subversives in their midst. 'Ten telltale signs to detect a nun.' But even I have to admit that the only one in evidence is compassion, as she hears a paralysed man sniffing beside her and tenderly wipes his nose.

Louisa is summoned to deal with a missing ticket. 'Duty calls,' she says apologetically. We take our places in the queue. Check-in counters are not built for wheelchairs and the staff seem more forbidding than ever as they peer down at the confined figures in front of them. I suddenly become aware of a commotion to my left. A middle-aged man has opened his suitcase and is tossing out the contents. Clothes fly everywhere, causing nothing more serious than confusion until a sandal hits his chair-bound neighbour, provoking an indignant howl. The man then throws down the case and twists his neck back and forth as though to ward off a persistent wasp. Two pilgrimage officials rush up to him. One puts his arms around his shoulders, gently calming him; the other gathers up the scattered clothes. Meanwhile Sister Anne consoles the victim, whose over-emphatic wails sound increasingly like pleas for sympathy and less like genuine pain. Jamie has captured it all on film and gives me a thumbs-up sign which is intercepted by Louisa who approaches, hand-in-hand with a little girl.

'That's Frank. I think he's on your list.'

'Oh yes, of course. The guy with Lyme disease.'

'No control of his emotions. The slightest thing can set him off. He used to be a churchwarden.'

'It must be hell.'

'And here's someone else you wanted to meet: Fiona, our young-est pilgrim, always excepting Dr Gilpin's baby, but we won't count her, will we?'

Fiona shakes her head solemnly. I ponder her mother's defensive 'personable' as I gaze at the discordant face with its elongated brow and elderly features, crowned by immaculately brushed golden hair. Her detached expression springs to life as, in response to my greet-ing, she pulls out a retractable tape measure and holds it against my left leg, disconcertingly close to the groin.

'Are you going to be in my film?' I ask, gently disengaging myself. Fiona looks confused and turns to Louisa.

'Of course,' she says. 'You're going to be the star.'

'Star,' Fiona repeats, clapping her hands.

'Right then. Shall we go and find Mummy and Daddy?'

'Yes, yes,' Fiona says, running off into the crowd.

'Bless!' Louisa says. She moves to follow, when a tall grey man with a bulging briefcase strides up to her. 'May I borrow you for a moment, Louisa? There's been a slight accident.'

'How slight?' she asks. 'Is anyone hurt?'

'No, nothing like that.' He whispers in her ear.

'Is that all?' she says with a laugh. 'No need to be shy. Sister Anne or Sister Martha should have some spares in the emergency bag.' The man hurries away. 'Pants,' she explains. 'One of the ladies couldn't reach the lavatory in time. Still, worse things happen at sea.'

On which note she hurries off, leaving me to speculate further as to why she was so happy to approve our film. Why should she expose the Jubilate to a medium that is notoriously inimical to religion? She cannot be seeking her fifteen minutes of public validation; her sights are set on something far more enduring, not to say eternal. She must have an unshakeable belief in the merits of her mission, along with the confidence that it will transcend anything that I and my camera might put in its way. She must have an absolute faith in faith.

I finally complete the check-in and line up with the crew for the departure lounge. Our equipment provokes the usual consternation at security. The days may have passed when my name alone ensured a rigorous body search, but the guards remain intent not simply to root out suspects but to cause the maximum discomfort and humiliation to everyone else. Impotent in the face of Sophie's official documents, they retaliate by checking every item in our bags, the only dubious ones they find being Jamie's magazines, which a jowly guard holds up with as great a display of distaste as if they were hard-core porn. Released at last, we move up to passport control where we are transfixed by a series of piercing screams.

The cause soon becomes clear. Not content with requiring people who can barely bend to remove their shoes and others who can scarcely walk to give up their sticks and totter through the scanner, the guards have forced Fiona to put her tape measure through the X-ray machine. Her mother tries to assure her that it has done no damage, grabbing the tape measure off the conveyor belt and pulling it open to show that it functions exactly as before, but Fiona is inconsolable. It is as though the magic powers with which she has invested it have been wiped out by the rays.

Lamenting that this is the one place that we are forbidden to film, we inch our way through passport control to the departure lounge. Dodging the passengers weighed down with duty-frees, we head for Wetherspoons, where Jewel is surprised by the number of lime-green luggage tags at the bar.

'Catholics drink,' I explain, buying a round.

We grab a table and are sitting down when Louisa catches sight of us and walks over. 'All present and correct,' she says, which may or may not be a question. 'Mind if I…?'

'Please do,' I say, half-standing as she draws up a chair.

'Ten years and it doesn't get any easier! Still, one last stretch and then it's Marjorie Plumley's turn. Squadron Officer Brennan reduced to the ranks. I can't wait!'

'But you must enjoy it to have gone on for so long.'

'I'm not sure *enjoy* is the word I'd choose, but I like to see it as my contribution – almost my vocation.' She gives another embarrassed laugh. 'Please don't think that I'm putting myself on a par with the nurses or sisters, let alone the priests. Not at all. But give me some letters to write or forms to fill or doors to knock on and I'm in my element. The Jubilate is a working pilgrimage. Which suits yours truly down to the ground. Everyone, from Father Humphrey to the youngest brancardier, is here to ensure that our hospital pilgrims get the most out of Lourdes.'

'What's a brancardier?' Jewel asks.

'What indeed? You must feel like you're back at school: it was weeks before I figured out that going to the Congo meant choir practice...! Brancardier was – is – the French for stretcher-bearer and it stretches – whoops! – back to the early days of Lourdes. We use it for all our male helpers, young and old. The women are called handmaidens.'

'Young and old too?' Jewel asks.

'Yes, although I fear there are more of the latter.'

'You're telling me,' Jamie says.

'Don't worry,' Louisa replies, in a voice that sends him fumbling for his beer. 'It's not as one-sided as it looks. There are two minivans full of young people currently making their way through France.'

'How long does that take?' Sophie asks.

'A couple of days. Believe it or not, they enjoy it. For one thing it's a lot cheaper. And they have the chance to make friends en route, as well as sorting out the music for the services.' She turns to me. 'I do hope you'll feature as many of them as you can. They're a real tonic. Some come back year after year, even though the work is quite menial. You should see the boys – I doubt if they so much as pick up a dirty plate at home – happily making beds and mopping floors. It's a chance to show viewers that teenage life isn't all about knife crime and hoodies. But the numbers have been steadily falling. We need more to sign up if we're to carry on taking as many of our hospital pilgrims.' It hits me that she is hoping to use the programme as a recruitment tool. To my surprise, I find myself less averse to the idea than I would have been half an hour ago. 'Between you and me, that was what swayed the committee in your favour. And when we sent out the release forms, not a single person said "no". I tell a lie. There's one couple we haven't heard from.'

My chest tightens at the thought of the constant struggle to avoid the two dissidents. 'Might they be open to persuasion?'

'Oh I'm sure it's just an oversight. They're first-timers so I don't know them, but the husband's – I think it's the husband's – mother is an old hand. I'll introduce them to you this evening.' She seems to sense my dismay. 'Or would you prefer it now?'

'If you wouldn't mind. We may catch them in shot when we arrive in Lourdes.'

Louisa leads me through the lounge, which feels sterile despite the clutter. We stop beside an elegant woman of about seventy, with her ash blonde hair swept up, neatly plucked eyebrows and a lightly powdered face. She sits flicking through a copy of the magazine that I filmed last year. Her baby blue jacket, opal brooch, cream silk blouse and black-and-white pleated skirt mark her out from the average pilgrim. She stands to greet Louisa, extending a perfectly manicured, slightly arthritic hand.

'Patricia, how lovely to see you again,' Louisa says, 'looking as chic as ever.'

'We try not to let the side down. Can't all be lilies of the field, can we?' She breaks off as if in doubt about the appropriateness of the reference.

'This is Vincent O'Shaughnessy, who's making a documentary on the pilgrimage.'

'Pleased to meet you,' I say, taking a hand that feels strangely weightless.

'We're all very excited about your film,' Patricia says.

'Me too.'

'Not that I watch much television,' she adds. My eyes drift to the copy of *Hello*, open at the story of a daytime presenter and her *long-awaited bundle of joy*. 'My husband – my late husband, that is – used

----
41

to say that scientists had shown how our brain waves when we watch TV are the same as when we're asleep.'

'Is that so?' I say, taken aback. 'Perhaps they meant when we're dreaming? At our most responsive.'

'Perhaps. You must be sure to let us know when it's on, so we don't miss it.'

'Patricia's one of our most treasured handmaidens. Ten visits now, is it?'

'Nine.'

'She's the queen of the dining room. Not silver service, gold. This year she's brought her son and daughter-in-law.'

'Yes,' Patricia says with a sigh. 'I finally persuaded Gillian. She's just popped to Boots for some aspirin. And this is my Richard.' She points across the aisle to a handsome man in his mid-forties with fine sandy hair, a strong chin, a strikingly clear complexion, and a frame that looks constrained by his jacket. He sits, shifting his gaze between the departure board and his wristwatch as if daring the times to differ. 'Richard, darling, this is Mr O'Shaughnessy. He's going to make a film of the holiday.'

'In the Grotto?'

'We'll certainly do some shooting there.'

'Shooting?' He sounds alarmed.

'With the camera.' I mime a tracking shot, which I trust will not be seen as condescending.

'I'm going climbing in the Grotto.'

'It's not that sort of grotto, darling, I've explained.'

'You can't stop me. I'm forty-six years old. You've no right to tell me what to do.' He starts to cry. Louisa pats his arm; I wince; his mother remains impassive.

'Please don't be alarmed,' she says. 'Sometimes he's worse than a child.' Her voice darkens. 'That's what he is now: a child. If only you'd known him before. He had fifteen men working under him, to say nothing of the casuals. The youngest president of the Surrey Rotary since the war, elected unopposed when his father retired. Then one day he had a haemorrhage on the golf course. Just like that. The blood poured into his brain and wiped out so many of the connections, so many of the hundreds of thousands – or is it millions? – of connections that make us who we are. And it's left him a boy. But a boy with the strength and ... and the urges of a man. Which is very hard: hard for him and hard for us. So we've come to ask the Blessed Virgin for a miracle, to give him back those connections, to give him back to himself.'

'Do you honestly expect one?' I ask, more abruptly than I intend.

'Aren't you a Catholic, Mr O'Shaughnessy?' she asks.

'With a name like mine?' I reply evasively.

'You're very like my daughter-in-law.'

'Really? In what way?'

'Faint-hearted. "What's the point of being a Catholic," I said, "if you can't ask God for a favour?" It's not easy for her. Richard can be a handful. It's no wonder she gets headaches. I sometimes think she doesn't want help from anyone. Are you married, Mr O'Shaughnessy?'

'No.'

'Really?' she asks. 'I'd have thought some bright young woman would have snapped you up years ago.'

'Some bright young woman did,' I say, refusing to elaborate.

'I brought Vincent over to discuss the release form for the filming,' Louisa interjects, sensing danger.

'Didn't I send it back? I'm sure I did.'

'Yes, of course. Everyone has, except your son and daughter-in-law. Well your daughter-in-law ...'

'I can't say I'm surprised. She worries herself to death over trivial things and neglects what's really important.'

'Perhaps you'd remind her?' I say, desperate to escape the skein of regrets and recriminations.

'Why not tell her yourself?' she says, gesturing to an approaching figure. 'This is my daughter-in-law, Gillian. Gillian, this is Mr Vincent O'Shaughnessy, the film director.' She cites my profession as if basking in the reflected glory of an Oscar-winner. As I hold out my hand to the tall, stiff, slightly frowning woman, I feel such a looseness inside me that I fear I may be losing control of my bowels. I cannot explain my response. She is undoubtedly attractive, with delicate features, full lips, piercing blue-grey eyes and chestnut hair pinned in a chignon, a style which, schooled in my mother's devotion to Princess Grace, I have long seen as a sign of refinement; but her looks are not the kind to make grown men melt. So I ascribe my fluttering stomach to pre-shoot nerves and a hurried breakfast rather than to her cool, firm touch.

She too is more elegant than the standard pilgrim in an ivory tailored jacket and knee-length floral skirt with a chunky suede belt buckled loosely around her hips, but the wooziness in my head keeps me from appreciating the effect. Smiling, I introduce myself but she ignores me.

'Where's Richard?' she asks, looking round and, although her words take unusually long to reach me, I immediately register her concern. 'I left him with you,' she says to Patricia.

'He was here a moment ago.'

'You're always saying you want to help and look what happens. You know you mustn't let him out of your sight.'

'That's not fair. I've just introduced him to Mr O'Shaughnessy.'

'He can't have gone far,' Louisa says with practised practicality. 'We'll soon track him down.'

'Such a fuss,' Patricia says, determined to save face. 'He's probably gone to the little boys' room.'

'I can take a look there if you want,' I say.

'More likely the little girls' room,' Gillian says, with revealing bitterness. 'But you're right. We're bound to find him if we spread out. I'd be glad of your help.' She looks me in the eye and the wooziness returns.

At that moment two security guards run past and the colour drains out of Gillian's face. It is as though, for all the threat of bombs and fires and robberies, experience has taught her to attribute any incident to Richard. As we follow the guards into Accessorize, her instinct turns out to be sound. The guards have grabbed hold of Richard, while a flustered woman slumps in a chair tended by a pair of salesgirls. A small group of passengers, drawn by the disturbance, watches from the lobby.

'Gilly,' Richard says, lurching forward to touch his wife. The guards tighten their grip on his arm, and he makes no attempt to resist. The guards exchange an uneasy glance as though recognising that this is not a cut and dried case.

44

'Oh darling,' Patricia says. 'What have you done now?'

'Nothing, honest! She was my friend. Gilly ...' He appeals to his wife who ignores him and crosses to the women.

'My son's had an accident. He's quite harmless.' Patricia addresses the guards as if they were waiters. 'You can let him go.'

'I'll take care of this,' Louisa says, proficient in damage limitation. 'Louisa Brennan, director of the Jubilate pilgrimage.' She holds out her hand to the nearest guard, who keeps his firmly on Richard. 'We're taking a group of sick – some very sick – people to Lourdes. This gentleman's had a brain haemorrhage which, among much else, has destroyed all his inhibitions. He has no awareness of what he's doing.'

To judge by his shamefaced demeanour, he has every awareness of what he has done, but it is not my place to comment. So I fix my attention on Gillian, who stands by the counter talking to the victim. I long to eavesdrop but fear that my presence is already intrusive enough. It is left to Louisa to bridge the gap, as she strides across to the cluster of women.

'I'm extremely sorry, Madam,' she says. 'Richard's one of the hospital pilgrims we're taking to Lourdes.'

'They ought to lock him up,' one of the salesgirls says.

'It was the shock,' the victim says softly. 'He came into the cubicle and wouldn't leave. So I panicked. I'm sorry.'

'No, you mustn't be,' Gillian says.

'And throw away the key,' the salesgirl adds.

'Is there someone we can fetch?' Louisa asks. 'Your husband?'

'No!' the woman shouts. 'No,' she says more quietly, 'he'd only get worked up. No harm done. Not even the shirt,' she says, examining the sleeves.

'You must at least let us offer it to you,' Gillian says. 'A token.'

'No, really. It's not necessary. I understand.'

'I'd like to. Please.'

'Well, if you're sure. Thank you. I'll go and change.' She stands unsteadily and, with an anxious gaze at Richard, moves into the cubicle. The two guards look relieved to find the matter settled with the minimum of pain and paperwork. At the same time, they are determined to protect themselves against repercussions.

'What time's your flight?' one asks Louisa.

'Eleven o'clock. We'll be called any minute,' she adds, as if this were further reason to let the matter drop.

'I knew it was something and nothing,' Patricia says, smiling at Richard. 'A silly mix-up.'

As she walks past to take charge of Richard, Gillian shoots her a glance that speaks of years of suppressed hurt and fury. I long to learn the story of a woman who I am now intent on including in the film. Moreover, I can no longer keep silent. I feel an aching need for Gillian to acknowledge me, if only as the unwitting cause of the confusion.

'It's my fault,' I say. 'I'm so sorry. I distracted your mother-in-law with talk of the documentary.'

'Yes, well, she's easily distracted. Maybe one day you people will learn that the whole world doesn't revolve around a camera. Not everyone's burning ambition is to appear on TV!'

'I'd put him straight on the plane if I were you, love,' one of the guards says. 'And take better care next time. The place is full of kiddies!'

'Oh God!' Gillian says, and, with her arm tucked through Richard's, turns to the counter to pay for the shirt. The guards leave; the onlookers disperse; a customer scans the shelves; and life returns to normal. To my chagrin, Patricia starts to apologise for Gillian.

'I wouldn't want you to think she's an uncaring wife.'

'I don't.'

'But it can be hard for her. Though I say so myself, he's a handful. It would be easier if she had children.' She sighs. 'She'd know from experience how to deal with him. That's where I could help. But she's proud. You've seen for yourself. And you know what they say about pride.'

'Well, we all fall sometimes,' I say quickly. Then, checking that we are not overheard, I make my pitch. 'I think that Richard and Gillian – and you, of course – would make a very interesting strand of the documentary. I hope you'll agree to be interviewed.'

'Really? How flattering! Who am I to refuse? If it helps put the message of Lourdes across … It is for the BBC?'

'A new series of *Witness*.'

'I can't speak for Gillian. She has a mind of her own.'

'I'm relying on you to persuade her. To work, it will need the entire family.'

'I promise to try my very best.'

Keen to escape while Gillian is still at the counter, I say a hurried goodbye to Patricia and return to the bar. No sooner have I sat down than the flight is called. We gather our bags and make our way to the gate.

'You took your time,' Sophie said. 'Anything special?'

'I got caught up in an ugly scene when one of our lot – a middle-aged guy with brain damage – broke in on a woman in a changing cubicle.'

'Why didn't you text us, chief? We'd have come over.'

'Have a heart, Jamie! You've got to allow people some privacy.'

'You are joking?'

To my surprise, I find that I am not.

The long delay in boarding gives us a further taste of the 'wheel-chair factor' that looks set to dominate the trip. I edge down the aisle, hoping for a smile from Gillian, but she is preoccupied with Richard's seatbelt and I have to be content with Patricia's skittish wave. I sit next to Jamie, who struggles to accommodate himself to the narrow seat, his one compensation being the 'well-stacked' stewardess whom he summons with embarrassing frequency.

'Enough, Jamie! It's humiliating,' I say, after he has pressed the bell for the fourth time, simply to ask whether it is *hot* in Lourdes.

'She's cracking, chief. She smiled then.'

'She curled her lip. What are you playing at? She's way out of your league.'

'Then she can lean back and relax. Leave me to make the running.'

'So far it's all been her: up and down the aisle! You're incorrigible. Do you try it on with every woman you meet?'

'Pretty much. It's the law of averages. Sooner or later, one of them's bound to break. You should go for it, chief. Good-looking bloke like yourself. Lighten up a little.'

'Thanks. I'll bear it in mind.'

I turn back to my novel, but Jamie's fidgeting makes it hard to concentrate. Retribution is at hand in the form of the captain's announcement when, in answer to 'the gentleman who asked about the weather on the ground', he informs us that conditions are normal for mid-June with a high of seventy-two degrees, a low of fifty-eight and sixty-nine per cent humidity. Jamie's embarrassment is capped when the stewardess swaps places with a male colleague who, bringing round a mid-flight snack, winks at him and, echoing his tone, asks if he would 'like to sample one of my buns'.

He declines.

On arrival at Tarbes, we are greeted by such a fleet of wheelchairs that several remain empty. I am amazed to hear the pushers speaking with Birmingham accents and immediately ask one of them for an interview. He identifies himself as Pete, a British Gas fitter, who travels here for a fortnight every summer with a gang of his mates. All the porters, all the attendants and all the baggage handlers are volunteers. 'Sounds weird, don't it? Coming away and staying in the airport. Most people can't get out of it quick enough. But we have a good laugh. And we go out on the piss in the evenings. Oh fuck, can I say that on the BBC?'

'We'll edit it later. Don't worry.'

'I made a promise to the wife,' he says with a diffident smile. 'We came here ten years ago when the kids were kids. She was fairly far gone with the big C. Breasts. Lungs. Ovaries. You name it.'

'But she was cured?' I ask incredulously.

'No, not at all. She died four months later.'

'So there was no miracle?'

'You tell me, mate? I'm down here, aren't I?' He rubs his knuckle against his cheek. 'Along with the rest of the lads. Coming to Lourdes made all the difference to Jackie. She said she saw so much goodness that she felt safe about leaving me and the kids. Oh fuck, now you've got me going.' That's one *fuck* I'm determined to fight for and I signal to Jamie to carry on filming as, without a jot of self-consciousness, Pete pulls out his handkerchief and wipes his eyes.

'Have you brought the children with you?' I ask, for some reason picturing surly teenagers.

'Fat chance! They're both grown up. One's a good Catholic girl; the other's more of a good-time girl. Oh no, she'll kill me! But seriously, mate, it's a very special place. Forget the Costa del Sol, this is the Costa del Hope.'

My fear that the filming will cause a delay proves to be unfounded, given the logistics of loading a dozen wheelchairs on to the coaches. Discreetly waiting till last, I clamber to the back where I pass Patricia sitting alone, a bag forbiddingly placed on the adjacent seat.

'Have you been deserted?' I ask lightly.

'Richard and Gillian took the coach to the Acceuil. Hospital pilgrims.' She mouths the *hospital* as if, even in this setting, it is taboo. 'Which hotel are you staying at?'

'The Bretagne.'

'Really? I'm at the St Claire.' Her tone hints at its superiority. 'I thought you'd be staying there or the Gallia Londres.'

'BBC cutbacks,' I say, with rare gratitude to the financial squeeze for sparing me this fellow guest, while plotting – precipitately, futilely – how my shooting schedule might compel me to spend a couple of nights at the Acceuil.

I am appalled by my readiness to conjure a romantic scenario out of thin air. I am a documentarist, not a drama director. My metier is facts not fantasies. Yet every relationship springs from a seed of fantasy, so why not this? For the first time in years I am open to the possibility of intimacy. No wonder I feel scared. But is it the prospect or the setting that scares me? Do I mistrust myself even more than Lourdes?

The questions hang in the air as I am distracted by Father Humphrey, who fills the forty-minute journey with a running commentary, first informing us that 'watches, tick-tocks and time-bombs need to be advanced by an hour,' then telling a succession of hoary priest jokes which draw the same enthusiastic response from his audience as their favourite hymns, and finally leading us in the Five Joyful Mysteries. I seek solace in the landscape, but the relentlessly flat countryside convinces me that south-west France looks better from 25,000 feet in the air. So I am doubly grateful when we reach town, dropping off passengers at three hotels on the way to the Bretagne. I note, with a mixture of relief and alarm, that there are only three other Jubilate guests besides ourselves: two elderly West Indian women, one with synthetic blond curls, and a gaunt middle-aged man with a disconcerting amount of luggage for a four-night stay. The short straw scratches my hand.

———

From the moment we enter the hotel it is clear that its three stars have been awarded very liberally. The walls are bare, apart from two large noticeboards plastered with information about current pilgrimages, a black-and-white poster for son-et-lumière at the town castle and a brightly coloured one for a funicular railway. The only decoration is a life-size statue of St Bernadette holding a chipped crucifix, with a vase of plastic lilies at her feet. A stylishly ageless woman with long fair hair, porcelain skin and half-moon glasses, an autumnal scarf draped artfully around her neck, looks up from her desk to greet us. We huddle behind Sophie who introduces us in fluent French, only to be trumped by the proprietress's flawless English. We fill in the registration forms while she perfects a look of exquisite boredom that puts me in mind of a penniless countess forced to open her stately home to hoi polloi. Her contempt seems more admissible when two plain girls in their early teens, dressed in bright pink shell-suits, run through the foyer, carrying cans of shandy.

'Tell us where's the shops please, Miss?' one asks.

'What is it you want to buy?' she replies coldly.

'Oh you know, things.'

'Ah *things*, of course. If you want souvenirs, there's the hotel gift shop. If you want clothes or shoes or cosmetics, climb the hill to the main square. If you want food, try the market. But, if you want *things*, I'm not sure that we can help you in Lourdes.'

Bewildered, the girl takes a gulp from her can and drags her companion outside. The proprietress returns her attention to us.

'Do you get a lot of British guests?' Jamie asks, with such exceptional politeness that for one ghastly moment I fancy he may be applying his law of averages to her.

'Oh yes.'

'Perhaps it's the name?' he says.

'Thank you, I have never thought of that,' she replies dryly. 'The meal times are printed on your bedroom doors. Breakfast is six thirty to eight thirty, lunch twelve thirty to one, and dinner at seven.'

'Seven to when?' Jewel asks.

'Seven.'

She hands us our room keys, each attached to an oblong block of a size that would make Mae West blush. 'When you go out, you should leave them on there.' She points to a half-filled board in full view of the door.

'What about thieves?' I ask, exercised by the lack of security. 'Surely someone could walk in off the street and pick them up?'

'The desk is always manned. We have never yet had a problem. Not even from gypsies. Of course there's always a first time.' She smiles grimly, as if she would welcome it in my case.

'I suppose they'd target the grander hotels,' I say, goaded to retaliate.

'We don't aim for *grandeur*, Monsieur,' she replies, opting for the native pronunciation. 'We're very basic Jesus.'

She turns back to her computer screen, underlining our dismissal. We go up to our rooms in a lift so rickety that Jewel starts to panic.

'Basic Jesus, indeed,' Sophie says with a snort. 'Did you see the *Hermès* scarf?'

Jamie and Jewel get out at the fourth floor, the latter so desperate to escape that she is willing to haul her case up a flight of stairs. With Jamie's foot wedged in the door, we agree to rendezvous in the street in an hour, to avoid the frosty foyer. Sophie and I brave the lift for a further floor. I drag my case to my room, which seems more suited to an anchorite than a pilgrim. The ceiling is low, so low over the window that I am unable to stand upright. A heavy oak wardrobe with a recalcitrant door faces the bed. The fixed coat hangers show that the proprietress has less faith in the probity of her guests than that of the passers-by. An oxblood carpet falls two foot short of the door where it is replaced by a floral runner. A small daguerreotype of nineteenth-century peasants hangs on an otherwise empty wall and a television sits on a metal arm above a frayed wicker armchair. I hurriedly unpack, draping T-shirts over the chair, spreading books on the floor, and placing my travelling photo-frame by the bed in a vain attempt to infuse the room with personality. Then I peel off my clothes: sweater, shirt and vest in one swoop, which even after thirty years fills me with a sense of defiance, take a tepid shower, dress and go downstairs.

The proprietress fails to look up as I rattle my key on the board. I dash outside and apologise for being late.

———

'How's your room?' Jewel asks.

'Functional,' I reply with a shrug.

'You're lucky,' she says. 'The plug won't fit my basin.'

'Very basic Jesus,' Jamie says.

'The sash on my window is broken,' Sophie says.

'Very basic Jesus,' Jamie and Jewel chime.

'There's no porn channel on the TV,' Jamie says.

'Oh please!' Sophie says.

'Hello!' Jamie replies. 'Has someone had a sense of humour bypass?'

'Shall we go over to the Domain?' I interject.

'Do you know the way?' Jamie asks.

'Director's intuition,' I say, pointing to a sign.

We edge through the milling crowds, down a narrow side street lined with cheap religious souvenir shops.

'Welcome to the town that taste forgot,' I say.

'The perfect place for Christmas shopping,' Jamie says.

'Sure, if all your friends are nuns,' Jewel says.

'I've never felt so Protestant in my life,' Sophie says.

We join the hordes streaming in to the Domain. The preponderance of elderly pilgrims feels strangely blasphemous, as if the miracle that they seek is eternal youth. Passing a memorial to a cured cardinal, we come across a line of officials, each one pushing an empty wheelchair that resembles a miniature brougham carriage.

'Do you think they belong to people who've got up and walked?' Jamie asks. I appropriate one of the proprietress's scowls. 'Sorry, chief.'

Once in the square we pause to take our bearings. Despite seeing them only six weeks ago on my research trip, I remain impressed by the twin basilicas: the lower one, bulbous, breasty, its gilded cupola gleaming in the afternoon sun, flanked by two flights of steps that lead to the upper one, its grey-and-white stone spires like a Disneyland model. Twisting around, I gaze past a crowned statue of the Virgin, down a long, grassy esplanade to the Breton Calvary, a rare image of the Son in a landscape that is largely maternal. An unintelligible prayer crackles over the loudspeakers, and a heavy, musky fragrance fills the air.

Sophie ushers us over a stone bridge, which spans a river so clear that the empty crisp packet being swept along looks even more of a desecration.

'Bet that's the Brits,' Jewel says, and no one chooses to argue.

'*Voilà*, the Acceuil,' Sophie says, pointing to a vast stone-clad structure like an open concertina, with two shimmering copper roofs. We walk towards it, past a small rockery with an elaborate fountain.

'So what's an Acceuil when it's at home?' Jewel asks.

'It comes from the French for welcome,' Sophie says. 'A kind of hostel.'

'It's fun to stay at the Y-M-C-A,

'It's fun to stay at the Y-M-C-A,' Jamie sings.

'You'll be lucky,' Sophie says. 'It's run by nuns.'

We walk into the lobby, dominated by a huge photograph of John Paul II, looking much like a hospital pilgrim himself as he sits slumped at the altar during his last Lourdes mass. A taciturn nun directs us to the third floor, where we enter a scene of complete disarray. Suitcases, rucksacks and shopping bags are piled high along one wall. Boxes of food, medical and cleaning supplies, rugs and windcheaters are stacked up along another. A uniformed nurse of indeterminate rank is handing out instructions to a trio of brancardiers, none of whom looks to be over twenty. Scanning their earnest faces, I wonder if they are here of their own accord or have been bullied into it by parents and priests.

I identify Kevin, a painfully thin lad with acne scars and a thicket of tawny hair, and ask if he will share his first impressions with the camera.

'First impressions of what?'

'Anything you like. The town. The journey. The pilgrimage. They're your impressions, not mine.'

Ignoring his friends' taunts, he takes out a comb and runs it through his hair. 'I've my reputation to think of,' he says shyly.

'This will do wonders for it, believe me,' I say, steering him into position and nodding to Jamie to start filming. 'It's early days yet, Kevin, but perhaps you can tell us what you're hoping for from your time in Lourdes?'

'Answers,' he replies with unnerving intensity. 'Why? Are you going to give us some?'

'Answers to what?'

'People come to Lourdes cos they're good people, right?'

'In the main, yes; I expect so,' I reply, taken aback.

'Then God lets them die. Why?' My studied silence forces him to expand. 'This morning, we passed a pile-up on the autoroute. A coach full of Poles ... Polish people. It skidded across three lanes, straight into the opposite traffic. There was blood and guts every-where. You could see the bodies.'

'No you couldn't, Kev.' One of his friends interjects. 'They were all covered up.'

'Well you could see the stretchers, so you knew they were there! And there was this stink of burning flesh.'

'Burning tyres, you dork!'

Kevin draws me aside. 'But they weren't ordinary Poles. They were pilgrims who'd been to Lourdes. Yesterday – maybe this morning even – they were at mass. Some of them were sick. Some of them were kids. Some of them were sick kids. Maybe some of them had been cured. What's the point of coming here then if God allows that to happen? Tell me: what?' I say nothing, signalling to Jamie to zoom in on Kevin's tortured face, confident that it is far more elo-quent than any doubts I might express.

I wind up the interview, leaving Kevin to resume his duties. Venturing further on to the ward, I spot Gillian outside the nurses' station.

'You're staying here?' I ask inanely.

'With Richard.'

'I thought it was only for hospital pilgrims.' The words slip out as though I had no more self-control than Richard.

'And their carers.'

'You're his carer?'

'So I'm told. I used to be his wife.' She disappears down the cor-ridor with an indifference more painful than either anger or con-tempt. I return to the dining room and to Sophie's announcement that Louisa has just summoned everyone to mass. It will be my first since my father's requiem and, for all my disbelief, I have a profound dread of saying or doing anything that will mark me out as a fraud.

We wait our turn at the lifts and go up to the chapel, which is spare, bright and anonymous. The Committee's concerns about the filming had centred on the services and we are careful to address them, standing unobtrusively at the back. The room quickly fills up. Some of the wheelchair-pushers reveal their inexperience, but good humour prevails, with even a head-on collision eliciting a cry of 'Hold on! I've not bought a ticket for the dodgems.' Once everyone is settled, Father Humphrey, his stomach straining his surplice, moves to the altar and declares that before the mass 'She Who Must Be Obeyed' wishes to say a few words. The epithet is greeted by titters from his flock and a show of diffidence from Louisa, who steps forward with a formal welcome. Claiming that no one pilgrim is more important than any other although some have more prominent roles, she summons those notables to the front: her deputy, Marjorie; the doctors, one, our gaunt fellow-resident at the hotel, the other, rocking a mewling baby; the head nurse, Anthea; chief handmaiden, Maggie; and chief brancardier, Ken. They stand in varying degrees of discomfort while Louisa runs through the programme. Among the pious hopes and practical details, she makes one remark that strikes a chord with me: 'I hope those of you who are seasoned pilgrims will forgive me if I repeat what I say every year: What we're doing in Lourdes is God's gift to us. What we do to one another while we're here is our gift to God.'

The mass begins, the sequence of Confession, Absolution and Gloria so familiar that it might be imprinted in my DNA. The opening hymn, however, comes as a surprise. 'Let There Be Love' is a saccharine ballad that might have been plucked from a Lloyd Webber musical, an effect accentuated by the accompaniment of guitars, flute and drums played by four of the young helpers. Our emotions are further manipulated by Fiona, who, with what appears to be official sanction, moves to the front and conducts the singing with her tape measure. It is hard to distinguish the Ahs from the Amens. Father Paul leads the prayers: for the sick; for our families; for priestly vocations; for the victims of the recent road crash; for those known to us who have 'gone home' since the last pilgrimage; for our fellow pilgrims; and, finally, for ourselves.

The gospel reading is St John's account of the paralysed man told to 'take up thy bed, and walk.' Father Humphrey expands on the theme in his sermon, assuring the sick that they are close to Christ and that their example and forbearance are an inspiration to us all. 'Remember that, however hard it may be for the human mind to fathom, all suffering has a purpose. The Blessed Virgin has cured many people in Lourdes but not St Bernadette herself, who was tormented all her life by asthma. When she was asked why, she replied that it was not for her to question the ways of God. "I'm happier on my bed of affliction," she declared, "than a queen on a throne." She had no more desire to suffer than Our Lord had on His cross, but she knew that it was one of God's gifts.' As he draws to a close, I wonder whether Lester and Frank and Brenda are grateful for their gifts; I wonder whether Fiona's parents and Tadeusz and Lucja take comfort from the knowledge of their children's proximity to Christ. Above all, I wonder about Gillian, sitting next to her inspirational husband, but the back of her head gives nothing away.

The sermon over, Father Humphrey asks two of the young brancardiers to bring up the Jubilate banner and calls on Father Paul to bless it. 'No one blesses like Father,' he quips, to the delight of his audience. Beneath the archness, however, I detect something more sinister. Out of the blue, my mind fills with images of castrati. Although the Church no longer emasculates its choristers, it continues to infantilise its congregations. The thought depresses me and I am grateful for the chance to bury it in the formality of the Eucharistic prayers, but the respite is cut short when Father Dave announces the Peace. I am wrenched back to my childhood and the dreaded moment each Sunday when I had to shake hands, first with Father Damian, whose clammy palm contained the threat of something more intimate, and then with Douglas, my fellow altar boy and weekly nemesis who, daring me not to squeal, turned the exchange into a Chinese burn. While nothing can ever compare with that, I watch in dismay as the room erupts in a tide of hugs and handshakes and kisses. Nor are we observers spared since, in swift succession: Louisa; Marjorie; a bald brancardier; Fiona and her mother; Sister Martha; and a young woman, who from her accent I take to be Lucja head towards us, extending both hands and greetings. Detachment is no longer an option as we are drawn into the heart of the crowd. Suddenly, an extraordinary sensation overwhelms me – if it is peace, then it is a peace that inflames every nerve in my body – as I first hear her voice, at once wry and sincere, and then slowly reach to take her outstretched hand.

GILLIAN

Thursday June 19

I turn away from the camera for fear that it will capture an emotion invisible to the naked eye. Vincent's film will be broadcast in November. Patricia will insist on watching it with us or, worse, on throwing a small party for her church or Troubridge Hall friends. We will sit in our allotted chairs in her airless sitting room, braving the constant round of crisps and crudités ('Richard, darling, I bought the olives pitted specially for you'), counting the minutes until the programme begins. Halfway through, we will see the exterior of the Acceuil, followed by a slow pan across the pilgrims gathering at the gate. 'Oh!' Patricia will cry, missing nothing. 'This was the morning we went on a walking tour of the town. I know because it was the first outing for my pink linen.' On cue, the camera picks out the suit, more Paris than Lourdes, but the audience's acclamations fade when it settles on the woman standing next to her, who might as well be in her nightdress, a woman whose every look screams morning-after ecstasy. My secret is out; my shame is exposed.

There again, I may be grateful for the record. In years to come, when I start to doubt my own memory, the film will bear witness to the moment that a decent man – a man of talent and discernment – chose me. The blissful smile on my face, the glow that I know must envelop me, will take me back to the spartan hotel room: to the lumpy mattress on which Vincent O'Shaughnessy – and somehow his full name matters – made love to me. It will conjure up a night when my body was once again the core of my being, when I was with a man who was healthy and lucid: a man who saw me as a woman and not just a cross between a call girl and a nurse.

I am aware that the experience can never be repeated. I am not looking for miracles, at least not for myself. I expect nothing more from him than courtesy and consideration for what remains of the trip. Nevertheless, I do not feel a single regret for what we did and, should I ever be tempted to waver, I will only need to switch on the tape. So let them think what they like of me! I search for the camera and smile.

'Didn't I tell you Lourdes would put a bloom in your cheeks?'

Patricia's voice drags me back to the present. 'You look positively radiant.'

'It must be the sun.'

'Have you put any cream on?' I shake my head. 'Here!' She fumbles for a tube in her bag. 'It can play nasty tricks.' I rub some on, to shield myself from scrutiny as much as from harm.

'It's done you the world of good,' she continues with disarming warmth. 'After all your shilly-shallying, aren't you glad you came?'

'I am.'

'I'll let you into a little secret. During the procession last night, I said a special prayer for you. Just a small one. There's someone we both know needs them more. But Our Lady must have heard. She has room in her heart for us all.'

'Yes, you're right. I think I've finally begun to understand the meaning of infinity.'

She gazes at me in confusion. 'Richard looks happy.' She gestures to her son who is sharing a joke with Nigel and a couple of brancardiers.

'He's excited. They're letting him push Nigel's wheelchair up the hill.'

'Is that wise?'

'He's discovered the appeal of helping someone needier than himself. It may pall, but then he only has one more day.'

'It'll all end in tears.'

'What?' Her words make me shudder.

'Tomorrow at the airport, when they go their separate ways.'

'Oh yes, of course.'

'Still, I'm sure he'll get over it. A friendship that springs up so fast can't reach down very deep.'

I study her face for a hint of a double meaning. 'Let's hope you're right.'

'Can we be having everyone please?' Ken's request cuts short our exchange. 'The *malades* and their carers in front. The rest of us forming an orderly line behind. Father Dave is ready to start.' At the sound of his name, the priest turns away from the group of youngsters with whom he is chatting, takes a last puff of his cigarette and grinds it underfoot. Temporarily relieved of my caring status, I stand back to allow the hospital pilgrims priority. As ever I am moved to see Linda, beanpole thin beneath several layers of clothing, pushing the hefty Brenda. Woe betide anyone who offers to help, as Matt found out at the Stations of the Cross. I am saddened to see Tess pushing Lester who, after his collapse yesterday, has finally accepted a chair.

'Still not too steady after the op,' he says stoically. 'Giving Tess a chance to make herself useful.'

'About time too,' I say, anxious not to betray her trust. 'Oh excuse me.' I fail to stifle a yawn.

'Rough night?' Tess asks with a glance at Richard.

'Quite the reverse.'

We set off past the miracle-working statue of the Virgin. The red tint to her crown puts me in mind of Vincent and, breaking all my own rules, I turn to look for him. He is at St Joseph's Gate, deep in discussion with Jamie and Jewel as they film the walk. All at once the few yards between us seem to extend for miles and a bitter chill sweeps through the air. I feel an acute need to make contact, if only by speaking his name. Jamie and Jewel are preoccupied and, besides, after last night the very thought of Jamie brings a blush to my cheek. So I opt for Sophie and, excusing myself to Patricia, hang back until she catches up.

It is not just her modishly eccentric clothes (today, a red-and-white stripy shirt and white skin-tight jeans with red question marks embroidered on the front and back pockets) that set her apart from the rest of us. She even walks differently, in the emphatic but effortless strides of one to whom people naturally give way. She is the kind of woman I like to pretend that I might have been in other circumstances but, in truth, the disparity runs far deeper. I know nothing about her background except to feel sure that it would not have stood in the way of her ambition. She would never have wound up as a secretary in a family construction firm, a position obtained through the good offices of the parish priest, who had no idea of the proprietary interest Mr Thomas Patterson took in his female staff. But if by some strange quirk of fate she had, she would never have quit her job to marry the boss's son, let alone agreed to wait the best part of ten years for children: children who would have given her marriage a heart; children who would have given her life a meaning; until, by the cruellest irony, her husband became her child. And if … but I have no wish to speculate what she would have done had she been left with Richard. Suddenly, the hypothetical becomes all too real.

I envy so much about her, but first on the list is her relationship with Vincent. Theirs is an easy, lunchtime, how's-things-at-home intimacy; ours a furtive, bedtime, somebody's-going-to-be-hurt one. But, even as I define the difference, I recall last night: the totally unplanned, desperately anticipated perfection of it. I feel his hands as hot on my breasts as if he had crept up behind me. I know now that, no matter how lonely the future may be, I would not swap places with anyone. At last I can understand the heroines of my schoolgirl romances who were willing to risk all for a single night of love.

'Vincent seems busy,' I say, trusting that I have not lingered too long on his name.

'He never stops. The way he works is to shoot as much as possible and then make the film in the editing. We have a schedule of course but, to quote him, it's a safety net not a straightjacket. He likes to be free to pick up whatever comes his way.'

I flinch, but her friendly smile reassures me. It is clear that Jamie has kept his promise to say nothing of Vincent's midnight quest, unless – and this is not an option I relish – he failed to realise that the woman in question was me.

'It must keep you in a state of panic.'

'More *creative tension*. At least that's my story. It only once turned pear-shaped, when he made a film about Estonian strawberry-pickers – Estonian strawberry-pickers in Kent, that is – and found that that was precisely what they were: Estonian strawberry-pickers. No ideological, generational tensions within the group. No East-West, poverty-affluence tensions outside it. Just twenty people picking strawberries and, two weeks later, no film. That was before my time, thank God! Excuse me, I ought to see if I'm needed.'

She walks over to Vincent who is standing in a shop doorway filming the ad-hoc procession as we file towards the bridge. For a moment his eyes meet mine and, with a barely perceptible nod, he indicates the gypsies camping on the bank. I feel my face breaking into a smile when I might have expected it to flush crimson. He switches his attention to Sophie and I switch mine to the road, which is steep enough to challenge even the fittest pilgrims. Some of the young brancardiers are wilting under the weight of their wheelchairs but Richard, licensed for once to exercise his muscles, forges ahead. Father Paul hurries forward to stop him, and I suspect that he has shot past the turning. He seems reluctant to head back but I keep my distance, happy to leave him in someone else's charge. I wonder if this is the new definition of my carer's role. I care ... oh yes, I will care for ever, but I no longer control.

Having gathered us together, Father Dave leads the way down a shabby side street to Bernadette's birthplace, an ancient mill which, with its cream plastered walls, wooden balcony and shuttered windows, resembles an artfully restored auberge. He beckons us closer, while waiting for the gaggle of visitors at the door to go inside.

'This is the Boly Mill, where St Bernadette was born on 7 January 1844, the first child of François Soubirous and his wife Louisa. The mill belonged to Louisa's mother, Claire Casterot, who initially lived with the family but, after Louisa gave birth to her second child, Toinette, in September 1846, Claire and her three younger children moved in with her eldest daughter, Bernarde, to give them more space.'

'More space?' A voice which a few hours ago was cooing in my ear now drips with scorn. 'They were at daggers drawn. It was a last-ditch solution.'

I am torn between a longing to listen to him and a fear that other people will overhear. 'In-laws,' I say with a smile which I hope will satisfy him, only to find myself addressing Patricia who has nudged forward.

'You'll see for yourselves how small the house is: just three rooms and the workplace, so it's no wonder that space was at a premium. Bernadette lived here for twelve years, until a string of misfortunes forced the family to leave. First, her father was blinded in one eye by a chip that flew off the millstone. Then her little brother Jean-Marie was gathered to the Lord.' I steal a glance at Vincent, whose face is impassive. 'François had long let his heart rule his head, giving extra measures to this one and selling on credit to that, but the advent of the steam-powered mills dealt him a mortal blow. Driven out of his own mill, he went to work for a rival who accused him of stealing flour and had him thrown into jail. Of course a few days later he was utterly exonerated, but it broke his spirit. In 1856, he took his family to a derelict hovel, Rives House, but even there the rent proved too high and, in 1857, just when you'd think they couldn't sink any lower, they moved into the *cachot*, the punishment cell of the former town prison, which a kind-hearted cousin put at their disposal.' He turns to Lester. 'Does that answer your question?'

'Perfectly, Father.'

'I thought so. Even through all the bad times the Soubirous remained loving and close-knit, and, before we take a look inside, I'd ask you to bow your heads in prayer for the family, an institution which is under greater threat than ever, yet remains the bedrock of our society, the place where we learn our Christian values.' Father Dave signals his intent by closing his eyes. I follow suit, but my thoughts are disturbed first by the background noise, which is amplified in the darkness, and then by the image of Vincent, whose prayers – were he to make them – would be full of reproof. I am pulled up by the 'Amen', which I emptily echo, and make my way to the front door, which is now clear.

Richard is wreaking havoc by trying to squeeze Nigel's wheelchair inside, despite Ken's protests. No longer the detached observer, I hurry to intervene.

'There's no room. Look at the stairs.'

'I can push it. Like this. See.' He tips the wheelchair right back, causing Nigel to giggle uncontrollably.

'Just stop it, please!' I say, unwelcome comparisons making me shrill. 'You're holding everyone up. Come in with me and catch up with Nigel later.'

'No. If Nigel can't go in, neither will I,' he says, in a mixture of solidarity and petulance.

'Don't worry, mate,' Vincent says, coming up from behind. 'How about we do some filming inside and show it to you both? Give you a sneak preview.'

'Before Gilly?'

'Before anyone.'

'Yes please,' Richard says. 'Then we can see it all from out here.'

Brushing aside my thanks, Vincent steps back from the door, leaving me to enter alone. I walk through the kitchen and mill, idly appraising the dilapidated machinery. Then I follow Claire and Martin upstairs and linger on the landing, taking an undue interest in the votive plaques as I wait for Vincent.

'It's very kind of you to help,' I say, when he finally arrives.

'Not at all,' he replies with a heart-warming smile. 'We're not planning on filming in here, so Jamie can wipe the tape once he's shown it to them.'

'Boys and their toys. I mean that in the nicest possible way.'

'I'm sure you always do.'

'So this is where it all began,' I say quickly, gazing at the room in which St Bernadette was born. The wooden wall-panelling and blue-and-white check counterpane look suspiciously pristine. 'It all seems a little sanitised.'

'And how! I was biting my tongue during Father Dave's homily ... sorry, history lesson.'

'Not very successfully. *More space!*'

'That was nothing. How about François Soubirous being *utterly exonerated*? Says who? He was simply released through lack of evidence. What's the big deal? Why not admit Bernadette came from a dysfunctional household? Or is the Church so fixated on happy families that it has to cover it up?'

'Let's discuss it outside,' I say, as Patricia and Maggie walk into the room. 'We're holding everyone up.'

'Ladies, you be the arbiters.' Vincent shoots me a mischievous glance as they simper. 'Do you like your saints squeaky-clean from the start, or would you prefer them to show a little human frailty?'

'Well, it's not up to us, is it?' Maggie replies. 'Take St Paul. He persecuted the early Christians and now he's at the top of the tree.'

'And Mary Magdalene,' Patricia adds. 'No better than she should be and yet she was the one next to Our Lady at the foot of the Cross. But if you mean St Bernadette, she was as frail and as human as any other young girl. Maggie, you remember the story Father Dave told us last year about when she was living with the Sisters of Charity and forbidden to go to the vegetable garden, so she threw her clog out of the window for a friend to fill it with strawberries.'

'Wicked!' Vincent says, with a smirk that cannot fail to escape my mother-in-law's notice.

'And one day,' Maggie says, 'she was even caught putting a block of wood inside her blouse to increase the size of her you know whats.'

'Sh-sh,' Patricia says, 'that's just hearsay. We don't want Mr O'Shaughnessy repeating it to all and sundry on the BBC.'

'Don't worry, ladies. Anything you say stays strictly within these four walls. Besides, as a hardboiled film-maker, I find this rebellious, provocative Bernadette far more to my taste.'

'Oh I didn't mean it like that,' Patricia says quickly.

'Of course not,' Vincent replies, with a wink that flusters her further.

We go back outside and find Jamie holding up his camera to replay the footage of the house to Nigel, who stares at it in frustration. 'Can't see,' he says, as Jamie points out each special feature.

'That's because you're not looking straight,' Jamie says, holding the camera a few inches away from his eyes.

'Gimme,' Nigel says, groping feebly for the camera.

'Not on your life,' Jamie says. 'It's more than my job's worth.'

'Can't see!'

'Don't mind him. He's a spastic,' Richard says casually about the man whom only this morning he described as his best friend ever, a category in which, when pressed, he included his wife.

'You mustn't use that word,' I say, fearful that he may have been overheard.

'You did!'

'I was speaking medically,' I reply, looking to both Vincent and Jamie for endorsement.

'I'm a spastic,' Nigel says, clapping his hands.

'Richard,' I say, desperate to move on. 'Since you've offered to push Nigel, you should do the job properly. Father Dave is waiting to get going.'

We join Father Dave on the short walk to the Lacadé Mill, which is billed in large lettering, as the *Maison Paternelle de Ste Bernadette*. Even to one unschooled in Lourdes lore, it points to a deep-rooted rivalry with the neighbouring birthplace. Father Dave explains that the designation derives from its being the only house that Bernadette's family ever owned and, unlike the Boly Mill, it remains in their possession, as we find out on being asked to pay an entrance fee.

'Somewhere along the line the spirit that gave free flour to the poor seems to have vanished,' Vincent says wryly.

In place of the room in which she was born, the Lacadé Mill offers the bed in which she slept on her last night in Lourdes before entering the convent of Nevers. The latter-day Soubirous may have been dispossessed of the birthplace, but they make up for it by accentuating their connection to Bernadette. Pre-eminent in the hall is a large family tree with an emphasis on the branch which, through the brother's second wife, still owns the house.

'It must be odd to have a saint in the family,' I say to Vincent, whose silent but eloquently critical presence has shadowed me through the building.

'But profitable.'

At the end of the visit we come to the gift shop, which sells the usual tawdry souvenirs at even more inflated prices than elsewhere in the town.

'Ten euros for a lavender bag?' I say, holding up one of the few acceptable items.

'But look at it this way! How often do you have the chance to be served by the great-great niece of a saint?' He points to the unsmiling middle-aged woman at the till and then to the photograph of her in christening robes embroidered by Bernadette herself in pride of place on the wall.

'This must be grist to your mill,' I say. 'No pun intended.'

'None taken,' he replies, studying a shelf on which plastic models of the Virgin and St Bernadette nestle next to fans, oven gloves, barometers, trays, flannels, pencil cases and key-rings embossed with images of the Grotto. 'Look, two for the price of one!' He picks up a laminated picture in which Christ's head morphs into the Pope's. 'What about this?' He winds up a small Madonna that warbles the Ave Maria. 'She's playing our tune!'

'People are looking,' I say as he rummages through the merchandise with open derision.

'The money changers aren't just in the temple; they've taken it over.' He ignores my warning and continues to delve. 'Wow, see this!' He presses the switch on a cherub cigarette-lighter. 'Come on baby, light my fire! Now this is sad. John Paul II at half-price.' He holds up a plaster statuette. 'Poor old Pope! I almost feel sorry for him. Marked down even in Lourdes.'

'Are you going to film here?' I ask, in a bid to distract him.

'I wish! Sophie and I tried to get permission when we came on our recce, but they're not fools.'

'*Vous désirez quelque chose, Monsieur?*' the illustrious saleswoman asks, as he jiggles a crucified Christ whose eyes open in alternate piety and pain.

'*Nous admirons vos objets d'art, Madame,*' he replies with a smile that she takes at face value. '*Malheursement nous prenons l'avion. Les restrictions de poids.*'

'*Nous avons des foulards et des choses en tissu pour Madame,*' she says, steering him towards a rack of garish scarves. Meanwhile, Richard, who has been looking round with Patricia, comes over with a miniature Eiffel Tower.

'I want this. Can I have some money?'

'But Richard, it's hideous.'

'It's my money.'

'That's amazing,' Vincent says, staring at the model. 'Show it to me, will you, Rich?' I wonder if the name is deliberate. 'Do you think it slipped in the wrong batch? Some tat-making factory sent it here rather than Paris? Or are they trying to cater for all markets?'

'I want it.'

'And you shall have it. On me.'

'You don't have to,' I say.

'It's my money,' Richard insists.

'I want to. Rich and I are old mates, aren't we?' He nudges Richard, who grins and almost drops the model. Vincent is so good with him that, against all reason, I construct an elaborate fantasy of his returning from Lourdes and moving in with us. My euphoria swiftly turns to despair. Quite apart from the logistics, I have slept with him only once. Once! I don't doubt his sincerity but, in his world, sex is as casual as a cup of coffee. He would be appalled by my schoolgirl scenario. At most this is – was – a holiday romance: two lonely people seeking solace in each other's company. Even if we were truly making love, rather than enjoying the quick bonk, screw or fuck with which I charge myself, there is no law that love has to last. I shall defer to Vincent and not attempt to match the human to the divine.

'Penny for them?' Vincent says. 'Or would you rather have a shawl?' He grabs one of the cloths and drapes it round my shoulders.

'What do you say?' he asks Richard. 'Shall we buy it for her?'

'I don't have my money.'

'It's a tea-towel,' I say, replacing it on the pile. 'We'd better go. Father Dave will be losing patience. I don't suppose he's on commission.'

Vincent raises his eyebrows. 'Okay, Rich,' he says, 'let's pay.' As he leads him to the till, I nonchalantly scan the shelves. My eyes fix on a Lalique angel, its elegant simplicity a reproach to the surrounding kitsch. I pick it up to admire.

'Oh that's lovely,' Patricia says, approaching. 'Show me. Are you thinking of buying it?'

'I was, until I saw what it cost. Two fifty!'

'Two euros fifty?'

'Come on, Mother!' I surprise myself by using her preferred form of address. 'Two hundred and fifty.'

'How can they? And for an angel! But it's so pretty.'

Vincent returns with Richard, who holds his packet like an ice-cream cone.

'Have you found something, ladies?' Vincent asks. 'An angel!' His studied ambiguity makes me blush.

'Gillian wanted to buy it, but I made her see sense,' Patricia says. 'The way they throw your luggage about these days, it's bound to break.'

Honour satisfied, she puts it back on the shelf. Vincent lifts it up, running his fingers over the chest.

'This reminds me of someone.'

'Fragile? Transparent?' I say, drawn to the game in spite of the danger.

'Luminous.'

Maggie appears at the door. 'Come on, slowcoaches. Father Dave has itchy feet.'

'I had athlete's feet,' Richard says proudly to Vincent as we walk out.

'You had something else,' I say sourly.

'I had blisters. They hurt.'

We make our way through the town to the *cachot*. Richard has abandoned Nigel in favour of Vincent, who promises him a 'man to man' chat as he guides him gently over the rutted pavement. I keep them firmly in sight, their implausible intimacy at once a comfort and a threat, while walking with Claire and Martin. I marvel at Claire's ability to conduct a normal conversation – one that is packed with the medical details normal for Lourdes – while constantly breaking off to encourage Martin who, even at this snail's pace, takes two shuffling steps to every one of ours. Her tender solicitude to his slightest need makes me doubly ashamed of my frustration with Richard. Is it that they share a profound bond, forged in the womb, denied to those of us who were coupled at the altar, or rather that she is a decent person who would never seek to escape her obliga-tions in nights of adultery and fantasies of divorce?

'You're a wonder,' I say, as she holds a tissue to his runny nose and tells him to blow.

'I'm his mother,' she replies, perplexed.

Somehow *I'm his wife* lacks the same ring.

We arrive at the *cachot*, where Bernadette and her family found refuge and which, according to Father Dave, occupies a similar place in the story of Lourdes as the stable in that of the Nativity. He leads us down a well-worn flight of steps into a cramped, cheerless room with a rough stone floor, bare plaster walls and a pervasive smell of damp. Not even the most hostile observer – I refrain from glancing at Vincent – could fail to be moved by the family's plight. Unlike the Boly Mill, there has been no attempt to disguise the squalor. A large rosary above the fireplace and two jars of irises on the ledge are the sole decoration. It is as though the authorities were determined to emphasise the inauspicious soil from which Bernadette sprang, an emphasis Father Dave echoes as he takes us through the tale. 'Remember Our Lord said: "Blessed are the poor in spirit." St Berna-dette herself said that, if there had been anyone poorer and meaner than her, then God would have chosen them.'

'Really!' Patricia whispers in a rare note of dissent. 'Has political correctness even reached Lourdes? It's her virtues he should be stressing not her income. Surely we can be poor in spirit whatever our station in life?'

She leads the way out, her reluctance to dwell in the cell or on its message widely shared. Only Lucja lingers, as though drawn back to the poverty from which she recently emerged.

'So what's the plan?' Vincent asks, accosting me in the doorway.

'You gave me a shock!' I play for time. 'I presume we're heading back to the Acceuil for lunch. You know how strict they are about timetables.'

'I'm learning. Your mother-in-law and Maggie have gone on ahead to set up.' I scan the crowd making its desultory way down the hill, but, while instantly alert to Richard walking alongside a young handmaiden, I see no sign of Patricia.

'It's strange that she should be happy to do all the dirty work here that she runs a mile from at home,' I say disloyally.

'Like Marie Antoinette playing at milkmaids on her farm.'

'She's not playing!' I exclaim, to the surprise of Derek and Charlotte in front. 'You may think me a hypocrite,' I add through gritted teeth, 'jumping into bed with the first man to show me a scrap of kindness. But don't tar the whole pilgrimage with the same brush!'

'Hey, what's brought this on?' He gives me such an affectionate look that, for a horrible moment, I am afraid I may burst into tears. 'I'm sorry. That was crass of me. I'm sure your mother-in-law is utterly sincere. Where would the world be without its charitable ladies?'

'No, it's me. I didn't mean to bite your head off. I'm a little overwrought.'

'Only a little?' he asks, smiling. 'Then you're doing better than me. Let's spend the afternoon together.'

'There's mass in the Notre Dame chapel.'

'Aren't you massed out?'

'Don't you have to film it?'

'I refer you to my previous question. There's a limit to the viewing public's appetite for Father Humphrey's quivering jowls.'

'I suppose there's not much point in my going since I can't take communion.'

73

'Why not?'

'Not without going to confession first.'

'So you believe that sleeping with me is sinful?' he asks, wincing.

'Don't take it personally.'

'Oh I'm sorry, I thought what we did was personal. Despite what you seem to think, you weren't just an anonymous fuck.'

'Don't be angry. I didn't say I regretted it. That's the problem; I'm revelling in it. I'm walking down this street, but my head – no, not only my head, my whole body – is back in your room … in your bed … in your arms. I said I'm not a hypocrite. How can I stand before the altar when I don't repent what we did? On the contrary, I want to repeat it.'

'That can be easily arranged.'

'I'm being serious!'

'So am I. Why do you have to go back for lunch? Richard is among friends.' Peering forwards, I see to my relief that the handmaiden has been joined by three young brancardiers. 'Let's go for a picnic. A Pic-du-Jer-nic.'

'What?'

'It's a mountain on the other side of town. We can take the funicular railway to the top. Didn't you see? There's a poster for it back at the Bates motel.'

'It's very tempting.'

'Is that mouth-wateringly tempting or Get thee behind me, Satan?'

'Probably both, but I'll opt for the former. After all, I'll only draw attention to myself stuck in my pew when everyone else goes up to the altar. But where will we find the food?'

'Leave that to me. This is your respite. The government has promised a better deal for carers and I'm here to deliver.'

'I've changed my mind. It's Satan all the way.'

'That's more like it. What time does your watch say? Ten past twelve. Meet me at St Joseph's Gate at one.'

The matter settled, he breaks away from the group and walks back towards the *cachot*. I press forward to find Richard, eager to make up for my imminent neglect. Tenderness mingles with apprehension as I see him chatting genially with two of the young handmaidens, Jenny and, I think, Eileen, their smiling faces a testament to his distinctive little boy/big man charm. His hands hovering above the smalls of their backs may appear innocent to Sheila Clunes, whose wheelchair is directly behind them, but my more practised eye detects danger. I sweep up and loop my arm through his, receiving a look of pure malice which, as ever, I try not to take to heart.

I occupy the walk back with descriptive chatter, designed to distract myself as much as Richard. At the Acceuil, I deliver him into Maggie's charge, explaining that I plan to slip away for an afternoon's sightseeing.

'Good idea! You deserve a break. Don't worry about Richard. He'll be fine.'

'What about mass?' I am confronted by Patricia who is dispensing handwash at the dining-room door.

'I've been every day this week. Surely I can miss one afternoon?' Her expression leaves no doubt as to whom she will blame should the long prayed-for miracle fail to occur.

'Are you going alone?' she asks suspiciously.

'Yes, of course.'

'If you wait till after lunch, I can come with you.'

'You should put your feet up. Anyway it'd leave too little time before the Blessed Sacrament procession. I promise I'll be back at five.' I head for the lift which, to my relief, is waiting.

'Watch out for your purse!' Patricia calls as I step inside, making me wonder if I may have misheard.

Such a tide of guilt engulfs me on my way through the Domain that I fear I may be forced back. Last night I could pretend, at least to myself, that Vincent's offer of a drink was nothing more than that. This afternoon I have no such excuse. I am skipping mass to meet my lover. Even if his intentions are pure, mine are not.

I have barely left the square when I spot him among the crowd swarming through St Joseph's Gate. I am amazed by my sharp sight, which I attribute first to love, then to Lourdes and, finally, to his conspicuous shopping bags. If it is love, it cannot be mutual, since he stares straight through me with no sign of recognition. Each step I take brings his anxiety into clearer focus. Half of me wants to run and reassure him, while the other half wants to steal up on him unawares so as to savour his delight. Suddenly he sees me and swings one of the shopping bags above his head, only to put it down fast before it bursts.

'Your carriage awaits, Madame,' he says, leading me out of the gate.

Having pictured us riding through Lourdes in a tourist buggy, I am grateful to find that his romantic spirit runs to nothing more reckless than a cab.

'You're mad! The meter's ticking.'

'We've no time to lose. A mere four hours – no, three hours fifty-six minutes (Madame is fashionably late) – before our next engagement.'

'Madame is unfashionably sweaty. I've rushed.'

'Then don't stand out here in the heat. Go in and … stick to the seats.' He gives me an apologetic smile as he ushers me inside and directs the driver to the Pic. We crawl through the town, my sympathy with jaywalkers shamefully diminished now that I am the one delayed.

At each left turn, the cross dangling from the mirror is struck by a blinding ray of light. 'Wouldn't that be just my luck?' Vincent says squinting. 'Death by dangerous crucifix.'

'Maybe it's a sign?' I say.

'Come on! You're not that credulous.'

'Joke! You're not the only one who's allowed a sense of humour.'

His pained expression melts into a smile as quickly as the laminated Christ turned into the Pope.

We arrange for the driver to pick us up at four, my preference, rather than four thirty, Vincent's; his protests that we will have barely an hour on the peak undermined by the sign announcing a six-minute ascent. We buy our tickets and take our place in a short queue behind a German couple whose young daughter voraciously licks a Mickey Mouse lollipop. She flashes a coquettish, gap-toothed smile at Vincent, whose eyes well up.

A cloud passes over her face and she tugs her father's sleeve. '*Warum weint der Mann denn?*' she asks. He turns round to find the tears now streaming down Vincent's cheeks.

'*Er hat zu viel Sonne in die Augen bekommen,*' he replies with a frown, pulling the girl in front of him. '*Deshalb müssen wir immer unsere Brillen tragen.*'

I squeeze Vincent's arm and stroke his hair, full of pity for his pain and frustration at my helplessness to relieve it. 'Don't worry, darling,' I say, feeling an intimacy that reaches beyond the flesh into the very marrow of our bones. 'I'm here. You'll be all right.'

'I already am,' he says with an effort. 'That's why it's so absurd. It's when I'm happy that I start to remember. And I'm truly happy.' He continues to weep, while deploring his feebleness.

I am so grateful for the arrival of the train that I barely wait for the passengers to descend before grabbing our bags and pushing him in. The one benefit of his tears is that they guarantee us a car to ourselves. I settle him on the hard wooden seat and hold him close, as he gradually shrugs off the past and returns to me.

My concern for Vincent overrides my usual fears about safety as we make our rickety ascent through the cedar and pine. Those fears return when we enter a rocky tunnel and the carriage begins to jolt.

'Relax,' he says, feeling me tense. 'This train's been running for a hundred years.'

'It feels as if that was the last time they had it checked.' I grip his hand. 'We make a fine pair,' I say, as we emerge into the light.

'Yes,' he says, 'we do.'

We arrive at the terminus, where I am relieved to find our fellow passengers heading for either the café or the entrance to the *Highest Grotto in Europe*, leaving us to set off for the peak alone. There are two paths: one wide and gentle; the other narrow and steep. True to form, he favours the latter. 'How are your shoes?'

'They're fine. I'm not so sure about my legs.'

'Wimp!' he says, spirits fully restored, as he clambers up a path which looks like little more than a gap through the bushes.

I trudge behind, my weariness intensified by the sweetly soporific scent of juniper and eglantine. Brilliant white butterflies, as powdery as pollen, flit in front of us. The beauty of the scenery almost reconciles me to the climb.

'Keeping up?' Vincent asks, without looking round.

'I'm right behind you,' I say, sensing that he too is starting to flag under his heavy bags. All at once he turns. 'Watch out where you tread. We don't want to wipe out some rare Pyrenean plant.'

'Of course not,' I say, amused by this blatant excuse for a pause.

We press on, both too proud to acknowledge any strain, before stepping out of the bushes on to a grassy knoll topped with an old observation platform and a giant masthead.

Vincent finds a shaded spot and sets down the bags, while I recover my breath. 'Aren't we going up to admire the view?' I ask.

'OK, OK. I admit defeat,' Vincent says, collapsing on the ground. He opens his arms and I happily sink into them. He is hot and sticky but, far from the revulsion I feel with Richard, I relish his every touch.

After taking the edge off our appetites, we turn to the food. He opens bags of bread and olives, cheeses and ham, pâté and salads, sausage and roast chicken, peaches, strawberries, and apple tarts.

'Do you like your women big?'

'I just like my women.'

'There's enough here for ten.'

'I wanted to go overboard. I wanted to be extravagant. I'm sorry, I'm sure it makes no sense.'

'Oh but it does. It makes perfect sense to me.'

'I went to the market. I couldn't resist.' He takes out a bottle and jauntily pops the cork. 'Wait for it!' He grabs a plastic cup as the bubbles gush out. 'Quick!'

'Champagne!'

'Well no, actually. Blanquette de Limoux. The local sparkling wine. I'm told that experts consider it vastly superior.'

'I'm told that too.'

'Champagne's a bit vulgar, wouldn't you agree? A bit two-for-one at Tesco?'

'Absolutely. I refuse to allow a bottle into the house.'

'Cheers, my darling. Here's to us.'

'To us,' I echo, wondering whether the toast will ever be more than an empty phrase. We both gulp the tepid liquid. 'Delicious,' I say after a pause. 'A distinctly superior woody tang.'

'Especially when it's served almost at boiling-point. You're a wonderful liar! I love you.'

For all my misgivings, we make considerable inroads into the food, our party spirits surfacing as, first I dangle a sliver of ham into his mouth, and then he scoops up some pâté on his finger, pressing it between my lips.

Suddenly, I am aware that we have an audience. '*Warum nuckelt die Frau denn an seinem Finger?*' the German girl asks her parents.

'*Die sind Englisch,*' her mother says, which makes me laugh.

'*Einen schönen Nachmittag noch. Die Aussicht von hier oben ist wirklick herrlich, nicht wahr,*' I reply. She looks appalled, as much by the realisation that she has been understood as by the prospect that this flagrantly immodest woman might engage her in conversation.

The Germans beat a hasty retreat, leaving us to refresh our intimacy with alternate bites of a *tarte Tatin*.

'Tell me,' I say, 'as a matter of idle curiosity, what was it about me that first attracted you?'

'Idle curiosity?' he asks, with a smile that rips through my defences. 'Sure! Though I can point to a moment more easily than a reason. It was when you took my hand at the opening mass. It was a touch … a feeling. No, it was *the* feeling. I knew at once that I'd found a bright, warm, wonderful woman: a woman who'd lived.'

'Really?' I ask, uncertain whether he is speaking of experience or years. 'But you must meet so many interesting people.'

'Perhaps what Father Dave said about St Savin applies to you? You've seen more in your quiet corner of Surrey than those of us rushing blindly around the metropolis.' Yesterday, I would have suspected him of mocking me; today, I am afraid that he may be deluding himself. 'Do you want me to go on?'

'Yes please,' I say, eager for anything that fleshes out the fantasy.

'There's a sadness in you, but it's a strength not a weakness: a brokenness that – no surprise – matches mine. And I've not even started on your smile.' He traces it with his fingertips. 'Your hair.' He runs it through his hand. 'The nape of your neck.' He brushes it with his lips.

'You're making me blush!'

'And your blushes, so innocently provocative! Your turn.'

'Oh I've not given it any thought,' I reply, terrified of saying something that he will find trivial.

'Liar!'

'Your honesty,' I retort. 'Your intelligence; your vivacity; your charm. Don't laugh! The fact that you weren't at all what I was expecting. Which made me want to look more closely at what you are.'

'And you're not disappointed?' he asks, with affecting diffidence.

'Quite the opposite. I'm even attracted by your views on the Church.'

'You're joking!'

'Not in themselves, I'm afraid, but because they're the antithesis of mine. My religion is so much a part of me; I could no more think of living without it than without an arm or a leg.' I shiver. 'Perhaps that's not the most sensitive comparison to make in Lourdes.'

'I promise not to tell.'

'I'm used to being with people who take faith for granted. Meeting you has been a challenge.'

'So long as you don't make it your mission to convert me.'

'Strange as it may seem, I'd like to keep you exactly as you are.'

'Thank you,' he says softly. 'That's another thing I love about you: you allow me to see myself through your eyes.'

I lean back against his chest, the baking sun mingling with the life-giving heat of his body. A few minutes later he leaps up. 'Come on, lazybones! Mattress temporarily withdrawn. It's time to explore.' He hauls me up and, after packing away the picnic in best Patricia mode, we climb the ramshackle flight of steps to the platform. The scenery is spectacular but, before I can take it in, Vincent points to the ladder running up the masthead. 'Shall we?'

'I dare you.' Flinging down the bags, he heaves himself on to the bottom rung. 'Don't you dare!' I pull him back on to the platform.

'Phew!' he says. 'For a moment I thought you might watch me go up.'

'And you'd have been fool enough to do it?'

'Faint heart and fair lady and all that.'

'Trust me, she's already been won.'

He slips his arm around my shoulders and we stand quietly marvelling at the panoramic view of the Pyrenees. I feel the same joy in nature as I did yesterday, more convinced than ever that such magnificence must be part of a divine plan, but no longer concerned to argue the case. We slowly turn to face each point of a landscape that lies, like a sumptuous carpet, at the feet of our love.

'Oh!' Vincent lifts his arm to his head. 'I can feel my ears popping.'

'Are we that high?'

'I am. Doesn't it make you want to throw everything up and come and live here?'

'*Everything*'s too easy. It's when you start putting names to things that it becomes hard.'

'Don't be so reasonable. Follow your dreams for once.'

'Such as? I'm too old to play at being Heidi.'

'I give up.'

'Yes, I think you should. We both should, leaving this as a perfect memory. I'll be the lonely woman you took pity on during filming. An anecdote to amuse your friends.'

'Do you think I'd ever do that?'

'No.'

'Then why say it?'

'Because I'm trying to make it easier for us. No, be honest, Gillian! I'm trying to make it easier for me. I can't live on dreams. I need to know what's real.'

'Is this real?' He kisses me, his own sweetness sharpened by the wine.

I let the kiss and the question linger before answering. 'This is too real.'

'I can't win.'

'You already have.'

We remain joined to each other, oblivious of the outside world, until a high-pitched 'Yuck!' forces us apart.

'Mommy, why are they kissing like that?' I peer at a ginger-haired boy, sporting a pirate hat and eye-patch, standing beside his parents, who are dressed even more bizarrely in matching mauve baseball caps, T-shirts and shorts.

'They're married, Victor,' his father says. 'Married people are allowed to kiss.'

His tone is so censorious that I contemplate flashing my ring. Vincent responds more aggressively. 'Yes, we are married. Only not to one another. Still, what can we do? My father saw her first. Have a good day!'

Leaving the trio dumbfounded, Vincent takes my hand and sweeps me off the platform, his attempt at a dignified exit thwarted by the wobbly steps. I hustle him down the hill, this time determined to choose the path myself.

'Don't you think we're breaking enough taboos already?'

'Smug git,' he says. 'He deserves all he gets.'

A cloud of melancholy descends on us as we take the funicular back to the bottom, where we meet up with the cab driver.

'*L'Acceuil Notre Dame, s'il vous plaît, Monsieur,*' Vincent says.

'*La porte de derrière,*' I add, compounding the gloom.

A web of side streets leads us swiftly to the Acceuil, where Vincent sees me to the door with strangely old-fashioned courtesy. 'At least it's *au revoir* not goodbye,' he says lightly.

'I should hope so, since we're due at the procession in ten minutes.' I take a precautionary step back. 'That was very special. Thank you for a truly wonderful afternoon.'

'It's not over yet,' he says, before returning to the cab.

I go indoors, thrilled by the promise with which he invests such routine words. The interlocking corridors confuse me, and I am obliged to an Irish pilgrim who informs me that 'the Jubilates' have already left for the Adoration Tent, so sparing me the need to find my way upstairs. Hoping to catch them en route, I hurry to the front of the building and along the riverbank to the meadow. The crowd is so dense that I despair of locating anyone, until the glimpse of a horn-playing Gabriel on a drooping banner directs me to the far side of the Tent. The moment I arrive, I realise my mistake. Everyone, from Louisa down, has put on the regulation sweatshirt, whereas I am wearing a prim-rose top that might as well be scarlet. Any hope of running back to the Acceuil is dashed by a burst of activity inside the Tent that signals the start of the procession. I decide to brazen it out and head for Richard and Patricia, who are sitting on a stone bench beside an elderly Scottish couple whose names I can never remember. Richard gives me a cheery wave and Patricia a withering look, but I am saved from further scrutiny by Fiona who, after measuring my leg, drags me off to her mother, who is guarding her collection of squashed flowers.

'They're lovely, Fiona. Did you pick them yourself?' I ask. She nods proudly, picking a buttercup from the bunch and holding it to my top.

'Yes. What a clever girl! They're the same colour,' Mary says. I force a smile, my gratitude for Fiona's welcome rapidly waning. We stand in edgy silence until Ken gathers us into line. 'First the wheelchairs. Next the rest of the *malades*. Then everyone else,' he ordains with the last-will-be-first Lourdes logic. Richard bounds up to me with Patricia on his heels.

'She won't let me go with Nigel.'

'Nigel's in a wheelchair,' Patricia says firmly.

'I can push him.'

'We had enough of that this morning. Besides, there are too many people.'

'What do you think?' Richard asks me.

'Your mother's right,' I say diplomatically. 'You walk with us.'

'I don't want to walk with you. You're not wearing your proper shirt. I'll feel stupid.'

'I'm sorry. I was late back from the town. I didn't want to miss the procession,' I say in my most placatory tone. 'Anyway, do you think God cares more about what we feel or what we wear?'

'What we wear,' Richard says with a grin.

'Thank you for that!'

'It's not a question of fashion but of respect,' Patricia says, determined to have the final word.

I step into line, the glow of the afternoon fading. Richard, with a rare sensitivity to my mood that does nothing to lift it, takes my hand. We inch towards the bridge where we converge with several other groups in an almost military profusion of banners. There we come to a standstill, sweltering in the heat, while our leaders discuss the arrangements.

'They're arguing over the order,' Maggie says knowingly, as she passes round paper cones of water.

'Shouldn't they have worked it all out before?' I ask.

'They did! Ken told me. It's the Poles, then the Catalonians – or is it Catalans? – then us.' I pull Richard's cone off his nose. 'But as usual, the Italians think that they have a God-given right to go first. And this lot aren't even from Rome!'

———

The impasse resolved, the Cracow contingent move to the front of the procession and the Milanese draw back, as if in a collective sulk. Just as we are about to set off, Vincent arrives with Sophie, Jewel and Jamie, all four clad in the official green.

'High drama there,' he says.

'Mediterranean temperament,' Patricia says, eager as ever to put the best gloss on everything Lourdes. 'Have you spent the afternoon filming?'

'Researching,' he says with a direct, if inscrutable, look at me. 'How about you?'

'We had a lovely mass,' Patricia says. 'Father Humphrey gave a sermon on broken people. How we're all of us broken but some of the cracks are easier to spot.' She strokes Richard's arm. He recoils.

'Did you enjoy it?' Vincent asks me.

'I'm afraid I skived off. I went for a walk around town.'

'Did you enjoy that?'

'It was nothing special.' My desire to punish him proves to be unsustainable. 'Yes. Yes, I did.' Patricia's eyes narrow.

'What about you, mate?' Vincent turns to Richard. 'Good afternoon?'

'I've been practising.'

'That's great.'

'Practising what?' I ask.

'Babies.'

'What?' I am gripped by a succession of alarming images.

'That's enough,' Vincent says to Richard. 'Remember it's a surprise.'

'I don't like surprises,' I say, considerably reassured to find that Vincent is party to this one.

'Me neither,' Richard says, 'but you always make me have them.'

We process along the Esplanade, turning back on ourselves to approach the Pius X Basilica. By the time we arrive at the bunker-like entrance, I am so caught up in the collective euphoria that I forget my aberrant top. Once inside, we move down a stark concrete aisle into a vast subterranean hall. We take our seats on one side of the raised altar, with a canopied dais for clergy to our left and the choir and organ to our right. Wheelchairs and invalid carriages are given pride of place, but even Brenda, who is determined to exploit her Lourdes privilege to the full, has to defer to the row of comatose pilgrims in hospital beds. I sit beside Richard, while Patricia is relegated to the back of the nave. Lucja slips in next to me with, to my amazement, Tadeusz on her other side. It is not only the first time I have seen him at a service, but the first time I have seen him holding Pyotr.

Lucja senses my surprise. 'He does it for me,' she says, with a mixture of sorrow and pride.

The Italian desire for precedence feels even more wrong-headed, since those of us towards the front of the procession are left to kick our heels – literally, in Richard's case – until those at the back arrive. The rows slowly fill, with many of the young brancardiers and handmaidens forced to stand in the recesses at the sides. When everyone is settled, representatives of each pilgrimage take their banner to be blessed at the altar, circling it with a dignity and precision that are all the more impressive for their being unrehearsed. I feel a deep surge of emotion at seeing Jenny, who has blossomed beyond recognition, carrying the Jubilate banner with Geoff. They are followed by two thurifers, causing dismay to several asthmatics, and a crocodile of priests and bishops including Fathers Humphrey, Dave and Paul. The Cardinal of Cracow brings up the rear, holding a glittering monstrance which he places on the altar, before walking backwards down the steps to take his seat beneath the canopy.

I abandon any attempt to follow the proceedings as each priest speaks in his native language with translations, chosen seemingly at random, relayed on giant screens. No sooner have I adjusted to a passage in French or German than the voice switches to Swedish and the translation to Dutch. The hymns are subject to the same linguistic lottery as the readings, and I whisper to Richard that it will be safer to hum. He jumps at the suggestion and I find myself beside a wayward bassoon. At the climax of the service, the Cardinal moves into the congregation and raises the monstrance to bless each section in turn. I feel none of the unease that I felt about attending mass. This is Christ coming to me in pity for my weakness, not me coming to him in defiance of my sin.

The Cardinal gives the benediction, after which the clergy and the banners process out and the congregation disperses with remarkable speed. As the organ thunders to a halt, I search for Vincent, defying him to have watched unmoved, but he is nowhere to be seen. Instead I am accosted by Patricia, who appears to have forgiven my impropriety in the joy of the service.

'You can always rely on a Cardinal in Lourdes,' she says, wiping her eyes. Richard giggles. 'I don't see why that's funny.' He ignores the reproach and laughs even more loudly, pointing to one of the crudely sketched posters of saints which hang from the roof.

'He's eating a strawberry,' he says.

'Nonsense,' she replies, reading the legend, 'it's St Jean Eudes holding the Sacred Heart.'

We walk outside and bump straight into Vincent.

'Fancy seeing you here!' Patricia says with deceptive airiness.

'I know,' he says, emulating her tone. 'The proverbial bad penny.'

'Did you enjoy the service?' I ask quickly.

'The choreography was impressive.'

'That's all?'

'I couldn't make head nor tail of anything else. How about you?'

'I couldn't make sense of it but I could understand it ... if you know what I mean.'

'Not exactly.'

'Then it must be a long time since you were in love.'

'We ought to be off,' Patricia interjects. 'We're holding people up. And we mustn't monopolise Mr O'Shaughnessy. People will talk.'

Her reserve fills me with foreboding. She may know nothing but she clearly suspects. Our sanctuary has been smashed open and there are eyes peering through the cracks.

'I wonder if I might borrow Richard?' Vincent asks.

'Like a library book?' Richard asks.

'To interview?'

'It's part of our surprise.'

'I have to go with him,' Richard says.

'I don't see why not,' I say, 'but it's half past six. There's only an hour before dinner.'

'That'll be enough.'

'I have to go!' Richard grabs Vincent's arm.

'Take care of him,' Patricia says anxiously.

———

'I'm not a library book!'

Vincent and Richard walk off, leaving me to return with a glacial Patricia.

'Are you sure you're being sensible?'

'What?' I did not expect such a direct challenge.

'Letting them go off like that. What do we know of that young man?'

'He's forty-two,' I say numbly. 'At a guess.'

'You know what I mean. You stopped Richard going out with his friends at home.'

'With good reason.'

'So you say. You should be grateful that they still took an interest.'

'Took advantage, more like!' I struggle to keep my temper. 'They behaved like idiots.'

'Surely you don't begrudge him a little fun? He's lost almost every-thing else.'

'Do you think he's the only one?'

'I've offered to help. You could pay someone. People must think we can't afford it!'

'I can't believe I'm hearing this.'

'All I'm saying is that you don't need to be tied to Richard twenty-four hours a day.'

'You object when I take myself off for a single afternoon.'

'It's not your going. It's where you go.'

'In *Lourdes*?' I ask incredulously.

'And who you go with. I don't want to see you get hurt.' Her voice is at once caring and cold.

'Don't worry! I'm a big girl.'

'Film people are notoriously feckless.'

'You shouldn't believe everything you read in the papers,' I say, hiding from the full implication of her words.

'They flit from project to project and person to person. I repeat; I don't want to see you get hurt.'

'Thought it was you!' Maggie lumbers up, bringing at least tem-porary relief. 'Been indulging my filthy habit in the bushes. Tilda and Ruth are looking after the *malades*.'

'Wouldn't you agree, Maggie?' Patricia leads the witness. 'Film people aren't to be trusted.'

'Can't say as I've had many dealings with them. Charles Hawtrey – you know, from the *Carry On* films – lived down the road before he died. I never met him myself but …' She mimes drinking.

I escape down the Esplanade and, to delay my return to the Acceuil, wander along the riverbank towards the Grotto. At first I shrink from the lime green sweatshirt in my path but, identifying the mop of blonde curls as Lucja, I wave. She walks up, carrying two large bottles of spring water.

'Do you want any help with those?'

'What?' She laughs. 'I am strong Polish girl.'

'You'll have to put them in your case. No liquids allowed inside the plane.'

'Yes, Tadeusz gives me warning. They will be burst all over our clothings. But they are for my mother.'

'Say no more!'

'She has come from home to look after the twins. We should be thankful.'

'I know all about those shoulds. Never mind! The sun's shining. And Tadeusz is spending time with Pyotr.'

'Yes. This makes me so happy. If there is nothing else – no, I must not say this so soon – but, if there is nothing else good that comes from here, it is that he is starting to hold Pyotr as if he has been one of the twins.'

'Has it taken him so long?'

'Being father to Pyotr is hard for Tadeusz. He does not have the faith of you and me.' I recall my struggle to reconcile a loving God with a damaged Richard and question her assumption. 'This is not because he is a man. In Poland, it is not like in England where the Church is for woman. In Poland, it is strong to believe. But Tadeusz, he does not believe in anything but himself. He wants to take no more orders, not from the priests, not from the Party. It is true, when he comes to England he has to take little orders: "Drive to this place!" "Bring this box to this place!" But he says he will soon be making his own business and giving the orders himself.'

'He seems a very enterprising man.'

'We are happy. We have the twins and they are growing up big and clever. I have a murmuring of the heart –'

'What?'

'Oh it is nothing. Nothing then and much more nothing now. I work in the morning and then I bring the twins home in the afternoon. It is a good life, but I am tired. Sometimes I am so tired. And so, sometimes, life is not so good in the night. You understand?'

'I understand.' I understand so well.

'I say this so as you know Tadeusz. He is a good man, but he is a man. And he met a woman. It was just for a few months. Then it was over. And I was pregnant. And Pyotr was born. And he blames himself. This man of reason blames himself like he was still in his grandfather's village. When the doctors told us what was wrong, he told me about this woman.'

'How noble of him! As if you weren't going through enough!'

'Perhaps he was thinking it would help if I had all the pain together?'

'Men ... no, I mustn't generalise. Yes, men seem to think that they can behave like shits and then we'll respect their honesty in admitting it. Poor dears, it must cost them so much!'

'Tadeusz asked if I wanted him to leave me. Leave? I had two three-years-old childrens and Pyotr. Leave? We were married in the church. So he stays. He stays now for one year and a half. He is a good father, a best father, to Agata and Filip. But he keeps away from Pyotr. To me, he has the feeling that even picking him in his arms will do him harm.'

'Yet he's looking after him now?'

'You must not laugh when I tell you it is a miracle. And if there is no miracle for Pyotr, there is still one for Tadeusz. He sees that he is not a bad man. He sees that his baby could have been born like this even if he has spent every minute he has spent with this woman with me.' She clasps the bottles to her chest as we enter the Acceuil. 'So what must I care if we will have a few wet clothings? It is a very little cost.'

I arrive at the Jubilate floor, refreshed by my short stay in someone else's story. We are soon called into dinner and, to my relief, Patricia's team is not on duty. The meal is marred by Richard's and Nigel's tacit agreement to mirror one another's movements. I am prepared to concede the slow-motion eating and napkin headscarves, but I draw the line when Richard crams three spoonfuls of spaghetti into his mouth.

'Nigel doesn't have your coordination. He'll choke!'

After raspberry jelly, which the two men remould into miniature breasts, we return to the bedroom, leaving the handmaidens to clear the tables and the brancardiers to arrange the room into a make-shift auditorium for the farewell concert. Richard monopolises the bathroom, his pride in his appearance one of the few remnants of his former self. As he stands at the mirror, an uneasy cross between Beau Brummell and Dennis the Menace, I feel a deep surge of affection for him.

'You're very thick with Vincent all of a sudden,' I say casually.

'I am not thick!'

'I mean that you seem to have a lot to discuss.'

'I'm helping him.'

'With his film?'

'Wait and see. You won't tell me your surprises.'

'That's true, I suppose.' Poor man! How he resents the 'wait and see' I apply to everything from food to outings. Yet the only way to maintain even a modest control over my life is to keep him in the dark.

We are summoned back to the dining room which has under-gone a rapid transformation. The tables have been pushed to one side and the chairs laid out beneath the window. Two drip-stands decked with balloons have been placed by the door and the Jubilate banner draped over the serving hatch. The room soon fills up. Patricia comes in with Maggie, pointedly taking a seat two rows in front of us. Vincent comes in with Jamie, who sets up his camera in the far corner. For all that he is following instructions, I am tor-tured by Vincent's disregard. Swiftly looking around, I join in the smattering of applause when Linda, with tinsel threaded over her glasses, pushes in Brenda, who is wearing a cardboard crown in a wheelchair garlanded with streamers. 'Queen!' Fiona shouts with wide-eyed enthusiasm, turning my admiration for their spirit into sadness at the masquerade.

Once everyone is settled, Father Humphrey takes the floor, to a roar of approval. He opens proceedings with a decade of the rosary, before launching into a comedy routine, great chunks of which, to judge by the response, have made as many appearances in Lourdes as he has himself. Patricia laughs immoderately at an account of the three nuns in a priest's life ('none yesterday, none today and none tomorrow'), that she would have deplored from anyone else. Only a quip that the favourite hymn in a crematorium is 'Light Up Thy Fire, Oh Lord!' falls flat. After a rare non-clerical joke ('horse sense is what stops horses betting on humans'), he solicits contributions from the floor. My fears of an embarrassing silence prove to be groundless when Sheila Clunes wheels herself forward to sing 'Danny Boy' in a quavering soprano, accompanied by the gentle guitarist from Saint Savin. She is followed by four young brancardiers, in precariously padded nurses' uniforms, who high-kick their way through 'Dancing Queen'.

An element of decorum returns when Frank, his eyes shut tight as though the slightest distraction might unbalance him, croaks 'How Much Is That Doggy in the Window?', his erratic tempo making it doubly hard for the accompanist to keep up. Martin then shuffles to the front and, with a supreme effort, makes a speech in which only the odd word – 'friends' or perhaps 'ends', 'love', and 'ease' – is intelligible. *Ease* turns out to be Louisa when, with thumbs twitching in clenched fists, he thanks her for her kindness and, nodding at the increasingly beleaguered guitarist, performs a version of 'The Shadow of Your Smile' which, despite having little or no connection with the tune, has our imperturbable director in tears.

Martin's song is so affecting that no one is ready to risk comparison, and his return to his seat is followed by a lull, which Father Humphrey threatens to fill with a second round of jokes. Then, to my horror, Vincent steps out and starts to speak. 'I want to thank you all for your kindness in allowing us to share in your pilgrimage. It's been a most enlightening experience in so many ways.' I have the chilling sensation that he is about to name them. 'I know that some of you had reservations about letting in the camera. I hope you'll feel that your trust has been vindicated when the film is broadcast later in the year. Now, if you'll indulge me a moment more, I too have prepared a party piece. But there'll be no filming. It's the director's privilege to call the shots. So come on up, Rich!'

Richard jumps to his feet with appalling alacrity and moves to Vincent, who places his hand on his shoulder. I struggle not to make comparisons as, with Richard gazing at Vincent and Vincent at the ceiling, they sing 'You Must Have Been a Beautiful Baby', directing the final refrain at me. Several people turn round, beaming congratulations as though I were a part of the performance, and I try to rescue a smile that has slipped six inches down my face. Only Patricia looks sour as if she too is trying to work out the implications of the double act.

'That was lovely, Richard. Thank you so much,' I say, as he bounds back to his seat, flushed with pride.

'I said you'd like it.'

'You were right. Was it your idea or Vincent's?'

'Mine!' he says, affronted.

'Good,' I reply equivocally. My attention is distracted by Father Humphrey's announcement of a special guest star, Fiona, who, despite tumultuous applause, has to be coaxed to the front by Mary. Her reluctance is not, as I presumed, the result of shyness, but of distress at her song having been pre-empted by Frank.

'Great minds think alike,' Father Humphrey says blithely. Fiona remains intransigent until he reminds her that 'there's more than one doggy in the window', whereupon she embarks on a version that bears even less resemblance to the original than its predecessor. At Louisa's suggestion, Fiona and Frank reprise it as a duet, with the audience supplying the canine chorus, ranging from Father Dave's Rottweiler to Marjorie's Chow. Then Maggie, urged on by various handmaidens, sings 'I'm a Pink Toothbrush, You're a Blue Toothbrush' to – or, at any rate, towards – a squirming Ken. Theresa, one of the nurses, follows with a love song from *The Lion King*. Finally, Mona, looking flushed, offers a soaring rendition of 'Climb Every Mountain', demonstrating that her talents are not confined to hymns.

'You've missed your vocation,' Sister Martha tells her, as she moves back to her seat.

'If I may have your attention a moment longer,' Louisa says, stepping forward. 'First, I'd like to thank all the wonderful performers for the very best show I can remember.'

'You say that every year,' Brenda says, with a cackle.

'It just gets better and better,' Louisa replies, without missing a beat. She then calls on Father Humphrey to draw the raffle. It could not have turned up a more fitting list of winners had it been rigged; as, in the view of one disgruntled loser, it was. The prizes having been claimed, with varying degrees of reticence, Louisa brings the formal part of the evening to a close. 'I'd like to remind you all that we're due at the baths at nine thirty. Meanwhile enjoy the rest of the party. The night is yet young.'

'Well I'm not,' Patricia says, turning to face us. 'So I'm off to bed. You should do the same, darling,' she tells Richard. 'All this excitement. I hope you'll sleep.'

'Oh Richard has no trouble,' I say, a veteran of his snoring. 'I'm the insomniac in the family.'

Fixing me with a knowing look, she moves away, to be replaced moments later by Sophie.

'Jamie, Jewel and I are going for a final stroll up to the castle. We wondered if you'd care to join us.'

'What a lovely idea!' I say, grateful for both Vincent's guile and her discretion. 'I'd be delighted. Can you hold on while I see Richard to bed?'

'Of course. Will you meet us at the hotel?'

'Why not?'

Why not indeed? It is the last night of the pilgrimage. After tomorrow, I shall never see Vincent O'Shaughnessy again.

VINCENT

Tuesday June 17

I have discovered why so many young people want to come to Lourdes. Forget serving God and helping the sick and all those other application-form platitudes. If last night is anything to go by, it's for the chance to hang out with their friends till the early hours and, what's more, to do so under the windows of clean-living television directors!

Am I showing my age? I pat my stomach for reassurance, but my head tells a different story. Where is the Vincent O'Shaughnessy I used to know, who would sit up until dawn righting the world's wrongs and then be hard at work at nine? Rolling a spliff at some nineties tribute party? Well, good riddance to him! He has no right to sneer at his elders. How would he like to spend a neck-cricking night on a threadbare bolster, struggling to drown out the clatter from the street, while a soft-voiced 'Peace be with you!' echoed insidiously through his brain?

I throw myself under a listless shower which seems to predate Bernadette, the dribble of water barely sufficient for its primary purpose, let alone its secondary one of washing Gillian Patterson out of my system. I step out smartly to brush my teeth, but the sight of the eager face in the chipped mirror is more than I can bear. 'In the first place,' I remind him, 'you're here to work. Lion's Share are paying you – a pittance, but that's a different story – to make a fifty-minute documentary, not to try to patch up your irreparable love life. In the second place, she's married and a Catholic, both of which should sound a thunderous alarm bell. In the third, fourth and fifth places, you are Vincent O'Shaughnessy and, even if she were interested in you, which as we've established she's not, you have absolutely no right to inflict yourself on another human being in an intimate context ever again.'

Relieved to have spelt things out, I put on my Jubilate sweatshirt, which gives me the surprisingly pleasant sensation of being subject to other peoples' rules. Steering well clear of the lift, I go down to the dining room, where the clamour of English voices depresses me. I stop to greet the two West Indian Jubilates who are sitting at a table by the door.

'Not on breakfast duty?'

'Not till lunchtime, thank the Lord,' the blonde-wigged one says, lowering her voice. 'Poor Mona suffers terribly from jet lag.'

'Really?'

'My Hector used to say I needed a sick-note when I went to the market. Still,' Mona says, pointing to the logo on her generous bosom. 'Let's pray that Gabriel blows some of the cobwebs away.'

I leave them ordering more bread, the English pronunciation of *pain* fuelling my suspicions of their self-lacerating faith, and join the crew by the window.

'Morning gang! How's tricks?'

'Wrong question!' Sophie says.

'Zambia was bad enough, but this place takes the biscuit!' Jamie says, scarcely giving me a chance to sit down. 'You're lucky I don't get the Union on to it, chief.'

'You're not in a union,' Jewel says.

'So I'll join. Forget the mattress that feels like a beanbag. Forget the death-trap lift. What about the plumbing?'

'It is a tad antiquated, I admit,' I say.

'Turn on the cold tap and the water's scalding.'

'Lucky you!' Sophie says. 'Even my hot was tepid.'

'I could have been scarred for life,' Jamie says, piqued at our lack of sympathy. 'And what about people with sticks who can't jump out of the way? Turn on the C and –'

'Wait a minute,' Sophie says. 'You are joking?'

'I'm bloody not. I could have got third degree burns.'

'What do you think the F stands for?'

'What F?'

'On the taps. C and F. *Chaud* and *Froid*. Not cold and freezing!'

'You div!' Jewel says to him. 'What next? Life-membership of the BNP?'

'We're in France,' Sophie says. 'It's in French.'

'I don't see why,' he says, refusing to back down. 'The staff speak to us in English. All the notices are in English. They even serve us Rice Krispies and Shredded Wheat.'

'Speaking of which, I'd better grab a bowl before they run out,' I say, as a smiling man with ill-fitting dentures walks past with a pyramid of Corn Flakes. I return to find Jamie and Jewel debating whether to ask for another roll. Concluding that Mr Bumble has nothing on Madame Basic Jesus, they decide not to take the risk.

'What sort of night did you guys have? Was anyone else kept up by the noise?'

'I could have sold tickets!' Jewel says. 'I gave up around six and went for a wander in the Domain. I bumped into the head honcho. You know, the priest who looks like Jamie in twenty years time – '

'*Très* amusing!'

'He told me that all the kids gather on the bridge at night for the crack. He came out with it bold as brass. "For the crack"!' Jamie bursts out laughing. 'You may find it funny but I didn't know where to put myself. I know the Church has become more liberal, but crack … do you think that's why there are so many gypsies?'

'Oh sure Jewel, they're all dealers!' Jamie says. 'Do you have any Irish blood in you?'

'Not unless you count Guinness,' she replies, perplexed.

'It's *craic*. C-R-A-I-C. Fun and games. I'm not the only one who needs to swot up on his C-words.'

We run over the day's schedule, sketching out a possible interview rota. 'I'd like to add Gillian and Patricia Patterson,' I say casually. 'The wife and mother of the guy who acted up at the airport. I'm sure they'll have a story or two.' Whatever my misgivings about Gillian or, rather, about my own attraction to her, I am determined to put the interests of the film first.

After breakfast, we send Jamie back upstairs to change into his sweatshirt.

'Must I?'

'It's for the photo,' Sophie says.

'But I won't be in it.'

'It's a sign of respect,' Jewel says. 'Besides, if the rest of us have to look like genetically modified peas, so do you.'

With Jamie duly homogenised, we stroll towards the Pius X Basilica for the International mass. I am amazed by the size of the crowd, which is more reminiscent of Oakwell on a Saturday afternoon than Holyrood on a Sunday morning. Crossing an avenue of pollarded plane trees, their lopped branches a cruel parallel to the

truncated human limbs everywhere on display, we position ourselves by the subterranean entrance and prepare to film the arriving Jubilates. The lime green is a useful marker, although a party
of Malaysian girl guides causes momentary confusion. We pick out
Tess and Lester, the former rosy-cheeked, the latter with a complexion to match his sweatshirt; Fiona, dragging her tape measure
along the path; Lucja, with her baby but not her husband; Maggie,
who breaks away at the door and sneaks into the bushes; and a
posse of priests.

Gillian, Patricia and Richard bring up the rear. Patricia greets us
with a regal wave, affording us a clear view of the amber brooch, like
a mute in Gabriel's horn, with which she has personalised her sweatshirt. Gillian fixes her gaze straight ahead, acknowledging neither
me nor the camera. Nevertheless, I take a perverse pleasure in the
thought that, if nothing else, we are united by our shirts.

Louisa walks past just as we finish filming. 'Ready when you are,
Mr De Mille,' she says with a shy smile. 'Wasn't he the one with the
crowd scenes?' she adds quickly. 'The basilica holds twenty-five
thousand. And on days like these it's standing room only. It makes
me quite weepy. So many people from every corner of the globe. A
truly catholic church. Oh, I don't want to offend anyone! Are you a
Protestant?' she asks Sophie.

'In principle.'

'It's the principles that cause the problems.'

We follow her into the church which, with its thick grey walls and
low concrete roof, could double as an underground car park, complete with shadowy aisles to shelter muggers. There is no decoration
apart from a few rows of small stained-glass windows, given a sinister glow by the artificial lighting, and a circle of posters of second-
division saints. We walk down to the lower level, a vast oval arena
with a raised altar at the centre. Beside it a tubular Christ hangs
from the cross, flanked by two skeletal mourners, whose brokenness makes a welcome contrast to the ribbed bulk of the building.
The sight of so many priests sitting through a service in which only
a handful can take part offends my socialist as well as my humanist
principles, and I long to see them gainfully employed.

'Do you think the collective noun for priests may be a *superfluity*?'

I ask Sophie, who gives me a guarded smile. 'If I weren't already a committed atheist, this would do the trick.'

After listening to the lengthy prayers, I feel a surprising sympathy for advocates of the Tridentine mass. At least Latin would leave us all equally lost. Louisa's 'truly catholic church' has become a linguistic hotchpotch, with one unintelligible language booming through the loudspeakers while another is flashed on the screen. 'They should give us headphones, chief!' Jamie whispers. I laugh, only to be admonished by a wagging finger from Marjorie, who is evidently fluent in Swedish (or is it Norwegian?) by way of Dutch. It is my first black mark and I am determined that it shall be the last. So, after asking Jamie to pan over the congregation, lingering on a few vacant faces, we switch off the camera and join the Jubilate youngsters in an aisle. Several, having abandoned all pretence of alertness, sprawl bleary-eyed on the floor, but Kevin, whose rebelliousness makes me nostalgic, directs his gaze at the altar in an expression midway between hatred and despair. As ever, adolescent angst is at its most intense when it focuses on God.

The mass ended, we walk out into dazzling sunlight.

'Looking for someone?' Sophie asks, as I peer down the path.

'Just looking,' I say quickly. This is one meeting that I cannot ask her to broker. Nonchalance is the key. So, putting all thoughts of Gillian to one side, I join the Jubilate pilgrims heading back to the Basilica Square for the group photograph. Striding more purposefully than I had intended, I find myself walking alongside a priest.

'We've not been introduced yet,' he says. 'I'm Father Paul.'

'Vincent O'Shaughnessy,' I say, shaking an unexpectedly calloused hand.

'You may not want to bother with me. I'm not on your list.'

'Please don't take it personally,' I say, angry at my need to apologise. 'We had to stop somewhere, so we went with Father Humphrey and Father Dave.'

'A wise choice. They're old hands. I'm comparatively new to this business.'

'Pilgrimage?'

'Priesthood. I've only been ordained five years.' I look at the weatherworn face and pepper-and-salt hair and wait for him to elaborate. 'I was a British Telecom engineer until I was fifty-four.'

'What happened then? Redundancy?'

'I can think of easier ways to earn a living,' he says, with a twin-kling smile that makes me feel contrite. 'I was married for just under thirty years: eight days under, to be precise. Rosemary and I had five children. Then she got cancer. Of the bones. The sort that tests your faith to its utmost.'

'And did it yours?'

'Most certainly. But it emerged stronger. Look, I'm happy to discuss it if you like, but you must have testimonies coming out of your ears.'

'They all make good background.' He laughs. 'I'm sorry, that sounded wrong. I'd like to hear. Truly.'

'On your own head be it. At first I was angry, so angry with God. I wanted to scream and shout and punch and kick. I used to wish He really were an old man in the clouds so I'd have somewhere to aim my fists. But, try as I might, my anger couldn't wipe out my faith. I could feel myself wilfully turning against the truth, like a spoilt child who can't get his own way. I stopped attending mass. I used to go every day, sometimes before work and sometimes after, and I really missed it. The strangest thing – and this may be hard for you to accept (it was for me) – is that I missed being one with Christ more than being one with my wife.'

'Yes it is … hard to accept, I mean.'

'Please don't misunderstand. I loved my wife; I loved her so much. She was the only woman I've ever wanted.' His once-in-a-lifetime love makes me feel shallow. Despite resolving to stick to my bystander's role, I have a compelling urge to make a similar dis-closure, but the last person to whom I would confess would be a priest. So I wait for him to resume. 'Rosemary insisted that I go back to the Church. She said she couldn't bear the thought of my losing everything.'

'Although she did.'

'I have to believe that she's gone to a better place.'

'Have to?'

'Do. But, if you're asking about doubts, then of course I have them. Didn't the apostles? Didn't Our Lord himself? I'd hate myself if I didn't have some doubts, although, in case it's your next question, that's not why I do. I still find it hard to believe that I'm Father Paul. Sometimes I catch my reflection in a shop window and wonder who on earth is that bloke in the collar. I never even noticed what was happening to me. Then one morning after mass – I was a twice-a-day man again – I cornered the priest in the sacristy and asked if he could spare a moment. It wasn't until I'd come out with it that I knew what I was going to say. "Father, how can you tell if you have a vocation?" I was frightened. I wanted to take back the words. I couldn't believe my nerve. "Ask God for a sign," he said. So I did. I mentioned to two old friends and one of my sons that I was thinking of changing my job. And they all said, quite separately, without the slightest hesitation: "You want to become a priest." What clearer sign could He have sent?'

'I don't know. The Bible seems to have plenty. Anything from plagues of frogs to the Four Horsemen of the Apocalypse.'

'If you'll forgive my saying so, you seem rather confused.'

'Sorry to disappoint you, Father, but most people would say I was boringly well-adjusted. I couldn't even drink myself to death when I tried. The trouble, if there is any, is that I was raised a Catholic. The last twenty-five years I've been able to put it all behind me, but being here – just seeing those kids serving at the altar this morning – has brought it all back.'

'Is growing up Catholic so much worse than growing up anything else?'

'Is that a serious question?'

'It is to me. I was on an ecumenical retreat not that long ago and we were asked to write down one word for how we visualised God as children. The difference between us and the Protestants was marked. Where we put *loving* or *kind* or *gentle*, they put *angry* or *authoritarian* or *all-seeing*.'

'In which case there must have been some crypto-Protestant priests in 1970s Yorkshire.'

'Did something happen to destroy your faith?'

'Lots.' I am distracted by the sight of a man walking past with a boy inexplicably dressed as Batman. 'Lots. But that's not why I lost it. I took a considered decision after weighing up the evidence. I used that greatest of evolutionary organisms, the mind.'

———

'And you think the world is entirely rational?'

'Not at all. But I don't mistake the irrational for the mystic. Just look around you – not at the world, but at Lourdes. Don't you find it paradoxical that people come all this way, some of them in great pain or with an immense effort, to petition God in a place where His failure is most apparent?'

'So you think illness and handicap are a sign of God's failure?'

'You disappoint me, Father. But the answer is "no". I think they are a sign – one of many – of His non-existence. Look at all these people surging towards the Grotto – the word *lemming* springs inexorably to mind. What is it they're after? Some form of cure, either for themselves or a loved one? Why waste so much energy when they know that, as good Catholics, they'll die and end up in Heaven?'

'By that logic, the whole Church should commit suicide. A massacre that would put Jonestown in the shade.'

'The thought had occurred to me.'

'Now you're being deliberately contrary.'

'Me? I'm not the one who prays for the Resurrection of the Body: an absurdity at the best of times but positively perverse in Lourdes.'

'By coming here, by bringing their sick, people are manifesting their faith in God's mercy. At the same time, like Christ, they proclaim: "Not my will but Thine be done."'

'I wonder which impulse is the stronger.'

'I can't speak for anyone else, but I know that the reason I come here is to be one with the sacred, to be in a place with a unique energy born of a hundred and fifty years of devotion. As for miracles: do I believe in them? Yes. Do I expect them? No. In our materialistic world we've put so many barriers in the way. But don't harden your heart. Remember that Christ healed people not just for their own sake but to be living witnesses to God's grace.'

'I feel sorry for the sick. As if all the pain and incapacity weren't enough, they have so much symbolic weight to bear. First there was Father Humphrey telling them that their suffering is an inspiration to the rest of us. Now you're saying that their cure would be a catalyst for conversion.'

'The burden isn't on them but on us. It's what we choose to see … no, how we choose to look.' We approach the Basilica steps on which a group of blind children is being coaxed to smile for the camera. Father Dave makes straight for us.

'Sorry to cut in, but may I have a word, Father?'

'Of course, Father. Excuse me,' Father Paul says to me. 'I've very much enjoyed the talk – and the challenge. I'm here all week, so should you ever feel like a second round ... Meanwhile, I know you have an agenda but, if you keep an open mind, who knows what you may discover.'

I accept the rebuke without demur and join the crew at the foot of the steps, while Louisa shoos everyone into place for the photograph. Catching sight of us hovering on the sidelines, she insists that 'our honorary pilgrims join in'. Jamie is excused by virtue of filming, and Jewel, who declares herself 'photo-phobic', wriggles out of it by holding a superfluous microphone. So Sophie and I represent the guests, taking a far more focal position than I would have wished, the one advantage being that I find myself next to Patricia or, rather, next but one to Gillian, who is remonstrating gently with her husband.

'Mr O'Shaughnessy, we're honoured,' Patricia says.

'Vincent, please.'

'Gillian, it's Mr O'Shaughnessy ... Vincent.'

'Vincent, of course! I knew it was one of the minor saints.' She smiles, as if to temper the insult.

'Oh dear, it's the same photographer who took us last year,' Patricia says.

'I'm told that a couple of families have it all sewn up,' I reply. 'Like everything else in this town, it's a monopoly. You might even say a mafia.'

'Not in Lourdes!' Patricia says, with such horror that I instantly change tack.

'What are the odds that he has some secret passion? He spends the morning on pictures of pilgrims, then in the afternoons it's views of mountains or soft-focus shots of wild flowers.'

'Or artistic nudes?'

'Gillian!' Patricia sounds as outraged as if she had been asked to pose.

'Flowers of another kind,' I say, heartened by the subversive note that has crept into the conversation.

'I wish they'd hurry up,' Gillian says. 'Someone here wants to go to the loo.'

'Not someone, me!' Richard shouts, to widespread amusement.

'Remember, darling,' Patricia says, leaning across Gillian. 'Think of the desert.'

'My last group photo was at school,' Sophie says to me. 'Two of the hockey team sprinted round the back while the camera panned over the rest of us. They managed to get themselves on both ends.'

'Don't try that here, or they'll hail a miracle!'

'I heard that,' Marjorie says, wagging her finger again.

No sooner is everyone settled than Louisa, who has been studying the shot over the increasingly impatient photographer's shoulder, insists on several of us moving around. I swap with Patricia for the sake of the 'wee' Scottish lady in the row behind, and find myself next to Gillian.

'Would you rather stay with your mother-in-law?' I ask.

'Oh Gillian doesn't care about that,' Patricia says, to a corroborative silence.

'But perhaps she won't want to be photographed beside such a dangerous sceptic?'

'You flatter yourself.'

'I'd rather flatter you,' I say quietly.

'You'd have your work cut out this morning. I'm hot and headachy. Richard was over-excited last night and fractious this morning. What's more, I hate having my picture taken.'

'I can't believe that.'

'Why not?'

'No one as beautiful as you can object to keeping a record.'

'Don't be idiotic.'

'I'm perfectly serious.'

'Is that what you mean by *flattery*?'

'I'm right, aren't I, Patricia? Your daughter-in-law's a very beautiful woman.'

'Well …' She sounds taken aback. 'I've never been able to fault her in the looks department. She doesn't always make the best of herself. But then who does these days?'

'So she shouldn't dislike being photographed?'

'What's the point?' Gillian asks, almost angrily. 'Are Richard and I going to pore over the albums in our twilight years? Sorry, but we're there already. And we don't have any children to take an interest. Just something else to be tossed on the bonfire when we die.'

'Really Gillian,' Patricia says, 'there's no call to be morbid! You still might like a souvenir.'

'I'll have plenty.' She taps her forehead. 'In here.'

'It's easy to forget. I know.'

'Then you forget for a reason. Everything happens for a reason. It must!'

Several heads turn in our direction, as I weigh up whether it is my place to reply.

'I didn't do anything,' Richard says, responding instinctively to her tone.

'I think we're there,' Louisa says, slipping into place on the front row. 'So long as no one grows in the next two minutes, Matt Hedley!'

'I can't always picture my mother,' Gillian says, 'and she only died five years ago.'

'So sad,' Patricia hisses in my ear.

'At times her face is as clear as any of these, and at others I seem to be seeing her at the end of a long corridor – no, a warehouse piled with stuff. How can a photograph begin to make up for that?'

'Now everyone please stand still like mouses. Imagine it is your "God Save The Queen". And say Camembert.' However lame, the joke has the desired effect.

'Camembert!' Nigel shouts thirty seconds later, replicating the effect for the second shot.

With an hour before we are due at the Grotto, Father Dave proposes that we visit the basilicas or relax by the river.

'I need to go to the toilet,' Richard says, as the group breaks up.

'Lavatory.' Patricia corrects him.

'I'll have to take him back to the Acceuil,' Gillian says.

'There are toilets over there,' I say, flouting Patricia and pointing to the colonnade.

'I don't like him going in on his own.'

'No problem. I can take him.'

She looks at me as warily as if he were six years old. I am struck by such a painful memory that I have to stop myself running out of the Domain. 'Thank you,' she says, freeing me from both suspicion and the grip of the past. 'That would be kind.'

'Then, if you're feeling strong, we can all climb to the old basilica.'

'Count me out,' Patricia says. 'I've seen it several times. I'm not as young as I was.'

'Slander!'

'More flattery?' Gillian asks.

'I'm happy to sit here and people watch.'

'I'm bursting!'

'Come on then, mate!' I turn to Gillian. 'Is there anything I should know? Will he need any help?'

'Only in remembering to wash his hands,' she says, with a faint smile. 'Don't look so worried.'

I lead Richard across the square. Ignoring his bladder, he seizes on every diversion, from a complacent pigeon to a young boy playing hopscotch with his grandfather's crutches. 'If we don't get a move on,' I say, 'we won't have time to go up to the church.'

'So what? Churches are boring.'

'Not always,' I say, determined to fulfil my loco-parental role. 'Do you go often?'

'Every single week. She won't leave me at home, even on a Sunday when I can't come to any harm.'

'She must like your company.'

'It's because she's frightened. A few years ago I had an accident. I very nearly died.'

'That's scary.'

'It was for her. I was unconscious for six whole weeks. I'm fine now, as fit as a fiddle – which is a stupid word – but she worries it'll happen again, at any moment. So it's best to do what she says.'

'That sounds sensible.'

'I used to be her boss, now she's mine.'

'Really,' I say distractedly.

'Don't you think that's funny?'

'Funny and sad.'

'You should laugh. People always laugh when I say that. "I used to be her boss, now she's mine."'

I take him into a lavatory whose gleaming white tiles match its sanitised smell. As we walk in, a young man helps an older man out of a stall, and I realise that we are in the one place where such a pairing provokes no comment. I stand to the side, striving to look nonchalant, while Richard uses the urinal. Then, following instructions, I lead him to the basin. His reluctance to accompany me seems to be based on something far deeper than the minor inconvenience of washing.

'My hands are dry. Feel. If they were dirty, they'd be wet.'

'They'll still harbour germs.'

'Germs! Everything's always germs. "Don't do that, Richard, it's full of germs." At school they said we're only here because of germs. If there weren't any germs, we'd die.'

'I'll wash mine too. Then if we die, we die together.'

He giggles and gives in, but his obduracy affords me a glimpse into the perpetual power struggle between husband and wife, which resumes as soon as we rejoin Gillian. 'You should wear your sunglasses, Richard,' she says, and he dutifully reaches into his pocket.

'Cool shades,' I say, as he puts them on.

'I chose them myself,' he replies, honour satisfied.

'So shall we go to the Rosary Basilica first?' Gillian asks.

'You're the boss,' I say.

'That's what I said,' Richard says.

'I'm glad to hear it,' Gillian replies, looking perplexed.

We climb back up the steps on which a group of Swiss pilgrims is the latest to be photographed, their pink legs in lemon shorts like the squares of a Battenberg cake, and enter the Rosary Basilica. Gaudy mosaics of the life of the Virgin glimmer from shallow side-chapels, while the Lady herself, surrounded by greetings-card cherubs, presides in gilded glory in the chancel. I walk round with Gillian, while Richard trails behind, intent on not treading on the paving cracks. As Gillian examines the mosaics, I sound a note of dissent.

'Michelangelo, thou shouldst be living at this hour!'

'I take it you don't approve.'

'That's putting it mildly.'

'Pity. I find them moving.'

'Have you ever been to Ravenna?'

'I'm afraid not.'

'Now those are mosaics! Christian too, of course, but there's something in them – an intensity; a precision; a power: I can't define it – that touches even an arch-heretic like me. That's what great art does.'

'Perhaps there's a place for great art and also for something … I don't know, a bit more basic? I'm sure it says something terrible about my taste, but I find these deeply poignant. Not the work of great masters, but the expression of a faith that isn't embarrassed by simple emotions. Look at the soldier over there, scratching his head in bemusement at the risen Christ.'

'I'm the one who's bemused. It's like a plate from a children's bible.'

'Perhaps it moves me because it's a link to my childhood? Or perhaps the same things that moved me then move me now? We'll have to agree to differ or, rather, to diverge. You take the high art road and I take the low.'

Her carefully chosen barb hits the mark. I decide that my best defence is flippancy. 'Well, for now, both roads are leading to the Upper Basilica, so let's see if we can find some common ground.' We emerge into the open and walk towards a steep flight of steps.

'Race you to the top?' Richard says.

'Don't be silly,' Gillian replies.

'It's exercise.' He runs up the first few steps.

'Don't go too fast.' He redoubles his efforts. 'Now he'll be all hot and bothered.'

'At least it gives me a chance for some time alone with you.'

'Why would you want that?'

'I ask myself the same question.'

'How about because some men are never happy unless they're flirting? Half the women on the pilgrimage are old enough to be your mother. Half are young enough to be your daughter. And the rest are nuns. Which leaves me.'

'Don't belittle yourself.'

'I'm not. You're doing that for me.'

'Since when does telling you I enjoy your company count as belittlement?'

'I'm sorry if I'm doing you a disservice, but it's not going to break your heart ... kill you. You and I come from different worlds. You have your reason for being here; I have mine.'

'Which is?'

'A miracle.' She stands still and stares at me defiantly, forcing the family behind us to an abrupt halt.

'So you believe in miracles?'

'Of course, since I believe in God.'

'A "let's cure Aunt Lily's cancer in Lourdes today and let's send a tsunami to Thailand tomorrow" God, I presume?'

'A God whose ways are far beyond human comprehension.'

'Just as well.' Sensing that she is losing patience, I soften my tone. 'In which case, if you don't mind my asking, why haven't you come here before? Your mother-in-law's been I don't know how many times and Richard fell ill – when was it? – twelve years ago?'

'Sometimes it's hard to act on your convictions. Other peoples' suspicion: other peoples' doubts get in the way. But I won't let that happen here.' Her vehemence is both a rebuke and a warning. 'I've finally come to a place where, for 150 years, miracles have been recorded and, even if ... even if I'm disappointed, I pray with all my heart that I'll win back that purity – that integrity – of belief, from which nothing anyone says or does can shake me. Does that satisfy you?'

'It answers me.'

'I'll take that as a *yes*.'

We reach the top, where Richard is waiting impatiently for the 'lazybones', and gaze across the burnished gold dome of the Rosary Basilica into the teeming square.

'So many people,' I say. 'Think how many visitors swarm here every year. Five or six million, all with their own hopes and prayers.' I refrain from adding *chequebooks*. 'Yet how many miracles have there been in total? Sixty something?'

'Sixty-seven,' a sonorous voice interjects. With his stomach concealed by the parapet, I have failed to identify the priest behind Richard as Father Humphrey.

'I'm obliged to you, Father!'

'The last was in 2005. In order to defend itself against its critics, the Church has set up a rigorous authentication procedure. In the first place, it defines *miracle* very strictly as "a cure that is beyond scientific explanation".

'But science is changing all the time.'

'Which is why the process is so rigorous. What's more, in Lourdes a miracle has to be "inexplicable, instantaneous and permanent". And it's ruled out if there's been any previous medical treatment.'

'Like what? Dialysis? Chemo? Or just aspirin?'

'I imagine something in between,' he replies smoothly, 'but, mercifully, I'm not the one to judge. Nor is any other priest or bishop or even the Holy Father. There are twelve doctors: independent experts. Perhaps you should raise the matter with them?'

'The film only lasts fifty minutes.'

'And for that you're willing to jeopardise your immortal soul?' His audacity astounds me. 'The problem with such a rigorous process,' he adds, 'is that it leaves no room for the thousands – literally thousands – of people who've had medical treatment that's failed and then have come here and been cured, in their own mind, miraculously. So to incorporate them, the authorities have created a second category of "authentic cure by grace".'

'Just how many thousands are there?'

'Around seven.'

'Well, even if you take that larger figure, you have to admit that the odds aren't too great.'

'The odds are immaterial when you're dealing with the Almighty. But I'm keeping you. During her thirteenth apparition, the Lady said to Bernadette: "Go tell the priest to build a chapel and let the people come here in procession." As you'll see, it's a very special chapel.'

Taking our leave of Father Humphrey, we enter the Crypt, the first of the three churches to be built on the site. We walk down a long passage lined with ancient gratitude into a white vaulted chapel dominated by a statue of the Madonna and Child framed by a golden nimbus. At the altar, a Vietnamese priest is saying mass for a group of his fellow countrymen.

'So what do you think?' I ask Richard, as Gillian slips off into a small side-chapel.

'The air feels wet.'

'That's because it's built into the rock.'

'Where's Gilly?' He looks around anxiously.

'Don't worry, she's over there.' I point to the chapel where, to my surprise, she is kneeling at the rail.

'Is it Sunday?'

'It is in Lourdes.'

'Shall we creep up on her?'

'Better not,' I say, striving for a laddish complicity. I watch him staring at his wife and wonder what he sees. Is she just a surrogate mother, her rules a constant source of resentment, or are there moments in the dead of night when the rational world is stilled and they once again become equals? I try to shake off the thought. As though aware of my scrutiny, Gillian stands and genuflects.

'All done?' she asks as she joins us. 'I'd hate to drag you away.'

'I'm infinitely draggable,' I say and follow her outside, where we climb a short flight of steps to the Upper Basilica. 'Two down, one to go!'

'For some of us,' she replies, 'it's not a chore.'

We enter a Gothic building of traditional greyness, relieved only by the mottled light of the stained-glass windows which, according to Gillian, tell the story of the Immaculate Conception; although, from where I stand, they might just as well be Napoleon's campaigns. The sweep of the high-vaulted nave, with no rood screen or statuary to obtrude, directs my gaze to the altar where, in place of the Crypt's benign if sentimental Madonna and Child, sits the ubiquitous symbol of Christianity's cult of death. Even in Lourdes, with its unique array of human suffering, the focus remains on the eternal suffering of Christ. Our most intimate moments are shared, not with flesh-and-blood lovers, but with the flesh and blood which, by some arcane mumbo-jumbo, is contained in the bread and wine. It would be easy to dismiss it all as a palliative, if I hadn't seen it blight too many lives.

I suddenly feel stifled and, not stopping to tell Gillian, hurry outside where, by contrast, even the hot, humid air feels fresh. I wait in the porch and, a few moments later, she comes out with Richard.

'Are you all right? I looked and you were gone.'

'I'm sorry. I didn't mean to alarm you,' I say, elated by her concern. 'It was my mobile.' I tap my jeans pocket over-emphatically. 'Sophie rang. The Grotto procession is about to start.'

We make our way down to the square and out to the drinking fountains where the Jubilate pilgrims have assembled. I excuse myself from Gillian and join the crew.

'We'd just about given you up!' Sophie says.

'Just checking out the lie of the land.' Jamie's smirk alerts me to my unfortunate choice of phrase. 'Ready to roll?'

'We've been ready for half an hour. You're the one who went AWOL.'

'Yes, *mea culpa* and all that. I gather Father Dave is going to begin by giving us some gen on Bernadette. You never know, it may come in handy. So let's go for it but keep him in close-up. We can always cheat a few reaction shots later.'

'All present and correct?' Father Dave asks. 'Would you move in a little closer? We're not Anglicans; there's no need to keep one another at arm's length.' He acknowledges the titter. 'That's better. Anything to save the old voice box. I shan't rattle on because I know that it's been a long morning and some of you are anxious for your lunch, eh Martin?' Martin chuckles at the sound of his name, emitting a string of drool which Claire discreetly wipes off his chin. 'But, for those of you who haven't been here before, and those of you who have but whose memories may not be what they were – '

'Guilty as charged,' Louisa interjects.

'I'll give you a quick rundown on Saint Bernadette and the Grotto. I'll be saying more about her on Thursday, that's for those of you who take the walking tour of the town. But, if you're anything like me, you won't be able to get enough of her. Just thinking about her brings tears to my eyes.' I signal to Jamie to zoom in on the evidence. 'The story begins one bitterly cold day in February 1858 when the fire went out in the *cachot* – that was the small punishment cell in which Bernadette and her family were living – '

'Punishment cell?' Lester interjects.

'Wait until Thursday. They had no money to buy logs so, with her sister and a friend, Bernadette came down to the river to forage for kindling. They were standing on the opposite bank – not far from where the church is now – when one of them saw a pile of wood in the grotto. It seemed like a miracle. Toinette – that's Bernadette's sister – and the friend immediately waded into the water.

Bernadette, who suffered from asthma, was afraid of catching cold so she asked them to throw in some stones that she could walk on. When they refused (a spot of girlish rivalry there, ladies?), she sat down and took off her clogs. All of a sudden she heard a sound like a gust of wind, and saw a lady in white standing in the grotto. Terror-struck, she grabbed hold of her rosary. The lady made the sign of the cross, prompting Bernadette to do the same. She began to pray. When she finished, she looked up to find that the lady had vanished. That was the first of eighteen apparitions in a period of just over five months.'

'Always to Bernadette alone?' I ask guardedly.

'She was the only one to see the lady, but thousands of people were there when she did. They saw her fall to the ground and drink muddy water from a hole she had scooped out herself when the lady told her to "drink from the spring and wash herself in it". They saw her so ecstatic that she failed to notice when the flame of her candle licked her hand for nearly ten minutes. And when the local doctor, a notorious sceptic, examined her afterwards, he could find no trace of a burn. He was among the earliest converts. Within nine months, seven people were cured of illness and blindness. And the legend of Lourdes was born.'

'So it was the magic not the message?' I ask, in a bid to draw him out.

'I wouldn't use the word *magic*, but yes. Human beings – and I include Catholics – are by nature a suspicious breed. We need signs. Our Lord said, "Blessed are those who have not seen and yet have believed." Precious few of us would pass that test. And of course Bernadette herself was disbelieved at first. Even her family accused her of lying. It makes me weep to think of what that little girl had to go through to bring Our Lady's words to us. But she refused to be worn down. And look now! This whole place is built on her testimony. Now, if you'll follow me, let's join the line which, I'm pleased to say, for once is not too long. After we've walked around, anyone who wants to can stay at the Grotto for private prayer. But, remember, lunch is at one on the dot. Maggie and the kitchen staff are implacable. Then, for those who can manage the climb, we've the Stations of the Cross at three.'

Taking my place in the queue, I move towards Gillian. 'I hope you'll forgive me monopolising your daughter-in-law,' I say to Patricia, who is standing beside her. 'But we were having a fascinating theological discussion.'

'She's a dark horse,' Patricia says, stepping back. 'Come on, Richard, we know when we're out of our depth.' Aware of having caused offence, I flash her my most ingratiating smile.

'You're starting to embarrass me,' Gillian says, as we wait side by side in front of the rock face.

'*Embarrass* is fine. It's when we get to *exasperate* that I'll start to worry.'

'Then start. What must she be thinking?' She looks at Patricia who is talking to Richard. 'The closest I ever get to a theological discussion is over whether to use Beeswax or Pledge on the pews.'

'Then it's high time for a change. Speaking of which, you don't really believe in these apparitions, do you?'

'I've already told you, you can believe in anything if you believe in God.'

'Don't get me wrong,' I say, resisting an easy riposte. 'I'm not suggesting that Bernadette was deliberately deceitful. I'm sure she thought that she saw something. The question is *what?* I never knew she had asthma. Maybe that's the key?'

'Asthma?'

'I'm no expert, but suppose the vision was a neurological response to an attack – even a mild one – brought on when she stepped into the freezing river.'

'But she didn't get that far. She saw the first apparition when she was taking her clogs off on the bank.'

'All right then. She had a shock when her feet touched the icy ground.'

'What about all the subsequent apparitions? The last one in July. It can't have been that icy then.'

'By then she'd invested too much in it. She was the victim of her own credulity.'

'She wasn't the only one. If *The Song of Bernadette*'s anything to go by – and I saw it every spring at school – the local priests were initially as hostile as the civic authorities. What swayed them was the sixteenth apparition, when the lady named herself as the Immaculate Conception. That was a new dogma proclaimed by the Pope only three or four years before. There was no way that an illiterate village girl could have known about it.'

'Not read about it, I grant. But the issue would have been in the air. She might have picked up on it without realising. The same thing happened at Fatima when the Virgin appeared to the three shepherd children and demanded the Consecration of Russia a few months after the February Revolution. It begs the question of why she always chooses the poor, the illiterate, the weak and the young – in a word, the gullible. Why not Voltaire or Stephen Hawking or, better still, Richard Dawkins?'

We edge closer to the Grotto, but all we can see are the pilgrims emerging on the other side. Some are so moved that, even though able-bodied, they have to be helped out by their friends or the Domain officials. Priests are right to talk about the *mystery* of faith, albeit not in the sense they intend. The mystery is how people can cling to a belief-system that has been the source of so much conflict and misery and violence and repression for the past two thousand years. I long to run up and down the line, forcing everyone to confront the truth: that God did not create the world, either in seven days or billions of years; that Jesus of Nazareth did not die for our sins but in a small-time religious uprising; that good and evil lie within our own control. Needless to say, I do nothing of the sort but wait patiently, a fake among the dupes.

'You're very quiet all of a sudden,' Gillian says.

'I'm sorry. I find this extremely painful. I understand how a nineteenth-century doctor might have been swayed by the lack of a scorch mark, but these people have access to the whole world on TV. Have they never seen the firewalkers in Fiji treading on red-hot coals without so much as a blister?'

'All right, let's forget the candle. What about the cures? Seven in the first nine months.'

'Yes. And I don't doubt they occurred. Faith healing is a well-documented phenomenon. There's a perfectly good natural explanation.'

'And a perfectly good miraculous one too.'

'So how come the cures are always for conditions that might have a psychological cause: the blind seeing; the lame walking, and so on? Why not the amputee sprouting a new limb?'

'That's disgusting!'

'Not for the amputee.'

We turn the corner and face the Grotto. I watch the pilgrims filing past, pressing their hands to the rock before wiping the condensation on their faces. A mother holds up a young boy who seems uncertain what to touch. Three Asian pilgrims shuffle forward on their knees. A nun causes a temporary blockage by prostrating herself on the ground.

'May I ask – purely out of curiosity – why you're so opposed to any notion of miracles?'

'That's easy. If I thought there was the slightest possibility of God intervening in the world – no, if I thought there was the slightest possibility of God, full stop – then I'd have to spend the rest of my life hating. How else could I cope with His arbitrariness, His favouritism, His cruelty?'

'So you'd judge Him by human standards?'

'Not human ... humane. Besides, according to your Church, God made us in His own image, so surely we have the right – no, make that the obligation – to apply our standards to Him? And if any human father had treated his children the way God has treated the world, He'd have had them taken away from Him thousands of years ago.'

'That's all very clever – '

'No, just true. On the one hand Christians profess to value modesty, and on the other they maintain that we stand at the pinnacle of creation. Excuse me? We're nothing but microbes who've outgrown their environment, a chance evolutionary process.'

'And isn't that the greatest miracle of all? You talk of the cruelty of God – '

'No, of Nature.'

'I think of the beauty, the kindness, the love. The love that I've felt all around me, the love that – no doubt you'll think this presumptuous – I've found in myself. And I know – don't ask me how, but I know it as surely as I know my own name – that it comes not just from inside me but from beyond. Now you can call that whatever you like; I call it God.'

She steps aside to wait for Richard and Patricia, who have lagged several paces behind. I move forward to join Jamie and Jewel at the Grotto which, up close, looks distinctly womblike, a hollow where the ancient Gauls might have worshipped Mother Earth. We film the Jubilate pilgrims in a similar act of devotion, focusing first on Lester and Tess, who linger hand-in-hand at the statue of the Virgin, and then on Matt, Geoff and Kevin, three of the young brancardiers, who lift Sheila Clunes out of her wheelchair and deposit her on the ground, where she kisses the spot on which Bernadette first prayed.

'Urgh!' Jamie says, 'think of all the feet that've trodden on it.'

'Not to worry,' I reply, 'they're the feet of the faithful.'

The momentary irreverence restores my spirits, which have sunk lower than I realised after my exchange with Gillian. If we were anywhere but Lourdes, I would blame a malignant spirit for urging me up on my hobby-horse to trample over both our affections. What do I know of the strains of looking after a brain-damaged husband, aware that there can be no let-up until one of them dies and, in the darkest moments, not caring which it is? What do I know of looking after anyone? Supposing our positions were reversed and it was me left with a wife who – for instance – had been horribly maimed in a car crash? How long before my pledges of devotion rang false and I hired a carer or, worse, put her in a home where weekly visits became first monthly and then confined to high days and holidays, as though she were an elderly aunt.

To be fair, I believe that I could cope with a child whose injuries simply compounded her need, a child whom I carried from sofa to bed as though she were her sane, strong sister who had dozed off in front of the TV. But a wife would be something else: a once powerful adult reduced to a state halfway between patient and captive. I think … I know that I would prefer her dead.

Does Gillian ever succumb to such treacherous thoughts? Or does *not my will be done, but thine, oh Lord* hold true, even in extremis? What does her faith mean to her? Is it the usual baptismal brainwash or is it rooted in something real? Is that what she means by the love she found in herself? In which case I should know better than to doubt it, since it has touched me more deeply than anything in years. But that is still no reason to pursue it. Even if she were a free agent

– or simply shared my taste for the furtive – our relationship would be doomed. We have nothing whatsoever in common. It is only in fiction that opposites attract; in real life they keep their distance.

The procession over, the Jubilate pilgrims stroll back to the Acceuil, apart from Tess and Lester who, still holding hands, stand staring at a bank of burning candles.

'Earth to Vincent!' Jamie calls, waving his hand in front of my face.

'Sorry. I was miles away.'

'Lunch!'

I follow the crew out of the Domain, braving the crowded streets as we search for a restaurant that is cheap (Jamie), music-free (Sophie), and vegan-friendly (Jewel). I am unusually compliant since I am conscious of no needs beyond Gillian. Without realising, I have regressed to a state of adolescent impotence where the only way to express my feelings for a girl was to ink her name on my arm. My mind is racing so fast that I can do little more than nod at the choice of the Café Jeanne d'Arc.

'Have they no shame?' Sophie asks. 'What does Joan of Arc have to do with Lourdes?'

'What does Shakespeare have to do with Barnsley?' I ask. 'But you still find his name above a local pub. Not everything in Lourdes is a sham!'

My outburst takes them by surprise, but I have neither the will nor the strength to explain, lowering my head to my *demi* and letting the conversation flow over it. While Jamie and Jewel discuss various remixes of tracks that I am too old to know in the original, and Sophie replies to messages and texts on her mobile, I reflect on my predicament, faced with the resurgence of emotions that I had thought were long dead.

'Would you please tell the court how you can be so sure?'

'Because I buried them myself, m'lud.'

To my relief, the others leave me in peace, attributing my silence to thoughts about the film. At the end of the meal Sophie calls for the bill, deftly divides it, and leads the way back to the Acceuil where we are to conduct the first of the afternoon's interviews: with Father Humphrey who is waiting for us in the Priests' Room. In spite of the plural, there is only one bed.

'We share it. Not at the same time.' He says with a chortle. 'Which-ever of us is on night duty.'

'Of course,' I say, immune to the bar-room humour. The monastic bed looks a tight squeeze even for one. Given my current concerns, I am convinced that his bulk is compensation. Moreover, with his mountainous gut overhanging his genitals, he must be able to break the golden rule of his Church and maintain that what he cannot see does not exist.

I invite him to share his experience of Lourdes. He responds with a potted life-history, peppered with the cringeworthy jokes which I used to think priests told to show that they were still one of the boys but which I now realise are a way to distance themselves from the awful reality of their lives. He starts with 'I was born in a Lancashire village so prejudiced that, when the postmistress asked what denom-ination of stamps you wanted, you'd reply five Roman Catholics and no Protestants,' followed by 'Would you like to know how I became a priest? When I was sixteen, my father told me the facts of life. There are nine in this family and only eight beds. You're out.' Just when the sense that he has mistaken the interview for an audition becomes overwhelming, he embarks on a long and heartfelt account of his stint as an army chaplain. 'We all know that it's hard for soldiers to readjust to civilian life,' he says. 'Let me assure you it's equally hard for priests. I've never felt so alien, so lonely and, to be honest, so dis-gusted with the people I was supposed to love. The men in the desert had been ready to lay down their lives – and some did, some did – to bring peace to a foreign land; I had parishioners who wouldn't lift a finger or, at least, put their hands in their pockets to help the home-less on their doorsteps. But God answered my prayers. I was in a bad way, on the verge of despair, when I received a phone call from the Jubilate director – not She Who Must Be Obeyed, her predecessor – to say that they were looking for a priest to lead their pilgrimage and a friend had suggested me. A friend indeed! At first I made up my mind to refuse. A trip to Lourdes didn't rate high on my list of priorities. But, thank God (and, believe me, I do every day), I had a change of heart. Here, I saw the same self-denying love I'd seen in the forces. I met men and women willing to set aside their own wants for the sake of others. Lourdes has given me back my faith in humanity when it was in danger of disappearing for ever. And, if that's not a miracle, I don't know what is.'

I am more grateful than ever for my pose of professional neutrality. After thanking him for his time, we leave the Acceuil and trek down the Esplanade to the Breton Calvary where, to the muted grumbles of a footsore Jewel and parched Jamie, I have arranged to film a joint interview with Maggie and Ken. It comes as no surprise that 'You don't want me; I'll crack the camera' Maggie and 'You'll have to take me as you find me' Ken have both dressed up for the occasion, with Maggie having added a garish gash of lip-gloss. They each describe the 'love affair with Lourdes' (Ken's phrase, Maggie's simper) that began on their first visits, Ken accompanying his elderly father and Maggie her pregnant niece.

'Steve – her husband – wouldn't come. He's an agnostic – not an atheist, mind, so there's still hope. He said to her: "Why not ask Aunt Maggie? She's a midwife. That way you'll have your very own medical team."'

I struggle to remain alert as they trot out their carefully polished anecdotes.

'I'm sure that none of this can be of interest to you,' Ken says over-modestly.

'On the contrary,' I reply, 'you've both been fascinating.'

The filming over, we make our way back across the Domain in a sweltering heat that shows no sign of abating, to the hillside above the basilicas, ready for the five o'clock Stations of the Cross. The precipitous path would appear to exclude the disabled pilgrims but, as we approach the first station, we find various helpers straining to push wheelchairs.

'Puts hairs on your chest,' Jamie says blithely to a handmaiden with a faint moustache.

We amble up to the Jubilates, who are easily identifiable by their sweatshirts, although some of the younger ones have changed into T-shirts and two of the boys have stripped off their tops. Looking around with studied indifference, I spot Gillian walking up the path with Louisa and wonder if she is deliberately seeking to keep me at bay, like a schoolboy sticking to a teacher when he knows that his tormentor is lying in wait at the other end of the yard.

Losing patience with myself, I search for Kevin, whom we are due to follow on the walk. He is angrily putting on his T-shirt after a reprimand from Marjorie. 'She says it's disrespectful. Why? Didn't God make our bodies? Didn't Jesus walk around in a loincloth?'

'I'm not too hot – sorry – on Messianic raiments. Still, a T-shirt makes sense if we're going to film you. Don't want to set too many female hearts aflame.'

'Oh sure! Have them switching off more like!' His pitiful lack of confidence takes me back thirty years.

'So, are you still happy to be our man on the Way of the Cross?'

'Don't see why not. Beats pushing a wheelchair. It's not my problem if the programme sucks.'

Jewel wires him for sound and we move up to the first station: *Jesus is condemned to death.* As Father Paul leads the prayers, I study the figures: Christ in *Ecce Homo* mode, guarded by four legionnaires in front of the Roman wolf. The lack of dynamism within the group and of any relation to the surrounding landscape makes it look both insubstantial and flat.

At the end of the prayers, we continue on a journey which, it soon becomes clear, is to be heavy on faith and light on art. At the third station, I realise that what the figures most resemble are plastic models that have somehow escaped from a cereal packet and landed in Lourdes.

I reserve the thought for possible inclusion in the voice-over and turn to Kevin.

'So Kevin, do you have any thoughts on the Stations this far?'

'Thoughts?' he asks, with mock incredulity. 'I'm not allowed thoughts. I'm seventeen. What do I know? I just do what my parents say, do what the monks say, do what the Bible says. Thoughts? Me? You've come to the wrong place if you want thoughts.'

By the seventh station: *Jesus falls for the second time*, Kevin appears to have had a change of heart. 'That's sick,' he says, pointing to a soldier holding back a jeering Jew with the tip of his spear. 'When were these sculptures made?'

'I'm not sure exactly. Some time before the First World War.'

'Jesus was Jewish, right?'

'Of course.'

'Have you seen how He's the only one who doesn't need a nose job?' I stare at the figure's hooked nose, ashamed at having failed to pick up the blatant anti-Semitism. 'It's all hypocrisy.'

'You talk of hypocrisy quite a lot.'

'Would you rather I shut my eyes to it like everyone else?'

'No, not at all. I wonder if you'd like to elaborate.'

'Oh yes, I'd like to,' he says fiercely. 'But you'd have every Catholic in the country writing letters of complaint to the BBC.'

'I'll take that risk.'

'Look at all these people gazing at Jesus with their holier-than-thou faces, but what do you suppose is going on in their minds? They pretend to be so devout, praying their rosaries, obeying the priests, but it's not worth dick!' His pained exclamation causes heads to turn but, to my relief, they are Tess's and Lester's. Counting on their indulgence to a fellow contributor, I motion to Kevin to continue. 'I know a man – let's call him Mr X – who claims to be a good Catholic, but does he give all his money to the poor? Does he shit! He makes more by buying their houses at auctions when they've been repossessed.'

'Rich men and needles: it's an age-old dilemma.'

'But there's worse. He's married, of course. And he sits at the dinner table with his wife and kids spouting on about sex and morals and the end of frigging civilisation as we know it ... is frigging OK?'

'Frigging's fine.'

'And it turns out he has a tart ... a slut ... a bit on the side. And when she gets pregnant, what does this good Catholic Mr X do? He tells her to have an abortion, that's what. And when his son finds out, he doesn't fall on his knees and beg for his forgiveness. Oh no! He packs him off to a boarding school run by a load of monks. More hypocrites. All paedos!'

'Come on!'

'I'm not saying they do stuff, just that they want to. Oh yes, you can see that they want to. And what did Jesus teach? Lusting after a woman is like having sex with her in your heart. Doesn't that go for boys too?'

'I suppose so, if you accept the premise.'

'It's all sick. It's all sex. It's just as bad on this pilgrimage. You know the doctor with the baby?'

'Yes,' I say, foreseeing a major edit.

'The father's one of the brancardiers. They met here two years ago.' I feel my heart leap. 'They got married and came again last year. The baby's three months old. You don't have to be a genius to do the maths. Any case, they admit it themselves quite openly.'

'Shouldn't people find love where they can? This is as good a place as any.'

'No, it's not!' he cries, and his face contorts in pain. 'It's supposed to be holy. St Bernadette was a nun. We should have our minds on God. See that woman!' To my dismay he points at Gillian. 'She came on to me the very first day we arrived.'

'Are you sure?'

'I know a pass when I see one. "Don't worry about me," she says, "I'm fit. Really fit." It's disgusting.'

I want to laugh out loud at the confusion but fear that I might compound the offence. We hike up the hill but are brought to an abrupt standstill by the Vietnamese group from the Crypt who have lingered at the ninth station.

At last they head off but, just as the Jubilates are about to take their place, a heated altercation breaks out at the rear. Although too far away to catch it, I see Gillian in its midst and presume that it must involve Richard. All my instincts are to rush to her aid, but I know that she would not thank me. So I hang back, happy for once to defer to a priest.

Father Paul quickly restores the peace – while leaving me absorbed in speculation – before moving to the front and offering up a prayer that we should each have the courage to bear our own cross, which seems somewhat perverse, given that Jesus is here falling for the third time under the weight of His.

He limits the period for private prayer out of consideration for the Dutch pilgrims who are hot on our heels. As we press ahead, I turn my attention back to Kevin.

'So it would be fair to say that the message of Lourdes has yet to reach you?'

'And it won't! I'm an atheist.' He glances sidelong at the sky, as if in fear of a retaliatory thunderbolt. 'I'm only here because I had to show willing – penitent (I don't think!) – or else they'll chuck me out of school. And I'm only there because I need my As to go to art college.'

'What did you do that was so terrible?'

'Drawing. Just drawing. Michelangelo drew nudes all over the Sistine Chapel, the Pope's private chapel, and they're masterpieces. I draw nudes and, because some sicko monk thinks he recognises himself, they're "obscene"; they're "sordid fantasies". Wait till I'm a famous artist. Then they'll be queuing up to interview me. Then people'll listen to what I say.'

'I'm sure.' Although I strive to expunge all trace of doubt from my voice, he looks at me with suspicion.

'Haven't you got enough? You won't use any of it anyway. You'll say you will, then you'll cut me out. Everyone always does.'

He rips off the microphone and hands it to Jewel. We have reached the twelfth station: *Jesus dies on the cross*, which seems an appropriate place to end. As I stand on the crest of the hill, with the three crosses framed against the trees, it feels that at last the landscape has become integral to the journey and, in spite of myself, I am moved.

'Another of your fans?' I am startled to find Gillian walking up to me and pointing to Kevin, who is striding down the path.

'Have you been watching me?' I ask, both gratified and alarmed.

'No, just the camera. For us ordinary mortals, it's as compulsive as a car crash.'

'I wouldn't want to put you off your prayers.'

'Now don't spoil it! I'm here to apologise for this morning.'

'No, I'm the one who should apologise. I don't know what got into me. I don't usually come on so strong.'

'Me neither. Telling you how you should live your life when I don't have the first idea what it's like!'

'That's easily remedied.'

'No need. Apologies accepted on both sides. Let's leave it at that.' She looks around in confusion at finding that she has outstayed the prayers.

'Have you given any more thought to an interview?' I ask as, to her evident unease, we walk together to the ridge. 'We're free straight after this.'

'I'm not, I'm afraid. It's gone six now. Dinner's at seven. Then the Penitential Service at half past eight.'

'Stop, too much excitement! Sorry. But how about after that? Won't you meet me for a drink?'

'You say *drink* as if it's not only in italics but you want me to acknowledge them.'

'You don't miss a trick.'

'Or a trickster.'

'You can always stick to tomato juice if it makes you feel safer.'

'It's not the alcohol that worries me. I know you think that we're all either fools or phonies. No, don't deny it! And you may have a point. But I came here with a purpose and, come what may, I mean to see it through.'

She hurries back to Richard, clasping his hand as they make the sharp descent to the thirteenth station, where *Jesus is taken down from the Cross*. I follow them from there to the fourteenth, where *Jesus is laid in the tomb*. I presume that we have reached the end and am taken aback when Father Paul guides us towards a fifteenth station, where *Jesus is risen from the dead*. As he waits for the stragglers to catch up, I move forward to question him. 'Surely there are only fourteen stations? Or were we labouring under a misapprehension, in that as in so much else, at Holyrood, Barnsley?'

'Don't worry,' he replies wryly. 'Your practice was perfectly sound. The final station was added here in the 1950s (Father Dave will be able to give you the exact date): a message of hope at the end of the journey.'

Much to my surprise, I find myself agreeing. Far from the kitsch image of my expectations, with plastic angels hanging from wires in the trees, it is a simple – almost stark – circular stone set in front of a crevice. For the first time the sculpture reaches beyond the biblical story to speak directly to me. Then, seeing Gillian standing with Richard, I recall her refusal of my offer. A shadow falls over the stone.

GILLIAN

Wednesday June 18

The prying finger between my legs jolts me awake. I pull it away like a nun on dormitory duty or, worse, at the mercy of illicit desires in the darkness of her cell. The rare relief of the single bed vanishes under sustained assault from the images cramming my brain. Dreams that usually slip out of reach with butterfly elusiveness now linger with shameful clarity.

In the adjacent bed, Richard kicks against a blanket that might have been me, and emits something between a snarl and a snore. I seize on the one moment when his incoherence is not an affront to speculate on his sensations. Is his mind equally muddled by night as by day, or is there some deeper level at which it still functions? Is there a parity, or even a compensation, in the unconscious which ensures that, while my dreams are empty delusions, his make perfect sense? A feral grunt as he thrashes and flails and buries his head in the pillow suggests not.

I swing my legs over the edge of the mattress, relishing the chance to map out my territory. Some women clamour for a room of their own; I would settle for a bed. I could return home and swap our marital double for companionable twins, but it would be too cruel to deprive Richard of the one place in which he still responds to me as a man. This sudden flood of compassion towards him disconcerts me. It smacks of the guilt offerings he used to make me, with their predictable pattern: clothes for a minor dalliance; jewellery for a serious affair. Am I seeking to atone for my mental infidelity with a similarly hollow display?

A knock on the door thrusts me headlong into morning.

'Just a second,' I call, jumping off the bed and grabbing my dressing gown from a chair. 'Come in!' The door creaks open to reveal the two young brancardiers I turned away yesterday, the helpers' helpers who, in Louisa's words, are 'here to give you the chance to relax and enjoy the pilgrimage too'. The reality is quite the reverse, their intrusion giving me three causes for concern rather than one. On most days I worry about Richard's inappropriate behaviour; today I worry also about my own.

'Come right in!' I say, gathering the flimsy gown around me and trusting that its lily-of-the-valley motif will offset any impropriety. I turn to draw the curtains; a formality, given the sunlight already streaming into the room. Matt ambles in, with bleary eyes, rumpled T-shirt and hair like a trampled cornfield. Kevin hovers behind, his sullen features emphasised by his defiantly unshaven cheeks. His manifest wretchedness brings out my maternal instincts, even as Matt's broad smile and gentle brawn bring out very different ones.

Before I know it, I am thrown back into the nocturnal landscape. Matt is eighteen years old! And no matter what the agony aunts – and, increasingly, nieces – in my magazines might say, an untried teenager, however potent, however grateful, is not this older woman's ideal. What is happening? Has Vincent O'Shaughnessy so unsettled me that my every thought – my every impulse – is sexual? Is the dream Gillian, brazenly turning the Grotto into a seraglio, the real me?

'Morning, boys!' I say, with an accent on their youth. 'You look like you had a rough night, Matt.'

'A gang of us went to the pub,' he replies sheepishly. 'It was wicked.'

'How about Kevin?' I try to deflect the scowl. 'Were you one of the party?'

'We've come to give Mr Patterson a shower,' he says, his bluntness a double rebuff.

'I didn't think you'd come to give me one.' My words seep out with no apparent relation to my brain. I turn in desperation to Richard. 'Right then, old boy. Rise and shine!'

He shifts groggily as my voice engages his nascent consciousness. 'It's his pills,' I say, feeling the need to apologise for a depth of sleep more suitable to one their age than his. 'Breakfast time!' I tell him, hoping for the reflex excitement of a puppy who has just learnt the phrase. But my hopes are dashed by the extended sequence of his wakening: first bewilderment; then panic at confronting the day deprived of familiar landmarks; next the partial reassurance of seeing my face; finally, pain and frustration at being dragged out of his dreams into a world over which he has even less control.

'Here are Matt and Kevin ready to help you up. You said you were tired of seeing the same old face every day.' In company I am careful to drop the *ugly*. 'Now's your chance!'

'Go away,' he replies, pulling the covers over his head in what may or may not be a game but I lack the patience to find out. As the two young men step aside, reluctant witnesses of our morning routine, I wonder if they are more disturbed by the evidence of brain damage or of marriage. Any illusions that the extended families of television soap operas may have left them will be stripped away by the petty power struggle being played out here.

Eventually my mixture of threats and blandishments pays off. He stands up with a wide stretch which, to my shame, his insouciance, Matt's amusement and Kevin's disgust, reveals an erection. I feign blindness, bustling him into the bathroom with the boys, praying that his loathing of being manhandled will counteract the female caresses that must have sweetened his sleep.

'He can shower and shave for himself,' I explain. 'You don't need help, do you, Richard?'

'I don't need help,' he repeats proudly.

'So just make sure that he has everything he needs: that the water's not too hot; that he plugs his razor in the right socket; that he doesn't spray his aftershave under his arms. Oh, why am I telling you all this? It's obvious,' I say, painfully aware that it would be quicker and easier to attend to it myself.

'In here, sir,' Matt says, as though Richard were wearing a dinner jacket rather than dubiously stained pyjamas. I give thanks for the deference that has steered him away from the ubiquitous *mate*.

I follow them to the bathroom door which Kevin slams in my face. Baffled, I walk to the window and watch the Irish pilgrims assembling outside the Acceuil. A priest glances up and I spring back for fear of embarrassing him. I drift around the room desultorily sorting out clothes, before spotting the Jubilate programme. Halfway through an account of today's service of anointing, I hear the Basilica clock strike eight and wonder what further humiliations to expect before it does so again.

Relieved of responsibility but not of concern, I focus my attention on the bathroom where the harsh splash of the shower is followed by the insistent whir of the toothbrush and electric razor. Intermittent shouts and muffled laughter give way to an ominous silence, after which Richard emerges, wrapped in a towel, led by a shaken-looking Matt and a soaked Kevin.

'Oh my goodness,' I say, as Kevin's glare threatens to dispel my sympathy. 'That shower's deceptive. Water comes at you from every angle.'

'Yeah, especially when it's chucked in your face!' he exclaims, prompting Richard to laugh. 'Look at me, I'm drenched! And my clothes are all back at the hotel.'

'It may not be ideal, but I'm sure I can find you a T-shirt of Richard's.'

'One of mine!'

'I'm not taking my clothes off for you!' His outraged tone makes me suspect a recent split from his girlfriend.

'Come on, Kev, don't be a prat!' Matt says. 'It's ninety degrees in the shade out there. You'll soon dry.'

'I'll sue. If I get pneumonia, I'll sue you. I'll sue the pilgrimage.'

'How about the Pope while you're at it?' Matt says. 'I'm sure the Holy Father must be personally responsible for the dicky plumbing.' He ruffles Kevin's hair, adding to his fury.

'Fuck ... get off!'

Matt turns to Richard. 'Does he need a hand with dressing?' he asks hesitantly.

'Not at all. You run along. Thanks so much. You've both been a tremendous help,' I say, resolving to refuse any future assistance that might be offered.

'Only we've got to do Mr Redpath in Room Seven.'

'You boys are wonders. Whatever they're paying you it's not enough.'

'They don't pay us anything,' Kevin says savagely. 'We have to pay them for the privilege of being here.'

'I'm sorry. I was being funny. Or rather, trying.'

The boys go out, leaving me to the familiar task of watching Richard dress. Cheered by my sanctioning of a blazer and cravat, he insists on putting on a sweater.

'You'll swelter.'

'It's *my* skin.'

'True.' Surprising us both by my compliance, I dispatch him to the dining room before taking my own turn in the shower, where I linger under the jet, soaping every pore. What I don't know, or rather, have no wish to discover is whether I am trying to wash away my night-time self or to become her.

I too spend longer choosing my clothes than the occasion might merit, nevertheless a trip to the countryside requires careful thought. As I run through my checklist: shoulders covered for the church and the sun; skirt long enough for a picnic; flat shoes for any uneven ground; I settle on my new lilac-and-white check dress with a white stole, a last-minute inclusion after Patricia's mention of the year she had 'cocktails with the Cardinal'. Ignoring the possibility of grass stains, I slip on the dress and relish its softness against my skin.

I make my way to the dining room, where my marital antennae immediately pick up Richard, sitting beside Nigel dipping crusts in an egg. Patricia gives me a discreet wave as she weaves around the tables replenishing cups. Whatever our private differences, I salute her sense of duty. No doubt at ninety she will still be volunteering at Troubridge Hall, serving lunches to old soldiers ten years her junior and doing so with no relaxation of her ruthless fashion code. Although she has been setting tables and doling out food since seven, her hair is as impeccably coiffed as if she had just emerged from the salon. Her jewellery is tastefully understated, especially the gold oyster-shell earrings which – I realise with a smile – turn her lobes into pearls. Her waxed apron printed with French herbs, a souvenir from Sissinghurst, is as spotless as the peach cotton twinset it protects.

Uncertain whether the wave is a greeting or a summons, I walk towards her. 'Good morning, my dear,' she says breezily. 'Your lie-in's done you the world of good. See how pretty you can look when you make the effort.'

'I haven't made any effort. No more than usual,' I insist, for the benefit of the two West Indian toast-makers to whom I have yet to be introduced. 'You're the one who deserves the praise. Waiting on everyone hand and foot while looking as spruce as ever.'

'Not hand and foot, dear. It's Fleur and Mona who do the donkey work.' She sighs in relief at having deflected the menial image. 'Have you met my daughter-in-law Gillian?' They shake their heads and hold out their hands. 'It's her first pilgrimage too, but I'm sure it won't be the last, not for any of you. Fleur and Mona are real assets to the kitchen. Mona was a school dinner lady so she keeps us all on our toes.'

'I can see they're working wonders,' I say, hoping that my gentle compliment will compensate for Patricia's condescension. This is a woman who makes a beeline for any black visitors to her church to prove her lack of prejudice, while lambasting the Anglicans down the road for appointing a West Indian vicar. 'It's all very well in Brixton,' she declared, 'but this is Dorking. The Church is supposed to console people not confuse them.'

Smiling at Mona and Fleur as warmly as if they had overheard the exchange, I move to my table. While accepting Louisa's argument that the number of special diets necessitates fixed seating, I suspect that she would bend the rules had she been placed alongside Richard, Nigel, Frank and Sheila Clunes. With Richard encouraging Nigel to play the clown (literally, given the eggshells on their noses), Frank chewing every morsel twenty times and returning to 'one' at the slightest interruption, and Sheila wolfing down her food in a constant bid to be first for seconds, I gaze at more congenial tables as wistfully as I used to gaze at more popular ones at school.

'Morning Sheila, morning Nigel, morning Frank!' I say, instantly regretting my mistake, as Frank's strangled reply is followed by a lengthy recount.

'Good breakfast?' I ask, prising the shell off Richard's nose.

'Ow!' he protests. 'It was finished.'

'I had two yellows in my egg,' Nigel says.

'That's a lucky sign,' I say.

'No, it's not,' Richard says. 'It's like eating twins.'

No sooner have I sat down than Patricia and Fleur head my way, advancing the rival attractions of tea and coffee. Placing my morning drug over family loyalty, I apologise lightly to Patricia, who takes the opportunity to linger at the table.

'Sorry I had no time to talk to you earlier, darling,' she says to an indifferent Richard. 'You arrived bang in the middle of the Corn Flake rush. Did you enjoy your breakfast?'

'I had two yellows in my egg,' Nigel interjects.

'Sh-sh. Don't speak too loud, or they'll charge you double.' Nigel giggles unrestrainedly. 'Aren't you eating anything?' she asks me. 'I'm sure we could rustle up an egg.'

'Thanks, no. I don't have any appetite.' I watch Sheila shovelling butter on her toast, and wonder what perversity prompts the caterers to shun the local baguettes in favour of thick, white – and increasingly stale – bread brought from home.

'You need to keep up your strength. Doesn't she?' She picks an unfortunate ally in Sheila.

'Is there any more toast?' Sheila asks. 'I still have a little hole that needs filling.'

Patricia purses her lips at such lack of restraint. 'Don't forget we have to climb the hill at Saint-Savin.'

'Not me! I'm in my chair,' she replies, with a grin far too wicked for Lourdes. Dismayed, Patricia turns back to Richard. 'You're looking very perky this morning.' Nigel's second burst of giggles makes her shudder. 'Did you sleep well?'

'No! Gilly stayed out all night and came back drunk.'

Patricia stares at me in horror.

'Don't be silly, Richard. I went for a quick drink with the film crew.'

'You came back singing.'

'Humming. I was humming. Though with my voice, I grant it's hard to tell.' I force a laugh. 'Elkie Brooks' "Sunshine After The Rain". I haven't heard it for years. Now I can't seem to get it out of my mind.'

'But why?' Patricia asks. 'It hasn't rained here in weeks.'

'It's just a song.'

'Still, it's put a bit of colour in your cheeks.' I cannot escape the feeling that she knows, or rather, imagines, since there is nothing to know. This makes it even more absurd that I should have extended the drink to the crew, as though there were something to hide.

'I'm a fine figure of a man,' Richard says abruptly.

'Yes, dear. But it doesn't do for you to say so yourself.'

'I didn't,' he says, affronted. 'She did.' He points to Louisa, who is patrolling the room, exhorting people 'not to rush but just to hurry on down to the coaches'.

I wonder what it is about the phrase that has stuck in his mind, leading him to repeat it so often over the past few days. I wonder, even more urgently, what it is about his mind that filters out some phrases while latching on to others. The man who was once a mystery to me in jest is now one in earnest. But what would I do if I found the key? Do I want to move closer to him or just to feel better about drifting away? In my current state, I suspect everyone's motives, starting with my own. Who was it said that a pilgrimage to Lourdes would bring me peace?

I urge Richard to use the loo before boarding the coach. 'But my bladder's strong. Go on. Feel.' A wave of repugnance turns first to pity and then to confusion, as he flexes his biceps in what may or may not be intended as a joke. We walk through a complex of white-walled corridors, as immaculate as the nuns who sweep them, and out into the open air. Ken stands beside the coaches directing wheel-chair-users into one and the able-bodied into the other. Richard's disappointment at being separated from Nigel grows on watching him being hauled up on a hydraulic lift. Louisa meanwhile fights a losing battle against the young brancardiers who steer their wheel-chairs across the courtyard as if in a stock car race. The girls look on, their expressions poised between admiration and scorn, instinctively drawn into a mating ritual that has flourished in these hills since the first cavemen brought back the bison. Or have I missed the point? Do they genuinely admire the boys' skill while scorning their swagger? Is mine the inevitable cynicism of one whose bison has been vacuum-packed for years?

Vincent walks into view, his curls as tight on his head as if he had just stepped out of a shower, an everyday image that gives me a singular thrill. He wears a moss green T-shirt and neatly pressed beige chinos, although it would be as absurd to suggest that he had chosen them for my benefit as that I had chosen my new dress for his. I bundle Richard on to the coach in a blaze of self-consciousness. Then, risking a glance at Vincent, I realise that my scruples are superfluous since he has yet to acknowledge my presence. Either he has taken my protests to heart or else he has lost interest: when we finally talked, he found that I was not clever or witty or charming enough or was simply too straitlaced. Did I misread the signs? Should I have fallen into his arms at the first sip of tomato juice? Or am I misreading them now? If he blames me for anything, is it for encouraging him to drop his mask, not least with the story of the friend and the murdered dog.

My mind is so preoccupied that I push past Richard into a window seat, usurping his prerogative. 'That's not fair,' he complains.

'Don't be such a baby!' I say, standing to swap seats, only to find myself staring at Lucja sitting in the row behind with Pyotr slumped in accusatory silence on her knee. Smiling feebly, I turn round and wait for what Patricia has promised will be one of the highlights of the week.

The journey out of Lourdes is dispiriting, as we crawl through streets that would be dangerously cramped even without the parked cars. 'Breathe in!' Father Humphrey yells, as we edge past a lorry unloading liquid gas. A near miss with a Spanish coach, which would provoke an ugly incident elsewhere, here leads to nothing more than a flurry of friendly waves and flourished crosses. With a missionary zeal that has lain untapped since the sixth form, I long to point it out to Vincent who sits, oblivious, several rows in front.

Father Humphrey passes the time by telling a series of jokes, of which only one, about a philanthropic American offended by an English bishop's prayer for 'our American succour', amuses me. Richard, however, takes the opportunity to tell one of his own. 'I have a joke.'

'I know. I've heard it.'

'How? It could be a new one.'

'It's not.'

'You don't know till I tell you.'

'Is it the one about the Irishman and foreplay?'

'How did you know?'

'I just knew.'

'How did you know?' he asks, with growing alarm.

'I didn't. I just guessed.'

'You don't know everything.'

We finally arrive at the autoroute and I feel a Boxing Day relief. It is only on leaving Lourdes that I realise how heavily the atmosphere of faith and expectation has weighed on me. I turn to look out of the window but, as ever, Richard blocks the view.

Father Humphrey hands the microphone to Father Dave with a

show of deference which, to the uninitiated (I picture one in particular), might sound like derision. As we trundle up the winding road, he leads us in two decades of the rosary, the familiar cadences gliding off my tongue. These are followed by the hymns 'Hail, Queen of Heaven' and 'Faith of Our Fathers', to which Mona adds such a thrilling descant that I find it hard not to applaud. Then, as fervently as he was praising the Virgin, he extols the beauty of the landscape and reports on its growing popularity for winter sports.

I marvel at the verdant slopes and snow-capped summits, which can be glimpsed even from my restricted viewpoint. 'Look, Richard, a ski-lift,' I say, trying to regain his favour.

'You can't ski.'

'I've never tried,' I reply brusquely. 'That doesn't mean I can't. There are lots of things I haven't tried that I might be very good at.'

He is as surprised by my tone as I am myself. 'I love you, Gilly.'

'I know you do,' I say, squeezing his hand.

'I love you more than all these mountains put together.'

'And I love you,' I reply uneasily.

'To your right,' Father Dave points out, 'is the Cirque de Gavarnie, or to us the Gavarnie Circus, a natural amphitheatre formed by millions of years of erosion. Those of you with sharp eyes might just be able to make out the waterfall which is the highest in France.'

'Are there elephants?' Richard asks me.

'It's not that sort of circus. More like a circus ring.'

'I know that,' he drawls. 'Like Oxford Circus.'

'Yes, that's right.'

'Like Piccadilly Circus.'

'That too.'

'You didn't think I knew that, did you? You're not so clever after all.'

'No, I'm not. I'm certainly not.'

'I love you, Gilly,' he says, smothering my hands with kisses. My perpetual hope of reaching through the mulch of his mind to a kernel of understanding turns to fear that at times he may understand too much.

The coach continues to Saint-Savin, a village so modest that we scarcely know we have arrived. We spill out into the main street or what may be the only street, two rows of terraced houses with the kind of shuttered windows that promise both privacy and protection. In front of us looms the church, a white stone building with fortress-thick walls topped by a conical turret which, it soon becomes clear, is not just Saint-Savin's main attraction but its entire *raison d'être*. To our left is a café with a bank of outdoor tables, at one of which sits a portly man in a pinstriped waistcoat who is either its proprietor or sole customer. Next to it is a general store with a stock of groceries, souvenirs, and ornate liqueur bottles that serve for both. A few doors down is an antique shop, its discreet sign barely distinguishing it from the houses on either side. The entrance is forbiddingly locked, but the window is filled with porcelain dolls and small clocks, all of which have stopped and several of which have missing hands, reinforcing the impression of a village outside time.

Ken's plea that we should wait by the coaches is widely ignored. Knowing how long it takes to disgorge the wheelchairs, all but the most obedient of us drift down the street.

'I'm just nipping into the café to buy Martin an ice cream,' Claire says.

'"Scream,' Martin echoes, with an anticipatory dribble.

'Would you like to join us for a coffee?' Tess asks as she and Lester follow.

'Or something stronger?' Lester adds, with a defiant grin.

'I'm fine, thanks. Enjoy.'

Several people, including Vincent, venture into the shop, while others stand outside choosing postcards from the carousels. Richard, who has been waiting for Nigel to roll off the coach, runs up and grabs my hand. 'Quick! Come on! You'll be left behind!' His concern is gratifying though unfounded, given the snail-like pace of the procession up the hill. Whatever Ken's many talents, the logical organisation of wheelchairs is not one of them. Some old-school sense of propriety prevents his allocating male pushers to female passengers, so that Jenny and a fellow handmaiden (I hear Moira ... Maureen) strain behind Sheila Clunes, while Matt and Kevin race up with the bantamweight Nigel. When the girls grind to a halt, Matt steps in with a mixture of gallantry and shyness, taking over from Jenny's friend. She in turn crosses to Kevin, who plants himself squarely behind Nigel, leaving her forlorn.

I stand beside Sister Martha, who gazes rapturously at the church.

'This place never fails to move me,' she says. 'I missed it last year.'

'Was your team on duty at the Acceuil?'

'No, I missed the pilgrimage. I caught the coxsackie virus from an asylum seeker in Plaistow.'

'But you're over it now?' I ask of the sinister-sounding virus, only to find from Richard's peal of laughter that, to him, it sounds like something else.

'Naughty lady!' he says, giggling. 'Naughty nun!'

'Shut up, Richard! You're not funny. I'm so sorry.'

'Not to worry. Water off a duck's back, or a penguin's, as Father Humphrey would say.' As she purses her lips, I suspect that Richard's misapprehension offends her less than Father Humphrey's routine ridicule.

We reach the church which, to my disappointment, turns out not to be white but a greyish-ochre, temporarily bleached by the sun. Patricia walks up to Mona and Fleur who are waiting in the shade of the porch.

'First in line, ladies,' she says cryptically. 'I wonder you've any puff left after all that singing.' Mona smiles, as serene as the stones that surround her. I step back. It is hard enough worrying whom Richard may insult without taking responsibility for his mother.

The rest of the group slowly climbs the hill, among them Vincent, whose coldness towards me is now so marked that a part of me – a very small, irresponsible part which I thought had died twenty years ago – longs for him to abandon all restraint: to run up and clasp me in his arms. Instead he is deep in conversation with Lester and Tess.

They join us outside the bolted door. 'No room at the inn?' Vincent asks pertly.

'It's the first year it's been locked,' Marjorie replies. 'There've been a spate of thefts from local churches.' She shakes her head. 'Of course it's all good practice for me.'

'The thefts?' Vincent asks innocently.

'Is he always this wicked?' Marjorie asks Sophie.

'Twenty-four seven.'

'The management! I'll be stepping into Louisa's shoes next year.'

'And they're big ones to fill.'

'Really wicked! Between you and me, I put it down to all the square-bashing when she was a young cadet.'

'Oh you mean literally? I'm sorry, I thought it was a figure of speech.'

'No, of course not!' She laughs nervously. 'I mean yes, of course. I'm so confused. It's this heat … Maggie!' She prises her away from Patricia. 'Will you ask some of your girls to take round the water? I'll just go and see if I can speed things up.' With a backward glance, she disappears behind the church. I find myself face to face with Vincent.

'*Wicked*'s the word!'

'Morning,' he says gently.

'Morning,' I reply, praying that he will attribute the inane grin forming on my lips to Marjorie's mistake.

'You're looking particularly luscious today.'

'Really? I feel frazzled.'

'Sweet dreams?'

'What?'

'Did you have sweet dreams?' he repeats with emphasis.

'Oh! No, I'm sorry. I never dream.'

'Everyone dreams. Whether they choose to remember them or not.'

'That's not true,' I say, more forcefully than I intend. 'My mother … at the end of her life she suffered from dementia. In the early stages, before she left us completely, she said the worst thing was not being able to dream.'

'I'm sorry. It must have been dreadful for you,' he says quietly.

'But worse for her.' I kick myself for having mentioned it. Suppose he thinks that dementia runs in families or, worse, wonders why two people so close to me should both lose their minds?

'So who was Saint Savin then?' he asks, in a neat change of tack. 'What wondrous feats did he perform?' He spots Father Dave. 'Ah, here comes the expert!'

'Expert on what? Are you in need of spiritual direction, my son?' he asks with a genial smile.

''Fraid not, Father. But when I am, you'll be the first to know. We were wondering about Saint Savin. Not on the A list, I suspect?'

'The Church venerates some ten thousand or so saints. Even a good Catholic such as yourself can't be expected to keep track of them all.' Vincent knows better than to reply. 'Saint Savin was born in Spain in the Dark Ages. Although how we who live in these benighted times have the gall to describe any other era as *Dark* is beyond me. He was the son of a wealthy nobleman who gave up everything – family, wealth, status – to devote himself to God. At some stage – I forget when exactly, but I'm sure there'll be a booklet about it in the church – he withdrew from the world completely, built himself a small hut and lived as a hermit for years – once again I'm a bit hazy on dates. He devoted himself to a life of prayer and poverty.'

'That's what puzzles me,' Vincent says. 'If God created the world and, for the sake of argument (or, more to the point, to avoid it), let's assume that He did, isn't that a kind of blasphemy? According to Genesis, He saw that it was good. More: He gave it to man to lord over. In which case why should anyone – no, I'll go further – what right does anyone have to withdraw from it? Surely it's our duty to enjoy it to the full?'

I refuse to catch his eye.

'Who's to say he didn't?' Father Dave asks.

'What?'

'Who's to say Saint Savin didn't sit – or, more likely, kneel – in his hermitage and experience overwhelming joy: that he didn't see as much of the world in his small patch of ground as any twenty-first century jet-setter?'

He makes his way to a group of brancardiers, leaving Vincent at a rare loss for words. Trusting in the power of my own silence, I smile and move to Richard, who is plotting with Nigel how to knock a limpet-like lizard off a cornice. I have just persuaded him to drop his pebbles when Louisa returns, followed by Marjorie and a dismayingly youthful sacristan. 'Success!' she cries. 'Not quite the key to the Pearly Gates, but it'll have to do for the time being.'

We enter the cavernous church. At first glance it appears as stark as a Baptist chapel, but gradually my eyes adjust and I make out the sanctuary with its black marble altar and richly coloured paintings, the vaulted transept with its golden Eucharistic Tower, the octagonal pilasters from one of which hangs a large wooden crucifix, and, most striking of all, the intricately decorated organ screen with its motifs of flowers, musical instruments and scores. I squeeze into a worm-eaten pew between Patricia and Richard, who grabs at the dust caught in the light from a turret window, and lean back to breathe in the spirit of simple piety emanating from every knot and crack in the wood.

Father Humphrey sits alone in the chancel while Father Dave and Father Paul celebrate mass. We begin by singing 'Let All Mortal Flesh Keep Silence', which Louisa accompanies on the organ. Her hesitancy is exacerbated by the audible clunking of the pedals, but the notes pouring out of the ancient pipes are gloriously mellow. In the last verse, displaying an irreverent streak as unsuspected as her musical talent, she pulls out a stop and the three wooden masks at the front of the screen open their mouths to sing along. Steve, who has clearly been primed, holds Fiona up to see, but her terrified howls cut through the Alleluias and he rapidly sets her down. As we kneel to pray, Richard twists alternately to left and right, playing one-sided peek-a-boo with the crucifix, whose haunted eyes seem to reach every corner of the church.

Father Paul stands to deliver his sermon. 'Many of us are parents,' he begins, and I sense Patricia tensing at my side. Never a fan of late vocations, she holds that the least such priests can do is to draw a veil over their past lives. I, as ever, take the opposite view and feel a pang for Father Humphrey and Father Dave whose childlessness is thrown into relief, until the thought of their spiritual parenthood turns my pity insidiously towards myself. 'All of us have parents,' he continues, in a less contentious vein. Patricia nods, while I add another failure to my list. My recent exchange with Vincent has reminded me how little I contributed to my mother's care. My father and sisters – and even my brother – recognised my prior responsibilities. What law or convention (for it certainly wasn't sentiment) required me to put my husband first? The readiness with which my mother forgave me makes it harder to forgive myself. Tears roll down my cheeks: heavy, gritty tears, as though I am passing through a further stage of mourning. I wonder if they are for my mother or for myself.

'As well as our earthly mother, we have a mother in heaven whose love for us is infinite,' Father Paul says. 'A mother who is always watching over us, interceding for us and willing us to do what is right.' I am curious as to how he defines what is right. Is it the words and example of her son, or the laws that the Church has built around them? Not even the holiest hermit could claim that they were one and the same. Christ made love the basis of His gospel, but what of those of us who have none, who are wives only in name, who are mothers only by the cruellest twist of fate? Am I to sacrifice heart to home for the rest of my life? Is that what God wants of me? Is that what Mary wants for me? I fumble in my bag for a tissue. Patricia puts her hand on mine and, while wishing that she had waited for me to wipe away the tears, I am grateful for the show of support.

At the end of the sermon, Father Humphrey moves to the altar to bless the oils. The three priests then walk into the nave and along the line of wheelchairs, anointing each person in turn. Nigel squeals as Father Dave makes the sign of the cross on his forehead. 'Hot! Burns!' He thrusts his hands beneath the blanket, shaking his head adamantly when Father Dave entreats him to hold them up. 'You burnt me!'

'Not me, Nigel. God. What you felt is the power of His love.'

Whether he grasps the distinction or simply responds to the clerical authority, Nigel lifts his hands. He screws his eyes tight as Father Dave turns up the palms and anoints them while praying: 'May the Lord who frees you from sin save you and raise you up.' Nigel blows on his hands, leaving Sheila who is seated beside him to supply an awestruck 'Amen'.

Having finished with the wheelchairs, the priests prepare for the rest of us. Father Humphrey moves into the centre of the nave while Father Dave and Father Paul take up places at either end of the transept. 'As you see, it's a very powerful experience,' Patricia whispers. 'But make sure you get Father Humphrey. He's the best.' For all that I shrink from the notion of competitive anointing, when Ken directs our row towards Father Paul, I sidestep and lead Richard into the queue for Father Humphrey. As if in consequence, the ritual is underwhelming and I feel nothing but the viscous smear of the oil.

Struggling to curb my resentment, I make my way back to the pew. I stop to assist a disorientated Frank who, from the broad smile on his usually twisted features, has taken his blessing to heart. A commotion in Father Paul's queue pulls us up short. Vincent is busy filming and I fear that he may inadvertently have caused offence until I see Tess slip to her knees. Lester has collapsed and, far from showing too little respect, Vincent signals to Jamie to switch off the camera. I watch from the confines of the pew while Dr Robson helps Tess lift Lester to his feet and, brooking no argument, leads him slowly to his seat. I prevent Richard peering round, while for once envying his lack of restraint.

'What did I tell you?' Patricia says. 'A very powerful experience.'

The mass ends and we file out, past a squat stone font with a troll-like figure on the base.

'It's medieval,' Patricia says, her reverence for the past increasing with age.

'It's very crude,' I say.

'No, that's intentional. Father Dave explained. It was made for a group of people – I forget the name – but there were thousands in Spain and France at the time. They were like lepers and weren't allowed to be baptised in the same water as everyone else. Isn't history fascinating?' I contemplate the line of latter-day outcasts and wonder if history is as remote as she thinks.

We plod through the ruins of the ancient cloister, our pace determined as much by the baking heat as the cracked path, to arrive at a large enclosed meadow that must once have housed part of the abbey complex but now makes for a perfect picnic ground. The brancardiers set out canvas chairs and spread tartan rugs on the grass, while Maggie and her team of handmaidens unload boxes of packed lunches. Patricia wanders over to help them. 'I'll make sure to save an extra-special one for you,' she promises Richard, to the fury of Sheila Clunes.

'There's Nigel!' Richard says, striding towards his friend whose wheelchair is parked in the partial shade of the archway. I follow, eager to learn more about the anointing which has visibly transfixed him. 'Father's hands. First, they're cold. Then they're hot. Then they're burning!'

'Me too. Is this a blister?' Richard asks, reluctant to be left out.

'What sort of heat was it, Nigel?' I ask gently. 'Was it like the sun is now or more like putting your fingers on an oven?'

'It was burning.'

'Yes, you said. But was it on the top of your skin or somewhere inside?'

'Just hot.'

'I know it's hard, but try to remember. Was it just where he touched you on your forehead and hands, or did it seem to cover you all over?'

'This is boring!' Richard says, digging his heel in a patch of primroses.

'It was hot. Just hot. He said it was cold but it was hot.'

The artlessness that made him unable to fake the incident makes him equally unable to analyse it. Anxious not to browbeat him, I shall never know whether he had a transcendental experience or merely an extreme reaction to the oil.

'Let's see if we can find a four-leaf clover,' Richard says.

'Yes!' Nigel shouts, straining against his protective strap as he watches Richard rip up clumps of grass.

With your luck you're bound to find one, I think meanly. 'Try not to overexcite yourself,' I tell Richard, before moving away to admire the landscape, a glorious vista which, whatever Father Dave might say, offers considerable compensations for the solitary life. The real test would be to withdraw from the world at the top of a tower block, finding God above all the squalor and din. I am shocked to hear myself sounding like Vincent but, when I look round, he is nowhere to be seen.

Instead, Maggie walks towards me with a tray of paper cups. 'Having a prayerful moment?'

'Kind of.'

'Don't let me stop you. I came to see if you wanted a drink. Wine or blackcurrant? Wine's on the left. They look the same but that's my little trick to make sure no one feels left out.'

'How thoughtful!' I say, stifling my surprise. I take a cup of wine and raise it to my lips as if toasting the view.

'Pretty as a picture,' she says, following my gaze. 'We've a café with a mural just like it on the front in Deal.'

She continues on her round and I turn back to the mountains. In the meadow a brancardier starts to strum his guitar and I am filled with a deep sense of peace. I sit on the sun-soaked wall above the steep hillside and close my eyes. When I open them again, I find myself staring at Tess.

'I'm sorry. I didn't mean to give you a shock.'

'You didn't.'

'I'm in need of some intelligent conversation.'

'I don't know about that but … sit down.'

'I've just been targeted by Brenda.'

'Don't tell me she's still trying to flog those bracelets?'

'She never stops. Apparently, they absorb all the negative energies and attract the positive ones. She ran down a list of conditions they're supposed to work for. If she'd said *cancer*, I swear I'd have hit her.'

'She means well.'

'She claims it's the one thing that's kept her MS from getting worse.'

'How much worse could it get?' She says nothing. 'I'm sorry.' She sinks down with a heavy sigh and flings back her head. 'How's Lester?'

'Don't ask! Sorry about all the hoo-ha in church. The heat and the incense and the hocus-pocus were a bit too much for him. He fainted. Nothing more dramatic. He's the world's least mystical person. With the exception of me.'

'So you didn't come to Lourdes hoping for a miracle?'

'The miracle was that we got here at all. It was touch and go right to the last minute. He was only allowed out of hospital on Friday. Don't mention that to anyone, please.'

'No, of course not.'

'My brother-in-law's brother-in-law – if you follow me – is on the Jubilate committee. Derek: the bald guy who hands round the hymn books at services.'

'Yes, he helped us when we arrived. I haven't spoken to him much.'

'He doesn't say much. He suggested we come for a break. Of course he sees it as rather more, but he knows what bad Catholics we are so he didn't push it. And he promised us loads of support.

So we thought: why not? It'll be our last chance to go away together. And it's easier to get childcare for a pilgrimage. My sister, his mum – everyone's willing to muck in. They wouldn't be quite so amenable to a week in Florida.'

'So where's Lester now? Taking a nap?'

'Not at all. He's being interviewed by your friend.'

'My friend?' I ask, knowing exactly whom she means but eager to hear the words out loud. The horror that they would have provoked yesterday has turned to pleasant surprise.

'The director.'

'He's not my friend especially,' I say, trying to draw her out.

'He was singing your praises as we walked up the hill.'

'We had a quick drink after last night's service. I challenged his views on the Church.'

'See, I was right! Intelligent conversation.'

No sooner has she said it than conversation runs dry, and we sit back in sunlight and silence.

'When I was a girl, they were healing rays,' Tess says after a pause. 'Now they give you cancer.'

'Is that what happened to Lester?' I ask, surprised.

'If only! His is in his bones. He's riddled with it. When he was first diagnosed he went to a visualisation group. You know: think of your diseased cells as monsters from outer space or Al Qaeda or something and zap them to smithereens.'

'I thought you said he wasn't mystical.'

'He's not, but our daughter is … was. She was going through her yoga and mung beans phase. He went for her sake, though he swears he gave it his best shot. He had to visualise himself in a field – something a lot like this, full of buttercups and daisies. But each time he tried, a bloody great cow would sneak up and shit beside him.' She starts to cry. 'Why did I tell you that? There must be a point. Oh yes, I've started visualising too. Though in my case it's not deliberate. I picture Lester's body as a rotten tree stump. His lovely body – '

'He's a fine figure of a man,' I say, wincing at the echo.

'A rotten tree stump crawling with maggots. And every time I hold him, I feel them wriggling on to me. What a bitch!'

I take her in my arms and rub her back, angry with myself for noticing the dampness. 'You shouldn't blame yourself. It's not Lester who repels you, it's the cancer. That strikes me as perfectly normal.'

'But we were more than normal! We're Lester and Tess. Our marriage was strong … whatever that means. I know what it means. It means us. I've never wanted another man. Not once in twenty-seven years.'

'There you are,' I say, holding back an avalanche of guilt.

'But I do now,' she says in a whisper. 'I want someone now. And not for comfort: not to cling to through the long sleepless nights when Lester is in hospital. But for sex: wild, passionate sex. I want to learn new techniques, new positions. I'm fifty-two.' She stands abruptly and starts to walk away.

'Where are you going?'

'I've no right to dump this on you. I can tell you're disgusted.'

'No, you can't. No, I'm not. Sit down, please!' I know that I should admit my own carnal feelings, that true friendship would be to show solidarity rather than merely mouth concern, but I'm too big a coward. 'You need some wine,' I say, spotting Mona handing round drinks. 'Promise not to move.'

'If you insist.'

I hurry over to Fleur and grab two paper cups. 'Here,' I say, returning to Tess. 'This should do the trick.' She accepts the cup gratefully, taking a large gulp.

'Either I'm in a worse way than I thought or this is Ribena.'

'What?' A quick sip confirms her finding. 'I'm sorry – I was warned. I'll change it.'

'No really, it's fine! Best to keep a clear head.' She smiles sadly. 'Twenty-seven years. Three great kids. The youngest takes his A levels next month. He should get straight As. He's a bright boy as well as a hard worker. But he can't ignore what's happening to his dad. I think that's what worries Lester most of all. He says he'll never forgive himself if he's responsible for Jake screwing up. Still, we can always look on the bright side. He won't be around to find out.'

'What do you mean?'

'Three months at the outside. Probably less.' I try not to betray my shock. 'He has a crack team looking after him: oncologists; pathologists; palliative nurses and, of course, his carer. Tell me, what sort of world is it that has to give caring a label? It should come as naturally as talking or eating.' I nod, trying to blot out the pilgrims who are mute or being fed. 'I'm not his carer – I'm his wife!'

'We all have to play different roles, ones we never expected.'

'Oh shit! Here's me droning on, without a thought for you.'

'Richard's as strong as an ox. He'll outlive us all.'

'So you'll still be a wet nurse at ninety?'

'I try not to look too far ahead. Besides, it's become such a part of me. Like a ring that won't come off in the heat.' I hold up my swollen finger. 'I know what you're thinking, so I'll say it for you: Life's so bloody unfair.'

'No, that's not what I think – though I'll grant you the *bloody*. I can live with *unfair*; I can even watch Lester die with it. What I can't live with is the illogic – the total lack of rhyme or reason, unless you believe in some celestial reason way beyond our limited understanding. And, as I said before, I'm too bad a Catholic for that.'

My own bundle of illogic bounds up to me.

'Gilly!'

'Yes, Richard,' I say, forcing a smile.

'Look!' To my amazement, he holds a four-leaf clover in his palm.

'You're so lucky! Show me!'

'Don't touch!'

'I'm not going to steal it.' On closer inspection I see that he has stuck an extra leaf to the stem with a film of sweat but, either because of Tess' story or simply her presence, I say nothing, allowing him to savour the deception. 'Good lunch?'

'We have to put all our rubbish in the bag. Where's yours?'

'I wasn't hungry. The heat,' I say, wishing the truth were that simple.

'You shouldn't be talking. People are going to sing. Come on!' He grabs my hand and pulls me off the wall.

'How about you?' I ask Tess.

'I'm the original Miss Corncrake. Besides I'd better check up on Lester. Thanks for listening.'

'My pleasure. I mean …'

'I know.'

Richard drags me into the heart of the meadow where he has laid his blazer on a rug. 'I bagged us two places,' he says with pride. I sit next to Linda, who squats stiffly beside Brenda's chair.

'Are you a singer?' I ask her.

'No, but Her Majesty here is. She won the Day Centre karaoke last Christmas with "Candle in the Wind".'

'I've won more than that, you daft bitch!' Brenda glowers at her. 'When I was eighteen, I was a redcoat at Clacton.'

'She's got the hump now.'

'Always showing me up.'

I link arms with Richard, who looks surprised, while three young handmaidens – Eileen, Lorna and Moira/Maureen – sing 'Bridge Over Troubled Water' to the brancardier's accompaniment. Their blushes at our applause deepen when Brenda shouts at Eileen: 'Pull your skirt down, girl! He's staring straight up it.'

Eileen jumps up as if stung. I turn to Richard, who is at once shame-faced and defiant. 'It's not me. It's him. See!' He points to the nearest man, who not only happens to be Father Humphrey but is fast asleep.

'Don't worry,' I say, anxious to defuse the tension. 'My eyes drift all over the place when I listen to music.'

'Not straight up a young girl's knickers, I should hope,' Brenda says sternly. 'Men! No control! Still you can't hardly blame them when girls wear their skirts up to their armpits.'

'I told you she'd got the hump,' Linda says.

Eileen's two friends stand up, even though one wears shorts and the other jeans. 'Richard didn't mean any harm,' I assure them. Which is more than I can say for Brenda who is thoroughly enjoying the consternation she has caused.

'Of course not,' Lorna says. 'It's my legs. Pins and needles. Besides, we should hand round some more water.'

'And I'll see if there's any rubbish,' Eileen says.

The three girls hurry off, leaving Brenda to reflect on their conduct. 'If I were Father Humphrey, I'd write to their parents. All "butter wouldn't melt", but I know what they're like underneath.'

'Rancid,' Linda says, with a complicit cackle.

'Come on, Richard,' I say. 'Let's find your mother.'

'I didn't do anything,' he says, as though threatened with the ulti-mate authority.

'I know. But we don't want her to feel neglected.'

We walk over to Patricia, who is standing with Maggie, Mona and Fleur in a huddle of matronly handmaidens. 'Ah there you are, my dears. I was just telling our friends here how Pattersons employed the first coloured welder in Dorking. It's no good giving me that look, Gillian. My daughter-in-law is so cp! In those days they were coloured. It was rude to call them black.'

'Times change,' I say.

'My husband – I wouldn't call him forward-looking but he was ahead of his time. He also hired a midget as a secretary. You remember, darling?' Richard looks blank. 'What was her name?'

'Nicola,' I say quietly, although Richard, as I later found out, knew her as Thumbelina.

'Nicola,' he repeats, as if grappling with the intimations of the name.

'She did the work of a woman twice her size.'

Patricia's remark reduces us to silence. I steal a glance at my watch, wondering how we are going to occupy the afternoon. As if in answer, Vincent strolls up.

'Afternoon ladies. Rich.'

'It's always ladies first,' Richard says grumpily.

'Force of numbers, mate. Good lunch?'

'It was cold.'

'Have you come to do some filming?' I ask quickly.

'We've enough shots of the Jubilates at play. If we're not careful, the viewers'll think it's one big jolly.' He turns to Richard. 'Speaking of which, I wonder if I can steal your wife.' His recklessness makes me gasp.

'They'll put you in prison.'

'They would if they knew what I was really thinking,' he says, smiling at Patricia, whose frown suggests that she has a fair idea. 'I want to interview a few of the villagers,' he adds. 'And your French is so good.'

'Gillian has a gift for languages,' Patricia says. 'She's always listening to the tapes. Even for countries where she's never been.'

'Let's go then if we're going,' I say, alarmed at where the conversation might lead.

'Don't be late back for the coach.'

'We won't,' Vincent assures them, moving to my side. I stride off, conscious of a tingling on my back, which I trust is the sun and not the weight of collective curiosity.

'Are you always this subtle?' I ask, on reaching the gate.

'You mean you've not seen any of my films?'

'Probably. I can't remember. Since Richard's illness we've watched wall-to-wall TV. That wasn't the right answer, was it?'

'Not really. Still you can make up for it when we get home. I've the entire O'Shaughnessy oeuvre on disc.'

'I'd like that.'

'Would you prefer it floppy or hard?' He pauses. 'I can't believe I said that.'

'Me neither.'

'Still, now I have, you may as well reply.'

'Good interview with Lester?' I ask, afraid that he will take my reserve for a ploy and even more afraid that he might be right.

'We got some usable material.'

'Material? Is that all we are to you?'

'It's my job. But it still touches me. Perhaps if I were to make a film about automated bank telling? But no, there'd still be people somewhere along the line.' He falls silent.

'Come on, you're missing your cue.'

'What?'

'Now you're supposed to say how I touch you.'

'Am I that cynical?'

'No, I'm sorry. I am. It's what comes of being a frustrated romantic.'

'We can do something about that.'

He drops all pretence of an interview as we amble aimlessly through the cloisters.

'What time are you supposed to meet them?'

'Who?'

'The villagers?'

'Come on! Even your mother-in-law didn't fall for that.'

'I take people at their word.'

'Since when? You've mistrusted me from the moment we met. But don't worry, I know it comes from all that frustrated romance.'

'Romanticism. Frustrated *romanticism*!'

'Either way we can sort it out. Hi ya!' Startled, I follow his gaze towards Kevin, who lies sprawled on a stone bench, holding up a book to shield his eyes from the sun. 'Enjoying yourself?' The instant he sees me, Kevin jumps up, pulling his shirt over his freckled stomach.

'Free time. That's what it says on the programme. What's freedom? The right to do what I like, when I like, how I like, without having to answer to anyone.'

'Whoa there!' Vincent says. 'We're on your side.'

'Oh sure!'

Such an absolute view of freedom seems suited only to a dictator or a hermit, and I start to see Saint Savin's withdrawal from the world in a whole new light. Reluctant to antagonise Kevin further, I ignore the connection and, instead, point to the dog-eared book that has slipped to the ground.

'Good read?'

'*A Season in Hell*. Rimbaud,' he says curtly.

'And?' I ask, refusing to be cowed.

'It's more than good. It's the only book I've ever read that tells the truth. He was seventeen when he wrote it. My age! Why can't I come up with something like that?'

'Perhaps you're not in hell?' I venture, to be met by a look of pure venom. He lies back and picks up the book, which he now uses to shield himself from us.

'See you then!' Vincent says. Receiving no reply, we move away and out of the cloisters. 'Poor kid! I hate to admit it but he reminds me a bit of myself at his age.'

'I can't believe you were ever that rude.'

'True. But then I wasn't that privileged.'

'And he hates women. He looks at me like I'm Delilah, Jezebel and Mary Magdalene – the impenitent Mary Magdalene – all rolled into one.'

'I hate to have to tell you, but he thinks you've got the hots for him.'

'That's not funny.'

'I don't know how high you score on teen-speak.'

'Abysmally low, I expect, but what does that have to do with anything?'

'You told him you were fit. To you and me and the Oxford English Dictionary, that means strong, healthy, physically able. But, to today's *yoof*, it means up for it, sexy.'

'But he can't. Oh my God, he did! We must go back and set him straight.' I turn and he grabs my wrist, dropping it as soon as he sees my expression.

'No, please don't. I almost did yesterday, but it'd only make him feel worse about himself – he'd be the smutty one.'

'What if he tells his friends?'

'I expect they'd agree: You're fit.'

I surprise myself by laughing. 'And to think I was worried about my rusty French!'

'Through here.' Vincent leads me out of the cloister and down the hill. I start to relax. Despite having no idea where we are heading, I am ready to put myself in his hands, at least for a couple of hours. I still have my doubts about him, but they are less to do with his character than his style. He has a trick of turning everything to his advantage which, however tongue-in-cheek, makes me feel manipulated. Besides, such a smooth operator is bound to have detected my weak spot. Everyone has one. Maybe credulity is mine?

'Watch out for the step!' He helps me over a splintery stile into an overgrown orchard, where I am hit by a powerful smell of honeysuckle and berries and lightly rotting vegetation. The lushness makes me queasy and I rummage in my handbag. 'Would you like a *Wet One*?'

'I beg your pardon!'

'A tissue!' I say, holding out the packet.

'I'd rather have a wet one.'

'Idiot!'

He wanders among the trees. 'What are these?' he asks, gesturing to the hard green fruit. 'Some sort of Pyrenean pear?'

'Quince, I think. Though they're a long way from being ripe.'

'And these?' he asks, lifting up a trailing bough.

'The berries look like juniper, but I'm no expert. If I'd known this was a nature walk, I'd have brought my *Observer's Guide*.'

157

'No, no guides. Not to plants, not to anything. Let's follow our noses, even if it means getting hopelessly, gloriously lost.'

'I've a sneaking suspicion you're not just talking about berries.'

'Am I that transparent? Good! Come on!' He leads the way through the orchard towards a shallow stream that marks the boundary with a neighbouring field. 'What are you waiting for?' he asks, as I draw back.

'A bridge?'

'Don't be such a wuss! What do you think those stones are for? Here, give me your hand.'

'You won't let go?'

'Don't you trust me?'

'I thought you'd already answered that.'

'Scout's honour.' He holds out his arm. Putting more weight on it than I would have wished, I step on to the first stone which, though slippery, is reassuringly stable.

'I feel like St Bernadette at the Grotto.'

'As long as you don't start seeing things!'

'No chance. I'm not that pure in heart.'

'I'm very glad to hear it.' He moves to the third stone and steers me on to the second. I stop to savour the heady combination of heat, light and gently lapping water when I am startled by a distant voice. 'Hello down there!' Vincent's firm grip saves me from taking a tumble, as I gaze up the hillside to meet Maggie's eager wave.

'Bloody woman,' he says under his breath, as he returns both her wave and greeting. 'Come on!' He leads me carefully over the two remaining stones to the safety of the bank.

'Thank you,' I say, before waving listlessly at Maggie. 'I didn't realise we were so conspicuous. What's she doing anyway?'

'Indulging her "filthy habit," I expect,' he says, in a wicked parody. 'Jamie and I are convinced it's a smokescreen.'

'Very witty!'

'While she indulges a far more intimate craving.'

'Thank you for that. It's a picture I'll always treasure.'

'We aim to please.'

'We're back on dry land. You don't have to keep hold of my hand.'

'I know I don't *have* to.' He makes no attempt to release it and I make none to break free.

'She's bound to tell Patricia she's seen us.'

'So? You're a grown-up. She has no hold on you.'

'No practical hold, it's true. But how about an emotional one? You'll think it odd, given the way I moan about her, but she knows me better than anyone. I suppose we share a sense of disillusion.'

'Don't tell me ... Men!'

'How did you guess?' He smiles, encouraging me to elaborate. After years of confiding in no one but Father Aidan, I feel the urge – no, the compulsion – to open my heart to a man I scarcely know. 'My father-in-law was a goat. No woman – well, at any rate no secretary – was safe. It was only twenty years ago (we're not talking the Middle Ages) but, far from objecting, most of the other girls were flattered. He wasn't bad-looking, it's true, but so slimy!'

'Did he try it on with you?'

'Of course. I was a woman; I was in his employ; I was fair game. He didn't get anywhere, I should add, and he backed off as soon as I started going out with Richard. But he never let up the innuendo. Endless insinuations: in front of Patricia, in front of Richard, in front of their friends.'

'And Richard did nothing?'

'Never. He'd stand up to everyone, except his father. I couldn't get to the bottom of it. I've known plenty of love-hate relationships, but never one that extreme. Half of him seemed to detest Thomas, while the other half wanted to be him.'

'Lots of sons have mixed feelings about their fathers.'

'And you?'

'Sure. Though mine were pitched somewhere between pity and scorn.' He seems taken aback by the rawness of the revelation.

'Even Richard's relentless womanising seemed to be modelled on his father's,' I add grimly. 'To prove that he was as much of a man. Though of course he failed when it came to delivering the goods – that is the children ... no, the goods! And Thomas now directed his digs at him: a long slow process of emasculation. Until one day I couldn't take any more and claimed – quite spuriously – that the problem lay with me. I was the one standing between him and his precious grandchildren. If he hadn't been such a pillar of the church, I'm certain he would have made Richard divorce me on the spot.'

'Isn't there some contradiction here?'

'Excuse me? There's a bloody great contradiction. But adultery was a matter between him and his priest. Divorce was a public scandal.'

'So Richard was the one with the problem?'

'No, not at all. At least not then. Now of course with all the drugs he's on, he has a zero sperm count. Which I suppose is one blessing.'

'But I'd have thought ... didn't you want kids?'

'No.' He looks surprised. 'I wanted *children*. Trust me, I'm not splitting hairs. Kids are for women with the luxury of choice. The irony, of course, is that we could have had them, but Richard insisted we waited. He'd worked out this master plan to build up his share of the business and sell up when he was thirty-five (which is why he could never be honest with his father). And it was the mid-nineties, so he was well on the way.'

'And then do what?'

'We were going to come south. Maybe here. The Pyrenees was on our list. Another irony! We wanted to watch our children grow up. He even talked of teaching them himself. That was Richard at his best. He'd have made a good father. It's important you understand that.'

'Me?'

'People. So now you know the story of my life. Shall we turn back?'

'Not the whole story. You're thirty-nine. Barely halfway.'

'Believe me, you might as well write *THE END* in capital letters. The rest is just repetition.'

We follow a furrow to the bottom of the field. The packed earth feels heavy underfoot. As we approach a clump of almond trees, a dog runs out and barks ferociously.

'Take care!' Vincent says.

'Don't worry. He's just marking his territory. Here boy!' He switches to a low-level growl and trots towards us. 'Aren't you the handsome one?'

'He may be rabid.'

'Nonsense. Look!' I crouch and stroke him with one hand, while holding out the other for him to lick. 'He wants to be friends.'

'Tough!'

'I thought you liked dogs.'

'Who's been spreading such libellous rumours?'

'Not even as a boy?'

'I never had one. According to my mother, they were riddled with germs. But then she said the same about library books. Why? Do I look like a dog person?'

'I just assumed. All the best people are.' I bury my blushes in the dog's muzzle.

'We did promise Pippa one for her sixth birthday, on the strict understanding it was a rescue dog. Celia wasn't going to support breeders when there were thousands of abandoned puppies looking for a home. I remember asking jokingly how she could justify having Pippa when there were all the kids waiting for adoption. It doesn't seem so funny now.'

'No.'

He sinks into a silence that it would be callous to break. Besides I am anxious to do nothing that might alert him to my confusion. How can I have been so crass? Must I project my own self-obsession on to everyone else? Why didn't I take Vincent's story last night at face value, rather than seeking to identify his 'friend'? As if refusing to associate with anyone so shallow, the dog emits a final snarl and darts off, leaving us to walk through the trees into the magnificence of the surrounding valley.

'So beautiful,' Vincent says, snapping out of his melancholy and gently pressing my hand. 'It takes my breath away.'

'Not just beautiful. Majestic. Mysterious. You can't tell me that anything this sublime is the product of chance.'

'Pure and utter serendipity. The glaciers melting. The formation of rivers and rocks.'

'What made the glaciers melt? Yes, I know. Global warming. And what made the earth heat up?' I cut him off before he can answer. 'There's always a scientific explanation. Like Chinese boxes. But when the very last scientist opens the very last box, what he'll find inside is God.'

'I admit it's easier to make out a case for God as we stand here than it is back in London or even Lourdes.'

'Because you're filled with the wonder of creation. There's none of the man-made mess in the way.'

'Actually, I'm rather fond of the man-made mess.'

'Then?'

'Because I'm filled with the wonder of you.'

'You really shouldn't say that.'

'Didn't the nuns who stuffed you with all that religion teach you to tell the truth?'

'Your truth?'

'What other truth do I have?'

'This.' I gesture to the landscape around us.

He does not reply, but stares into the distance. I follow his gaze but my eyes have started to blur. I wonder why we are both so determined to set out our spiritual stalls. Are we trying to prove to each other that we have nothing in common and should walk away before it is too late? Or are we making our positions clear, so that neither can cry foul in the future?

'Suppose I were to grant your hypothesis. Do you believe that any God who could create all this – the vastness, the splendour and so forth – do you truly believe that such a God would care whether two people – two deeply frustrated romantics (I think we've established that) – choose to share a few moments of intimacy?'

'The Church says that God doesn't make that kind of distinction. What's great or small to us is one and the same to Him.'

'I'm not interested in what the Church says but what you say. Take this.' He leans over and plants his lips on mine, drawing back before I have time to register my surprise. 'Has anything changed? Are God and His majesty and mystery in any way diminished?'

I know that he expects me to reply, but I can think of nothing but the sweetness of his breath: the rightness of the kiss. 'Part of me wants to sleep with you so much,' I say, afraid that my words fail to make any sense, let alone convey my full meaning. 'And not because I'm frustrated – not just because. But it's not that simple. There's Richard.'

'There always will be. That's an epitaph, not a life.'

'I told you about his women.'

'That's all in the past.'

'Not entirely. Please hear me out – this is very hard for me. When I first found out, I was distraught. All that talk about how different he was to his father and it turned out he was exactly the same! I threatened to leave. He begged me to give him another chance. He even called on Patricia to persuade me.'

'From what you've said, I'd have thought she'd have been glad to see the back of you.'

'Better the daughter-in-law you know? She was surprisingly supportive. Well, she'd been through the same thing herself. I can't swear she said "all men are beasts", but it's what she implied. What she did tell me – and this I remember perfectly – was to stick it out; things get better after twenty years.'

'And you believed her?'

'On the contrary, it's what convinced me to leave. There's a lot I admire about Patricia – no, truly! For a start, she never let Thomas drag her down. When he looked elsewhere, so did she.' Vincent grins. 'Don't get too excited. I'm not talking men here but church work and charities. There was no question of her kicking him out, so she made the best of what she had. She never became bitter or sorry for herself. She's always kept herself busy. Of course it's a strategy! But it's one that she's put to good use.'

'But it wasn't one for you.'

'Not at all. The way I saw it I was still young. I was a qualified secretary. And I had this gift for languages. I thought I'd try for a job with the EU or even the UN. But it was a big step and – you won't be surprised to learn – I kept putting it off. Then I discovered a note to Richard from Nicola, one of the secretaries, and ... let's just say there was a physical disparity that turned my stomach. I could no longer look at him the same way. At last I was spurred into action. Then the day before I was planning to go – do you really believe things happen by chance? – I had a phone call from the woman's mother. She – the daughter, that is – had been with Richard when he'd had the haemorrhage. She'd gone with him to the hospital.'

'Your mother-in-law told me he was playing golf.'

'For once she's not being cagey. I felt she had enough to deal with as it was. I did tell Thomas, but he died not long afterwards. Patricia and Lucy – that's Richard's sister – think it was seeing Richard so impaired that killed him.'

'And you?'

'I'd say he had a lucky escape. Richard was in a coma for six weeks. Six weeks when we knew nothing and feared the worst. Then he came round and I realised that the worst had just begun. What's more I realised I'd have to be part of it. What kind of a woman would abandon her brain-damaged husband?'

'A brave one?'

'Maybe in the world of the BBC. I even wondered if God was punishing my decision to leave by forcing me to stay.'

'You're not serious?'

'Though maybe He was making it easier for me: knowing that, when the crunch came, I'd never have had the guts to go.'

'There's still time to find out.'

'Is there? There's something else I should tell you.'

'You mean there's more? Don't worry, there's nothing that'll make me walk away,' he says, so tenderly that I can hardly bear to continue.

'Richard lost so much of who he was but he didn't lose his libido. If anything it grew stronger when he lost all inhibitions. Once he was back on his feet, a couple of his friends started taking him out for the odd evening. At first I thought they were being kind. Then I realised they were having a laugh at his expense. Or maybe it was a bit of both. All I know is they were taking him to visit girls in the local brothels –'

'In Dorking?'

'You'd be surprised. It took me a while to realise what was happening. He was always so much more overbearing when he came home, but I put it down to the drink. Then I started to get symptoms: itching, lumps, blisters. Must I go into details?' I long for the anonymity of the confessional. 'He gave me herpes. Most of the time it's dormant. I can go for months – years even – without symptoms. Then all of a sudden … boom! And who's to say what triggers it? Stress? Well I've had my fair share of that this past week: bringing Richard here; meeting you.'

'Meeting me?'

'It may even be the sun,' I say, refusing to be deflected. 'It's not just the prospect of Richard on the beach that keeps me away from the Caribbean.'

'I'm so sorry,' he says. 'You've had a rotten deal. But if, as you say, you have no symptoms …'

'That's just it. I think I may be having an attack now. It's hard to tell. There's a rawness, a tingling – oh, you don't want to know! You're right – it's tough but I have to live with it. Though it doesn't do much for my self-esteem, or the thought of a new relationship. Which is why, whatever my feelings for you, I can't just jump into bed, let alone join you for a quickie behind that rock. There's a lot more to sort out first.'

I wait for him to reply, but he says nothing. Then he turns and kisses me full on the lips for several seconds, although it is not a kiss that bears any relation to time. It is only when he moves away that I realise that its message is goodbye.

'Thank you for being so candid with me. I'm humbled – I know how difficult it must have been. And there's a lot I'd like to say in return, but it'll have to wait until later. It's gone four now. We'd better hurry back if we don't want to miss the coach.'

'Of course,' I say, equally eager to escape.

As we make our way down the path, he seems shrouded in thought. Both my mind and my body are numb, but gradually a few sensations return: first confusion, then pain, then anger. At the very least I had expected a greater acknowledgement of what my admission had cost me. Even the emptiest praise would have been preferable to this silence. On the other hand, I have lost nothing but the chance of heartbreak. The knowledge that our relationship was built on sand is strangely cheering. At a stroke, all the conflicts and doubts that have plagued me since meeting him are resolved. There are two – no, two and a half – days left of the pilgrimage. I shall return to Lourdes and pray for a miracle.

We reach the stream but, when he holds out his hand, I shake my head and walk across alone.

VINCENT

Wednesday June 18

We drive through Lourdes nose to tail with a coach full of African children whose faces, squashed against the back window, are too like those on charity appeals to elicit a light-hearted response. Since the narrow streets predate Bernadette, I resist the urge to see them as indicative of the religious mindset. Nevertheless, as we inch past a lorry unloading liquid gas, I question the providence that consigned such momentous apparitions to such an ancient town. 'Breathe in,' Father Humphrey shouts to a few sycophantic titters and widespread embarrassment about his girth.

A Spanish coach pulls out too fast at the crossroads, provoking a stream of very un-Lourdes-like invective from our driver, who adds to the danger by turning to the passengers to solicit support. Father Humphrey seeks to calm him with a fulsome tribute to his steering, before asking everyone to join in a round of applause, which is prolonged to the point of parody. 'And let's not forget the one who guided Christophe's hand,' he says. For a moment I suspect that he may be proposing a similar round to the Lord, but he contents himself by leading us in His Prayer.

Scarcely drawing breath, he embarks on a full-blown comedy routine. I reflect on the direct line that stretches from the bread and circuses of Roman politicians to the communion wafers and wisecracks of Catholic priests. As I sit through his extensive repertoire of nun jokes, I feel an unexpected sympathy for Sister Anne and Sister Martha. What is it that makes priests as obsessed with nuns as their smuttiest altar boys? Still, I suppose it keeps them from being obsessed with those same smutty altar boys.

Beside me Sophie is texting her boyfriend, her sporadic chuckles a welcome counterpoint to the fawning laughter echoing through the coach.

'Giles?' I ask, when she finally signs off.

'He's in Abu Dhabi. Some legal stuff for the airport.'

'What time is it over there?'

'Not a clue. But it's Sophie time, twenty-four seven.'

'I look forward to meeting this paragon.'

'He's not your type.'

'I'm relieved to hear it.'

'I mean you won't like him.'

'How come you're so sure?'

'The job. The friends. The club. The car. The gym. The parents. The cottage. The politics.'

'But none of that has stopped you?' I ask, wincing at the exhaustive list.

'Of course not,' she says, as affronted as if I had questioned her affection for her old nanny.

Despite dabbling in Bohemia, when it comes to love and marriage she retreats to Wiltshire. Giles has replaced Gregory, whose brash announcement that he went to school at Windsor Comprehensive let even an oik like me in on the joke. Maybe such tribalism makes sense? Throughout my childhood my great-aunt's marriage to a Methodist was presented as the ultimate betrayal. 'A *primitive* Methodist!' my mother pronounced, as though it were a reflection on his character. With similar relish, she seized on their granddaughter's recent civil partnership as the inevitable result.

'She's "married" a nurse!'

'What's his name?' I asked disingenuously.

'Susan,' she replied, with a shudder.

Just as some delight in putting up social barriers, others delight in tearing them down. I can think of one very bright, very beautiful and very big-hearted woman whose love for the cocky young BBC director with a spleen as large as his ego was, to his amazement, prompted by him alone and not an attempt to punish her patrician parents: a woman for whom the only meaningful distinction was talent. She should have stayed closer to home, marrying some decent, dim man who gave her security if not excitement, propriety if not challenge, fidelity if not passion. Instead, she fell for a cheap womaniser, whose mixture of cowardice, vanity, restlessness and opportunism, not to mention, lust, destroyed both their lives.

Would I behave any differently if I fell in love again?

Do I think so badly of myself that I need to ask?

I would be as true to any future love as Sister Anne and Sister Martha are to God.

So what perversity makes me pursue a married woman?

———

She is sitting some five or six rows behind me, yet I am as alive to her presence as if she had swapped places with Sophie. Just to know that she is so close makes my heart leap. Controlling my desire to turn, I keep my gaze fixed on the window. Having scared her off yesterday, I had to prove that I was no threat and so confined myself to a nondescript nod as she boarded the coach. This strange blend of anticipation and self-denial brings its own rewards, like a child hoarding his sweets to savour at bedtime or, more to the point, a monk mortifying his flesh in the hope of eternal bliss. My grin baffles Sophie. 'Come on!' she says, '*Sucker* and *succour*: it's not that funny!' It takes me a moment to realise that she is alluding to Father Humphrey's joke.

The excitement intensifies. I gibber like a baby and fizz like vintage champagne. I long to transform the coach into the set of a Hollywood musical, dancing down the aisle, partnering each of the women in turn – Marjorie, Tess, Lucja, Patricia, even Maggie – as I head for Gillian, whom I sweep off her feet and across the floor, which expands to the size of a ballroom. On and on we waltz until the final frame freezes and the credits roll over us, locked forever in an image of perfect harmony.

Who cares if I never make the film or, indeed, any film, while Douglas Simcox, fresh from his triumph with the Mugsborough housepainters, is whisked away to a glittering career in L.A.? Real life has never seemed so beguiling. Not even the dull drone of the rosary can shake my mood. Father Humphrey has relinquished the microphone to Father Dave, who injects a serious note into the proceedings, his appeal to the Virgin coinciding, consciously or not, with our reaching a more precipitous stretch of road. He invites a moment of audience participation, or as he calls it, hymn-singing, leaving me free to examine the prospect from the window and, more pressingly, my prospects with Gillian.

We have, as Father Dave reminds us, arrived at the halfway point of the pilgrimage; I intend to make it a turning point for Gillian and me. With the free time scheduled for this afternoon, Saint Savin should be the perfect place to test our feelings which, transplanted from the hothouse of Lourdes, will have room to breathe. In the mountains we will be surrounded by nature, not hemmed in by history. We will be Adam and Eve without the accretions of myth.

Mundanity sets in when, with a nod to his former profession, Father Dave praises the surrounding countryside. 'They're developing the region for winter sports. A poor man's Biarritz. It's been a godsend for Lourdes. Half the hotel staff come up here out of season.'

'If you can't fleece them in the Grotto, fleece them on the slopes,' I whisper to Sophie.

'Do you ski, Vincent?' she asks.

'Is that a serious question?'

'No, of course not. I'm trying to be the irritating Sloane in your flesh!'

'The answer is *no*, I'm afraid. I was a wooden-crate-down-slag-heap kind of boy.'

'I was a Verbier-every-February kind of girl. So what? It's never too late to start. There's nothing to beat it. The fresh air. The purity. That feeling of being on top of the world.'

'And then it's downhill all the way.'

We come to a stark iron bridge spanning a picturesque ravine. 'Hands up anyone who can tell me who built it?' Father Dave asks. 'No, not you, Maggie! We know you know. Yes, Frank?' He walks down the coach to catch the muffled reply. 'The builders,' he repeats for our benefit. 'The builders!' He laughs. 'Yes, that's certainly true. But who was behind it? Go on then, Maggie.'

'Napoleon.'

'That's right. Legend has it that he was camped with his army on one side of the river and he fell in love with a young lady on the other. So, to facilitate their – how shall I put it? – *amour*, he had his engineers build the bridge. The path of true love and so on.'

'How about the path of true adultery?' I say to Sophie. 'Isn't that forbidden by his Church, or are emperors given papal dispensation?'

'I'm off duty.'

Twenty minutes later we arrive at Saint Savin, stepping off the coach into streets that are almost deserted. The rows of shuttered windows seem designed to deter the casual glance as much as the impromptu visit. I feel a chill down my spine in spite of the blistering heat.

'I wasn't expecting a red carpet, but this is seriously spooky,' Jewel says as she joins me.

'They're probably all in church. Two childhood sweethearts tying the knot.'

She looks at me open-mouthed. 'Would you mind repeating that?'

'Why?'

'The christening of the village idiot's baby perhaps, or the funeral of a downtrodden peasant. Since when did childhood sweethearts enter your calculations?'

'Am I that predictable?' I must be on my guard. Rose-tinted spectacles are doubly unseemly at my age.

We watch while the lengthy decanting process begins on the second coach. Jamie leaves Father Humphrey and walks towards us, as the hydraulic lift is released and the first wheelchair laboriously lowered. 'Next time, how about behind the scenes at Formula One motor-racing, chief?' Jamie asks.

'Sure! Fine! Why not a six-part series?' I reply, irked to hear my own impatience echoed in his.

'So what's with the padre?' Jewel interjects.

'He's all right is Father Humph. He drinks; he swears; he gambles. Him and me and some of the brancs are having a poker club tonight.'

'Deal me in,' Jewel says.

'No way. Women *verboten*!'

'That's sexist!'

'What else do you expect of the Church?' I ask, in a bid to restore my reputation.

'It's cool he's cool,' Jamie says. 'He says the Church doesn't mind a game as long as the stakes are low.'

'Some of these kids have no money at all. They've had to scrimp and save to get here.'

'We're playing for peanuts.'

'What's peanuts for you may be a tidy sum to them.'

'No, peanuts. You know: salted, dry roasted.'

Eager to escape, I head into the shop for a bottle of water. Maggie, in an accent so thick that for once the French have no need to feign incomprehension, is explaining the purpose of our visit to the proprietor. Her '*service de huiles*', complete with extravagant gestures, so perplexes him that I suspect he may direct her to the nearest garage. 'He remembers us from last year,' she says, seizing on his wary smile.

'Or perhaps it's just my filthy habit,' she adds, pointing to a packet of Marlboro, which he hands her with marked relief.

'Who can forget that?' I ask, wondering why, given her obvious desire for penance, she doesn't just cut out the middleman and say a Hail Mary after every puff.

Clutching my bottle of Vittel, I join the crowd climbing the hill, pausing to greet Mary and Steve, who carries a chortling Fiona on his shoulders, before moving up to Lester and Tess. 'Morning,' I say to a respective grunt and echo, as Lester fights for breath and Tess struggles to support him. I want to help, but the fear of offending him paralyses me. I am back on the kerb with the blind man, praying that his innate road sense will relieve me of the need to intervene. A nagging suspicion weaves through my mind that my reluctance to touch him springs less from regard for his dignity than from a primitive horror of contact with his disease. Keen to dispel it, I edge closer to his side. 'Bloody steep,' I say. 'No wonder the coach-drivers won't risk it. Anyone like a hand?'

'Go ahead,' Lester says, wheezing. 'Heaven help me if I ever become dependent on her.'

'The feeling's mutual, mister,' Tess replies lightly. 'Tomorrow there's no argument. You're getting a chair.'

Taking Lester's free arm, I am shocked by its adolescent boniness. 'Still on for your grilling after the service?' I ask, to distract us both from the uneasy contact.

'You bet! Can't miss my moment of glory.'

'Are you happy with what you've got so far?' Tess asks me.

'By and large. Everyone's been so frank. Not just on film. Last night I went for a post-penitence drink with Gillian Patterson. Have you talked to her at all?' I ask casually.

'Not as much as I'd like,' she replies. 'She's an inspiration. I can't imagine what it's like to have your husband …' She stops; Lester coughs; and I describe my chat with Gillian, ostensibly to fill the gap, but also from an aching need to speak her name out loud. Given the urgency of their own concerns, they are less likely to question my exhilaration than Jewel. As I babble on, we pass two young wheel-chair-pushers who are making even slower progress than we are. A quick glance at their passenger explains why; it is Sheila Clunes.

A second glance revises the explanation; Matt, who was previously paired with Kevin, has linked up with one of the handmaidens – literally, given their interlocked fingers on the back of the chair. I smile, at which she instantly breaks away. Why? Do I emanate disapproval? Or does middle age preclude me from any understanding of love?

Determined to prove otherwise, I make my way towards Gillian, who stands among the crowd in the porch. Discretion prompts me to address my remarks to Marjorie, and I engage her in the gentle ribbing of which the pilgrimage ladies are so fond. I overplay my hand and she flees to the safety of Louisa, leaving me with Gillian, which would be the perfect outcome had I not lost the power of coherent speech. Her radiance reduces me to banalities. The charm of her dress persuades me never again to disregard fashion. Celia cared little for clothes, foraging in charity shops with all the relish of one who grew up with a Harrods charge account. She had a grace and a glow and a youth that made even a cheesecloth skirt look stylish. Gillian is different. A troubled life – or simply a longer one – requires more adornment … I must stop this! It is absurd – not to say, distasteful – to compare a wife of ten years with a woman I have known for two days.

Nevertheless, the mere fact of my doing so convinces me that my feelings for Gillian are real. My mind is a mass of contradictions that somehow make perfect sense. I am at once light-headed and weighed down, as though I were split in two, and yet for the first time in years I feel whole. I worry that all this is happening too fast. It was months before Celia and I were able to speak of love to one another: in my case, because I had been taught to mistrust my emotions; in hers, because she had been taught to mistrust men. But here I am speaking of it – if not to Gillian, then at least to myself – after just two days. Have I become more perceptive or less discriminating? Am I responding to Gillian herself or to my own loneliness? Does this impetuosity come from being in France, home of the *coup de foudre*, or from being in Lourdes, home of lost causes?

Her expectant gaze only accentuates my confusion. There is something different about her this morning. It is not her hair which, a few tantalising wisps apart, remains coiled in its chignon. It is not

her skin, although two days in the sun have lent its natural creami-
ness a hint of bronze. It is not her eyes, which have the same quick-
silver quality as when we sat in the hotel bar last night. It is her
mouth. She has chosen a lighter lipstick. If only I knew more about
make-up! Celia despised that too ... No, stop there! What does it
mean when a woman who has always worn plum switches to pink?
Is she signalling that she is ready for romance? Or has she simply
run out of her usual shade?

There is so much I want to say to her but, instead, I come out with
an archaic, almost flippant compliment (since when has *luscious* fea-
tured in my vocabulary?). I follow it with an equally inane question
about her dreams. No wonder she looks lost. What do I expect her
to reply? 'Yes, and you played the lead in all of them, shinning down
a chimney – ' or some equally phallic symbol – 'to rescue me from a
dragon with Patricia's face and Richard's tail'? I am so on edge that I
challenge her most casual remark and she responds with an account
of her mother's dementia. The thought of her suffering torments me,
and I long to ensure that she never has to go through such an ordeal
again. That longing feels even more quixotic when I realise that she
goes through something similar every day and that her only way out
lies in Richard's death. However hard I try, I cannot bring myself
to wish for that. He may not be the man he was – he may scarcely
be a man at all – but he still *is*. And, if I have learnt anything from
Lourdes, it is how much of life remains on the margins.

I strive to change the subject and, catching sight of Father Dave,
ask about the church's patron saint. The news that he was a hermit is
not encouraging. For all my antipathy to Bernadette or, more accurately, the sentimental cult that has grown up around her, at least she
engaged with the world. Saint Savin withdrew from it, abandoning
family and friends (as soon as we return to Lourdes, I must ring my
mother) and any hope of leading a productive life. However abhor-
rent it may be to me, I am afraid that such conduct may find favour
with one who is prone to renunciation. I have to show her that if the
concept of sin means anything, then it is the rejection of all that is
good; all that is happy; all that is beautiful in the world. In a word, it
is the rejection of love.

I would go further and say that the true sin is to surrender one's free will to an oppressive and outmoded ideology, but prudence prevails and I put the case for worldly pleasure in terms that any catechism teacher would approve. So I am doubly nonplussed when Father Dave poses a question that is both simple and unanswerable: 'Who's to say Saint Savin didn't sit – or, more likely, kneel – in his hermitage and experience overwhelming joy: that he didn't see as much of the world in his small patch of ground as any twenty-first-century jet-setter?' His message hits home as if he were bellowing it from a pulpit – no, precisely because he is not bellowing it from a pulpit but rather intimating it in the porch. If I had stuck to my small patch of ground: if I had not sought satisfaction elsewhere, I would not have destroyed my marriage. We would still be a family rather than two mourners and one grave.

I hereby swear by all I hold most sacred, by the memory of that family which, with the bitterest irony, gives me the chance to redeem myself, that, should I be offered another taste of love (no, it is too late for self-protection), should Gillian return my love, then I will make it my whole world. I will not be diverted by a passing fancy; I will not look for meaning in a chance encounter; I will not seek fulfilment in a stranger's sheets.

Louisa and Marjorie return, accompanied by the sacristan brandishing keys, and we follow them inside. I am instantly hit by the scents of beeswax, incense and dust, along with a hint of stale flesh, that take me back to my childhood. For once I am happy to sit quietly in my allotted pew, stilling my racing mind among the cosy certainties.

'Look, chief,' Jamie says, pointing to the angular wooden crucifix hanging on a pillar. 'His eyes follow you all through the church.'

'Not just the church, Jamie, life!' I say jokily. 'Every good Catholic from here to Timbuktu knows that the eyes of the Lord are on him day and night.'

'Scary!'

The truly scary part is that, even sitting here as a rational adult, I feel the eyes boring into me. I wonder if I shall ever escape, focusing on the familiar irritations of the service to sustain my dissent.

Midway through proceedings, Father Paul moves to the pulpit. 'Many of us are parents; all of us have parents,' he begins, before expounding on the nature of family. I never cease to be amazed by the ease with which priests pontificate on an institution from which they are themselves safely removed, like staff officers in support trenches sending foot soldiers over the top. Although, at least in Father Paul's case, the officer has risen from the ranks.

After a concluding paean to the Holy Family, he steps down, whereupon Father Humphrey moves to the altar to bless the oils, and we prepare to film. Any hope of slipping unobtrusively out of the pew is thwarted by the tightness of Jamie's squeeze. I fix my attention on the ritual. I am intrigued by the notion of priests as shamans channelling a spiritual power which, to judge from the recipients' faces, touches them deeply. The big surprise is Lester, who tumbles to the ground the moment Father Paul signs the cross on his forehead. Tess cries out, and consternation ripples through the church. To my dismay, Jamie lowers the camera. 'Sod's law, chief,' he whispers. 'Tape jam! I'll nip out and change it. Be right back!'

I nod tersely, but the shot is lost. By the time Jamie returns, Lester has recovered and resumed his seat. The rest of the service proceeds without incident and, at the end, we walk out past a crudely carved font at which the initiated gaze with reverence.

'Do you think it's pre-Christian?' Sophie asks.

'No,' Ken interjects behind her. 'Sorry to butt in, but I couldn't help overhearing. It was made especially for the Cagots. They were a group of medieval pariahs – the lowest of the low – not just in France, but across Europe.'

'Why?' Sophie asks. 'What had they done?'

'No one knows, at least not according to Father Dave,' he replies with a laugh. 'Some experts think it was because of their ancestry (which may have been Arab); others because they were lepers or cretins.' He looks uncomfortable. 'That's in the strict medical sense. Either way, they had to wear special clothes and keep themselves apart.'

'Even in Church?' I ask.

'I'm afraid so,' Ken says. 'They had their own door and were made to stand behind a rail. Sometimes they weren't allowed to take communion at all and, when they were, it was handed to them on a long stick. So whenever you think the Church is set in its ways, it's as well to remember that some things have changed.'

As we make our way outside, I catch sight of Gillian walking through the cloisters with Richard and Patricia. I long to join them but, in the first place, I can think of no suitable pretext and, in the second, I have to concentrate on the matter in hand. The film may be billed as a 'personal journey', but it is a journey into faith not love. So I turn back to the church and wait for Lester and Tess to emerge. He recoils from the heat, but straightens himself up the moment he sees us.

'Are you better?'

'He's fine,' Tess answers for him. 'Just a little giddy.'

'I was dehydrated,' Lester says. 'I feel a bit of a fraud. Everyone looking at me as if I've had some kind of mystical experience.'

'People should mind their own business,' Tess says.

'Brenda was quite resentful. She's been coming here for years and never felt a thing.'

'Cow,' Tess says.

'We can postpone the interview if you like,' I say.

'That sounds like a good idea,' Tess says.

'Nonsense. I'm looking forward to it,' Lester says. 'If you'll give me ten minutes to grab something to eat.'

'Of course. As long as you're sure.'

'Never more. I just need to build up my strength.'

We follow them through the ruins of the ancient abbey and into a large enclosed meadow, where their fellow pilgrims mill about, spreading rugs, sipping wine and opening hampers in festive mood. All thought of disease and disability has vanished. Even the shadow of death has been wiped out by the midday sun. It feels like a vision of paradise: not Eden, for which it is both too casual and too crowded, but the Greek Golden Age, at least as it appeared in the vast Victorian canvas of frolicking nymphs and shepherds that made such an impression on me as a boy.

Two latter-day nymphs hand us our packed lunches. My analogy breaks down as we contemplate the pork pie, apple, chocolate and crisps.

'Helps keep our minds on higher things,' I say.

'How?' Jamie asks, 'when all we can think of is our stomachs.'

Father Humphrey stands in the middle of the grass and struggles to make himself heard. 'Has everyone got their meal?' He is greeted by a chorus of assent. 'Good, because I'm not sure I've got the hang of the loaves and fishes routine yet. Shall we say grace?' The silence is broken by a gust of laughter from the edge of the field where Patricia, Maggie and some of the helpers are gossiping out of earshot. A concerted 'Shush' prompts them to bow their heads.

'Jesus Christ, King divine
You changed water into wine.
Please forgive us foolish men
When we change it back again.'

His levity seems to suit the alfresco setting, although Louisa's smile is visibly forced. 'Did you like that? You did? I'm not sure She Who Must Be Obeyed would agree.' Louisa's smile wavers. 'All right, let's have another go. Bless us, O Lord, and these Thy gifts which from Thy bounty we are about to receive – and which Frank Maloney already has received.' Frank looks up at the mention of his name, piecrust speckling his chin. 'Through Christ Our Lord. Amen.'

Frank's impatience generates affectionate laughter, which sets the tone for the meal. I blame my lack of appetite on the heat, a factor that has clearly not affected Jamie, who scoops up my entire lunch, along with Jewel's pork pie. In this light, his earlier remark about waste and starvation in Africa seems particularly glib. Refusing him time to digest, I lead the way to the cloisters, picking up Lester en route.

'Are you happy to stand?' I ask him. 'We can dig out a chair if you'd rather.'

'I'm good. Honestly. It's amazing the difference a pork pie can make.'

'How about here?' Jamie asks, indicating a spot beside a buttress. 'The stone makes an interesting background and the sun won't be in his eyes.'

'Fine by me.'

'And me,' Lester says, moving into position.

'Right!' I launch straight into the interview. 'Lester, you're with the Jubilate as a hospital pilgrim. Am I correct in thinking that, unlike most – if not all – of the group, you are not a believer?'

'Yes. That is no, I'm not. I don't know if it's from conviction or just circumstance. Until recently, when I was diagnosed with cancer – terminal cancer – I never thought much about God or death or anything otherworldly. Well you don't, do you, when you have a family to support (not just financially) and a business to run? You have your work cut out dealing with the state of the garage roof, never mind the state of your soul.'

'But things have changed?'

'Well obviously – though not that much. Perhaps I'm hedging my bets a little? Who was it said you might as well believe in God because, if you're wrong, you've lost nothing and, if you're right, you'll be on the winning side? I've not gone that far but I'd say I've grown a little less dogmatic in my disbelief.'

'Has coming on the pilgrimage helped that?'

'Not yet. I've been very moved by the way people cope with their disabilities. Who wouldn't be? But, if they're anything like me, they won't want to hear that. Some of my friends think I should be fighting harder, but it's no use. Every time I start to ask: "Why me?", I hear my own voice answer: "Why not me?" Don't get me wrong; if you could wave a magic wand – or, better still, something more scientific – and blast the cancer to kingdom come, I'd be first in the queue. But as far as I know, you can't. There's no law says I have to live three score years and ten, let alone four score years and senile. I'm just grateful for what I've had.'

'And what you have left?'

'There won't be much of it. Two months – three, if I'm lucky. It's hard to take in because I don't feel that bad. A bit breathless every now and then. Some cramps in my stomach but, if you didn't know better, you'd think they were indigestion. That's why I left it for so long. By the time this film is broadcast, I'll be dead. It's difficult to get my head round. This will be the last people see of me. So perhaps you'll give me a moment to say thank you to everyone: to all my friends; my mum and dad; my two sisters; the greatest kids any man could wish for; and most of all my wife, Tess, my Tess ...' He starts to sob. 'I'm sorry, I didn't know it would hit me like this. She'll kill me. Well she would if it wasn't too late.'

'Do you find humour a useful weapon?' The question rallies him and he rubs his eyes.

'Not intentionally, no, but I suppose I must. Here we are, in this gorgeous countryside: the sort that makes some people feel that there must be a God, but makes me feel that there's no need for one. How could anyone be morbid or depressed in the midst of all this?'

'Does that make it harder to leave it all behind?'

'Not in the least. I know I'll be leaving other people to enjoy it, although, with luck, they won't be riddled with cancer. That's why I'm happy to be here. I know that most of my fellow pilgrims are hoping for a miracle cure or, at any rate, some kind of spiritual revelation. I just want the chance to spend time with my wife before the disease really kicks in. And, if you'll allow me, I'd like to say a few words directly to her.'

'Of course.'

'I don't want her to grieve. If I've learnt anything from all this, it's that life is short. She mustn't waste hers on regrets. And I trust my boys not to make things hard for her. I expect them to support her in everything she does, including – especially – moving on.'

His words touch me deeply, and I am relieved to be able to wrap up the interview and let him return to Tess.

'What now, chief?' Jamie asks. 'Do you still want to go for the Polish guy?'

'Let's wait till we're back in Lourdes.' I turn to Sophie. 'Would you speak to him? We've earned a break. It'd be a crime – ' Even as a hyperbole, I baulk at *sin* – 'not to take the chance to explore the landscape.' Sophie gives me a wry smile as if she suspects my motives, but I refuse to respond. We walk back into the meadow, past Fiona who is holding up a toy windmill, willing its sails to turn without a breeze, and Frank who is blowing the seeds off a dandelion clock. He stares forlornly at the bare stem, rocking on the balls of his feet, until Louisa hurries over and calms him with a hug.

'Strange,' I say to Sophie. 'He's the last person I'd have thought she'd develop a rapport with.'

'Maybe that's why?'

We almost trip over Father Humphrey who lies prostrate on a rug, like a small hillock, his sleeves rolled up to reveal two beefy forearms, one of which is marked with the faint outline of an anchor. I am intrigued by this hint of a former life, but my speculations are curtailed when Geoff, egged on by Father Dave, waves a buttercup under his nose. He snorts in his sleep until Geoff, exceeding his brief, pokes the stalk into his nostril. He sits up with a jolt amid widespread laughter, which he takes in good part.

'The dead awakened and appeared to many,' Father Dave says, repeating it moments later for effect.

I slip away to join Gillian, who is standing in a group at the far end of the meadow. As I walk over, I see her sneak a glance at her watch which cheers me, although it may just be that she is checking the time for Richard's pills.

'I wonder if I can steal your wife,' I say to him.

'They'll put you in prison.'

'They would if they knew what I was really thinking.'

I am surprised by how readily she agrees, and wonder if it is due to enthusiasm for my company or fear of my indiscretion. She strides ahead, as if to convince any casual observer that we are leaving separately. Once through the archway she relaxes and asks about my interview with Lester, showing a gratifying familiarity with my schedule, before pretending to take my request for her translation skills at face value. We stop to talk to Kevin who has chosen to dramatise his alienation by sprawling on a bench in the middle of the cloisters, like a lone wolf baying outside the city gates. His wretchedness adds to my unease. I have no plan or goal other than to be with Gillian, and yet I have too many teenage memories of trudging through Barnsley, desperate for a deserted bus shelter, to be happy leaving things to chance. So, assuming an air of confidence, I propose that we head down to the fields at the bottom of the hill, praying that we won't be met by a locked gate, let alone an irate farmer with a gun.

Fate (I refuse to credit a higher power) smiles on us, as I guide Gillian over a rickety stile and into an ancient orchard. The atmosphere is deliciously mellow, with luminous butterflies fluttering over lush foliage and strange fruit. The beauty of the setting enhances hers, or she encompasses it, or perhaps it is just that for the first time in years I feel at one with nature. I am wondering how best to take her hand without its seeming either forced or threatening when, by a stroke of luck, we arrive at a stream and she needs my help to cross.

I have a wild impulse to lose my balance and land us both in the water in the hope that, crawling out, she will throw off her soaking clothes – among other constraints – and make passionate love to me on the bank. But, given my record with romantic schemes, we are more likely to hobble back to the coach on twisted ankles. Besides, how can I risk ruining such a delightful dress?

I have to be content with keeping hold of her hand and, either because she has come to trust me or else because she has a compelling need to unburden herself, she embarks on the story of her unhappy marriage. Halfway through – although she has already declared it to be *THE END* – we are confronted by a snarling dog. She bends down and beckons it to her, ignoring my warnings of deadly disease.

'He wants to be friends,' she says, letting it slobber all over her arm.

'Tough!'

'I thought you liked dogs.'

'Who's been spreading such libellous rumours?'

'Not even as a boy?'

'I never had one. According to my mother, they were riddled with germs. But then she said the same about library books. Why? Do I look like a dog person?'

'I just assumed. All the best people are.' She refuses to elaborate, burying her face in the dog's fur, and I realise that she has totally misinterpreted what I told her last night. Half of me wants to burst out laughing, while the other half is offended that she should think me so craven as to offload my humiliation on to an imaginary friend. But, given her account of her philandering husband and his lecherous father, it is no wonder that she sees all men as self-serving liars.

We walk further into the valley but, rather than surrendering to its charm, we dispute its creation. The familiar battle-lines are drawn. To Gillian, the magnificent landscape is conclusive evidence of God's design; to me, it is the fortuitous result of millions of years of rock formation. But, however much I reject her views, I am enchanted by their expression, a split that leaves me confused. All the earnest debates at college as to whether it would be a betrayal to sleep with a Tory pale beside the one now engaging me. Can a committed atheist (no bet-hedging agnostic here) truly love and respect a Christian, and a Catholic to boot? As I gaze at her face, the loveliness of her lips far surpasses the words flowing from them, and the answer comes back a resounding *yes*.

Seizing the moment, I kiss her: a kiss as far removed from last night's beery fumble as these mountains from a child's mud-pies. Steeped in my own sense of the sacred, I ask: 'Has anything changed? Are God and His majesty and mystery in any way diminished?', but, rather than replying, she returns to the subject of her marriage. I am caught in a tide of emotion: first, joy as she describes how she had been planning to leave Richard, which proves that, whatever else, she does not regard her vows as inviolable; then, horror as she recounts the full extent of his betrayal. Fearing the worst from the roster of itching, lumps and blisters, I am weak with relief on hearing that it is only herpes. I long to make light of it, explaining that the virus was rife during my early years at the BBC. But I am afraid of accentuating the gulf between our worlds.

Moreover, I feel that her honesty demands as much from me but, before I can speak up, I need a more intimate setting, less pressure of time and, not least, a measure of Dutch courage. So I kiss her as tenderly as possible, and promise that we will talk later.

'Thank you for being so candid with me. I'm humbled – I know how difficult it must have been. And there's a lot I'd like to say in return, but it'll have to wait until later. It's gone four now. We'd better hurry back if we don't want to miss the coach.'

The earth is hard underfoot, but I feel as though I am sinking into a quagmire. What right have I to sit in judgement on Richard? He is not the only husband to have cheated on his wife. He, at least, had his father's example to lead him astray, whereas I had a father who was faithful all his life to his youth-group sweetheart. So what's my excuse? When Celia left, I vowed that I would never again hurt another woman, even if it meant that I could never again be close to another woman. Now I find myself reaching out to Gillian, whose past gives her a dual claim on my fidelity. Why should she trust me when I cannot trust myself? Or must I rest my hopes on greying hair and a waning libido?

Gillian rebuffs my attempts at conversation, as if she can read my guilt and already regrets her disclosure. We head back into the village to find everyone preparing to leave. She thanks me for the walk as if I were a tour guide, and moves to Richard, who is watching his friend Nigel being wheeled on to the lift. Either from a reluctance to separate them or, more likely, a desire to escape from me, she steers Richard into the second coach. Desperate for distraction I join Kevin, who looks more isolated than ever now that Matt is chatting with the handmaidens.

'Did you finish your book?' I ask.

'She had us picking up litter,' he says, pointing to Louisa. 'Even apple cores. I told her they're biodegradable. I'm surprised she didn't take before-and-after pictures of the grass.'

'You may find it hard to believe, but I promise you things get better.'

'Even for them?' he asks, with a nod at the wheelchairs. Stumped for an answer, I step into the coach, sitting beside Sophie who is glued to her iPod. The trip back to Lourdes feels endless which, despite the dull road and the lack of a commentary, I attribute to Gillian's defection. Meanwhile, I run through some questions for Tadeusz. He refuses to be filmed in any kind of religious setting, which poses problems in a town where the only cinema is permanently devoted to the life of Bernadette, but Sophie is confident of finding somewhere suitable along the river. So, leaving our fellow pilgrims at the Acceuil, we take the path past the Saint Bernadette church and up to the Adoration Tent, where the landscape starts to become wooded. We stop beside an ancient beech tree with two low branches protruding at almost perfect right angles to the gnarled and twisted trunk.

Tadeusz stands uneasily as I ask the first question. 'Tadeusz, the rise in British Catholicism in recent years has been largely ascribed to Polish immigrants. Are you part of this trend?'

'I have no love for the Church. I have much love here.' He strikes his chest in a way that suggests the violence of his emotion rather than its depth. 'I have love for my wife; I have love for my childrens; I have love for my fellow peoples; but I have no love for the Church. I was married in church for the sake of my wife. It is big thing for her; it is small thing for me. I have my childrens christened in church for the sake of my wife. It is big thing for her; it is small thing for me. Then we have third baby, Pyotr. At first we are happy he is such a good baby since he does not cry. But he does not cry for too long. He does not move his eyes like this ... how you say?'

'Blink.'

'Yes, he does not blink. And I cannot say: God has done this for reason. Yes, it would be big thing for my wife; but it is big thing for me also. I cannot say that, if we fall down to our knees and if we follow what priests tell us, then God will heal Pyotr and all the other Pyotrs. No, all I can say is: Life is not perfect. We do not need rules – if they are Catholic rules or communist rules, it makes no difference – that punish us when we are not perfect. We need only to admit that this is who we are and it is for us and only for us to do the best things we can.'

'Then why have you come to Lourdes?'

'Because of love, like everyone else. But not like everyone else for love of God. It is for love of Lucja and for love of Pyotr. No, this is not always true.' His face clouds over. 'It is for love of Lucja and for love I try to find for Pyotr. And this is all I have to say.' He pulls off his microphone to emphasise his withdrawal. 'I am sorry. This is not what you want to hear.'

'It's exactly what I want. Thank you.'

'But it is not what I want to say. I must go.'

'Are you sure? We've no more filming until the Torchlight procession. Can I take you for a drink? Or will Lucja be waiting?'

'She is always waiting. She has made it her life.'

I arrange to meet the crew at the hotel and take Tadeusz to a small café on the edge of the Domain. It is packed with early diners and the conversational din is exacerbated by the synthesised plainsong blasting from the loudspeakers. I order two *demis* and try to draw him out.

'How long have you been living in England?'

'Seven years,' he says impassively.

'Are you happy?'

'This is not a question. I mean it is not a question I can reply. Some of my friends, they move abroad to make new life. Some of my friends, they stay at home to make new country. I cannot make this choice. Let me explain. There is house in Oldham, two streets away from us, where family were killed ... stabbed with knife. Woman, her mother, her father and her two childrens by husband. It is good house: much light with many rooms and big garden. But no one wants to live in this house and so it sells for little piece of its worth. This is one house. How can I live in country where peoples were killed all around?'

'Too many ghosts?'

'No, it is more real than this. It is friends of me. Men and women who are stronger than me, who fight and who are destroyed. So we come to England to make new life. But Lucja changes. She reads English magazines. She thinks to make new life means to build new kitchen. Every time she speaks begins with "need". Do not mistake – I still love her. But this word – this "need" – comes between us. And through my work – I drive van for drinks company; I am not Polish plumber – I meet Susan.' He falls silent. 'Excuse me. I am not quiet with happiness or with sadness, just with thoughts. Susan was waitress. She wanted me for funny times, nothing more. And I am man. Which means I am fool. And I think of nothing more than what is to be man in bed with Susan.'

'You're not alone, mate.'

'It is different from being man in bed with Lucja. With Susan, it is nothing but bed. With Lucja, there is always "we need new socks for Filip; we need new shelves for wall." Once, when we are loving, she stops and puts on light (ever since we have childrens, she no longer wishes to love with light) and she picks up pen for shopping list. She says she is sorry but, if she does not write list down, she will forget. This is bed with Lucja. But she is pregnant again and we are happy. And I tell Susan and she ends with me.'

'She feels bad about Lucja falling pregnant?'

'She feels bad; she feels boring? Who knows? She says one thing but I think she means another. And I am glad to be back with Lucja: to be father and mother – this is what we do best. Then we learn truth about Pyotr: why he does not cry; why he does not blink (you see, I remember). And I tell Lucja about Susan – '

'Really? I understand why you'd want to make a fresh start, but wasn't she going through enough already? Weren't you?'

'You think I feel bad about me and this is true, but it is not because I feel responsible for Pyotr. I feel bad because life is so small, that Lucja cannot be Susan and Susan cannot be Lucja, that Tadeusz cannot be so many men and that Pyotr … that Pyotr cannot be anything. Doctors tell us that he will not live for long, that in his small life he will have many diseases and he will not be able to fight them. This makes me feel very bad, but I also feel good to know that there will be ending. And of course I feel bad because I feel good. And most of all I feel bad because Lucja blames herself for Pyotr: that she works too hard to buy things – magazines things – and she is so tired that baby is born weak. So I think, if I tell her about Susan, I will make her blame me. For once I am glad of her Church, since it is better she blames me than she blames herself.'

'And did she?'

'No, she didn't blame me or, if she did, it was small blame. She blamed herself for pushing me away, for pushing me to Susan. Now we come together again in bed and I feel great love for her. But it is different. It is love with colour of sadness. I want her to be happy. I work many hours; I make much money; I can buy her kitchen. But, since she has Pyotr, she is not caring. She spends so much time in church. Is she praying for Pyotr? Does she really believe – not with mouth but in heart – that if she prays enough times, God will make him well?'

'Why not ask her? You've been honest about everything else.'

'Because it is too important. If she answers "yes", it makes space between us too big.'

I feel his story as if it were my own in translation. 'But you're here?'

'Yes, her church pays for trip. I tell her to bring her mother. It is her dream to see Lourdes. But no, Lucja says if I won't come, then she won't come too. So I am come – and now I must go. I must help her with Pyotr before meal. This is strange. I find how much more I want to help since I am here. Do not mistake. This is not miracle. There is no magic, no Madonna. It is just peoples. I see parents carrying childrens and husbands pushing wives, and women like Brenda and her friend. I do not like these women; I cannot pretend. But when I see their love to each other, I think: Tadeusz, you can be this loving to Pyotr. No, I think: you are already this loving to Pyotr, but you are too afraid to show it.' He stands up. 'This is big surprise.

If you ask friends, they tell you: Tadeusz, he is man of little words.'

'Then I feel even more honoured that you've used so many on me.' His hand hovers over the bill. 'No, this is mine. I'll catch you later at the procession.'

He walks out of the café and I know that I should return to the hotel, but I need some time to myself. I may be growing mawkish in my middle age, but I find that so much of both Lester's and Tadeusz's stories resonates with my own. When Lester urged Tess to move on, it was as if he were speaking not just to her but to me; when Tadeusz described how he and Lucja rebuilt their relationship after his affair, he pointed the way for one who has been far too inclined to wallow in guilt. If I were a religious man – and Lourdes holds out that possibility, however violently I reject it – I might conclude that, far from my choosing the two interviewees, they were chosen for me. Why else did I schedule them on the very afternoon I was moving closer to Gillian? But I prefer to believe that coincidence is one of the happier outcomes of living in a world without God.

'*Mademoiselle!*' I err on the side of caution. '*Encore un demi, s'il vous plaît.*'

The question I have to address is not why I was told the stories, but what use to make of them. For years I have scoffed at the concept of Catholic guilt, even as it held me in thrall. It is what kept me from opening my heart to Gillian this afternoon. I could not bear to see my own unworthiness reflected in her eyes or, worse, drowned in her compassion. So I backed away, just when she needed me most.

My conviction that I will destroy any chance of love has led me to harden my heart against it. The irony is that, after so many years of loneliness, my most intimate relationship is with the woman whose gospel of guilt I blame for blighting my hopes of intimacy. Is it any wonder that I deplore the cult of the Madonna? At last, however, I feel strong enough to break the mould. I am ready to place my trust: not just in Gillian (that's easy!), but in myself. Which means accepting the fallible man whom Celia and Pippa loved, rather than the fallen man who was given to me as my birthright and whom, despite every effort, I have been unable to shake off.

My head is buzzing. Is it the air or the alcohol? Like Tadeusz, I have no need to share someone's faith to be moved by its manifestation.

Come what may, I am determined to declare myself to Gillian tonight. After texting Sophie that I will be ready in half an hour, I head back to the hotel to freshen up. I retrieve my key, smiling wanly at Madame Basic Jesus, who has lost much of her mystique since Jamie reduced her to Madame BJ. As if on cue, she dabs her lips and I feel my smile broadening. Once in my room I take a stuttering shower, scrubbing myself like a nerve-racked teenager. Trusting that any excess after-shave will evaporate outside, I join the crew in the lobby and lead them to the Acceuil, where the pilgrims are assembling for the procession. Great excitement greets the news that the Jubilates are to be at the front, a position which Ken, an old hand at Lourdes diplomacy, has secured by sending five young brancardiers to be stewards in the Basilica Square.

Our first place remains relative, since the procession is as ever led by pilgrims in beds: some propped up on pillows; others with sheets like shrouds; most attached to drips. Although there are fewer than at yesterday's International mass, the cumulative effect is of a hospital being evacuated during a fire.

Jamie weaves through the crowd, enjoying the challenge of the chiaroscuro, picking out our chosen pilgrims, their faces lit up by candle flames in the gathering dusk. I follow him to Gillian and her family, where I take the opportunity to linger.

'Are you filming the whole procession?' Patricia asks.

'Just odd moments. Then we'll go for an overview once it reaches the square.'

'It's my favourite service of the week. All of us walking together in the darkness. So powerful.'

'Of course,' Gillian interjects. 'The interplay of light and shadow. The Nazis recognised that.'

'It's nothing like it!' Patricia says, with a shudder.

'That's my line,' I say to Gillian.

'I'm sorry. I didn't realise. Do you have the copyright?'

'There's no call to snap at Mr O'Shaughnessy,' Patricia says. 'He's only doing his job.'

I let that pass. 'Is anything wrong?' I ask Gillian, whom I note with interest has changed into a navy trouser suit, with a white V-neck jumper and long red scarf.

'I'm just tired, I guess. This is a very emotional place. You can lay yourself open in ways that aren't always wise.'

'I don't know,' I say, trying to sound both knowing and neutral. 'Sometimes the benefits can take time.'

I rejoin the crew as the procession moves slowly down the Esplanade towards the Breton Calvary, from where it turns back past the Pius X bunker and up to the Basilica Square, like a snake swallowing its tail. The crowd is so vast that, when the Jubilates reach the square, some of the later groups are still waiting to set off. Babel is redeemed as the jumble of prayers crackling over the loudspeakers is intercut with the universal Ave Maria. Even I am impressed by the concerted surge of ten thousand candles at every repetition of the phrase.

Entering the square, we are herded towards the steps by a series of stewards, including Kevin, who wears his official armband like a badge of shame. 'It's humiliating,' he says. 'Loaning us out like plates for a church supper.'

'You're doing a great job,' Sophie says.

'A great job is working with slum kids in Calcutta or Tutsi refugees in Rwanda, not a load of coffin-dodging – '

'Stop now!' I say.

'Why? You're not filming.'

'Stop, because you don't mean it,' I say. 'And you'll regret it later. I know.'

'Think you know me better than I know myself?'

'I think I know you because I know myself.'

'You're as bad as all the rest of them.' He sees a group of Swiss pilgrims breaching an invisible barrier. 'No, stay in line. *Pas permis. Pour les chaises roulantes.*'

Jamie, Jewel and I climb the ramp to the upper level from where we have a spectacular view of the Esplanade. 'No one can accuse us of playing down the numbers now, chief,' Jamie says, sweeping his camera over the panoply of lights below. With the shot in the can, we pack up filming for the night and head back down to the square. I struggle to detect the Jubilates in the crush and finally spot them by the steps, following the service. A large statue of the Virgin rests on a plinth in front of the Rosary Basilica with ranks of robed priests behind it, forming a great swell of clerical stomachs, prominent among them Father Humphrey's. To the left, representatives of each pilgrimage hold up their banners. A cursory glance at the lime green, conspicuous among a sea of reds, purples and silvers, reveals that Marjorie, Frank, Geoff and a young handmaiden whose name I can never remember are doing the honours for us.

I edge towards Gillian and find myself alongside Louisa, who immediately hands me a candle. 'I always carry a few spares just in case,' she says, reminding me of the knickers at the airport. I hold it sheepishly and squeeze between Gillian and Patricia, who seizes the opportunity to give me a light.

Richard plays with his candle, jiggling it like a sparkler before mingling its flame with Gillian's. Both flare up, whereupon she whips hers away and he turns his attention to mine, which is promptly snuffed out. I feel mildly aggrieved, until Gillian leans across and relights it.

'You've revived my flame,' I say pointedly.

'Anyone would have done it.'

'No, they'd just have relit my candle.'

We both laugh, and I feel her mood lighten. We hold each other's gaze with only the drone of the prayers to root us to the world, when a burst of flames behind the statue makes me jump.

'What's that?'

'*Lumen Christi*. The light of Christ.'

'Trust Him to put me in the shade.' She turns back to the service and I am afraid of losing her. 'Come for a drink with me.'

'We had a drink yesterday.'

'And you're still here to tell the tale!'

'I have to help Richard get ready for bed.'

'I'm sure he'd be happy with one of the handmaidens.'

'I'm sure he would,' she says sharply. 'Wasn't the Departure Lounge enough for you?'

'Maggie's a handmaiden. So's Mona,' I reply, chastened. 'Or how about his mother?' Before she can object, I tap Patricia on the shoulder. 'Sorry to disturb you, but I wonder if you can help? I want to show Gillian the view from the Upper Basilica and she's worried about leaving Richard.'

'Someone has to see him back to the Acceuil and into bed,' she interjects.

'I'm his mother – you only have to ask. All this special treatment! She'll be expecting the leading role in the film.'

'It's not a casting couch,' Gillian snaps, turning swiftly away as if to keep the remark from registering. 'Richard!' She grabs his wrist, just as his candle strays perilously close to a blind girl's ponytail. 'Take care!' He chuckles, and I am not convinced that the peril was accidental. 'Vincent and I are walking up to the old church.'

'Me too,' he says.

'No. You'll find it boring. We're going to pray.' I am both surprised and encouraged by the lie. 'Besides, don't you want to go back with Nigel?'

'He's at the front so he can see.'

'Not for much longer. Stay close to your mother.' She kisses him warmly, which I suspect may be as much for my benefit as for his. We steal off, our defection doubly brazen at the climax of the service. I take her hand under cover of the crowd, only to run into Kevin, who turns away in disgust, his disillusion with the adult world complete.

'So,' she says, 'do you really want to show me the view?'

'Far more, I fancy, than you want to pray. Your call: steps or ramp?'

'Steps,' she says, and we climb to the upper level, gazing over the balustrade into the square. 'It's so beautiful. Don't laugh, but I feel as if each one of us is a spark of light that merges into a single stream. Have you noticed the way the lights down there are reflected up above?' She points to the sky. 'This afternoon you said it was easier to get a sense of God in the country – '

'For some people.'

'Yes, of course. Well it's certainly easier to get a sense of the universe. Look at all the stars! Even the brightest are usually hidden from us in the city. And when you think how many … Did you know that there are more stars in the universe than heartbeats in the history of mankind?'

'Say that again.'

'More stars in the universe than there have been heartbeats in the history of mankind.'

'Are you sure?' Loath as I am to offend her, I cannot let the claim pass unchallenged. 'If you think how many you and I alone will have in our lifetimes …'

'I know. And how many millions of "you and I"s there have been since the world began. But a wise old man told me.' She laughs. 'No, it's true, I promise; I did some research. Isn't it amazing? If we talk of trillions of trillions, it just sounds like another impenetrable statistic. But if we talk of the human heart ...' She smiles, and one heart misses a beat.

'It's a beautiful image,' I say, 'but doesn't it make you doubt your belief in a divinely ordained universe with a special place for us?'

'*No* to the first and *yes* to the second. Whoever said that we had a special place?'

'Genesis for a start,' I reply, suspicious of the question.

'I don't take it literally, any more than you do. Far from shaking my belief in God, the infinity of stars actually strengthens it. Even if there were only a fraction of their number, it would be utterly inconceivable that on one of them – if not on many – there weren't intelligent life, indeed, far more intelligent life than ours. If I thought that we were the be-all and end-all of creation, then I really would despair. Are we the best that God can come up with? The answer is *no*! There'll be life forms on other planets that are much more worthy – much more expressive – of Him.' She peers down at the square. 'See how small everyone down there looks to us. Think how much smaller we must look to God. It's a sign of His boundless love that He still cares for us. I'm sorry –' She breaks off as if in embarrassment. 'But that's what I believe.'

I stare at her in awe. I have been treating her beliefs as though she learnt them at her mother's knee or, at any rate, kneeling in a convent school chapel. In setting them out, she has shown them to be far more considered.

'Thank you,' I say, 'it's a fascinating proposition and one I'll need time to digest. Though you won't be surprised to hear that I see things differently. To me, one of the most admirable things about human beings is our self-belief. It may be an illusion, but good on us for perpetuating it! What could be more heroic than to maintain a sense of purpose on the edge of the void?'

'Will we ever find anything to agree on?'

'Lots. Besides, respect counts for far more than agreement. Look at Tadeusz and Lucja.' I want to look at them more closely now I know everything that their marriage has endured. 'They hold dia-metrically opposite views, but that doesn't stop them loving each other.'

'I love Richard.'

'But do you respect him?'

'It's turning chilly. Let's go and get that drink.'

Eager to agree, I suggest that we exit by the upper gate rather than return to the square where the crowd is already dispersing. We walk down an unlit tree-lined road, whose sinister aspect is intensified by the rustle of leaves and the occasional feral squeal, and arrive at a small row of shops. I gape at the effrontery of names – The Myster-ies of Mary, The Grace of God, The Sacred Heart of Jesus and Notre Dame de Lourdes – which are as shrewdly designed to reassure cus-tomers as their merchandise is to exploit them. Even at this late hour the aisles are full. Pilgrims sift through the ubiquitous baskets of Madonnas, crucifixes and Bernadettes, with all the hunger of their counterparts in a Soho sex shop, an image I prefer not to share with Gillian. Instead, I guide her towards the Gallia Londres hotel where we head straight for the bar, which is less crowded than it was last night.

'What can I get you?'

'I'd better stick to tomato juice.'

'Dare I ask for a Virgin Mary?'

'You dare!'

The waitress, a filigree crucifix nestling in her puckered bosom, takes our order and we start to relax. 'I wanted the chance to clear the air,' Gillian says. 'We only have two more days here – one full one – and then we go our separate ways. I'd hate to leave you with the wrong impression.'

'What do you mean? I only have the very best – '

'Please, let me finish! Then you'll have your turn. There's some-thing unreal about Lourdes: that is it's a place where everyday reality is put on hold and something more intense – more mysterious – takes over. I'm afraid that I – that both of us – have let it go to our heads. Don't get me wrong. I'm flattered by your attention. When a man shows an interest, for whatever reason, it makes me feel ... well some of the same sense of possibility as when we were looking at the stars. It's done me a world of good to meet someone who takes me seriously; who wants to know how I am, not just how well I'm coping; who cares – or seems to care – about me.'

'There's no *seems* about it.'

'Thank you, but please wait one more moment. This isn't easy to say. I allowed myself to get carried away this afternoon. I took advantage of your good nature – '

'What?'

'By landing you with all that stuff. No wonder you ran a mile.'

'Stop there! That's just what I was afraid you'd think: that's why I was determined to get you on your own tonight. I'd have dragged you off by force if necessary.'

'Patricia would have loved that.'

'I couldn't bear it when you were talking about Richard's affairs as if he were the dirty one and I was squeaky-clean. Believe me, I'm no better than he is. Worse. I don't have his family history as an excuse. My father only ever looked at one woman his entire life (he didn't look at her very much, but that's another story – sorry, bad joke). I didn't tell you everything last night about Celia and Pippa.'

'You had no call to. It's private.'

'Not from you.' Having spent years seeking women to help me blot out the past, I have now found one with whom I can share it. 'I loved Celia with all my heart. Before that, *love* had been a catch-all word for everything from Christmas cards to foreplay. Suddenly it was something real: a word with millions of different meanings for millions of different people, but one that was unique and unequivocal for us.'

'She must have been very special. I wish I'd known you both in those days.'

'Yes … no. I wish that for everyone else, but not you. And the odd thing is it no longer makes me feel disloyal, let alone guilty. You're right; she was very special. Beautiful, so beautiful, clever, sensitive and strong. Although we couldn't have come from more different backgrounds, we shared the same values and ideals and, perhaps most important of all, the same sense of humour. You'd have thought that would be enough for any man. But not for Vincent O'Shaughnessy. There was a part of me that was never satisfied. I lived in a world with illicit opportunities on every corner, or, at least, in every bar.' She glances around her instinctively. 'I told myself that my casual affairs were of no consequence. If anything they strengthened my marriage since I went back home refreshed and reinvigorated, having fulfilled my genetic imperative. And I accuse the Church of sophistry!' I gulp my drink which, unlike Gillian's, is appropriately Bloody. 'Then, eight years ago, when I was making a series about London Zoo, I went out after work with a young woman (a researcher not a keeper). One thing led to another and we ended up at her place. It was half-past eight when I remembered I was supposed to pick up Pippa from her friend's. There was no way I was going to let that stop me from getting my jollies. So I called Celia to say something had come up: a giraffe had gone into labour; which she'd have been bound to tell Pippa about the next day – had Pippa been alive the next day. Now you see what a lying, cheating bastard I am!'

'You don't have to put yourself through this.'

'I've put myself through it every day for the past eight years. Where was ... oh yes! Celia was furious since, as she'd been reminding me for weeks, she'd invited some big-shot impresario to the house to meet one of the Russian pianists she represented. Everyone had left, but she'd had a few drinks and didn't want to drive. I told her to ring for a taxi, but she said it would take too long. For the sake of a fuck – some meaningless fuck with a woman whose name I can't even remember; no, worse, whose face I can't even remember – I was willing to sacrifice my daughter. A cheap fuck!'

'Everyone's staring at us.'

'They won't all speak English, or has Hollywood made *fuck* universal? Sorry, sorry.' I offer a general apology to the room before turning back to Gillian. 'Or should that be *mea culpa*? So where was I? Oh yes, on Battersea Park Road with a German juggernaut hurtling around the corner. Did you know that European lorries have a blind spot when they're driving on the left? Did you?'

'No.'

'Nor did I. At the inquest the driver was exonerated. The coroner made a recommendation about fitting more effective mirrors but, when I last checked, it had still to be taken up. Celia was above the legal limit for alcohol and so, in most peoples' eyes, she was culpable. But not in mine.'

'Was she hurt?'

'You mean injured?' She nods. 'Two cracked ribs and a broken wrist. I envied her her pain.' She lays her hand on mine. I leave it as long as possible before reaching for my glass. 'There was even some talk that she might be charged, but the matter was dropped. Perhaps they thought she'd suffered enough?' I struggle to remain composed. 'Would it have made any difference if I'd been the one at the wheel? Would quicker reflexes have enabled me to swerve? Who knows? And what makes it so unbearable is that I'll never know. At least if there was a God, I'd find out when I got to Heaven and St Peter read out a list of all my sins before damning me to Hell.'

'Would there be no one to speak up for you?'

'Oh yes. And although you've never met her, you know who it would be. That's what makes it even harder. And it's also why I backed away from you this afternoon. You think I'm different from Richard, but I'm exactly the same. Groin-led.' She replaces her hand on mine. 'I'm not asking for sympathy.'

'If you were, you wouldn't get any.'

'Pippa was six. If she were here today, she'd be fourteen: a young woman. How can anyone make sense of that? She was so beautiful. I know every father says the same thing, but in this case it's the truth.'

'I can believe it.'

'No, she took after her mother. She was lucky in that, if nothing else. Sometimes I wish I'd lived in an age when child mortality was a commonplace. Isn't that the sickest thing you've ever heard?'

'No.'

'It should be. Celia stopped speaking to me after the funeral. I mean she stopped talking. It wasn't that she wanted to punish me; there was nothing left to say. I think we both went a bit mad, but even that didn't make us closer. We were as remote from one another as we were from the world.'

'How long did that last?'

'Weeks, months: I can't honestly remember. All I know is that Pippa died in July and I was alone by Christmas. I threw myself into my job. I was offered compassionate leave, but the only compassionate thing would have been to load me with so much work that I couldn't see beyond it. One night I came home to find Celia had shaved her head. She never referred to it and neither did I. People assumed that she had cancer. I think she found misplaced compassion easier to bear. Not long after, she moved back to her parents. Officially it was only temporary, but we both knew she would never return.'

'Do you still see her?'

'No, only a couple of times since the divorce. It helps that she lives in Scotland. I'd like us to be friends, I really would. We had so much together; it can't all have been smashed. But she's moved on. The last thing I'd want is to burden her with my grief.'

'And have you moved on?' she asks gently.

'On?' I ponder the question. 'No, but I have moved round, which may be the best I can hope for.' I laugh, which sounds alarmingly like a sob. 'The pain doesn't die but, in time, you find better ways to deaden it. In the early days all I had was drink. Once when I was in Sainsbury's buying whisky – it somehow felt less compromising from a supermarket – I was sure I saw Pippa. How, I don't know; I could never have mistaken her face. But all I saw was the hair: the flame-coloured curls down to her shoulders. I reached out my hand to stroke it – so happy, so grateful, just as the girl's mother came up the aisle. She screamed. The next thing I knew, I was grabbed by a pair of security guards and frogmarched into an office. When I realised my mistake, I broke down. Tears poured down my cheeks – all the tears I'd been holding back since Pippa died. You wouldn't believe that one body could contain so much fluid. The police were called, along with my boss at the BBC, who explained about the accident four months before. At a stroke everything changed; the villain became the victim. The police referred me to a bereavement counsellor, who I saw for a couple of months to satisfy my friends. Not that it did any good. Packaging my grief into two weekly sessions felt like another form of infidelity.'

'What kind of a world have we made for ourselves when the slightest touch becomes suspect?'

'Would you have said that if she'd been your child?' She stares into her glass. 'Fuck! See, that's how insensitive I am!'

'Of course you're not. Quite the reverse.'

'Do you want to know the worst thing? I still have the feel of that girl's hair on my hands. Not Pippa's. Not the daughter whose hair I kissed and stroked and brushed and smelt for six years, but a stranger's: a child I touched for at most a few seconds. Why?'

'Let's go to bed.'

I look at her in bemusement. 'Sorry?'

'Please don't make me say it again.'

'I didn't tell you that as a come-on.'

'I never imagined you did.'

'Even I have better lines.' As mistrustful of myself as ever, I wonder if I am telling the truth or if, at some subconscious level, I bargained on her responding to my confession.

'I'm not throwing myself at you.'

'Of course not!' I say, scared that she might be having second thoughts. 'It's all been the other way round.'

'I don't suppose you've been entirely celibate since … in the past eight years.'

'Not entirely, no. I've had a few women. To relieve myself; to punish myself; in some perverse way, to prove that I'm still alive and yet not worthy of life at the same time. But no one I've truly cared about. Not till now.'

'No more! If we talk about caring, we'll talk ourselves out of it. Let's just stick to tonight or, better still, the next couple of hours.'

'Of course.' I wonder whether her pragmatism is innate, or if the years of looking after Richard have hardened her. 'Shall we go back to my hotel?'

'We can hardly go back to mine!'

'I could book a room here.'

'And tell them what? Our car broke down on the way to Biarritz and we've walked here without any luggage? We might as well sign the register Mr and Mrs A. Dulterer.'

'We're in France.' She looks at me wryly. 'No, you're right. I'm at the Bretagne. It's a ten-minute walk.'

We are both so nervous that we make it in six. I pick up my key, which feels more than ever like clocking in, and stand before the proprietress's desk as if it were Sister Theresa Anthony's at primary school.

'*Madame … je regrette mais je ne connais pas votre nom.*'

'It's of no consequence.'

'*Je vous présente Madame Patterson. Une de nos pèlerins.*'

'If you have come to watch the television, you will find many of your compatriots in the bar. We have Sky Sport especially for our English guests.'

'Thank you, but we have pilgrimage business to discuss,' I say, abandoning the linguistic struggle. 'It's quieter in the room.'

'Of course, Monsieur. There are two very respectable chairs.'

I summon the clattering lift and lead the way to my room. Halfway down the corridor I remember the photograph of Pippa by my bed, which I fear will prove a greater deterrent to Gillian than all the priests in Lourdes combined. Improvising fast, I announce that the main light-switch is broken and ask her to wait by the door. Then I hurry in and turn on the bedside lamps, first popping the photograph into a drawer. The low wattage has the unexpected bonus of bathing the room in a semi-romantic haze.

'It's not the Ritz, but I can at least offer you a drink. No tomato juice, I'm afraid. Vodka, vodka or vodka.'

'What the hell! In for a penny.'

'I'll fetch a glass.' I search the bathroom and come back with a cloudy tooth mug. 'Or the Lourdes equivalent.' I pour her a generous measure. 'Here, have a Minty Mary.'

'Whenever I've imagined having an affair – don't look at me like that; I said an affair, not an orgy – it's always been in France.'

'Alain Delon? Daniel Auteil?'

'The man was immaterial.'

'That's nice to know.'

'I meant that I pictured a small hotel. Shutters on the windows. Vines climbing up the walls. A millrace down a leafy path.'

'You had everything planned.'

'I had everything dreamt.'

'And here we are. Skegness circa 1980.'

'Believe me, this'll do fine.'

'I wanted you the moment I saw you.'

'Please don't say that.'

'Why not?'

'It makes me feel arbitrary, expendable. Just a face in the crowd.'

'No, it wasn't just your face; it was something deeper. Your spirit, your aura, the energy you give out.'

'I think someone's had too many Minty Marys.'

'Then let's try something else.' I kiss her, and for the first time I have no fear of being rebuffed. I let my tongue savour her mouth, as if the confusion of taste and touch will transport us to a realm beyond the senses. After a while, she breaks away and rests her head on my shoulder. I lace my fingers through her hair, marvelling at the richness of every strand, before lifting her face and covering her cheeks with kisses. 'You're tickling,' she says with a smile. 'No, don't stop!' I want to obey, but there is so much of her still to explore and I am worried that the 'couple of hours' she specified in the bar may be all that we have. I slip my hands under her jumper and run my fingers over her skin. She flinches.

'I'm sorry. Are my hands cold?'

'No. Gentle.'

Moved, I press my lips to her breasts while caressing her stomach. I feel her shiver and myself stir. She is slimmer than I had expected and I thrill to the suppleness and fragility of her flesh. As I reach downwards, she clasps my wrist.

'No, not like kids in the back row of a cinema.' She points to the bed. 'Can't we make use of all the facilities?'

'Of course.' I kick off my shoes and pull down my trousers, wondering whether she will be gratified or alarmed by my erection.

'I never thought I'd make love to another man. Now I know that all we need is a condom.' She catches the look of dismay on my face. 'You do have one? I assumed …'

'What? That I never leave home without one? Whatever you may suppose, I don't make a habit of this.'

'No, of course not.'

'Is it absolutely essential?' I ask, hating myself for broaching a subject that causes her pain. 'You said you weren't sure about the symptoms.'

'I'm still not. But that's not the only reason to take precautions.'

'Oh, I see.'

'As I've told you, Richard's drugs have reduced his sperm count, so I'm not on the pill.'

I have no wish to think of Richard, let alone his sperm count, and I refuse to be thwarted by the lack of a condom like a teenager too bashful to talk to the barber. 'I'll nip down to Reception,' I say, pulling up my trousers and shuffling on my shoes.

'You're not going to ask that ogress?'

'For a condom? God no! But I'll find out where the nearest chemist is. I'll be as quick as I can. Promise you won't run away?'

'What do you think?'

'There's BBC World and yesterday's *Guardian*. Have some more vodka.'

I give her a final kiss and go out. I bound down the stairs two at a time, imagining myself on a chivalric quest. Madame Basic Jesus looks more disapproving than ever, as she stares at me over the top of her glasses.

'Would you be kind enough to direct me to the nearest *pharmacie*?'

'It's nearly midnight, Monsieur.'

'Don't you have late-night shopping in Lourdes?'

'Yes of course, until eight o'clock every evening. Do you or your *friend*' – never has a rolled *r* sounded so forbidding – 'have a problem?'

'Just a slight headache. Nothing serious.'

'Wait here. I will fetch you a pill.'

'Please don't go to any trouble. It'll pass.'

'It's no trouble, Monsieur. The health of our guests is our premier concern.'

She retreats to her inner sanctum, leaving me in an agony of frustration. Racking my brains, I think of Jamie, whose 'nothing ventured' philosophy must lead him to prepare for all eventualities. A quick glance at the key-board confirms that he is in his room but, before I can entreat his help, I have to wait for Madame to play her part in a charade of my own instigating.

'Here you are, Monsieur.' She comes out and hands me a foil strip containing two huge pills. 'One for now and one for the morning.' My throat constricts.

'Do you swallow these whole?'

'Mais non, Monsieur. They are *suppositoires*. Far more effective. If you need any help – '

'No really. That's very kind.' I quail. 'I'll manage.'

'I was on the point of saying that you have your pilgrimage doctor in the hotel. I'm sure he'll be happy to oblige.' She dismisses me with a disdainful smile. I dash up to the fourth floor and pound on Jamie's door, oblivious of the sleeping neighbours.

'Who is it?' he shouts, in a voice that is reassuringly alert.

'Vincent.'

'Can't it wait, chief? I'm busy.'

'It'll only take a moment.'

'I've got company.'

I start. Has Jamie been conducting his own romance? Notwithstanding his catholic tastes, he would be hard-pressed to find a suitable candidate among the Jubilates. The gruesome prospect of an amorous Maggie or Marjorie gives way to the growing fear that he may have played the media card on one of the more impressionable young handmaidens. Doubly determined, I knock again.

'It's an emergency!' After checking that the coast is clear, I call through the door: 'I need a condom.'

'What was that?'

'A condom!'

The door springs open and I tumble on to Jamie, who stands in his shirtsleeves holding a hand of cards. He steps aside, revealing his *company*: Father Humphrey, who sits in a clerical stock over a vast string vest; Father Paul who, either less hot or more reserved, has merely loosened his collar; and two of the older brancardiers. 'We're playing poker, chief,' Jamie says with a grin.

'So I see,' I say, struggling to retain a thread of dignity. 'Who's winning?'

'Father Humphrey of course,' says Father Paul, who alone comes to my rescue. 'Look at his nuts!'

'Do you have business to discuss with young Jamie here,' Father Humphrey asks, 'or is it just a social call?'

I feel a spark of hope that some unique acoustic in the room may have muffled my words, but Father Humphrey's smirk, not to mention Jamie's guffaw, douses it.

'Just a word about tomorrow's schedule, but it can wait.'

'Are you sure, chief?' Jamie asks, dragging out my humiliation. 'You said it was an emergency.'

205

'You know me, ever one to exaggerate.'

'Because if there's anything I can do to help.'

'Not at all. I'll see you at breakfast. Enjoy the game.'

I leave his room feeling three foot tall, and walk up to mine, where I find Gillian laid out on the bed like a gift that will have to be returned. I sit down beside her, gently stroking her back.

'Here,' I say, handing her the foil.

'What are these?'

'Headache pills.'

'I don't have a headache.'

'You will when I tell you that the chemists are closed. Jamie … Jamie can't help.' I think it wise to draw a veil over his guests.

'You asked him?'

'Don't worry, he promised to say nothing. Meanwhile we're back where we started. Please don't say it's a sign. If you do, I swear I'll throw myself out of that window.'

'Of course it's a sign: one that you should be more resourceful. I'm not giving myself to a wimp.'

'What can I do?' I ask, desperate for a hint that she may be joking. 'Raid the kitchen for sausage skins?'

'That's disgusting!'

'Besides it's a continental breakfast. We could steal a car and drive to Biarritz. It's only a couple of hours. No, I know! Why didn't I think of it before? Listen, what can you hear?'

'It sounds as if someone's having a party.'

'Near enough. The kids from all the different pilgrimages meet on the bridge after dark and let their hair down. I'll try them.'

'You can't! They're young. Good Catholics. They'll be shocked.'

'Take it from me, every good Catholic boy over the age of sixteen keeps a condom in his wallet, just waiting for what the Lord will provide. Though, if my experience is anything to go by, it'll be well past its expiry date. No, forget I said that. Think of all the mortal sins I'll be saving them from. Don't go away!'

I race down the stairs for the second time in half an hour. To my relief, Madame BJ has been replaced by a male receptionist who greets my parting wave with a friendly smile. I head outside and down the surprisingly busy street. After two sleepless nights, I now welcome the proximity of the bridge. Young brancardiers and hand-maidens are bunched along its length: some leaning against bollards; others squatting on the pavement; an intrepid pair perched on the parapet, gazing into the fast-flowing waters of the Gave. After checking that there are no Jubilates nearby, I head for a group of boys, whose fair hair and Nordic features, caught by the moonlight, bode well for our mutual understanding.

'Hi there,' I say. 'I'm sorry to butt in. Do you speak English?'

'Naturally,' one of them replies with singsong vowels.

'You may think this odd, but do you happen to have any spare condoms?' They look at me blankly. 'Condoms. You know: Durex; johnnies?' I am rapidly running out of euphemisms. 'French letters?'

'You wish to post your letters?' another asks. 'You must make inquiries at the hotels.'

Fearing that the language barrier is too great to surmount, I resort to gestures. 'Do any of you have something to put on this?' I point to my crotch. 'I'll pay.'

Their outraged faces prove that gestures are equally open to mis-interpretation. I want to set them straight, but the mood has turned ugly. 'Fuck off!' one shouts. A second spits and a third crushes his beer can. Heads turn in our direction, and I find myself subject to whatever sixth sense protects clean-living youths from predatory older men. Reluctant either to entangle myself further or to confirm their suspicions by turning tail, I brave the row of hostile stares and continue across the bridge. On the far side, I come to the *Café Pub, Au Roi Albert*, a beacon of light in a row of closed souvenir shops. While I know better than to expect a condom machine in the Gents, I hope to meet one customer with some sympathy and, more importantly, some solution for my plight. But a glance through the glass door reveals Pete, the widower from the airport, standing at the narrow bar with a crowd of his mates. There is something about his heartfelt faith that humbles me and, for all his jokes about his 'good-time girl' daughter, I refuse to offend it with my request.

Forced to admit defeat, I turn right down a small side-road, willing to walk for miles to avoid recrossing the bridge. Nowhere but Lourdes could two people go through so much, only to be kept apart by the lack of a condom. Even if I manage to buy some tomorrow,

I fear that the moment will have passed and Gillian be back with Richard. I walk down to the river, where I see the small gypsy encampment which is, according to Father Dave, a sign of Bernadette's universal appeal and, according to Madame Basic Jesus, the source of every unsolved crime in the town. Either way I feel a rush of hope and, trusting in the solidarity of the outcast, I leap over the chain-link fence and scramble down the bank.

GILLIAN

Tuesday June 17

The basilica bells offer a welcome alternative to the brashness of the alarm; the fitful birdsong offers a welcome corrective to the measured bells. Reminding myself that I never sleep well in a strange bed, I stand and move to the window where an overemphatic stretch threatens to crick my back. Lourdes at seven in the morning looks eerily similar to Lourdes at seven at night. A nurse in a navy blue uniform walks down the path with a nun in a dove grey habit. An old man pushes an unseen passenger in a hooded wheelchair. A blonde girl in a dun-coloured blouse carries a furled banner towards the river.

I am distracted, first by a knock at the door and then by an elderly handmaiden who walks straight into the room without waiting for a reply. Should I be touched by the assumption of innocence or angered by the disregard? We sat next to her at the flight gate but, hard as I try, I cannot remember her name. Still, if she can ignore the niceties, so can I.

'Good morning, my dear,' she says.

'Good morning. I'm afraid I've forgotten your name.'

'Ruth,' she says. 'Plain and simple. When I was a girl, how I envied all the Angelicas and Antonias, but I've grown into a Ruth. Did you sleep well?'

'Like a log,' I say, effortlessly reverting to social mode.

'I've come to collect your dirty sheets.' I see her cast her eyes over the sleeping Richard and wonder whether she intends to drag him out of bed.

'Oh!' I say, surprised at the level of service. 'I'd no idea you changed the sheets every day.'

'Only the soiled ones.'

'We don't soil our sheets,' I reply coldly.

'Are you sure?' She sounds unconvinced.

'Quite. Richard has perfect control of his bladder, though not all his biological functions. And so have I.'

'Splendid! You're the kind of guests we like.' She turns and walks out briskly. 'Don't forget, breakfast in half an hour.'

I watch in stunned silence as she leaves. Has my life been reduced to this? You can put out your best bedlinen for the Pattersons. No need for a mattress protector with the Pattersons. Count on the Pattersons for a stain-free weekend.

A second knock cuts short my ruminations. 'Come in!' I call, determined to give myself at least the illusion of choice. Two young brancardiers hover at the door, one of them the boy who behaved so oddly yesterday.

'Morning,' the other says, with breezy confidence. 'I'm Matt; this is Kevin. We've come to help.'

'How amazing!' I say. 'You wouldn't get this level of service at the Ritz.'

'I've never been to the Ritz,' Kevin says.

'Neither have I.'

'Then how do you know?'

'Leave it out, Kev,' Matt says.

'Just a turn of phrase.'

'We've come to help Mr Patterson get ready,' Matt says.

'Really? That's very kind but quite unnecessary. We manage perfectly well by ourselves.'

'He's on the list.'

'Then I suggest you cross him off it. He might react badly. He's not used to being touched by men.'

'Can't have gone to a Catholic boarding school,' Kevin says, with disturbing flippancy. Then he smiles, revealing unusually small front teeth. 'Just a turn of phrase.'

'Well if you're sure,' Matt says.

'Positive.'

The boys walk out: Matt with reluctance, Kevin with relief. I brace myself and move to wake Richard, aware that this marks the end of my repose as much as his. He responds with his habitual resentment, as though the return to consciousness is the first of the many indignities to which he will be subjected during the day. I lure him into the bathroom with the promise of excitements which I trust he will forget in the morning rush. I slip off my nightdress before switching on the shower, a precaution which proves to be justified when he waves the shower-arm above his head, sending jets of water across the room. Bowing to the inevitable, I soap myself at the same time, brushing off his routine groping while pondering the irony that we now take a joint shower from necessity, when we once did by choice.

Discouraging his fascination with the drenched floor, I lead him back to the bedroom where he refuses to put on the Jubilate sweatshirt. 'It looks like sick.'

'Which is very practical,' I reply, my patience exhausted. 'If you are sick, you won't have to change it.'

'Yes, I will. You'll say I smell. I want to wear this one.' He picks up a powder blue polo shirt which complements his colouring. I feel a stirring of affection for him and, not for the first time, wish that there were some way to exploit his innate dress sense. Might a brain-damaged stylist take his place alongside a blind piano tuner? 'You can change into that later,' I say quickly, as much to distract myself as him. 'There are two occasions when we have to wear our pilgrimage shirts. Today for the official photograph and on Thursday for the Blessed Sacrament procession. I'm wearing mine too.'

'I'll look like a girl.'

'You'll look like the group.'

He sits listlessly on the bed, and I seize the chance to thrust the sweatshirt over his head. He turns suddenly, grabbing my wrists. 'Richard, let go! You're hurting me!' The pain is intense, but I dare not shout for fear of attracting attention. 'Please stop!' He drops my wrist, which I press hard in a bid to disperse the pain around my body. I sniff and wipe away the tears which are welling in my eyes.

'You're not crying?'

'Don't worry, it's over.'

'You're not crying! It's just a game.'

'I know you didn't mean it.'

'You shouldn't pretend to cry. It makes me feel bad. Here.' He taps his head and his own eyes start to water.

'I know it's just a game, but you shouldn't play so roughly,' I say, taking advantage of his docility to slip his arms through the sleeves. 'Just gentle games from now on.' He puts on the rest of his clothes and slumps on the bed, lost in a world that is as closed to me as nuclear physics. I pull on my sweatshirt and skirt and brush and pin up my hair, the one physical feature of which I remain proud and which, despite the leverage it allows him, I have refused to cut short.

'Come on,' I say, my preparations complete. 'Breakfast!' He shows no sign of having heard. 'Aren't you hungry?' I ask, prising him off the bed and hoping that it does not provoke a tantrum. Luck is on my side, since he follows me compliantly to the door.

'I've done nothing wrong,' he says, dragging his heels, 'but I'm in prison.'

'What on earth are you talking about? You're in Lourdes.'

'There are electric wires running across the door.'

'Look, I've just walked through it.'

'That's because you've turned them off.' He looks at me with heart-rending helplessness.

'Come on,' I say, linking arms. 'We'll both feel better once we've eaten.' On reaching the dining room, I am forced to revise my opinion. Sister Anne stands by the door holding a tub of anti-bacterial handwash, which she squirts on everyone who passes through. Richard recoils.

'I've just washed my hands. They're clean. See!'

'I'm sure they are,' she says. 'But this will give you added protection. When you leave church, you dip your fingers in the holy water even after you've been to mass.'

Richard stares at her and, as if the last twelve years were all a dream, spits out with controlled venom: 'You cunt!' Then he thrusts his hands under her nose. Stunned, she squirts the handwash and he rubs his palms together.

'I'm so sorry, Sister,' I say, 'he doesn't know what he's saying.'

'Yes, I do,' Richard says, 'it's that – '

'Come on!' I push him into the room and turn back to the nun. We exchange that look of pained compassion which I suspect is ubiquitous in Lourdes.

Louisa walks over to greet us. 'Morning,' she says. 'Sleep well, I trust? Good!' Her brusqueness makes the question even more rhetorical than usual. 'We've a busy day ahead, so I'm sure you'll be wanting your breakfast.'

'Should we sit anywhere?' I ask.

'Only on the first night. From now on we prefer to stick to fixed seating. With so many special diets, any chopping and changing causes havoc. You'd find a gluten-free turning into a lactose intolerant. Isn't that so, Patricia?' She addresses my mother-in-law, who has come to coddle her surly son. 'I was saying: you just can't get the staff these days.'

'Too true!' Patricia says, as ever more sympathetic for the loss of a maid than the loss of a limb. 'I don't know what I'd do without my Rose. She's a treasure.' She gives me a look which is part appeal, part warning. I turn away in case I should unwittingly reveal that 'her Rose' left fifteen years ago after a distressing encounter with 'her Thomas', to be replaced by a succession of contract cleaners. Still, if I am to enjoy a week's respite from reality, why shouldn't she?

'We've put you on a table by the window,' Louisa says. 'See, you have a glorious view over the Domain.' The view is partially obscured by a huge woman who is about to swallow an entire croissant. 'Have you met Sheila Clunes?'

'We bumped into each other at Stansted. I'm Gillian, this is Richard.' Sheila glances up.

'Sheila has one of our healthiest appetites,' Louisa says. 'Bless!'

'I have a little hole that needs filling,' Sheila says, cramming the croissant into her mouth.

'Aren't you going to say hello to Gillian and Richard?' Louisa asks.

'Hello Gillian. Hello Richard,' she says, spluttering crumbs into her neighbour's orange juice. He is too busy counting on his fingers to notice.

'This is Frank,' Louisa says, ruffling his hair and pressing his head to her bosom in a manner which, were their positions reversed, would surely be labelled *abusive*. 'Frank likes to chew.' That seems to be all he likes since he does not look up, either at Louisa or us, but quietly returns to zero. 'And last, but by no means least, this is Nigel. Oh dear, you seem to have slipped!' Without more ado, she reaches under his arms and heaves him upright.

'Richard,' Nigel says, banging his spoon on the table.

'No, I'm Richard,' Richard says.

'Richard,' Nigel repeats.

'No, I'm Richard.'

'He understands you,' I interject, 'he's saying hello.'

'I know that,' Richard says to me, contemptuously. 'We're just playing. Aren't we, little man?' He plumps himself in the vacant chair next to Nigel.

'Not there,' Louisa says. 'That's for the handmaiden to cut up Nigel's food.' Her appeal comes too late, since Richard has already made himself at home to the extent of dipping his spoon into Nigel's cereal.

'No, Richard, that's Nigel's,' I say, finding my worst fears of a week of communal eating confirmed.

'Don't worry. There's plenty more. It's good for Nigel to have a friend,' Louisa says, dropping her voice. 'He doesn't have an easy time of it. He's thirty-eight, but he lives in a home for geriatrics. You can't blame the local authority. It's the only residential place they have available. What makes it particularly cruel is that he has a mental age of six.'

'He should get on well with Richard then,' I say sadly, 'although at least he had thirty years' grace in-between.'

No one would guess it to see him rolling Nigel's wheelchair backwards and forwards. My instinct is to intervene, but I take my cue from Louisa's indulgent smile. There are sufficient helpers on hand to deal with any breakages and bruises.

'Do you like being pushed around?' Richard asks Nigel.

'I like it,' he replies.

'I get pushed around,' Richard says, with a rancour that shocks me. 'And I don't have a chair.'

How I envy their instant rapport! As a girl, I made friends within moments of meeting. Pushing forty, I vet every new acquaintance as if for membership of MI5.

'You sit here, Gillian.' Louisa directs me to the empty chair between Frank and Sheila. 'I'll get someone to bring you a bowl of cereal.'

'I can fetch it myself. Really. There's no need.'

'Oh but there is,' she says firmly. 'A little bird told me you wouldn't let the young brancardiers help you with Richard this morning.'

'He doesn't need … I mean you have so many more deserving cases.'

'We'll be the judges of that. We have more than enough helpers. So promise me you'll make use of them. I know it can be hard to let go, but we're here to give you the chance to relax and enjoy the pilgrimage too.'

'I promise,' I reply and, to my relief, she seems satisfied, She walks away, to be quickly replaced by Charlotte, a small, elderly hand-maiden with buck teeth and twinkling eyes.

'Would you like some orange juice, my dear?' she asks, in such effortlessly patrician tones that I understand Patricia's re-engagement of Rose.

'Thank you. That would be lovely.' Her trembling hands as she lifts the jug make me doubly embarrassed. While Frank calculates the correct ratio of chews per mouthful, I calculate how many meals I am destined to spend at this table: two more today; two tomorrow (since we are having a picnic lunch at an ancient abbey); three on Thursday; one on Friday. Maybe my pilgrimage should include a fast?

I decline all offers of food. If I had an appetite, the sight of Sheila Clunes dripping honey from her toast to her chin to her plate would destroy it. I am pleased, however, to see Richard eating heartily, until I realise that he is not actually swallowing but engaged in an unspo-ken contest with Nigel, to see who can stuff the most spoonfuls of Rice Krispies into his mouth. I am about to intervene, when Nigel splutters all over the table.

'You pig!' Sheila Clunes shrieks. 'You dirty, disgusting pig!' For a moment I fear that she is going to breach the ban on physical violence but she confines herself to a bitter tirade, the commotion attracting the attention of the entire dining room. Louisa and Derek hurry over, arriving just as Richard, with unsuspected delicacy, wipes the milky mulch off Nigel's cheek.

'What's wrong, Sheila?' Louisa asks.

'He's a pig! Look!' She points to the regurgitated cereal.

'Worse things happen at sea,' Louisa says. 'We'll soon have that cleared up.' While waiting for a handmaiden to bring a cloth, she stands behind Frank and ruffles his hair. He makes no response but returns to his little finger and resumes counting.

Derek gazes approvingly at Richard and Nigel. 'Looking out for one another already. That's what Lourdes is all about.'

'I'm going to look out for Nigel,' Richard says staunchly.

'That's the spirit,' Derek replies.

'I'm going to look out for him at every meal.'

Derek and Louisa move off. A handmaiden wipes the table. I am touched by the evidence of Richard's newfound compassion, while reminding him that toast tastes better eaten through the mouth than the nose.

'I'm not eating it,' he says, as if to a simpleton. 'I'm showing Nigel my moustache.'

Nigel, at least, seems to relish the sight. Moments later the young doctor comes to wheel him away for an injection. 'Anticonvulsant,' she whispers to me.

'I had a needle in my brain,' Richard says proudly to Nigel as we follow them out, leaving Sheila and Frank to continue eating.

We assemble outside the building at eight o'clock, which seems premature for a service that begins an hour later in a church a few hundred yards away, but that is to ignore the logistics of a Lourdes procession. Ken looks baleful as he barks out commands which are erratically obeyed. Like a ten-year-old boy playing soldiers, he marshals us into a line that is regularly broken when people step out to fetch sunshades, exchange greetings and distribute water. I intervene to stop Richard accepting the wheelchair that is routinely offered to every *malade*, a term rendered all the harsher by the coarse English accents. It feels cruel to separate him from his new friend, but I refuse to tempt fate by letting him claim a phantom handicap.

'Do you want people to think you can't walk?'

'I don't care. My brain doesn't work properly, which is more dangerous than Nigel's legs.'

Once again I am left to speculate on the extent of his self-knowledge. 'The exercise will give it oxygen.'

'You'll be sorry if I fall over.'

'Nonsense!' Louisa interjects, as she hurries past with a sun hat. 'You're a fine figure of a man.' Far from bridling at the interruption, Richard looks smug.

'If I can't go at the front with the chairs, then I'll go at the back.'

'If you insist.'

'The very, very back.'

'Wherever you like, as long as you stay in line.'

I see no sign of the film crew and, to my surprise, feel a tinge of disappointment. Yesterday at the airport I was unduly sharp with the director (Victor? Gilbert? Hubert?). I did my best to make amends during the evening mass and, fanciful though it might seem, I would swear that we shared something more than the collective Peace. I would like the chance to build on it, not least because his sensitivity and intelligence (the glint in his sea-green eyes) make a welcome change from the doleful antics of Frank and Sheila Clunes. But he is here to work and I am here for Richard. I am not one of his chosen interviewees and I have no intention of pushing myself forward. Nevertheless, I cannot deny the spark of … what: sympathy? solidarity? that I felt when I held his hand. Victor? Robert? Clement? How can I have forgotten his name?

Patricia strolls up and rests her hand on Richard's, only for him to brush it away. I have to admire the skill with which she camouflages the rejection, swatting an imaginary fly off his sleeve. 'Your first procession, Gillian,' she says, as piously as if it were my first communion.

'Yes.'

'It's good to see everyone wearing their Jubilate shirts. No distinctions. All one body, even the disabled.'

'Yes.' I repeat, distracted by the glimmer of her brooch.

We pass a fresh-faced young priest who might have walked straight off a Fra Angelico fresco. Patricia gives him an unctuous smile.

'Did you see his hair?' she asks, as we walk on.

'Beautiful,' I say of the russet locks spilling down his neck.

'He's just trying to be clever.'

'Our Lord had long hair.'

'Our Lord wore a loincloth,' she says, peremptorily.

I compose myself as we process around the Esplanade and down the steep incline to the church, where we find the crew waiting for us at the entrance. I decline to play to the camera and fix my gaze straight ahead. We walk into a building reminiscent of a vast nuclear bunker, along a ramp lined with primitively painted posters of saints, and down to an egg-shaped nave with a ribbed concrete ceiling like an upturned boat. The pews are already packed, but neither the wealth of humanity nor the brightly decorated altar can relieve the brutality of the design.

Given the lack of seats, I suggest that we join the Jubilate helpers in one of the shadowy recesses bordering the nave. Patricia objects. Spotting a modest gap on a distant bench, she makes a dash for it, flashing a gracious smile at the Mediterranean family on the other side who, realising that she is in earnest, shuffle their already cramped bottoms closer together. That done, the three Pattersons, one triumphant, one indifferent and one embarrassed, squeeze into the vacated space.

'See,' Patricia whispers to me, 'all these people need is a push.'

Conscious of activity behind us but unable to distinguish it over the sea of heads, we watch the lengthy procession on a giant screen. First, representatives of the various pilgrimages, holding up banners, file down the nave and around the altar before vanishing from view. Then a line of priests and bishops, with a cardinal at the rear, approach the altar, kneel and kiss it, before taking their designated seats opposite the choir. Every so often the director – or whoever else selects the shots – cuts away to the conductor waving his hands like a schoolboy tracing an hourglass figure or a potter throwing a dimpled vase. At slack moments the screen fills with stock footage of the Virgin, St Bernadette or a chalice. At others, the camera pans over the congregation, lingering on the wheelchairs at the front. Richard jumps as he spots Nigel, his face fixed in a permanent grin, nodding out of time with the chorale.

'That's Nigel,' he says to Patricia, who looks blank. 'That's Nigel,' he says to me. I nod and smile. The fortuitous sighting keeps him busy, as he fixes his eyes on the screen in the hope of another. Meanwhile, the officiating priest welcomes pilgrims from around the globe, listing their many different cities and organisations, each of which is greeted with warm applause. At the mention of Barcelona, I clap with particular vigour, a compliment which our disgruntled neighbours resolutely fail to return to the 'Jubilates from the UK'.

The prayers, spoken in French, German, Swedish and Italian, with simultaneous translations into German, Spanish and Dutch, remind me of the woman I once wanted to be: someone with a world of language at her fingertips. I feel cheated when an American voice booms over the loudspeakers, rendering my one skill superfluous.

The linguistic duplication drags out the service and I am grateful for Richard's preoccupation. The Communion is equally protracted, the congregation lining up in front of scores of priests who are dotted around the church. Anxious not to be accused of queue-jumping after our appropriation of the bench, I steer Richard and Patricia away from the Spaniards towards a huddle of wheelchair-bound Jubilates. We stand behind Brenda, the woman with the ferocious sales pitch, as two young Irish girls walk among the *malades*, offering them cups of water.

'Can I give you some?' the larger girl asks Brenda.

'Have you got one with gin in it?' she replies.

'Excuse me?'

'Gin! Gin!' she cackles. Heads turn. The priest looks up from his current communicant. Marjorie rushes forward to silence Brenda. The two girls scurry away.

'She's got multiple sclerosis; she's a lesbian; she lives in Hull,' Patricia hisses in my ear, leaving it unclear which of the three distresses her the most. She breaks off on finding herself next in line for the priest. Richard follows, opening his mouth to receive the Blessed Sacrament. I turn away wondering why, given his wholesale regression to childhood, it should offend me so much that he takes communion on the tongue like his mother, rather than in the hand like me.

We emerge from the subterranean gloom into blazing sunlight. Marjorie is waiting for us at the entrance.

'Straight up to the square for the group photograph! I don't need to tell you where to go, do I?' she asks Patricia.

'Of course not,' she replies, her pleasure at being deemed a doyenne overriding her dislike of being taken for granted. A silver-haired brancardier who knows her of old comes up to greet her. My mind drifts during the introductions and I spend the next few minutes trying – and failing – to catch his name. He explains that six months ago he was diagnosed with high blood pressure and ordered to take more exercise, hence the pedometer on his belt, which he slips off at Richard's insistence. Having shown him how it works, he enters Richard's statistics – a procedure complicated by his refusal to acknowledge his weight in kilograms – before clipping it on to his waistband. Richard dashes up and down the path, narrowly avoiding both wheelchairs and crutches, before returning to announce triumphantly that he has 'lost eight calories'.

Eager to clear my head, I leave Richard in his mother's charge and press on, finding myself alongside Claire, the softly spoken woman with the cerebral-palsied son, whom I met at the airport. She supports his elbow as he limps along, dragging his left leg with his right foot turned inwards, his arms bent and his hands pressed to his chest like a child mimicking a begging dog.

'Hello again,' I say. She smiles warily. 'Did you do the International mass on your previous pilgrimages?'

'Oh yes, it's one of the highlights. Martin looks forward to it, don't you, love?' He emits a sound like escaping gas. She strokes his hair protectively. His right hand flails as if to flick her off, but his face beams. 'Let me do that again.' She strokes his hair and sniffs it. 'Oh you smell so good.' He giggles and dribbles down his chin. 'I'm sorry,' Claire says to me, 'but I can't resist. He's so clean. He had his second shower of the year this morning.'

'When was the first?' I ask inanely.

'Last night,' she says, with a laugh. 'Last night.' I am afraid that she might burst into tears. 'He's getting so big now that I can't manage on my own. Of course we do our best. A strip wash every day. But there's nothing to beat the smell of freshly showered boy.' She nuzzles his neck and I try not to stare at the patch of drool on her sweatshirt.

'It must be hard for you.'

'It's harder for Martin,' she says sharply.

'I didn't mean – '

'I understand. But I won't be made a martyr. People who know – who knew – me far better have tried. When Martin was born and everyone was throwing in their pennyworth, it was my mother – my dear, sweet mother who always wanted everything to be just so – who put it best. "God doesn't make rejects," she said. And she was right.' Looking at Martin, his broad smile a sign that he knows we are talking about him even if he cannot make out what is being said, I am inclined to agree. 'Martin isn't my cross or my trial or my burden; he's my son.'

'Still, you must need help.'

'Why?' she asks, and I glimpse the steel in her soul. 'Martin's father has offered to find people.'

'I'm sorry. I didn't realise you were married, still married.'

'I'm not. He left three years after Martin was born.'

'Men find it so hard to cope with imperfection, especially in a son,' I say, thinking of Richard's father. My words tail off as I watch a middle-aged man tenderly leading a boy dressed as Batman into the Basilica Square, his prominent hump artfully concealed beneath the flowing cape.

'He said it wasn't Martin he couldn't cope with but me, or rather me and Martin together. Do you have children?'

'No.'

'I'm sorry. Yes, even though Martin's my only child, I'm sorry. And I make no bones about it. Do you need some water, love?' He shakes his head. 'All fathers are a little jealous of their sons – that's where the psychiatrists have got it the wrong way round. But the father of a boy who's special (I drop the *needs*) is the worst. I understand now, though at the time … let's just say I found it more difficult. He wanted to keep Martin out of sight. He wanted to have more children. How could I when I knew I'd have to devote every ounce of my strength to Martin? No rejects, remember! So he left and he found someone else. Helen – his wife – is very good with Martin. He goes there sometimes at weekends, although I won't allow him to … Martin wouldn't be happy to stay overnight. They have two children. Boys. Arthur and John. They're good with Martin too. You like Arthur and John, don't you, love?' Once again he emits the disconcerting hiss. 'But they're not special. Not at all.' Her eyes fill with tears. 'I'm sorry – I didn't mean to witter on like this, but you'll find that's the way of things in Lourdes. When I was at school, a friend had a phone with a party line. I asked my mother if we could have one. "We have a line to ourselves," she said, making it clear that a party line wasn't quite the thing. But it still sounded much more exciting. And Lourdes is like that. You spend the week listening in on other peoples' lives. Some of them are happy, and some are sad, but they're all inspiring.'

We enter the Basilica Square and head for the patch of lime green at the base of the steps, parting company when Patricia beckons me to join Richard and herself in the front row. I watch the director filming, until he too is brought into line when Louisa, living up to her nickname, orders 'our honorary pilgrims' to join in. I must stop thinking about him. It is absurd to assume that the man must be as interesting as his job.

Vincent – his name is Vincent, of course: St Vincent Ferrer, St Vincent de Paul – squeezes in beside Patricia and then, after Louisa's realignment, beside me. I feel a little faint in the heat. After some schoolboy provocation, he amuses himself by flirting with me. This is not the delusion of a lonely, middle-aged woman since he openly admits it.

'Perhaps she won't want to be photographed beside such a dangerous sceptic?' he says to Patricia.

'You flatter yourself,' I interject.

'I'd rather flatter you,' he replies, as if the flagrancy excused the offence.

He even appeals to Patricia, conclusive proof that his remarks are not to be taken seriously. Plaudits pour out of him like a salesman's patter. He ought to realise that words, however lightly spoken, can stir up powerful emotions. He ought to know better than to use – let alone repeat – the word *beautiful* – to a woman with a brain-damaged husband, who has not received a compliment without the taint of compassion in years.

Whatever his game might be, it is clear that he has no real interest in me. I am just a convenient nobody on whom to try out his sweet nothings. I resolve not to reveal my hurt, pointing out that any photographs that Richard and I collect will quickly gather dust. This in turn conjures up thoughts of my mother, and I blurt out my fear of forgetting her face to a man I have only just met. Are my confidences as indiscriminate as his blandishments? Or is there something in the Lourdes air that cuts through the usual constraints?

'Now everyone please stand still like mouses. Imagine it is your "God Save The Queen". And say Camembert.'

The polite titters that greet the photographer's remark build into a gale of laughter when Nigel responds to it thirty seconds after everyone else. Following a second shot, Father Dave gives us an hour's free time, during which I propose to visit the basilicas. Then Richard announces that he needs the loo. I reflect glumly on all the films that have been ruined and trips curtailed in similar circumstances. 'I'll have to take him back to the Acceuil,' I say, whereupon Vincent volunteers to take him to the Gents in the square. This is so far beyond the call of duty that I wonder whether he might be gay. I gaze at him quizzically, at which he looks so pained that for a moment I fear that I may have spoken out loud. I instantly accept his offer.

I am at a loss as to why Vincent should be so keen to insinuate himself into our company. Might his compliments be sincere after all? I watch him lead the way across the square, his arm draped loosely around Richard's shoulder, like two teammates heading for the pitch. For his part Richard, usually so averse to another man's touch, makes no attempt to wriggle free. I leave Patricia to 'people watch', a neat way to dignify her nosiness, and walk over to join them, trailed by a pair of persistent pigeons.

As soon as they return to the square and I persuade Richard to put on his sunglasses, I suggest that we go up to the Rosary Basilica. We enter a building which in scale and decoration could not be more different from the underground basilica. It is indeed shaped like a rose, with its semicircle of richly ornamented side-chapels clustered like petals around the high altar. My eye is drawn to the monumental image of the Virgin above the apse, her girlish smile and undeveloped body highlighting the sublime yet terrifying fate to which she has been called. She is attended by a flight of inexpressive cherubs who, as in one of my favourite bedtime stories, seem to be waiting for birth to give them identity. Nostalgia turns to pain as I am seized by the thought of my own unborn children: the weight of emptiness within my womb. I quickly look up at the dome, with its garland of red, white, lilac and golden roses, before I betray myself to Vincent.

We walk around the side-chapels: Vincent and I examining the mosaics; Richard absorbed in the geometric patterns on the floor. Vincent mocks the picture-book piety of the images, but his censure fails to dampen my enthusiasm. On the contrary, I welcome the chance to champion the workmanship. My scope for comparison may be limited – to my regret, I have never been to Ravenna – but

I am able to judge it on its own worth. Not all art has to convey nuances and ambiguities. There is a place for direct viewpoints, primary colours and clear lines.

'We'll have to agree to differ or, rather, to diverge. You take the high art road and I take the low.'

My remark appears to shake his man-of-the-people persona and he hustles me outside and up the steps to the Upper Basilica. While Richard races ahead, Vincent resumes his banter. I refuse to oblige him by either leaping into his arms or playing the affronted wife. Instead I stop short, reminding him that I am here for a purpose and will not be deflected. 'You and I come from different worlds. You have your reason for being here; I have mine.'

'Which is?'

'A miracle.'

At last I have voiced the word out loud. Up till now, whenever I mentioned Lourdes I made it sound like Bath or Baden-Baden, where the water has medicinal properties; for the first time I have proclaimed its miraculous ones. People have been cured here of many hopeless conditions and they can – they will – be again. Moreover, if the cure derives from God's grace rather than the pilgrim's merits, who is to say that He won't choose Richard?

Vincent, however, will not be appeased, attacking first the premise and then the probability of a cure. He stresses how few there have been over the years, fumbling for the exact number, until a priest leaning over the parapet comes to his aid.

'Sixty-seven.'

Vincent seems as taken aback as I am by Father Humphrey's intervention. My initial amazement that he has made the climb gives way to fear of what he will think on seeing me tête-à-tête with a man who is not my husband. Moreover, having caught the last part of our conversation, he is bound to associate me with Vincent's scepticism. As they argue over definitions, I deplore the concern for other peoples' good opinion that not only reveals my inherent shallowness but makes me unworthy of the smallest miracle.

Leaving Father Humphrey to contemplate the view, we enter the Crypt, passing down a long corridor covered with ex voto plaques. 'Tributes from all our satisfied customers,' Vincent says with a smile.

Richard opts to walk with his neck bent back and his eyes fixed on the vaulted ceiling, forcing several people, including a woman with a pushchair, to scatter. Once inside, I leave him with Vincent, whose readiness to help says far more about his regard for me than any amount of talk. I am gripped by an overwhelming urge to pray and, refusing to feel inhibited, step into a small side-chapel. Kneeling at the rail, I acknowledge that the only good opinion I require is God's and implore His forgiveness. My Amen coincides with the click of a camera. I spring back to find an Asian tourist sprawled on the floor, taking my picture.

I feel indignant and defiled, but his deep bow as he returns to his group pre-empts my protests. I am disturbed that he should have chosen me over all the other worshippers and hurry back to Vincent and Richard.

'All done?' I ask Vincent. 'I'd hate to drag you away.'

'I'm infinitely draggable.'

I take Richard's hand, thankful for his compliance, and lead the way outside and into the Upper Basilica, a drab grey building in which even the ubiquitous plaques lack the marbled richness of those in the Crypt. I walk down the nave, motioning the men to follow. Vincent complains about the obscure design of the stained glass.

'They tell the story of Our Lady,' I say, examining the windows. 'See, there's Pius IX proclaiming the dogma of the Immaculate Conception. And there she's appearing to Bernadette.'

'You have to look very closely,' Vincent says.

'Isn't that what you expect when people watch your films?'

Pleased with myself, I steer Richard towards the sanctuary, where he is drawn to the array of Sacred Hearts dotting the walls.

'Will you be my Valentine?'

'I beg your pardon?'

'My Valentine,' he repeats, pointing at one of the Hearts.

'Oh!' I reply, dismayed. 'Aren't I already?'

Searching in vain for Vincent, I wonder whether he has grown bored with the church or with us. Surprised by my own concern, I tear Richard away from the hearts and towards the porch, where we find Vincent waiting.

———

'Are you all right?' I ask. 'I looked round and you were gone.'

'I'm sorry. I didn't mean to alarm you. It was my mobile.' He taps his trouser pocket, and I feel something inside me stir. 'Sophie rang. The Grotto procession is about to start.'

We make our way down the ramp in the full glare of the midday sun and spot the Jubilates flocking around the drinking fountains, their lime green sweatshirts clashing with the verdant landscape beyond.

'Thank you for letting me tag along,' Vincent says. 'I really enjoyed it. Now I'd better get down to some work.'

'Thank *you* for looking after Richard. He appreciated it.'

'And you?'

'I appreciated it too.'

Drawing Richard away from the taps, I join Patricia, who is chatting to Maggie and Charlotte.

'Are you feeling well, Gillian?' she asks. 'You look a bit flushed.'

'It's just the heat,' I say, covering my cheeks.

'It can be treacherous,' Maggie says. 'The first time I came here, with my niece, I told her: "You're lucky Aunt Maggie's a trained nurse."'

'Did you have a good time, darling?' Patricia asks Richard.

'We went into three churches.'

'That's nice,' she says distractedly.

'How many churches are there in the whole world?'

'I know there are 365 in Norwich,' Maggie says. 'Or is that pubs?'

Father Dave gathers us together for a brief introduction to the life of Bernadette. It has been familiar to me since school when, inspired by the annual showing of the classic film, I longed to follow her example and prove myself worthy of a similar visitation. Neither her abject poverty and cramped sleeping quarters, nor her illiteracy and ill health could dampen my zeal. It was a real-life Cinderella story, with a celestial Fairy Godmother and a divine Prince Charming. My fervour reached its height when I discovered that her exhumed body was incorrupt, just when my own was growing fleshy and assertive. I was sure that if Our Lady had appeared in Lourdes and Fatima, she could make her way to Reigate, but the nuns insisted that she would never choose such a heathen country, infested with atheists and Anglicans.

A tug on my sleeve drags me back to the present. 'Quick, let's get in the line,' Richard says. 'It's time to go through.'

'It's not a race.'

'I know that, but we can still be the first.'

We join the queue alongside Patricia and Maggie, a step behind the Polish couple with the docile baby. The woman smiles, while the man stares straight ahead.

'I don't like the grotty,' Richard says.

'Grotto, darling,' Patricia says. 'And you love it.'

'No, I don't,' he replies firmly. 'It's a grotty grotto.' Patricia looks pained; Maggie smiles supportively.

'It used to be very grotty,' Father Dave says, walking up to Richard. 'Though I don't think that's what gave it its name.' He laughs. 'It was the town rubbish dump. Which is why Bernadette came here scavenging for wood. What does that tell us today?'

'How do I know?' Richard asks tetchily.

'That we can find God in the most unexpected places.'

'Like toilets?'

'Richard!' his mother says, for once objecting to more than just the word.

'God is everywhere,' Father Dave says, brushing off the remark, 'in everything we are and do. Even our most basic human functions.' He moves away, leaving Richard bemused.

Vincent takes advantage of a break in filming to join us. 'I hope you'll forgive me monopolising your daughter-in-law,' he says to Patricia. 'But we were having a fascinating theological discussion.'

I flinch. Patricia may be many things but she is no fool. For all the allure of TV exposure, she can only be pushed so far. She steps aside with bad grace, leaving us to pick up our talk, although it is clear that Vincent has less interest in listening to my arguments than in convincing me of his. I am amazed by the ease with which I engage in the kind of intellectual debate that I usually find so intimidating. Far from bumbling inarticulately, I hear myself voicing thoughts that I have never consciously formulated. Moreover, while I may be unable to prove that the apparitions were genuine, the rapture on the pilgrims' faces as they approach the Grotto leaves me in no doubt of the genuine devotion that they have inspired.

Vincent's blanket cynicism starts to grate, and I am eager to shake it off before my own walk through the Grotto. So, leaving him to rejoin his crew, I stand back and wait for Richard and Patricia.

'You've remembered us at last,' Patricia says sourly.

'I was only a couple of steps ahead.'

'I'm not sure I care for your television friend. He's a bit too pleased with himself for my liking.'

'You were all over him yesterday.'

'Nonsense! I was just trying to put him at ease.'

As we arrive at the Grotto, Patricia walks in front, pressing her hand reverently to the rock face, prompting Richard to go one better, standing on tiptoe to touch the overhanging ledge and following it round as far as possible, as though rapt by a playground game. I walk behind, longing for some sort of epiphany, but my mind is racing and all I feel is a blast of damp air. No sooner have we reached the end than Patricia announces that she must return to the Acceuil to prepare for lunch.

'Would you rather go with your mother or sit here quietly with me?' I ask Richard.

'Are you praying?'

'Half.'

'I'll go back.' He kisses me softly on the cheek and moves off with Patricia. As I watch them cross the bridge, I feel an unexpected rush of compassion. I bow my head, but my prayers and thoughts are pulling in opposite directions. I may have held my own in conversation with Vincent, but he has vanquished me the moment I close my eyes. Contrite and confused, I return to the Acceuil, welcoming lunch as a kind of penance. No Ash Wednesday fast could be more exacting than a mealtime with Frank and Sheila Clunes.

After a statutory rest, we head back through the Domain to the hillside behind the basilicas to walk the Way of the Cross. Patricia has opted out, deeming the path too steep for 'these old legs', a phrase that drew an unsavoury chuckle from Richard. Several of the older pilgrims have followed suit but, despite Louisa's warnings about the rough terrain, there are three Jubilate wheelchairs.

'More work for the Lourdes mountain rescue team,' she says, shaking her head.

'Is there such a thing?'

'You're looking at it,' she replies, before signalling to Father Paul that he should start.

I glance at the crew filming Kevin and feel a flicker of envy that is especially unworthy when I should be meditating on the Cross. I contemplate the first station but, whether because I am still under Vincent's influence, respond to it aesthetically rather than spiritually, finding the drab bronze tableau as artificial as the glade in which it stands. The universal gospel should adapt to any setting but, far from being timeless, the stiff figures in their Roman robes seem anachronistic and, far from transforming the world, the Passion story looks lost in the landscape, an insignificant adjunct to the beauty all around.

I walk on, preoccupied.

'Brace yourself, Bridget!' Richard whispers in my ear.

'What?'

'That's what he says.'

'Who?'

'The Irishman!'

'Oh, I see. Very good.' I force a laugh.

'That's wrong.'

'The joke?'

'No, you! You shouldn't laugh when you don't think it's funny. Like being friends with someone you don't like.'

'I'm sorry. My mind was – '

'It's wrong!'

My guilt increased, I plod on. As we reach the seventh station, I dismiss the thought that I too am weighed down by a cross. But as Richard drags his heels, complaining about heat, tiredness and 'digestion', leading me to half-cajole, half-drag him up the hill, the burden becomes unbearable.

Father Paul truncates the prayers in consideration of the oncoming groups, but his courtesy is not reciprocated. We are brought to a halt by a party of Asian pilgrims who linger at the ninth station. When they finally set off, Linda has trouble getting Brenda's wheelchair to move. I wonder whether to lend a hand but, thankfully, Matt steps in first.

'Do you want some help?'

'No, we don't!' Brenda snaps. '£53.10 a week carer's allowance she's paid. And what does she do for it? Sweet FA!'

I feel my cheeks sting, but Linda seems unruffled. 'Yak, yak, yak! Miss High and Mighty. I'd like to see you try to get by without me.'

'Ladies, please!' Father Paul hurries over. 'Is there a problem?'

'It's him!' Brenda nods at Matt who stands, nonplussed. 'Sticking his filthy mitts all over my chair. "Do you want some help?" I know their help. Give them an inch!'

'An inch!' Linda repeats smugly.

'First, it's the chair; next thing, their hands are everywhere. They think I can't feel anything but I can.' She rounds on Matt. 'I can!'

'But I never touched you,' he says, ashen-faced.

'No, we know. No harm done,' Father Paul reassures him, before turning back to Brenda. 'But if you do need help, perhaps one of the handmaidens, or me?'

'Let her do it,' Brenda says. 'Lazy cow! Look!' She nods at the tableau in front of her. 'Our Lord flat on the ground, pinned down by the Cross. And Simon of Cyrene holding up the end as if nothing's wrong. That's you, Madam,' she screeches at Linda, 'Simon of bloody Cyrene!'

'Yak, yak, yak,' Linda says blithely. 'It's like she's slowly sinking in cement. It's swallowing her up bit by bit. Pity it's not reached her mouth.'

'I heard that!'

'You were meant to.'

Richard watches them, as engrossed as by a row on reality TV. I pull him away, for fear that someone should accuse him of involvement. Father Paul steps forward and leads us in prayer: 'Lord, help each of us to accept the cross that is our lot, be it pain, illness, betrayal or bereavement. Give us the grace to know that You are carrying it with us so that we can move on with You to new life. Amen.'

We continue along the path but, despite vowing to treat the camera as if it were CCTV, I find myself drawn to it at the twelfth station on seeing Kevin tear off his microphone in mid-interview and stomp down the hill. I wonder what Vincent can have said to provoke him, but as I walk across to find out, a more assertive Gillian takes my place.

'Another of your fans?'

'Have you been watching me?'

'No, just the camera. For us ordinary mortals, it's as compulsive as a car crash.'

'I wouldn't want to put you off your prayers.'

'Now don't spoil it!' I say, disarmed by the gentle teasing. 'I'm here to apologise for this morning.'

'No, I'm the one who should apologise. I don't know what got into me. I don't usually come on so strong.'

Honour is satisfied on both sides, but I am conscious of a very different conversation taking place beneath the words. I linger in defiance of all my good intentions until I find that the prayers have ended and Father Paul is leading the Jubilates down the hill. I am left behind, my distraction doubly culpable as I gaze at a weeping Mary Magdalene.

Eager to return to the path, I refuse Vincent's offer of a drink and, grabbing Richard, who stands spinning on the spot, hurry to rejoin the group.

'Ow!' Richard protests, 'you're making me dizzy.'

'*I'm* making you dizzy?' I reply, deflecting my frustration. 'You're the one going round in circles – I'm walking in a straight line.'

I recite the prayers at the thirteenth and fourteenth stations, but am reduced to silence by the fifteenth: *Jesus is Risen from the Dead*; which is represented simply by a rough-hewn stone rolled away from the rock. The landscape is no longer the backdrop to the story; it is the story. The biblical figures have been abandoned and we are the living witnesses, not to a historical event but to an eternal mystery that is re-enacted every day. I long to share my excitement with Vincent, but I am aware that my responsibilities lie elsewhere and, quashing any sense of disappointment, steer Richard back down the hill and through the Domain.

We return to the Acceuil and go straight to dinner, which is slightly more tolerable than breakfast and lunch, if only because the distaste for salad shared by three of my four fellow diners makes the meal that much shorter. The fourth seems not to care what he eats so long as it is well chewed. After a brief coffee break during which Richard and Nigel play an anarchic game of ludo, we make our way to the St Bernadette Chapel for the Penitential Service.

'Another church, another concrete monstrosity,' Vincent whispers, as he greets us at the entrance. 'Have you thought about my offer?'

'What offer's that?' Patricia asks sharply.

'They want to interview me after the service.'

'Don't forget to mention the Holy Redeemer. Father Aidan will appreciate it.'

Patricia flashes Vincent a smile, which I fear that he will take as genuine, and ushers us into a building which is even less attractive inside. Rows of utilitarian benches face a stark wooden dais backed by olive green screens. A cat's cradle of steel piping covers the ceiling with, above the altar, a huge disc with the crucified Christ. Father Humphrey leads a service which supplies much of the warmth that the decor lacks. The hymns, sung to the slightly discordant strumming of two young brancardiers, are once again conducted by Fiona, with her flexible baton. After a wildly uncoordinated version of 'Guide me, O thou great Redeemer', Father Dave steps forward to deliver a sermon on the three 'p's of pilgrimage: prayer; perseverance; penitence.

'We all say our prayers, don't we?'

'I do,' Nigel says, to a roar of laughter.

'And we all persevere on our journey towards God? That's not a question you need answer out loud.'

'I do,' Nigel repeats, to a similar response.

'But the most important of the three is penitence: to admit that we are miserable sinners who are dependent on God's grace. And what lies at the heart of sin? Think for a moment how it's spelt: S – I – N. What's the letter at the centre? *I*. And the letter at the centre of the word is at the centre of the deed. I'm the one who's responsible for sin. It's putting myself first instead of God. So now let's acknowledge what we are, both to God and to one another. Put up your hands if you're a sinner!' Fathers Humphrey and Paul, who are with him on the dais raise their hands to a murmur of approval. A young brancardier thrusts up both of his, despite his friend's attempt to

234

pull one down. Richard waves his right hand as if trying to attract attention (is it Father Dave's or God's?). Patricia lifts her arm at the elbow as though her mild arthritis exempts her from such emphatic profession of sin as everyone else. The entire congregation is a forest of hands, with one exception. His cameraman has his hand in the air; his sound recordist has her hand in the air; his producer has her hand in the air; his own hands lie clasped in his lap.

At a stroke I feel my sympathies transformed. Is this the epiphany for which I yearned at the Grotto? Far from condemning his defiance, I am full of admiration for his resolve. This is a man who will not put profit over principle or convenience over conscience; this is a man who will not be swayed by emotion or led by the crowd. And, while it may be reading too much into a single gesture, the 'I' at the centre of sin has never felt more certain. This is a man who has broken the ice of my heart.

At the end of the service I seek out Derek, who is escorting Nigel back to the Acceuil. He agrees to take Richard, who has no qualms about deserting his wife in favour of his friend. I walk up to Vincent, who is talking to Sophie in the vestibule.

'So,' he says. 'Are you giving in to temptation?'

'Must you put it like that?'

'Subtlety has never been his strong point,' Sophie says.

'Judas!' Vincent says, with a flourish.

'Have fun,' Sophie says, walking off.

'We intend to.'

'It's only a drink,' I say firmly. 'There can be no harm in that.'

'It depends whether you're putting the *i* in inebriation or the *u* in drunk. Shall we go?'

We make our way through the Domain, past the huge Torchlight procession in which we are due to take part tomorrow. As we weave through the crowd, Vincent is sunk in thought, and I wonder whether he already regrets having invited me. We reach St Joseph's Gate but, instead of heading for one of the nearby cafés, he leads me deeper into the town.

'Is that one over there no good?'

'We're going to a hotel.'

'Not yours?' I ask, more primly than I intend.

'No, not mine,' he replies with a smile. 'The Gallia Londres. It was your mother-in-law who put me on to it. She says it's the best in Lourdes.'

I refrain from pointing out that, like so many of Patricia's recommendations, it will be based on hearsay rather than experience, and follow him into an old-fashioned lobby, lined with plush armchairs and display cabinets crammed with antique china.

'I presume we can have a drink without staying here?' he asks warily.

'There's an easy way to find out,' I reply, walking over to check with the receptionist. 'Yes, it's fine,' I report back.

'You speak French?'

'Passably. And you?'

'Don't ask. Not that it matters here. You don't need a French phrasebook in Lourdes, just a medical dictionary.'

'Are you always this hard on everyone?'

'Usually. But I'm even harder on myself.'

We walk through an anteroom hung with nineteenth-century prints of religious orders into a spacious bar, decorated with heavy chandeliers, festooned columns, Empire furniture and urns of drooping lilies. We take our seats, and a waitress in a low-cut blouse better suited to her granddaughter fetches our drinks. Vincent downs his double whisky in two gulps, and I am perturbed to find Patricia's anti-Irish prejudices popping into my head. He summons the waitress for a refill.

'I hope it's not anything I've done,' I say quickly.

'Of course not. Well, maybe by association. That bloody service.'

'Ah that.'

'Yes that. At the end, when I was waiting for you – just on the off-chance – I saw this guy, Dennis, I don't know if you've met him: early twenties, light brown hair, motor-neurone disease, in a wheelchair.'

'There are several …'

'Quite. Just one of many. Which is why I didn't pick him to interview. He was waiting for one of the brancs to push him back to the Acceuil. He looked miserable, so I asked what was wrong. He answered in that tortuous way: you know, as if every word had its roots twisted around his gut.' I nod. 'It turned out to be what Father

Paul had said about everyone going to confession at least once during the pilgrimage. Dennis couldn't think of any sins to confess. "That's all right, mate," I said, "I'll give you some of mine." But he couldn't see the joke. He's terrified that, with nothing to confess, he can't be absolved and he'll be shut out of heaven.'

'That's very sad – '

'Sad! It's tragic. He's a young man. He should be sinning all over the place, but he's paralysed. He can't touch himself, let alone anyone else.'

'But he's the exception. It doesn't apply to the rest of us.'

'Doesn't it? I don't believe in God but if I did, I'd give Him far more credit than the Church does. Can you think of any more loathsome creed than that God created the world to reflect His own glory, for which He demands our constant praise? That's not love; it's narcissism to the nth degree! When you give someone a present, you don't wrap it up in a load of conditions. You want them to enjoy it to the full, to make it their own.'

'You can't argue against God from an analogy.'

'Well, you sure as Hell can't argue for Him from the facts! Look at all the suffering in the world.' As the waitress brings him his drink, I wonder whether his interest in me is primarily as a sparring partner. 'I promise you, I'll just say this one thing and then I'll shut up.'

'You'll just say this one thing and then you'll be blotto.'

'Trust me, it takes more than a couple of whiskies.' He drinks more moderately than before. 'Where was I? Oh yes, suffering. Good Catholics like you – I mean good people who happen to be Catholics, not good Catholics who happen to be people – spend their lives trying to work out how God can allow us to suffer. And, as I pointed out to Father Paul this morning, nowhere do you see that suffering more vividly than in Lourdes. Instead of tying yourself in knots trying to defend the indefensible, why not look at it the other way and ask how, with so much suffering, you can allow yourself to believe in God?'

'I won't give you the standard answer that, if there were no suffering, free will wouldn't have any meaning.'

'No, please don't.'

'But, after Richard's haemorrhage, a priest – yes, I'm sorry; it was a priest and not a therapist or a counsellor – said something that has helped me a great deal over the years. He said that pain and suffering were necessary to remind ourselves that there's another life beyond this one: to stop us becoming complacent and accepting second-best.'

'Next time you see him – I trust that he's still in good health (I'd hate to think of him suffering) – '

'What is it that makes you so angry?'

'Tell him that there are some of us who are quite happy to settle for second-best so long as we can enjoy it, and those we love – and even those we don't love – can enjoy it too: some of us who believe that life is meant for living, not for saving up for some eternal pension plan.'

'That sounds like a recipe for hedonism.'

'And what's wrong with that? *Hedonism* has such negative connotations in a culture shaped by Christianity, but wanting – and giving – pleasure can be a very positive thing.'

'I suppose it depends what you mean by *pleasure*. Some people find it in living for other people.'

'Do you?'

'I never think about it,' I reply, anxious to remain detached. 'I don't have any choice. Richard requires constant attention. What should I do? Put him in a home and walk away?'

'No. That is it's not for me to say.'

'No, it's not – it's really not. My life may be a shadow of what it was – of what it could be – but it's not nearly such a shadow as his. When we married, I vowed to love him in sickness as well as in health. Is sickness limited to something quick like cancer or a coronary? Is permanent brain damage excluded by the small print?' I stand and start to leave. He grabs hold of my hand.

'Forgive me,' he says. 'Please don't go. Not like this. Sit down. Have another drink. Please.' I waver.

'It's still tomato juice. That's not changed.'

'Anything you like.' He summons the waitress and orders more drinks.

'It may surprise you to learn that peoples' lives aren't a television programme you can shoot and edit at will,' I say, as she walks away. 'You've known me for two days – you don't know me at all.'

'I know you're not happy.'

'No, really? My husband has lost half his brain cells – should I be jumping for joy?'

'Isn't there something you could do just for you? Do you have no unfulfilled ambitions?'

'Yes, to dance Sleeping Beauty. Now for your next trick ...'

'That's fascinating! Tell me more. How old were you when you first knew?'

'About the age Richard is now. I went to classes for years, but it all came unstuck when I hit puberty. Boobs.'

'I see.' His gaze is sympathetic rather than prurient.

'They grew too big. I tried starving myself, but they just went on growing. You've no idea what it's like being fourteen and a size 32D. The sneers from the other girls; the assumptions from the boys; the suspicion from my mother, who was convinced they'd lure me into sin.'

'And did they?'

'Only the shallow end.'

'I'm sorry.'

'So you should be. But thanks for asking. I don't often get the chance to talk these days. They say widows have it bad once the first wave of sympathy dies down. In my case that was about ten years ago.'

'You can talk to me.'

'I thought I was.'

'I mean *talk* talk.' He looks at me with all the seriousness of a six-year-old, but a six-year-old who is the antithesis of Richard.

'What about you? I've owned up to my Margot Fonteyn fantasies. Did you want to be a TV director as a boy?'

'As a boy, I didn't have a TV. I grew up in a town where people would gather outside Radio Rentals in the evenings to watch the sets flickering in the window. There was no sound, but they still stood there. What does that tell you? That they were poor? That they were sheep? That a picture's worth a thousand words?'

'Where was this?'

'Barnsley. In Yorkshire.'

'But your family's Irish?'

'My great-grandfather came over to work in the pits in the 1880s. It's still a source of deep shame to my mother. My dad sat at a colliery desk all his life, but he might as well have come home black with dust.'

'She can't have had an easy life.'

'She didn't make it any easier. She was – she is – a bright woman, but I never saw her read a book, just the *Dowry of Mary* and *Catholic Fireside* magazines with their syrupy stories of wise old priests and plucky Irish nursemaids. Her life has always revolved round the church. She loves all the festivals, but it's funerals that are her real treat. She just needs to sit next to you on the bus and she's on her knees beside your coffin. "I go to pay my respects," she says. The only superiority she feels safe to show is over the dead.'

'Do you have any brothers or sisters?'

'Neither. She took one look at me and decided to cut her losses. Shortly before he died, my dad told me she'd had such a difficult labour that the doctor advised them not to risk another. I'd take a bet she held a gun to his head.'

'You make her sound very strong-willed.'

'Let's just say she visits the doctor when she wants a second opinion.'

'What about friends?'

'What about them?'

'Does she have many?'

'A few fellow parishioners. Bitter, unfulfilled women working out their frustrations on their families. Not that my mother's the worst.' His eyes glisten. 'I had a friend (this is hard!). When he was twelve or thirteen, his mother caught him jacking off with his dog in his bedroom. I mean the dog was in the bedroom, not that he was jacking off the dog.'

'Yes, of course.' I smile wanly.

'First thing next morning his mother went to the priest and asked him what she should do about it. "Get rid of the dog," he said. Now, let's give him the benefit of the doubt. He may have meant: "Put a card in a newsagent's window", but she took him at his word. That afternoon, when my friend came home from school, he found she'd been to the vet and had it put down.'

'But the dog wasn't to blame!'

'Neither was my friend! Though he got his revenge. He had a Saturday job in the abattoir and a cousin who was an altar boy. And ... well, I expect you can guess the rest. They switched the blood with the communion wine. So on Sunday morning when the priest took a swig – and I mean a swig, no symbolic sip for him – he spat it out all over the sanctuary.'

'You're making it up!'

'I swear, on my mother's life.'

I weigh up the oath. 'Where is he now – your friend, not the priest?'

'I've no idea. We lost touch when I moved down to university. Sussex.'

'To study film?'

'Politics. I wanted to change the world. Don't laugh. Not that there was much politics left in 1985. To have changed anything at all, I should have read economics. So when I got my degree, I took the classic route of the impotent Leftie and joined the BBC. I've worked for it one way or another ever since.'

I note that he has said nothing about his private life and wonder if it is an established strategy to draw out others while revealing as little as possible about himself. 'Is there a Mrs O'Shaughnessy?' I ask tentatively.

'You mean, apart from my mother?' He gives me a wry smile.

'Yes.'

'There was once. Celia.'

'That's a lovely name.'

'She was a lovely person. I still find it hard to talk about her. She was so perfect, I couldn't imagine what she saw in me. Even her parents made me feel at home, well as much as they could given that they own a large chunk of Lincolnshire. They see themselves as bastions of tradition – in every sense. Her father's more likely to buy a new coat for his horse than for his wife. The first time we met, he told me he'd worn the same jacket for twenty-five years. I thought that meant he was proud of his figure ... We still keep in touch. They send me a smoked salmon every Christmas.' He laughs mirthlessly.

'Even though you and Celia are divorced?'

'Who told you that?'

'No one. I just assumed.' To my horror I realise that he may be widowed.

'And you're quite right! Vincent O'Shaughnessy: a man so impossible no woman can bear to stick around!'

'Not at all. But the world you move in: the late hours, the hothouse atmosphere.'

'Yes, the stresses and strains of a media marriage … if only things were that simple! Still, Celia's well out of it. And there's no one who wants her to be happy more than me. She's married to the kind of man she should have gone for first time round. They live in a hunting lodge near Inverness with their two children, Rob and Fergus (I'm glad at least they're boys). I hear occasional news of them from my former mother-in-law. I think she thinks she's being kind.'

'What about you? Did you and Celia have no children?'

'Yes one: a daughter.'

'Does she live with her mother?'

'She's dead.'

'Oh no, I'm so sorry. I had no idea.'

'Don't worry, it's fine. Well it's not, of course; it's not fine at all, but that's life. She was knocked down in Battersea eight years ago. She was six.'

'A car crash?' I ask, determined to avoid further misunderstanding.

'Yes. The doctors swore it was instantaneous. But were they telling me the truth or what I wanted to hear? I know she was dead by the time the police arrived, but who's to say that in those few short moments she didn't suffer unspeakable agonies?'

'And you?' I ask. 'Are you still suffering them now?'

'I'm forty-two. She was six.'

'A moment ago, when you were denouncing the Church, you said that the secret of life was to be happy.'

'Quite. But I never said that I'd found it.'

'Would you like another drink?'

'No thanks. Contrary to appearances, I'm not a complete soak. All I want is to sit here talking to you.'

'It's eleven fifteen, I really must go. They'll be wondering where I've got to.'

'I haven't spoken to anyone like this since Celia left. I haven't felt about anyone like this since Celia left.'

'Please don't say that.'

'Why not if it's true?'

'It means I have to respond. And the only possible answer is "no".'

'You haven't heard the question.'

'I don't need to. We've only just met.'

'What was it our saintly director said yesterday? "What we do in Lourdes is God's gift to us. What we do to one another while we're here is our gift to God."'

'You don't believe in God.'

'But I do believe in one another. And I believe – I know – that we have something: an energy, a bond, call it what you will. I'm sitting three feet away from you but I can feel the beat of your heart, the rush of your blood.'

I too feel the bond, although I am less certain of its effect. Then, before I can object, he leans across the table and seals it. I am both relieved and affronted, as when a nurse plunges a needle into my vein while still seeming to swab the skin.

'You shouldn't have done that.'

'Why not? The pilgrimage rules talk of protecting vulnerable people. You can take care of yourself.'

'Can I?'

'And if you can't, I know someone who'll gladly apply for the post.'

'I must go,' I say, standing. 'Don't worry, I'm not offended. But I am late.'

'I'll walk you back.'

'There's no need. This is one town where a woman alone at night is safe.'

'Not according to the proprietor of my hotel. She claims that the streets are full of marauding gypsies.'

'I'll take the risk. I really need to clear my head before I go back to Richard.'

'Of course,' he says quietly.

'I've had a lovely evening. Truly. And I hope we can do it again. But in company, not on our own. And please, when you see me tomorrow, don't mention any of this.'

'Should I pretend to have forgotten your name?'

'I'm serious. Think of us as strangers on a train who've opened up our hearts during a long journey.'

'A journey that will last another three days.'

'But one of us has already changed seats. Believe me, it's for the best.'

'No, it's not. But if that's what you want.'

'Thank you.'

As I move away, I wonder whether returning his kiss, albeit on the cheek, would be a gesture of goodwill or a provocation. Suspecting the latter, I give him my cheeriest smile and leave.

VINCENT

Thursday June 19

Any hope that Jamie might have kept his mouth shut is dashed as I approach the table. 'I didn't know you were a fan of Mendelssohn,' I say, cutting through a snatch of the 'Wedding March'.

'Just getting in some practice, chief!' he replies.

'So,' I say, eager to avoid Sophie's and Jewel's pointed glances, 'what's on the menu this morning? Croissant and cereal?'

'How did you guess? Though I'm sure if you told them you need to replenish your strength,' Sophie says wryly, 'they'd be able to rustle up some sausages or a steak tartare.'

Jewel squirms.

'I doubt Madame BJ would approve of that.'

'She wouldn't want you flopping about – ' Jamie leaves an excruciating pause – 'before a busy day.'

'No need to worry about me,' I reply, refusing to feel inhibited.

'That's not what I heard.'

'What did you hear, Jewel? I'm all ears.'

'Far be it from me to listen to idle gossip. '

'Perish the thought!'

'But Jamie said you knocked on his door.'

'Hammered on it. Practically broke it down.'

'Right. Hammered on his door in the middle of the night, desperate for a condom.'

'And?'

'Which rather suggests that you had company … female company.'

'Not necessarily,' Jamie says.

'Oh please!' Jewel says, rolling her eyes.

'I don't see why it should suggest that I had company of either sex. There are plenty of other uses for a condom.'

'Right,' Sophie says. 'You had something stuck in your teeth and you'd run out of dental floss.'

'No, no!' Jewel says. 'He'd cut his finger and wanted a waterproof bandage.'

'No,' Sophie says. 'He wanted to blow one up for a draught excluder.'

'No, no – ' Jamie says.

'He wanted to make a hot pad for a stubbed toe!' Jewel says.

'No, no – ' Jamie says.

'He wanted to store the candle wax from the Torchlight procession!' Sophie says.

'No, no,' Jamie says. We all look at him expectantly. 'You've made me lose my thread!'

'Enough!' I say. 'All right, I admit it – I had someone with me last night. Now can we drop the subject? As for you …' I turn to Jamie. 'Is it too much to expect a little discretion?'

'What do you mean, chief? There were four other blokes in the room, two of them priests!'

'Why? Did Father Humphrey say something?'

'Didn't he just! You sure put the kibosh on the game. First thing today he's going to round up all the women, plus a couple of the tastier brancs.' He pulls a face at Jewel. 'And force them on pain of … you know, sounds like extermination.'

'Excommunication?' Jewel says.

'That's it – *excommunication*, to fess up which one of them it was.'

'You're having me on?' I ask, feeling nauseous.

'You should have heard him! "Not in all my time in Lourdes … bringing the pilgrimage into disrepute …!" He wants you both on the next flight home.'

Two thousand years of Church repression are embodied in a single priest. I am planning how best to defend myself and to protect Gillian, when Sophie intervenes. 'Don't be a brute, Jamie. Can't you see he's really worried?'

'What?' I ask.

'Honest, chief, look at you!' Jamie says. 'Father Humph was pissing himself. He said it was the best laugh he's had in years.'

Not sure whether to hug him or hit him, I compromise by tapping my spoon on the crown of his head which, to the delight of Jewel and Sophie, gives off a faintly metallic ring. I move to the cornflake queue, where my paranoia returns when the middle-aged man in front winks at me. To my relief, I realise that he has a severe tic.

I rejoin the crew who are busy speculating on the identity of my companion.

'So who is she then?' Jamie asks me. 'One of the handmaidens? A couple of them are quite well-stacked.'

'Thanks for that, Jamie!' Jewel says. 'They're women, not supermarket shelves.'

'They're also young enough to be my daughters.'

'I didn't say *young handmaidens*,' Jamie says defensively. 'I'm not ageist.'

'But it wasn't one of the handmaidens, was it, Vincent? Or one of the *malades*. More like someone in between.' Sophie's voice tells me that she knows and her smile that she approves.

'You don't mean Linda?' Jamie asks. 'She's in between. Here, you're not the filling in a lesbo sandwich?'

'Linda and Brenda are …' The word *partners* dies on my lips as I realise that fidelity is not my strong suit. 'Gay.'

'That wouldn't bother Jamie,' Sophie says. 'He'll go for anything with a pulse.'

'Yeah yeah!'

'Forget the pulse,' Jewel says. 'I spoke to Frankie Sewell, the AD on the pathology doc. She said that by the end of the shoot there was a distinct whiff of formaldehyde about him.'

'Enough now!' I say, feeling sullied by association. 'I'll tell you her name – Sophie's already guessed it – but I swear that if one of you so much as breathes it, Jamie Proud, I'll personally cut your balls off, and hand them to Father Humphrey on a communion plate.'

'Cross my heart and hope to die!'

'It's Gillian Patterson.'

'But she's …'

'Yes?'

'She's great,' he says, a moment too late. It does not augur well when even Jamie's first thought is that she is married.

'You will be careful,' Jewel says, proving that of the three she is the one who is genuinely concerned for me. 'We wouldn't want you to get hurt.'

'I promise. Besides, I may not see her again on the pilgrimage, let alone once we leave.' Even as I speak, I am drawing up a plan of campaign. 'We have a packed schedule.'

'Not this afternoon,' Jamie says.

'It's earmarked for an interview with one Gillian Patterson,' Sophie says.

'She hasn't yet agreed to take part.'

I let the rest of the conversation waft over me as I finish my cereal, desperate to keep the vanilla scent of her skin and the lemony tang of her hair from being swamped by the burnt, dark smell of the coffee. I struggle to wipe the broad grin off my face as I relive our lovemaking. It has been so long since I looked to anyone for more than temporary relief that I had forgotten the joy and peace and the extraordinary intimacy that can seep through a woman's skin. How remarkable that an act of adultery should relieve me of so much guilt!

The thought lingers to mock me. Given my previous record, I would be wise to stop trying to anticipate the future and allow myself to enjoy the present. But there is something in me – in us (no, I lost the right to generalise when I boarded up my heart after the crash) – that refuses to trust my happiness to chance.

The waitress pours me a cup of coffee which Sophie, looking at her watch, tells me that I have no time to drink. I take two scalding gulps before we hurry down to the lobby and make our way to the Acceuil. It is hard to fix my mind on work, but at least we are spared another service since we are taking a tour of the town's monuments led by Father Dave. A quick glance reveals Gillian prominent among the assembled Jubilates, although her yellow top is eclipsed by Patricia's pink trouser suit and Maggie's *I ♥ Bernadette* T-shirt. As if by magic she meets my gaze, turning the surrounding hubbub to the trill of birdsong.

'Let's be having you all please,' Ken says, eager as ever to whip us into shape. 'The *malades* and their carers in front. The rest of us forming an orderly line behind. Father Dave is ready to start.'

I watch Gillian chatting with Lester and Tess and, to my surprise, feel no urge to join them. Unlike yesterday, when the so-near-yet-so-far frustration left me desperate for the least contact, I am content just to see her enjoying their company; to admire her affability and charm, while knowing that I alone have witnessed the other side of her: the passionate lover giving herself, body and soul. When she stifles a yawn, I am thrilled to be the only one to realise why she is tired. 'Richard had a rough night,' I hear her say, deceit adding an edge to romance. My head tells me that every one of the fifty or so pilgrims on the walk has a claim to her attention; my heart tell me that she exists only for me.

Father Dave approaches me as we cross the Esplanade. 'Do you know the story of this statue?' he asks, pointing to the Crowned Virgin.

'No,' I say, wondering why every statue in Lourdes has to have a story when such a wealth of human stories abounds.

'It originally pointed the other way, towards St Michael's Gate, but on its very first night it turned to face the Grotto and has done ever since.'

'Is this some sort of wind-up?'

'Not at all. It's been well documented.'

'How? I don't recall any CCTV footage in those days, so were there photographs taken before and after? Not that they'd prove anything. Bored kids – I suppose they have them in Lourdes – could have sneaked in and switched it round.'

'All I can do is give you the facts – it's up to you what you make of them. The legend goes that, if you say three Hail Marys in front of it, then you'll be sure to return.'

'Have you?'

'Of course. Every time. And it hasn't failed me yet.'

We walk to St Joseph's Gate, where we film the Jubilates streaming out of the Domain; footage which, even as we shoot it, I know will end up on the cutting room floor. After last night I am more determined than ever to focus on the essentials. All the painters and poets (not to mention, their biographers), who make heartfelt pleas for the primacy of love, have long struck me as disingenuous, seeking to justify the hours that they spend between the sheets rather than at their easels or desks. Not any more! Love transforms not just the artist but his work. Women – I don't claim to be either balanced or inclusive – not only touch the heart, ravish the senses and fire the spirit, but concentrate the mind. Far from creating a distraction, Gillian will inspire me to greater things.

I laugh, which to my embarrassment comes at the exact moment that Fiona, having slipped away from her parents to measure

Martin's leg, gets the tip of the tape caught in his open fly. The two mothers, Mary and Claire, vie with each other in a pantomime of apology. Although Fiona's eagerness to measure the world must bear some relation to her failure to understand it, I wonder why she should have a particular fondness for inside legs. Are they simply at a convenient height, or is there a darker impulse at work which, in later life, will transform a harmless eccentricity into a dangerous obsession?

Determined to arouse no one's suspicion – let alone Jamie's and Jewel's mockery – I cast a sidelong glance at Gillian, who is deep in conversation with Sophie. I am surprised to see them together and wonder, with a mixture of excitement and alarm, whether they are talking about me. No sooner have I spotted them than Sophie slips away and joins us outside a shop selling rosaries the size of flagellants' chains. While Father Dave leads the group across the bridge, I risk a fuller look at Gillian who, with her usual intuition, returns it with a flustered smile. I direct her attention to the four nondescript tents on the opposite bank. Pace Madame BJ, I would offer their occupants not just the run but the freedom of the town. From now on, whatever the election, I shall vote for the party that offers the best deal for gypsies. Like a rambler campaigning for the right to roam, I shall fight for the rights of Roma! So what if they made me pay over the odds for the condoms? This is Lourdes; miracles do not come cheap.

We arrive at Bernadette's birthplace where, feeling constrained by the crowded courtyard, I tell Jamie to switch off the camera and enjoy the tour. Not even proximity to Gillian, however, can reconcile me to Father Dave's paean to the Soubirous family who, despite injury, penury, industrial change and, worst of all, the death of a child, are cast as first cousins to the Waltons. At the end of his homily, Father Dave asks us to pray for today's families as 'the place where we learn our Christian values'. Watching Gillian bow her head, I acknowledge that Richard is not the only obstacle to our happiness. She may be praying for his health, world peace, or even for me, but I suspect that she is sticking to the brief. Longing for a glimpse inside her mind, I consider offering 'a penny for your prayers', only to reject it as in every sense mean, as well as uncomfortably close to standard practice.

A commotion at the door is a sign that not everything in Lourdes is designed for the disabled. Nigel is caught in the gap between the authentic past and the accessible present; Richard, undaunted, is trying to shove him through.

'I can push it. Like this. See.' He tilts Nigel's wheelchair.

'Just stop it, please!' Gillian says, taking me back a few hours to when she was the one left helpless with laughter as I discovered the sensitive spot behind her knee. 'You're keeping everyone waiting. Come in with me and catch up with Nigel later.'

'No. If Nigel can't go in, then I won't,' he says, with a blend of loyalty and spite.

Seeing Gillian's frustration, I am quick to intervene. 'Don't worry, mate. How about we do some filming inside and show it to you both? Give you a sneak preview.'

'Before Gilly?'

'Before anyone.'

'Yes please,' he says. 'Then we can see it all from out here.'

Shrugging off Gillian's thanks, which I trust will find more private expression later, I go in search of Jamie, whom I find sharing Maggie's 'filthy habit' behind the mill.

'There's been a slight change of plan. We are going to film inside the house after all.'

'But you said ...'

'I know. This isn't for public consumption. Nigel's wheelchair won't fit through the door so he and Richard are stuck outside. We'll show them the highlights on camera.'

'How thoughtful!' Maggie says. 'I knew the spirit of Lourdes would touch you in the end.'

'Yeah, it touched him in a big way last night,' Jamie says, as I drag him off. 'This Richard – he wouldn't happen to be Richard Patterson?' he asks, as soon as we are out of Maggie's earshot.

'And your point is?'

'Just asking. So you want me to put company property to your private use. Very dodgy. I'll have to square it with the Union. I know, I know – I've been meaning to join for years.'

'What would the Union say to a pint at lunchtime?'

'Make it two and you're on.'

I follow Jamie into the house, afraid that Gillian will have long since exhausted its limited appeal but, to my delight, she is standing at the top of the stairs, seemingly fascinated by the cracks in an ancient beam. I take advantage of the narrow landing to graze her thigh and, during a lull in the stream of visitors, am poised to steal a kiss when Patricia and Maggie arrive to thwart me. Addressing my remarks to them but my point to Gillian, I ask how human they like their saints. They reply with twee anecdotes about Bernadette's childhood, which are compounded by Maggie's prudery. I smile in disbelief at her 'you know whats'. The woman was a midwife! Did her patients give birth through their *front bottoms*?

We return outside, where Jamie is showing the footage of the house to Nigel for whom it all remains a blur.

'Don't mind him. He's a spastic,' Richard says lightly.

'You mustn't use that word!' Gillian says.

'You did!'

'I was speaking medically,' she replies, looking to Jamie and me for support. I shake my head in mock disapproval. I know how human I like my saints.

'I'm a spastic,' Nigel says, clapping his hands, to the amusement of a bevy of Belgian schoolgirls who file past with an escort of unusually indulgent nuns. Two of the girls giggle and point at Nigel. Maggie shoos them away, at which one sticks out a purple-stained tongue.

'Did you see that?' Maggie asks, outraged. 'I don't know what's got into young girls today!'

'I don't know what's got into the nuns,' Patricia says. 'If ever I misbehaved at school, I was given the ruler.'

As we walk the short distance to the Lacadé Mill, otherwise known as the *Maison Paternelle*, it is clear that, whatever the competition between the two mills during Bernadette's lifetime, it has intensified since her death. They flaunt their rival attractions: the one offering the room in which she was born; the other the bed in which her mother died and she herself slept on her last night in Lourdes. I am intrigued as to how today's Soubirous, who emphasise their relationship to the saint in the large family tree in the foyer, are viewed by their fellow citizens. Are they revered for the prosperity that their ancestor has brought to the town, or resented for their self-importance, like the couple in medieval Jerusalem who used to infuriate their neighbours by referring to the Virgin as 'Cousin Mary'?

Wandering around the cheerless rooms, I feel a tinge of pity for the vain attempt to generate interest in the few paltry objects left over from a lifetime of poverty. That soon evaporates when we reach the shop, which is in every sense the climax of the tour. The souvenirs themselves are no shoddier than those on sale elsewhere in town, but the setting highlights their commercialism. I rummage through the Bernadette handbells and nightlights, oven gloves and fridge magnets, pointing out the worst excesses to Gillian, who struggles to remain composed. To her marked relief I turn to Sophie, who is standing by the till sniffing a bar of cellophaned soap. 'I came for a cure for cancer and ended up with this lousy T-shirt,' I say, holding up a garish *Our Lady of Lourdes*.

A cuckoo clock shaped like the Grotto, with Bernadette kneeling at one side, strikes the hour. 'Kitsch or what?' Sophie asks. Before I can reply, the face springs open and a miniature Virgin slides out to a mechanically warbled Ave Maria.

We stare at it open-mouthed. 'We must ...' I say. 'Would the budget stretch?'

'Don't even go there! Look out, the manager has her eye on us. She'll call security.'

'She already has,' I say, indicating the Virgin who, after the eleventh Ave, retreats into the clock. I move back to Gillian, picking up a laminated portrait of Christ whose expression shifts from rapture to agony at a flick of the wrist. The proprietress, despairing of a sale, intervenes, directing us towards a rack of scarves which, though less obtrusive than the other items on display, are equally gaudy. The only one to find anything to his taste is Richard, who lumbers up to Gillian with a model Eiffel Tower. Its innate vulgarity, together with its utter inappropriateness to Lourdes, tickle me, and I offer to buy it for him. Overriding Gillian's objections, I take him up to the till to pay.

'It's in Paris,' he says to the salesgirl who wraps it. 'I like Paris more than Lourdes.'

We return to Gillian, who stands with Patricia appraising a small glass angel. It is no surprise to find her drawn to the one stylish item in the shop.

'Gillian wanted to buy it, but I made her see sense,' Patricia says. 'The way they throw your luggage about these days it's bound to break.'

I am affronted that anyone, let alone Patricia, should deny Gillian anything, and have to stop myself snatching it from the shelf and offering it to her on the spot. Instead, I carefully lift it down and, with a glance at Gillian, stroke the smoothly amorphous chest, making her blush.

'This reminds me of someone.'

'Fragile? Transparent?' she asks defiantly.

'Luminous.'

I replace the angel on the shelf, resolving to call in and buy it later, to give it to Gillian at a more opportune – more intimate – moment. 'An angel for an angel,' I say to myself, and wonder if it is lack of practice or of soul that makes the words sound so trite.

We return outside, where Father Dave gathers everyone together for the walk to the *cachot*. Hearing Matt and Geoff discussing songs for this evening's concert, I suddenly see a foolproof way to make a public profession of my love for Gillian. Everything hinges on convincing Richard, and I grab him while he is showing off his Eiffel Tower to Nigel.

'Sorry to disturb you, but we have business to discuss, man to man.'

'Man to man,' Richard repeats blithely to Nigel. 'So you can't come.'

Any guilt I might feel about using Richard as a ventriloquist's dummy vanishes in my excitement. For two days Louisa has been pressing me to take part in the concert, insisting that anyone who works in TV must be a practised performer or, at the very least, have a fund of stories about the stars with whom he has rubbed shoulders at the BBC. Having taken my refusal for aloofness, she is sure to welcome my change of heart. I shall explain that I am not appearing on my own account but to support Richard, who wants to pay tribute to his wife. It is the perfect cover and will suit us all: Richard will have his moment centre-stage; I will speak out without fear; Gillian will be confident that she alone can see my lips move.

'Can you sing, mate?' I ask, facing up to the first hurdle.

'Like a log. Ask Gilly.' He searches for his wife, who is walking a few steps behind us with Claire and Martin.

'No, we mustn't. It's important to keep this a secret. Do you understand?'

'Of course. I don't like surprises but I like secrets.'

'This will be our secret, yours and mine.'

'Not Gilly's?'

'No.'

'Good. She's always making me do things. All day long. I told her that in some countries abroad, men are allowed to hit their wives.'

'Really?' I say, gritting my teeth.

'And their mothers too,' he says gleefully. 'Their wives and their mothers and their aunts and their sisters and their cousins … their girl cousins. The man's in charge.'

'But not in England.'

'No, not in England,' he says sadly. 'I used to be her boss, now she's mine.' This time I play my required part, although the laughter is hollow.

'Well we'll surprise her by singing a song in tonight's concert. Just you and me. Would you like that?'

'A song with words?'

'Some, yes. Not too many.'

'Do I know them?'

'You tell me. What are your favourite songs?'

'"God save the Queen"!' he replies after a pause. 'God save our gracious Queen, Long live our noble queen,' he sings lustily. The elderly handmaiden in front turns round, as if she suspects mockery.

'That's great!' I cut him short. 'But it's not quite what we're looking for. Gillian may be a queen to you and me, but she's not the Queen. We need something personal.'

'I can do "Me and My Shadow". We sang it – Dad and me – at a party. And Lucy held a torch at the side so you could see our shadows on the curtain. She made them large and then small. And everyone laughed and clapped. Everyone clapped and said I was good.' His eyes fill with tears to which he seems oblivious. 'Everyone clapped.'

'And they will tonight, mate, I promise. We'll sing a love song to Gillian.'

'A love song?' he asks uneasily.

'A lovely song. Funny too.' A tune pops into my head. 'And I know one that's just the ticket. If I write out the words, can you read them?'

'Course I can! It's my brain that was hurt, not my eyes.'

'I want you to read them so often that you know them by heart. But you must promise not to show them to Gillian.'

We arrive at the *cachot* and, while waiting for the rest of the group to assemble, I borrow Sophie's clipboard and write out the lyrics of a song that was a staple of my childhood. My mother had a record of it by Bing Crosby who, after *Going My Way* and *The Bells of St Mary's*, was not only her favourite film star but almost an honorary priest. She would sing it when she was doing her housework, complaining – unconvincingly – that she could not get the tune out of her head. Being barely out of nappies myself, I naturally assumed that the 'beautiful baby' was me but, in line with her view that emotional deprivation was an essential part of growing up, she immediately set me straight, explaining that: first, it was only girls who 'drove the little boys wild'; second, the words were addressed to an adult; third, I had never won a prize, nor was I likely to unless I pulled my socks up.

Thank you, Mother, for leaving me with such an indelible memory of other peoples' happiness.

Father Dave leads us into the *cachot*, the former punishment cell where the family sought shelter after being evicted from the mill. Now practically empty, it would only have boasted a few sticks of furniture at the time. In spite of myself, I worry about the sleeping arrangements: the parents in one bed and the four children in the other.

'How old were they all?' I ask Father Dave, whose smile remains fixed while his furrowed brow shows that he catches my drift.

'Bernadette was fourteen; Toinette eleven; and their brothers, Jean-Marie and Justin, were seven and three.' I am both reassured by the girls' seniority and surprised that no one else in the group seems to have shared my misgivings. Yet, as I gaze at their open trusting faces, what would once have felt like culpable naivety now feels like blessed innocence.

The close cell and cloying story intensify my need for a few hours' break from all things Bernadette. As soon as we are back outside, I seek out Gillian and put forward a plan. My exhilaration at her willingness to skip mass fades when I learn that it is because she believes herself to be in a state of sin. After thirty years of attacking the Eucharist, I am in danger of becoming its advocate. If generals are given communion before they send troops into battle, is she to be denied it because of an act of love? On her own admission she is more of a widow than a wife, so the 'sin' is a mere technicality. How can any God, let alone the God she invoked last night – the God who created more stars than heartbeats – condemn her heart for beating a little faster?

Careful not to squander my advantage, I refrain from further argument and persuade her to join me on a mountain picnic. Leaving before she can change her mind, I trek back up the hill in search of Sophie and Jewel, who have sneaked into a confectioner's.

'Take your time,' I tell Sophie, who is wavering between nougat and truffles. 'The Gillian Patterson interview is definitely off. We're not filming until the procession at five.'

'Great!' Jewel says. 'Ken told me of this amazing salad bar tucked away behind the bridge.'

'Count me out, I'm afraid. I need some fresh air. I'm going for a walk on the Pic-du-Jer alone.'

'Is that *alone* alone?' Sophie asks, 'or alone-without-us alone?'

'It's alone-don't-ask-questions alone. So I'll meet you back at the Acceuil at half-past four.'

'Take care, Vincent,' Jewel says gently.

'Don't worry. I shan't stray too far off the beaten track.'

'I wasn't speaking literally.'

'Neither was I.'

My first stop is the Lacadé Mill to buy Gillian her angel. Undeterred by the price, I hand it to the assistant, admiring her elegant wrapping, until the Virgin of the Clock makes a midday appearance, to remind me that time is short. I hasten to the nearby market, its abundance of meats and cheeses and fruits and pastries in stark contrast to the gimcrack goods on sale elsewhere in town. Extravagance is my watchword; I want to provide a feast that is the opposite of the meagre fare we had yesterday at San Savin. I want to throw away more food than we eat, without a single thought for African famine or sustainable farming. I want a world where there is no one to be happy or loved or fed but us.

I buy pâté and sausage, cooked chicken and freshly sliced ham from an extravagantly mustachioed butcher, whose stall is hung with spikes of offal like the results of mediaeval torture. I buy sheep's and goat's cheese from a farmer who refuses to let me take the quality of his produce on trust. I bypass the fish stall, where the streaks of silver, grey and pink among the ice offer uneasy intimations of mortality, to buy a lettuce as crisp as a rosette and tomatoes as shiny and round as billiard balls from a vegetable stall laid out like a herbaceous border, and strawberries, peaches, cherries and grapes from a fruit stall, whose apple-cheeked assistant is the perfect advertisement for her wares. I hesitate only over the price of champagne at the wine stall, prompting the proprietor to suggest a local sparkling wine which he considers '*mille fois mieux*'. Spitting out an imaginary mouthful of champagne, he cleanses his palette with the Blanquette de Limoux, kissing his fingertips for emphasis.

I buy two bottles.

With only twenty minutes left until my meeting with Gillian, I set off briskly for the Domain, when I realise that I have forgotten the one crucial item. Spotting a green cross flickering on the far side of the road, I head for the pharmacy where I wait behind two old ladies. My admiration for the chemist's patience disappears during the first old lady's litany of ailments which would doubtless be cured by a baby aspirin. When she eventually leaves, weighed down by a bag of pills and potions, the second old lady takes her place, brazenly lifting her skirt to show how her support stockings dig into her doughy thighs. At last it is my turn and, still smarting from last night's humiliation, I ask the chemist if he speaks English.

'A little, Monsieur. How can I serve you?'

'Do you sell condoms?'

'Of course,' he says, his relaxed smile proving there is still one dogma-free zone in Lourdes. Pointing to a display right in front of me, he asks about my preference in size and flavour. Remembering the old 'small, medium or liar' joke, I opt for *medium* and, thankful that Gillian is not so fastidious as to make taste a factor, for *flavourless*. I buy two packets, counting on there being less wastage than with the food, and, conscious of the time, hail a passing taxi to take me down to St Joseph's Gate.

Leaving it with the wine as surety, I hurry into the Domain, planting myself in the centre of the path, to the irritation of several wheelchair pushers who are forced to swerve. There is no sign of Gillian, and I am starting to fear that I might have missed her when the basilica bells send out a reassuring peal. As I gaze expectantly at every passing woman, I wonder if she may have had a last-minute change of heart. Perhaps Richard is playing up or, worse, she has found out about the song and failed to grasp my intentions? My apprehension grows, and I picture the food rotting in the bags: cheeses running on to strawberries; sausages bleeding on to tarts; baguettes crawling with weevils.

Suddenly she drifts into view and I wave one of the bags over my head like a victory flag. I should never have doubted her. It would have been no more than I deserved if she had stayed away. This is absurd! I have promised her an afternoon's break and, for that if for nothing else, I must give myself one too. She moves to my side, tantalising me with the delicate fragrance of rose and jasmine. I long to clasp her in my arms, so tightly that our flesh dissolves but, alert to any stray Jubilate, I make do with mouthing a kiss.

'Your carriage awaits, Madame,' I say, leading her out to the taxi, where I tell the amused driver to 'brrm brrm' up to the Pic.

That is easier said than done. I share the driver's frustration at the tourists who step blindly into the road as if the patron saint of Lourdes were not Bernadette but Christopher. Yet, given the calm, easygoing Vincent I am keen to project to Gillian, I greet his hoots and imprecations with no more than a sympathetic shrug. In any case, I prefer not to look out of the window, since the pervasive reminders of human misery – the hydrocephalic boy; the burns victim with the Halloween face; the double amputee strapped into his chair like a skittle – are hardly conducive to romance.

A more painful reminder awaits me at the funicular, where we stand in line behind a young German girl whose smile threatens to unman me. It is not her face or even her missing front tooth that make me think of Pippa (although I still treasure the tooth that she placed under her pillow three days before the crash) but, of all things, her lollipop. I bought Pippa an identical one at a fair on Clapham Common that last summer. I also won her a goldfish at a coconut shy after so many throws that, according to Celia, I might as well have bought a shoal of carp. Memories of that day flood back, bringing tears to my eyes. I am torn between wanting to fix the images in my mind so that I can pore over them at leisure, and wanting them to fade before they cast a shadow over the afternoon.

If time is circular, then one part of me is still at that fair, facing the combined might of Celia and Pippa on the dodgems – the dodgems! – as surely as another part stands here with Gillian, as she ushers me on to the train. Yet, despite the physicists' theories, for me at least, the movement of time is all one way. Time past is time lost beyond recovery. People don't live in the past; they fail to live in the present. So I must look ahead, before today becomes another missed opportunity and the source of tomorrow's tears.

As the funicular judders up the mountainside, a growing awareness of Gillian's unease lifts me out of my introspection. After bawling like a baby, I am glad to assume a more dominant role when she clutches my hand in the tunnel. We alight at the top where the air is at once muggy and refreshing. To my relief, our fellow passengers head for either the café or the cave, leaving us to climb to the observation post unhindered. Both from a need to regain control after my outburst and a renewed sense of adventure, I insist that we shun the signposted path in favour of a wilder one hewn from the rock. I swiftly regret my choice as we scramble through clumps of tendon-twisting tendrils and calf-lashing ferns, and bemoan my misplaced gallantry in refusing to let her carry even the lightest bag.

'Keeping up?' I ask, not daring to stop.

'I'm right behind you,' she replies, with disconcerting vigour. I press on but, just as I am about to step over a broken branch, it rears its head and slithers into the undergrowth. I stifle a cry, telling myself that it is harmless and warning Gillian to watch out for the plants, before resuming the hike. Reaching the top, I make straight for a patch of short grass which, thankfully, harbours nothing but ants. I sink on to the ground and, moments later, Gillian sinks on to me. I am dripping with sweat but she seems not to notice. Normal constraints have been abandoned. With her, I need feel neither embarrassment nor shame.

'Shall we eat?' I ask.

'You mean there's more?'

Reluctant to let her go, I try to open the packages using one hand and my teeth, but she objects, insisting that we lay the food neatly on paper-bag placemats. I am now so hungry that, far from impressing her with my munificence, I fear that I may have under-catered. We seek to satisfy two appetites at once, serving each other with an intimacy that makes the meal, if not the prelude to an immediate act of love, then the promise of an imminent one. Our idyll is shattered by the German girl who, having finished her lollipop, seems to have absorbed some of Mickey's more irritating characteristics. She squeaks at her parents who stare at us in disgust, until Gillian sends them packing in a language which, now more than ever, I wish I could understand.

'What did you say to them?'

'They left. What does it matter?'

'Why the mystery? Tell me, or I may have to use force!'

'Will it hurt?'

'No, but it may tickle.' I approach her knee, fingers poised.

'All right, I give in! I told them you were my lover: that we'd met long ago on a pilgrimage and now we come back once a year for a day of unbridled passion.'

'You told them all that in a single sentence?'

'German's a very succinct language.'

The glaring implausibility makes me wonder if, beneath the jokiness, she is sketching out a possible scenario for our future: an annual reunion on the anniversary of our first meeting. Some couples travel to refresh their relationship; we would be travelling to keep ours alive.

I feel a momentary chill and, dispensing with the proprieties, take a swig straight from the bottle. The fizz of the wine, the warmth of the sun, the splendour of the view and, above all, the thrill of her presence cast an intoxicating spell. I feel invincible and, although we are at the top of the hill, yearn for new peaks to conquer. I help her to her feet and lead her to the platform.

'Shall we?' I say, pointing to the ladder running up the central masthead.

'I dare you.'

Rising to the challenge, I start to climb. Even the bottom rung makes me dizzy but I refuse to lose face and, gripping the rusty rail, gingerly lift my foot. Fortunately, she knows enough of male vanity to pull me down before I can do myself any harm.

Safe on solid ground, we gaze at the Pyrenees which stretch out at our feet like a stage-cloth. If the mountain up which Satan took Christ had been one of these, He would have yielded to temptation on the spot. But the very beauty that convinces me that everything is possible has the reverse effect on her. She has been a stranger to happiness for so long that she thinks its door will be barred to her for life. The only comfort I can offer her is myself, which I do, not by speech but by touch. As we revel in each other's company, we face a second intrusion, this time from an American boy dressed as a one-eyed pirate.

'Mommy, why are they kissing like that?'

'They're married, Victor,' his father says. 'Married people are allowed to kiss.'

His smugness enrages me. 'Yes, we are married,' I say. 'Only not to one another. Still, what can we do? My father saw her first. Have a good day!'

Let them build a wall round their son if they like, but not if it encroaches on my land, obscures my light and prevents the birds in my trees from nesting!

We clamber off the platform, leaving the family stunned. Grabbing our debris (even incestuous adulterers respect the environment), Gillian hurries me down the hill, the memory of the snake reconciling me to her choice of path. We wait in deepening gloom for the funicular and, by the time it disgorges us at the foot of the hill, I face a withdrawal more brutal than that from any chemically induced high. The driver picks up our mood and, after three questions about the visit, which Gillian answers for both of us, we return to the town in silence. I drop Gillian at the Acceuil, reassured to know that we will be meeting again very soon, albeit with several thousand other pilgrims in procession, and continue to St Joseph's Gate. Switching on my mobile, I find two messages and three texts from Sophie, the final 'Where r u?' followed by a line of question marks that spills off the screen. Eager to postpone her reproaches, I text back that I am on my way and ask the crew to meet me by the statue of the Crowned Virgin.

I arrive to be met by a concerted look of disapproval, which I seek to deflect with a breezy smile.

'Back in the nick of time!'

'For what?' Sophie asks. 'Midnight mass?'

'Come on! A little nervous tension can be creative. Get the juices flowing for the final day.'

'Seems like yours have been flowing already, chief,' Jamie says. 'All the way down your kecks.'

'What? Oh Hell! Grass stains.' I twist my neck to see. 'Are they on my back as well?'

'What does it matter?' Sophie says. 'They'll be setting off any minute. Here!' She hands me a Jubilate sweatshirt, which I gaze at blankly. 'For the procession!'

'Where can I change? There's no time to go back to the hotel.'

'Here,' Jewel says. 'I'll hold your bag.'

'Right here?'

'No one's looking,' Sophie says.

'Come on, chief,' Jamie says, 'flash the flesh!'

Feeling as bashful as a boy on a beach wriggling out of his trunks behind a skimpy towel, I pull off my T-shirt, which inevitably sticks on my head.

'Hey Mr Macho Man,' Jamie says.

'Wow, Vincent!' Jewel says. 'I never knew you had such a hairy chest.'

'So? I'm a mammal, aren't I? Are we going to stand here all day discussing my secondary sexual characteristics? I thought we were pushed for time.'

I lead them swiftly towards the bridge, to find the procession stalled in a dispute over precedence.

'First shall be last,' Louisa says, 'except, it would seem, if you come from Milan.'

'Is there a problem?' I ask her.

'Latin temperament! The older I get, the happier I am to be Anglo-Saxon. Ah ha,' she says, as Ken races back from the front line to give her the thumbs-up. 'They appear to have reached a compromise. By the way, try not to include any shots of Gillian Patterson this afternoon, would you?'

'Really? Why not?' My heart ricochets in my chest, as thoughts of spies, secret courts and anathemas flash through my brain.

'She's forgotten to put on her sweatshirt. Idle on parade!'

'Of course,' I say, heaving a sigh of relief. 'Something similar happened to me once.' I am gripped by a memory so powerful that I have to share it with someone, even Louisa. 'My parents-in-law threw Celia – my wife, well at the time, my fiancée – an engagement party. She forgot to tell me it was black tie.'

'Heavens! Did you turn up in jeans?'

'No, far, far worse: an off-the-peg suit from Burton's.'

Louisa looks at me with unexpected fondness. 'Please, forget I mentioned it. Film whatever you like. We're all one in the eyes of God.'

Grateful for her sympathy if not her logic, I leave her and join the Pattersons, flirting with danger, or at least with Gillian, under her mother-in-law's nose. Sensing that she is uneasy – and not just about her anomalous top – I walk away to meet Jamie and Jewel at the Breton Calvary, filming the procession as it wheels around the Esplanade and into the underground basilica, which exudes a far more welcoming air than it did on Tuesday.

'Have they changed the lighting?' I ask Jamie, who shakes his head. 'Or rearranged the seats?'

'What's wrong?' Sophie asks. 'Will there be a continuity problem?'

'Only in the commentary. I was too quick to run this place down. It wasn't designed to be a jewelled chapel for the elite. It has to house thousands of people every day.'

They look at me in astonishment. 'You didn't eat any dodgy mushrooms on your walk, did you, chief?' Jamie asks.

'Ha ha! All I'm saying is that we shouldn't compare it with

Westminster Abbey when its job is to be more like Wembley Stadium.'

A steward checks our permit with undue officiousness before steering us into a recess beside the choir, from which we film the procession as it files down the nave. The profusion of priests and bishops is much as before, the key difference being that the Cardinal bringing up the rear carries a golden monstrance, shaped like a sunburst. As he places it on the altar, I feel a lump in my throat, which is no less real for stemming from nostalgia rather than faith.

The service is as incomprehensible as its predecessor, with only the occasional English passage and French word (*seigneur, dieu, ciel*) to keep me on course. Somehow I find the mystification less irritating than before. The prayers provide a setting for my own reflections as my mind, no longer confined by the concrete, soars to the peak of the Pyrenees.

As soon as we are back outside, I take my leave of the crew and arrange to meet them at eight for the evening's concert.

'Communing with nature again, chief?' Jamie asks slyly.

'Not at all. I'm rehearsing my party piece.'

'You're not thinking of performing?' Sophie asks incredulously.

'Stranger things have been known.'

'What are you planning to do?'

'Wait and see! I did wonder about a chorus of "When Irish Eyes Are Smiling" accompanied by Frank on the spoons, but I couldn't answer for the consequences.'

'It's official,' Sophie says, 'you're out of your mind.'

Leaving Sophie shocked, Jewel worried and Jamie unflatteringly excited, I walk to the top of the ramp where, once again, I find myself waiting for the Pattersons to emerge from the church.

'I wonder if I might borrow Richard?' I ask, after some desultory chatter.

'Like a library book?' Richard asks.

'To interview?' Patricia asks.

'It's part of our surprise.'

'I have to go with him,' Richard says.

'I don't see why not,' Gillian says, 'but it's half past six. There's only an hour before dinner.'

'That'll be enough.'

'I have to go!' Richard grasps my arm with a force that makes me tremble for Gillian. I struggle to keep up my smile as I prise him off.

'Take care of him,' Patricia says anxiously.

'I'm not a library book!' Richard shouts back as we walk away.

Patricia's words haunt me as I lead him down the riverbank. Is it guilt that makes a mother's routine concern sound so desperate? Richard may not be the only obstacle to my happiness, but he is the greatest. It would take a saint not to speculate on his – on its – being removed. I watch him clamber on to the low stone wall, stretching out his arms and feigning a wobble as though on a tightrope. If he were to fall, or if I were to stumble and knock him off ... but he is too strong and the water too shallow. On the other hand, if he were to try the same trick on the main bridge with its fifty foot drop ... This is wrong! Even to fantasise about his death is a denial of everything I believe: everything I am. But what's the alternative? I can't just wave Gillian goodbye at the airport as though she were Louisa or Maggie. She is worth fighting for; we are worth fighting for. As if to show me that the fight is more equal than I might suppose, the strains of a Spanish prayer float across from the Grotto. I have love on my side; Richard has God.

'Where are we going?' he asks. 'This is boring.'

'Wouldn't you rather we rehearsed – practised – outdoors, enjoying the weather? We can't go back to the Acceuil since Gillian might hear.' Nor can we go back to my hotel, since the mere idea of Richard lumbering about the room in which I made love to Gillian fills me with revulsion.

'I don't like *kindergarten*,' he says, jumping down on to the path.

'What?'

'In the song. It's a silly word.'

'Oh, I see. Of course. But it's a rhyme. "When you were only starting to go to kindergarten ..."'

'Why can't it be farting?'

'That wouldn't be very nice. Remember it's about Gillian.'

'She farts.'

'That's enough now!'

'She pretends it's me but it's not. Sometimes in bed ...' He puts his lips together and trumpets a fart.

'It's *kindergarten*, all right? We do it properly or not at all.'

He doesn't have to die. We could put him in a home: a private one with his own room and furniture. Money wouldn't be an issue. According to Gillian, they did very well from the sale of the family firm. The key thing is to make her see that it would be for his benefit as much as for ours. He would be far happier among people like himself: look how quickly he bonded with Nigel! If all else fails, I could move in with them. We could build the husband equivalent of a granny flat, an annexe for him to live in with a carer. Gillian could keep an eye on them during the day.

Since when did my fantasies become so functional?

We arrive at the thicket where I interviewed Tadeusz. 'How about here?' I ask.

'I don't like trees.'

'All trees or just this one?'

'Trees with low-down branches. Branches should be up in the air.'

'How about here then?' As I lead him towards a silver birch, its slender trunk rising to a crest of dense foliage, I blot out the image of a falling branch inducing another haemorrhage.

'Why are you shaking your head?' Richard asks.

'Am I?' I reply, unaware that the image was so close to the surface. 'Sometimes I try to push away a nasty idea that's stuck.'

'Me too.'

'Really?'

'Only it won't always go.'

As soon as we have settled on a spot, I run through the lyrics, which he insists that he knows by heart. I am surprised to find him so alert, and wonder if he has made sense of it or simply learnt it by rote. I then run through the tune, assuring him that it will be easier when we have the guitar accompaniment.

'Will we have to play it?' he asks anxiously.

'Don't worry. I'll speak to one of the brancardiers.'

We struggle to match the words to the tune and it is immediately clear that, for all his bravado, his knowledge of the song is limited to the first two lines, which he repeats again and again in the same self-congratulatory croak. He grows frustrated and fractious at my efforts to assist him, stumbling over every other word until I realise that the best I can hope is to sing the song alone, with him as a kind of echo. Trusting that he may fare better with the movement, I demonstrate a simple routine – falling on one knee at the end of a verse and throwing out my arms minstrel style – which I ask him to copy. His crude parody makes me despair of both his cloddishness and a tribute that risks descending into farce. Nevertheless I refuse to give up, even when he starts to rebel.

'Singing to a baby's stupid,' he says, tugging at a creeper.

'Not a baby, a woman. A woman you love who was once a baby.'

'Gilly.'

'If she's the woman you love,' I say, longing for a confession that might exonerate me.

'Of course. I love her more than the whole world, more than all the stars in the sky.'

'More than all the heartbeats in the history of mankind?' I ask, horrified that she might have shared the thought with him.

'What?' he asks, with reassuring bemusement.

'Just another way of saying the same thing.'

'Why are you singing it,' he asks abruptly, 'if we're singing to Gilly?'

'I'm not. I'm here to help you. You wouldn't want to sing on your own, would you?'

'Yes … no … yes … no.' He seems to be genuinely torn, as he rips the creeper from the trunk.

'Hey, what's the matter? Don't worry. You're doing fine.' He slumps to the ground, head in hands, looking more lost than ever.

'I try – I try so hard, but sometimes I do things wrong,' he says, as if letting me into a secret. 'Sometimes my head's not right.' A tear rolls down his cheek. 'I used to be different once.' He gazes up at me. 'I used to be like you.'

I crouch beside him, feeling a profound need to be on his level.

'Do you remember those times?'

'Of course. I'm not stupid.'

'I'm sorry, I didn't mean …'

'Gilly shows me pictures and I remember the day we got married.'

'She shows you that, does she?' I try to squeeze the pain out of my voice.

'We had a cake with three floors. Some was sent abroad.'

'To your family?'

'We had all my family. All Gilly's family. All my friends. And my best friend, Jonathan.'

'Your best man?'

'That's what I said! He made a speech. Everyone laughed, except Mother. Gilly can't remember what it was. She should.'

'Well, you can't either.'

'But she has the pictures. She won't let me see him any more.'

'Jonathan?'

'She won't let him take me out on our own.'

'Why's that?'

He gives me a sharp look. 'Sometimes my head makes me do wrong things.' He says it so plaintively that, despite knowing what those wrong things are, I cannot hate him.

'You're not the only bloke to do things wrong; it's part of being a man: part of being a male that is, not part of being a human being,' I add quickly, even though the distinction will be lost on him.

A young couple walk past, hand-in-hand. Richard watches them with a glint in his eye. 'Shall we meet some girls?'

'What?'

'Just you and me. Not Nigel.'

'What girls? Where?'

'In a bar,' he says impatiently. 'You've got some money.'

Half of me wants to help him to whatever solace he can find; the other half wants to throttle him. 'What about Gillian? Won't she be upset?'

'She's always upset. But we won't ask her.' He chuckles uproariously, as if at a private joke.

'We can't today. We don't have time. We have to go back to the Acceuil to sing at the concert … the party.'

'She's always telling me what to do. I used to be her boss, now she's mine.'

'Yes, you've said that already.'

'Did I?' His face darkens and he bangs his head against the trunk. My murderous fantasy returns to shame me and I wrench him away.

'Don't worry, mate. Everyone repeats things all the time.'

'Do you?' He looks at me hopefully. 'All the time?'

'Never stop. Come on!' I stand and pull him up with me. 'Don't forget to go over your words again in your head,' I say, leading him out of the thicket. 'But don't let anyone hear or it'll spoil the surprise.'

I deliver Richard back to the Acceuil in time for dinner, finding Gillian by the Jubilate nurses' station, talking to Lucja and Sister Anne.

'At last!' she says. 'I thought you'd kidnapped him.'

'I'm not a kid!' Richard says resentfully. Gillian ignores him.

'Right now, is someone going to tell me what's going on?'

'Our lips are sealed,' I reply. 'Aren't they, Rich?' He shows his agreement by pulling his lips over his teeth and muttering incoherently through them.

'I'll find out, I warn you. I always do,' she says, in schoolmarmish tones that I find disturbingly sexy.

'Remember, Rich, we men must stick together.' He mumbles and mimes his assent, while the shadow passing over Gillian's face makes me wish that I had chosen a less loaded phrase.

'Well, now that you've set my husband against me,' she says lightly, 'do you have any other tricks up your sleeve?'

'Up my sleeve. In my shirt. Wherever,' I reply, with a smile that I trust will placate the nun while enticing her.

'Right, Richard,' she says, bundling him into the dining room. 'Food! That is if you deign to open your mouth.'

I return to the hotel, where the lingering fumes of sweat in the lift send me racing to the shower. I scrub and scour and brush and floss and dab and squirt, with an eye less to the farewell concert than the more intimate celebration with which I intend to follow it, before joining the crew in the bar, where I immediately order a round in a bid both to honour my promise to Jamie and to make up for my earlier absence. Sophie is glum, having failed to hear from Giles all day despite repeated texting, and Jamie's 'Give the guy a break – he might have been pissed and banged up in jail,' is no help. She has nonetheless dressed for the party, with a spangly black top and plum velvet trousers. Jewel has put on a khaki cotton sweater with leather patches, which should bring back memories for Louisa, and a calf-length denim skirt with oversized buttons down the side.

Jamie wears his usual plaid shirt and frayed jeans, along with a neckerchief pushed through a leather ring that makes him look like an aged and hirsute boy scout.

We make our way to the Acceuil and up to the rudimentarily decorated dining room, which exudes the same strained cheer as a hospital ward at Christmas. Before the concert starts, I have to finalise two arrangements. First, I seek out Alan, the young brancardier who, having taken on the lion's share of the guitar accompaniment at the services, is now moving into the secular field. I find him in the day room rehearsing 'Danny Boy' with Sheila Clunes, who lacks the brogue which alone might make its mawkishness palatable. I congratulate her with all the sincerity I can muster, although this clearly fails to compensate for my refusal to include her in the film.

'I'm not talking to you,' she says. 'Where's my pusher?' Her shout brings a young handmaiden rushing down the corridor to wheel her away.

'I know where I'd like to push her,' I say to Alan, who looks shocked to hear such feelings, even in jest. 'I wonder if you'd also play for Richard Patterson and me, well him really. I'm just helping him to serenade his wife. "You Must Have Been a Beautiful Baby." Do you know it?'

'I don't think so.'

'It's before your time. Before mine too,' I add lamely, wondering what it is about his guileless gentleness that makes me so self-conscious. 'I don't have any music, I'm afraid.'

'No problem, I only play by ear. You hum it and I'll see if I can pick it up.'

He proves remarkably adept, although I suspect that he may find himself floundering when he has to deal with Richard. 'He can be a little erratic,' I explain.

'Try keeping time with Fiona! I bet you it'll be fine. The concert's just a bit of fun. Besides, everyone's so tanked up on free wine they never notice when anything goes wrong. In fact they look forward to it.'

'Great!' I say gloomily. Envying his composure, I go in search of Sophie, whom I find perched on a laundry basket in the corridor, staring disconsolately at her phone. I resist any 'watched pot' analogy for fear of losing her goodwill, which I shall need if she is to be my emissary to Gillian.

'You know I've become friendly with Gillian Patterson.'

'Come on, Vincent, I'm not one of the nuns!'

'No, of course not.' Stung, I see why Giles might have taken the opportunity to stray. 'I was wondering if you might ask her out after the show.'

'What?'

'On my behalf.'

'You mean "my mate really fancies you"? Aren't you old enough to do your own dirty work?'

'That's just it – I don't want her to think it's dirty. If I ask, she'll assume it can only lead to one thing.' Sophie snorts. 'She'll feel pressurised, compromised. That bloody conscience of hers will start working overtime.'

'Whereas this way she'll be able to kid herself!'

'Exactly.'

'What is this? *High School Musical 3*?'

'It's our last night here. I don't want to waste it. Please.'

'Whatever,' she says wearily.

'That's great, Sophie – I owe you. Now I'd better check that Jamie and Jewel are on the case.'

I join the crowd heading for the dining room, finding myself alongside Patricia and Maggie. 'Let's ask Mr O'Shaughnessy,' Patricia says.

'Ask me what, ladies?' I reply, with a rush of alarm.

'Did you know there are more churches per person in Trinidad and Tobago than anywhere else in the world?'

'Strangely enough, that's one statistic that seems to have passed me by.'

'Mona swore to it. I told her: "It's no wonder you people are always smiling."'

'And what did she say to that?'

'She smiled.'

Patricia and Maggie enter the dining room, avoiding the empty seats beside Gillian and Richard in their eagerness to sit at the front. I confer with Jamie and Jewel, agreeing that we will film any of our core interviewees who take part, with the strict exception of Richard. First up is Father Humphrey who, with his wheezy vowels and quivering chins, might pass for the compère at a workingman's club. He starts by leading us in a decade of the rosary, neatly ensuring that even the lamest of his subsequent jokes is greeted with relief. He is followed by Sheila Clunes, who trills 'Danny Boy' to an ovation that owes more to tact than to taste; four young brancardiers, who camp up 'Dancing Queen' with a relish that is lost on the current audience; Frank, who grunts 'How Much Is That Doggy in the Window?'; and Martin, who stammers 'The Shadow of Your Smile'.

The protracted pause after Martin's song encourages me to move forward. Before summoning Richard to join me, I pay an impromptu tribute to the audience's hospitality and trust. Conscious that I must now exhibit a similar trust – namely, that they will not yawn or gaze at their watches, let alone compare our version with a slicker one playing in their heads – I call on Richard, who leaps up like a newly promoted understudy. I glance at Gillian, whose face is a rictus of horror. Anxious to reassure her, I tell Alan to strum the opening chords. 'Ready, Rich?' I ask. He nods, remaining silent long after Alan has begun the first verse. He gradually relaxes and mouths the odd word. On the fifth line, I turn to find him staring me full in the face. I take his shoulder and twist him very slowly towards the front. His mumbling grows louder, although scarcely more coherent, until we come to the final couplet:

'You must have been a beautiful baby

'Cause baby look at you now.'

As if aware that it is his last chance, he belts it out straight at Gillian, which emboldens me to do the same. To my relief, she is smiling broadly, having banished – or at any rate concealed – her fears. After milking the applause, Richard returns to his seat and I rejoin Jamie and Jewel, ignoring the ironic edge to their compliments.

'I've got to hand it to you, chief,' Jamie says. 'Talk about covering all bases.'

'I just wanted to help Richard thank his wife.'

'That's what I like about you, Vincent,' Jewel says. 'You're all heart.'

There is a further lull after our performance, not, I fear, because nobody feels confident to top it, but because of an unwitting duplication in the programme – too many doggies in the window – which requires all Father Humphrey's diplomacy to resolve. His success is rewarded by a double act from Fiona and Frank, which is even more mismatched than Richard's and mine. After that Maggie, with unsuspected gusto, sings 'I'm a Pink Toothbrush, You're a Blue Toothbrush' to Ken, who looks as if he would rather suffer both halitosis and plaque. One of the nurses sings a nondescript love song, before Mona brings the show to a close with a stirring rendition of 'Climb Every Mountain'.

Louisa steps forward with her usual blend of diffidence and determination. 'If I may have your attention a moment longer.' The hubbub dies down. 'First, I'd like to thank all the wonderful performers for the very best show I can remember.'

'You say that every year,' Brenda interjects.

'It just gets better and better. Now we've one final duty – or I should say, pleasure – to perform. The raffle. Thanks to your generosity every ticket has been sold, which will enable us to offer two subsidised places to hospital pilgrims next year.' This prompts the loudest applause of the night. 'So, if I may call on Father Humphrey to do the honours.'

'Got your tickets ready, Vincent?' Sophie asks.

'All five of them,' I reply, 'thanks for that!'

'Sh-sh!' Maggie shouts, clutching her stubs as reverently as a rosary.

'*Rien ne va plus,*' Father Humphrey calls out, as he plunges a pudgy hand into the bag. 'Third prize – a 2lb box of Belgian chocolates, courtesy of our sponsors, Harringtons of Stroud, goes to number 26.'

'That's mine. Mine!' Sheila Clunes shrieks, pushing herself forward so fast that I half-expect the sixty-eighth miracle of Lourdes, with her leaping out of her wheelchair to tear the voucher from his hands.

'If there is a God, He has a sense of humour,' I whisper to Sophie, just as her mobile goes off.

'Shit! Sorry.' She slips out of the room.

'Occupational hazard,' Louisa says indulgently. 'Well done, Sheila. Promise not to eat them all at once.' A roar of laughter prompts her to bite her lip. 'Now our second prize please, Father.'

'Our second prize is … what is our second prize?'

'A two-hour session with a beautician and stylist followed by a unique personalised portrait at a studio near you, courtesy of another of our sponsors, Cyril's Photographic Galleries,' Louisa reads out.

Father Humphrey jiggles the bag and pulls out a ticket. 'Number 333.' There is no response. 'All the threes – three hundred and thirty-three. Come on! Someone must have it.'

'Over here!' one of the brancardiers shouts. 'Don't be shy, Kev.'

'Kevin, lad, is it you?'

'I've got the ticket, yeah,' he says grudgingly.

'Well come up and get your voucher.' As Kevin trudges to the front, I detect a measure of pride beneath the truculence.

'I can give it to my mum,' he says.

'She may prefer to have a picture of you,' Louisa says gently.

'Does it include a plastic surgeon?' Geoff calls out.

'Don't mind them, Kevin,' Louisa says. 'They're just jealous.'

'I don't!' Kevin says, his face resuming its habitual scowl.

'Finally, we have tonight's star prize. A weekend for two in Lourdes, courtesy of our tour operators, Remington Travel who, I'm sure you'll all agree, have once again done us proud.'

'And the winner is …' Alan strums a few suspenseful chords on the guitar as Father Humphrey dips his hand into the bag. 'Number 158. Who has number 158?'

No one speaks until Jamie, peering over my shoulder, exclaims: 'It's you, chief.'

'What?' I look with horror at the offending ticket.

'This way!' Jewel says, as everyone claps.

'Well this is a turn-up!' Louisa says. 'Come on out, Vincent.'

'I think someone must have paid a secret visit to the Crowned Virgin,' Father Dave says, adding to my misery as I creep to the front.

'Here you are, sir,' Father Humphrey says, handing me an envelope. 'You'll be back again sooner than you thought.'

'It's a fix,' Brenda shouts. 'A bloody swindle!'

'Now now, Brenda,' Louisa says, in mollifying tones.

'Yes, it's all so as you can get your ugly mug on TV,' Brenda shrieks at Louisa, before rounding on Father Humphrey. 'Call yourself a priest? You should be ashamed. And you!' She turns to Linda who sits, tinsel dangling over her face and a brimming glass of wine in her hand. 'Get off your bony arse and take me back to the room. That's if you're not too pissed.'

'Watch out!' Linda says. 'The royal knickers are in a twist.'

'Something else'll be twisted in a minute. Get up!'

Linda stands tipsily and pushes Brenda out of the room.

'Oh dear,' I say, 'I'd be happy to give the holiday to her, or anyone else for that matter.'

'Nonsense,' Louisa says. 'Every year it's the same. Isn't that so, Marjorie?'

'I'm afraid Brenda doesn't always enter into the spirit of the occasion,' Marjorie says. 'Once she won second prize: a bottle of perfume – which I must say she … Anyway, she raised merry hell because it cost less than the third prize.'

I rejoin Jamie and Jewel who are now openly smirking, as Louisa winds up the proceedings. 'Well done to Vincent and to all our winners. And to all our losers, because they're winners too,' she adds, with the usual Lourdes logic. 'I'd like to remind you that we're due at the baths at nine thirty. Meanwhile, enjoy the rest of the party. The night is yet young.'

Alan strums his guitar and Louisa herself moves to the piano, while handmaidens bring round wine and Coca-Cola. Sophie returns, looking relieved. 'Sorry about that. It was Giles. He's been in meetings all day. He left his mobile at the hotel. Everything's sorted.'

'I'm very glad. Now remember, you have a matter of a similar nature to arrange.'

'I'm changing my job description – dogsbody, nursemaid and dating agent.'

As she walks over to Gillian, I turn to Jamie and Jewel for distraction. 'Are you two hitting the bars?'

'Not at all,' Jewel says. 'We're off to the Solitude to join the brancs and girls in a game of charades.'

'Just remember some of them lead sheltered lives,' I say to Jamie. 'We don't want a repeat of the *Fanny by Gaslight* incident.'

Sophie comes back with the news that Gillian will meet me at the hotel as soon as she has settled Richard. I thank her warmly and hurry out of the room in the hope of triggering a general exodus. Nobody stirs.

I walk over the bridge to find the path blocked by the Torchlight procession which, yesterday, formed such a felicitous prelude to my encounter with Gillian. As I wait for a convenient gap, an old man with a wall eye wordlessly offers me a candle. Reluctant to offend him but refusing to dissemble, I shake his hand, which is itself waxy, and indicate that I am just passing through. I cross in front of a party of African nuns, whose black faces and white habits feel gloriously incongruous, and hurry up to St Joseph's Gate and back to the hotel. While not even Madame BJ's basilisk stare can daunt me tonight, I am relieved to see her young assistant at reception. I explain that Gillian will be arriving shortly and ask him to show her to the bar. One glance at the beery Liverpuddlians watching football is enough to change my mind. I return to the foyer and tell him that I will wait in my room.

I sit, stand and lie down, flicking through my newspaper and notebooks, as time plays its usual tricks. I hide the crystal angel under the pillow, ready for a chance discovery when she rests her head. I am torturing myself with all the reasons for her to cry off when a knock at the door makes me jump. '*Entrez*,' I call, finding to my delight that it should have been '*Entres*'.

'I told the receptionist to ring.'

'I like to catch you off-guard.'

'I'm always off-guard where you're concerned.'

I leap up and kiss her: first delicately, even tentatively, to re-establish contact; then rapidly and repeatedly, to make her laugh; then deeply and at length, so that nothing can come between us.

'I need to sit – to lie – down a moment,' she says eventually.

'*Mi casa es tu casa.*'

'Spanish too? I thought you weren't a linguist.'

'Is it Spanish?' I ask with a grin. 'No wonder that Swiss guy looked confused.'

She stretches out on the bed, plumping up the pillows in a thrillingly proprietorial way. I perch on the edge, frightened of moving too fast.

'Sophie knows?' she says.

'Jamie told them both. But don't worry. They're utterly discreet.'

'What must they be thinking?'

'That I'm a very lucky man. That we are very lucky people. That we should seize every scrap of happiness we can.'

'I see you've picked a crew who share your philosophy.'

'Are you angry with me?'

'Of course not. Why should I be?'

'Because of the song.'

'I was touched ... well, taken aback and a little terrified, but touched. I was touched.'

'Apart from anything else, it gave me a chance to get to know Richard.'

'And?'

'I now realise that among all your other virtues you have the patience of a saint.'

'I thought you had no time for saints.'

'Only plaster ones.'

'Patricia knows too.'

'Why? What's she said?'

'Nothing. She didn't need to. Her face said it all. Ever since I came back this afternoon.'

'She had to know sometime.'

'No, she didn't.'

'She does if we're to have any future.'

'What? Like "Excuse me, Mother-in-law, but would you look after your son while I spend the weekend with my lover?"'

'Why only the weekend?'

'It's so easy for you. You have no ties.' She catches sight of Pippa's photograph which, this time, I had not thought to remove. 'This wasn't here yesterday.'

'I put it in the drawer.'

'You were that sure I'd be coming back?' She sits bolt upright.

'Not at all. I slipped it in when we arrived. The business with the light switch.'

'Yes, of course.' She relaxes.

'It shows what a difference one day can make. Last night I thought you might be upset, put off. Tonight it never crossed my mind. I want you to share in every part of me, the past as much as the present.'

'She's so pretty,' she says, lifting the picture to the light. 'She has your eyes.' Then, setting it carefully down, she takes hold of my face and kisses my eyelids. 'Such expressive eyes.' I rest my head on her shoulder and her touch becomes almost maternal.

'Nothing in this world is easy,' I say. 'The Church has got that right at least. For two people to have as much as we do, someone else will always lose out.'

'But does it have to be someone weaker?'

'Is Richard really that weak? Or is his weakness his strength? You said yourself that, if his brain weren't damaged, you'd have left him years ago. You feel as guilty as I do, only with far less – with no – cause. Guilty for an act of God! Somewhere deep down, you think God did this to Richard to stop you breaking your vows. So is it a blessing or a punishment? Either way it's destroying your life. I'm sorry.'

'Why, if it's what you believe? How you must despise me!'

'You know that's not true. It would be easier if I did, or at least if I was bored by you or as indifferent to you as I am to Mary or Claire or Tess.'

'She's looking to have an affair.'

'Who? Tess?'

'Forget I said that! She was overwrought. She's so worried about Lester.'

'When will you realise that you can trust me?'

'I'm sorry – I'm so confused. Didn't you promise me a drink? I'd kill for a Minty Mary.'

'No need.' I pick two glasses off the chair. 'I pinched them from the dining room this morning. I'm equipped for every eventuality.' As I pour two large vodkas, her eye falls on the condoms lying on the bedside table.

'So I see.'

'Well I couldn't afford the bootleg version two nights on the trot.'

'You've bought six,' she says, fingering the packets.

'As I said – every eventuality. Budge up!' I sit beside her on the bed. 'Cheers!' I clink the glass she holds loosely in her hand.

'So what happens next?' she asks.

'We make love.'

'And then?'

'We make love again. Sorry, I know that wasn't the question, but I think we should take things as they come. I don't mean *slowly*. Quite the reverse. Just that we should face each problem as it presents itself.'

'What about the problem that's already here – that's asleep half a mile up the road?'

'Some men take on their partner's children – I'll take on Richard.'

'That's easy to say. It's not all fun and games and party pieces.'

'No, Miss.'

'I'm being serious.'

'So am I. If it's what you want, we'll find a way.'

'The trouble is I don't know what I want!' She lets her head fall on the pillow. 'Ow!'

'Oh hell, I forgot! You haven't hurt yourself, have you?'

'I'll survive. What is it?' She lifts up the pillow and pulls out the package. 'A present for the chambermaid?'

'Hardly. It's for you. Every angel should have a spare.'

'You've lost me. What is it?'

'Open it and see.'

GILLIAN

Monday June 16

'Wakey wakey!' Patricia shouts superfluously through the door. 'My hands are full.'

'Come in,' I say, pinching my cheeks.

'I've brought you a cup of tea.' She sets it down on my bedside table.

'That's kind, thank you.'

'I can never sleep well the night before I travel. Shall I draw the curtains?'

'I'll do them. It's fine.'

She pays no attention. 'It's a lovely day. Someone up there's watching over us.' She gazes at the garden. 'Which is more than I can say for your borders. You can take the rustic look too far. Still, I'm sure you've a lot to occupy you.' She turns to my primary occupation. 'How's Sleeping Beauty?'

'Still sleeping.'

'It's a gift. When he was a boy, his father used to say he'd sleep through World War Three. That's when we still thought there'd be one.' She kisses his forehead, causing barely a stir.

'Right. I'll leave you two to get ready. I only have to p my coat on.'

'We have an hour and a half before the car comes.'

'I'm sorry but it's the way I am. No point trying to change me now. I'll wipe down your worktops.'

'I'd rather you didn't.'

'One less thing for you to worry about. Take advantage of me while you can.'

She heads downstairs to reassert ownership over my kitchen, where she has been creeping about since six o'clock, in an attempt at silence that grates more than noise. I suspect that even now, with Pattersons sold, Thomas dead and Richard ... well, Richard, she holds that everything I have comes courtesy of her. For all her fawning over her son, she never gave him credit for any initiative. No matter how much business he brought in, she shared Thomas's view that it sprang from the goodwill he had inherited when he joined the firm. Throughout his working life he felt humiliated at having to remain

Mr Richard in deference to his father. By the time his father died, he was plain Richard, with no status at all.

I taste the tea, which is predictably weak: a single 'as it comes' when Richard first took me home, having established a pattern for life. Has she never considered that nervousness at meeting my prospective mother-in-law might have made me eager to please? At what point in subsequent years did it become impossible to set her straight? Or has she known all along and been secretly laughing at my cravenness? The thought is too appalling to contemplate.

I give Richard a gentle shake. He turns to me groggily and starts the day with a slurred invective, a gust of stale breath and a routine fumble with my thigh. I push away his hand and apply my usual mixture of carrot and stick. 'Breakfast time. Your mother's downstairs.'

'What's she doing here?' he asks, a tremor followed by a frown.

'She stayed the night, don't you remember?' I hustle him out of bed and into the bathroom. 'We're going away, so give your teeth an extra-special brush.' He moves to shut the door. 'Why so coy all of a sudden?'

'Mother,' he replies, slamming it in my face.

I return to the room and make the bed, venting my resentment of Patricia on the pillows. I should have stuck to the original plan of picking her up on the way to the airport rather than letting her twist my arm. 'It will be one less thing for you to worry about in the morning. And you'll be doing me a favour,' she said, shamelessly playing the old lady card. 'I have to put Toby in kennels the day before, and I don't feel safe in that big house all on my own.'

At least she keeps herself active. I dread to think what will happen when she grows frail or incapable. Will I have to look after the mother as well as the son? By rights that task should fall to Lucy, whose annual visits home are as routine and joyless as dental check-ups. I would feel more aggrieved were it not for her hints of some childhood murkiness involving Thomas, which she blames Patricia for ignoring. Having watched him operate at the office, I am loath to pry.

Richard emerges from the bathroom. 'Your clothes are laid out on the bed,' I say, prompting a snicker on which I prefer not to dwell.

'Go downstairs as soon as you're dressed and your mother'll make your breakfast.'

'That's your job.'

'I have to get ready. We don't have much time. The driver'll be here in an hour.'

'What driver?'

'To take us to the airport, remember? We're going on holiday.'

'No, we're not. We're going to church.'

'We're going to Lourdes, on a pilgrimage.'

'I know that – I'm not stupid,' he says sharply. 'To sing at the cave and hold candles and pray with the priests.'

'Very good,' I say, impressed by his memory if disturbed by its slant. 'All that will make you hungry, so be sure to eat up.'

I shower and put on the Liberty print skirt that Patricia has bought me for the journey, a gift that I would have received with more grace had it not come with a reminder that 'first impressions count'. I gaze rebelliously at a pair of trainers, which I slip into the top of my case before dragging it downstairs. Patricia hears the clumping and dashes out of the kitchen.

'You don't need to do that. I arranged with the taxi firm – the man will bring down all the luggage.'

'It isn't heavy.'

'That's not the point. He's been paid.'

I follow her into the kitchen where Richard is eating a boiled egg in a yellow chick eggcup that Patricia must have unearthed from the back of a cupboard. Has she no qualms? It is bad enough that she should connive at his infantile antics without ferreting through my shelves.

'Everything's out on the table,' Patricia says.

'Thank you. Richard, stop playing with your food! Can't you eat properly just for once?'

'I think this visit to Lourdes is going to do you a lot of good,' Patricia says.

'If nothing else, it'll be a break. It's our first week away since … well, in years. People aren't exactly showering us with invitations.'

'I hope you won't take this the wrong way – as you know, I'm the last one to criticise – but you're a bit too inclined to feel sorry for yourself. Seeing all the severely handicapped people, some no better than vegetables (not that you heard that from me!), will show you how well off you are.'

'I can't wait,' I say, taking a bite of cold toast. For all her cod psychology, Patricia has failed to realise that the last thing I want is to see people worse off than myself. I am well aware that, in the roll call of victims, I rate fairly low. Hello, Mr Double Amputee, have you met Mrs Sprained Ankle? But the ankle still hurts. I don't want it put in perspective; I want it cured.

'Mother?'

'Yes, darling.'

'What's an Irishman's idea of foreplay?'

'Finish your egg, Richard!' I interject.

'I don't know, darling. You tell me,' Patricia says abstractedly.

'Brace yourself, Bridget!'

'That's not funny,' I say.

'You laughed. Two times!'

'I was being polite,' I reply, eager not to lose face in front of his mother.

'You mustn't repeat that on the pilgrimage, darling,' she says, enjoying my discomfort. 'There may be someone called Bridget. In fact I'm sure there will.'

I picture a coachload of Bridgets and shudder. I cannot believe that I agreed to join them. Since Thomas's death, Patricia's annual trip to Lourdes has been the highpoint of her year. Yet the louder she has sung its praises, the surer I have been that it is not for me. 'It's a tonic,' she says. 'The *malades* – I find it helps to think of them in French – are so grateful for everything; they give us back far more than we give them.' It is clear that she has not abandoned her usual priorities! For years she has been urging me to go. 'You owe it to Richard. What kind of message does it send to God if you can't make the effort to take him to the Grotto?' But I have resisted her blandishments, more afraid of the message that God would send to me by leaving him as he is. Then this spring, without further reflection, I said yes.

Why? Did she catch me at a moment of weakness? Had I said no so often that it no longer rang true? Am I hoping to revive my schoolgirl devotion to St Bernadette by going in her Jubilee year? Or is there some secret part of me, hidden behind the vanished hopes and vanquished efforts – a part I am afraid to acknowledge even to myself – which believes that Richard can be cured?

Life would be so much easier if I were an apostate or an atheist, railing against a cruel or a nonexistent God but, try as I might, I have never been able to shed my faith. From as far back as I can remember, it has been the one constant in my life. Even in the darkest days of Richard's haemorrhage and my mother's dementia, when belief in divine will was more of a burden than a blessing, I could not shake the absolute conviction that God *is*, that it is my understanding, not His goodness, that is flawed.

'There's a reason why God has given you this challenge,' Father Aidan told me, after visiting Richard in hospital. 'He never gives any one of us more than He knows we can bear. It may take you a lifetime to figure out His purpose, but you must never doubt it.' And I never have. I go to confession and mass, and say my prayers every day, even though 'Thy will be done' rings hollow from one who is forever pressing Him to see things her way.

'Faith that moves mountains' may be overstating it, but I have always believed in miracles: not just the easy, everyday ones of beauty and birth: the scent of a flowering rose or the smile of a newborn baby (not that that is always so easy); but the tricky, transcendental ones: the blind seeing; the lame walking … the brain-damaged recovering their wits. There have, however, been so few in recent years – even in Lourdes – that it is hard to see why God should spare one for Richard. On the other hand, it is not as if health were a finite resource, like the rainforest, that he could only enjoy at someone else's expense. Doctors prolong lives every day. They are forever finding cures for previously chronic conditions. It is simply a matter of time before they discover a way to reverse the effects of a haemorrhage. So I am asking for Richard's recovery to be brought forward a few years: more like an experimental treatment than a suspension of natural law.

I must take care not to expect too much, exposing myself to disappointment. Instead of looking for the lightning flash when Richard steps out of the baths, brain cells fully restored, I should look for the gentle glimmer when I step out, fortified for the years – the decades – ahead with a *malade* who is not grateful for anything. That, too, would be a miracle in its way.

The doorbell rings and Patricia leaps up, unbuttoning her house-coat to reveal an immaculately pressed skirt and blouse. 'That'll be the driver. You let him in, Gillian. Send him upstairs for the other cases.'

'Of course.'

Patricia goes to 'the little girl's room', re-labelling it for Richard on her return. 'I am not a little boy!' he says, bridling at the inadvertent slur. I make a last-minute tour of the house, which Patricia deems to be unnecessary – despite having left her bedroom window open – before joining mother and son outside.

'Is that everything, love?' the driver asks Patricia, whom he correctly judges to be in charge.

'Quite. Except for one thing. I'm sure you won't mind me mentioning it.' She flashes him a steely smile. 'I am not your love – I'm your passenger. At least I will be if we ever set off.'

'Yes, of course, lo … Missus,' he replies, cracking his fingers. 'No offence meant.'

'And none taken.' Patricia steps graciously into the front, leaving Richard and me to squeeze behind with the hand-baggage. No sooner has she settled than she twists round, just far enough to show the driver that he is not party to the conversation. 'I'm sure you'll like the Jubilates, Gillian,' she says. 'They're a friendly bunch. No airs and graces. You might have found my other pilgrimages a bit intimidating. On one – I can laugh about it now – we had a hand-maiden from Argentina. She owned half of … I forget the name of the capital.'

'Buenos Aires,' the driver volunteers.

'She flew to Lourdes in her private jet,' Patricia continues, tight-lipped. 'Then in the dining room, instead of gathering a pile of dirty plates like everyone else, she picked them up, one by one, and handed them to her maid.' Despite her disapproving tone, I suspect that she secretly admires such fastidious piety. 'You'd never get that with the Jubilates. Our only concern is the comfort and enjoyment of the *malades*. Though between you, me and the gatepost, I sometimes think it does more harm than good. They come to Lourdes for a week where they're made to feel special, then they go back home where the rest of the year they're ignored.'

The driver snorts; I swallow a laugh; Patricia gives me a furious look and turns back to the front, sitting in silence for the rest of the journey. Mightily relieved, I attend to Richard, who is drawing big-breasted women in his breath on the window.

We arrive at the terminal just as a coach carrying our fellow pilgrims draws up, a synchronism that delights Patricia. 'Be good enough to fetch us a porter,' she tells the driver, with the assurance of a seasoned traveller on the Orient Express or, more accurately, an avid reader of Agatha Christie.

'Don't worry,' I countermand quickly. 'I'll pick up a trolley. Richard, you wait here with your mother.' I hurry into the vestibule, returning to find Patricia engulfed by a group of Jubilates. She introduces me to several and, while I fail to keep track of their names, the breadth of her smile is a reliable indicator of their place in the pecking order.

A bald man in horn-rimmed glasses directs us to the check-in desk. 'You don't need to bother about him,' Patricia says, after greeting him like a long-lost brother. 'Derek. He's in charge of travel. Bit of a loner. Hello again!' She waves at a tall poker-backed woman with severely cut pepper-and-salt hair and a large gold crucifix. 'This is Marjorie, our deputy director. She keeps us all on our toes.'

'Not you, Patricia. I gave up trying long ago,' Marjorie replies, only to contradict herself by insisting that we wear our name badges, despite Patricia's claim that 'surely everybody knows me by now?'

The claim appears to be borne out by the number of people who come up to greet her. Any semblance of a queue breaks down as passengers roam around, abandoning their cases to chat to friends, to the despair of both Jubilate organisers and airline officials. A nun, whom in the melee I identify as either Martha or Mary, holds up her mobile to show Patricia some pictures of the asylum seekers with whom she works. Patricia, whose belief that we are all sisters under the skin fails to stand up to scrutiny, glances at them casually, breaking off at the sight of an elderly woman in a dusty pink raincoat, with short white hair, a whiskery face and a prominent mole on her chin.

'Maggie!'

'Pattie!' As they fall into one another's arms, I marvel at Patricia's tolerance of the diminutive.

'Maggie, meet my son Richard. No, don't disturb him while he's quiet!' We watch Richard pushing the baggage trolley back and forth, as though cleaning a persistent carpet stain. 'This is my daughter-in-law, Gillian. Gillian, you've heard me talk about my friend, Maggie, from Deal.'

'Of course,' I say, as though the name were never off her lips.

'Maggie and I have been on nine pilgrimages together. Gillian is a Lourdes ... this is her first time.' Maggie looks at me with a mixture of complacency and compassion. 'I've told her there's nowhere to beat it.'

'Nowhere in the world. I just wish that it weren't in the blessed EU.'

'Really?' I ask, presuming that she shares the other Maggie's loathing of Brussels.

'I have a filthy habit.'

Bewildered, I flash her a noncommittal smile. Meanwhile, I am distracted by a young girl with Down's Syndrome who strolls up and down the queue measuring various legs and cases. She approaches me, holding her tape measure loosely against my thigh.

'Hello,' I say.

'This is Fiona,' Patricia interjects. 'Do you remember me?' Fiona responds to Patricia's stiff smile by sliding towards Richard and pressing the tape measure to his leg. He grins and extends it to his groin.

'No, Fiona, you mustn't bother Richard,' I say, pulling her away. 'He's doing a very important job looking after the luggage.' She stares at me in confusion.

'I'm so sorry,' a flustered woman rushes up to us. 'She does so love to measure things.'

'I'm big,' Richard says with a chuckle which, to my relief, she ignores.

'I know that some people find it disconcerting.'

'Not at all. She can measure me whenever she likes,' I say lamely. 'But she'd do well to avoid Richard.'

'Of course,' she says brightly. 'Come along, darling, let's find

Daddy. I'm Mary, by the way.' She holds out the hand that was clutching Fiona. 'I hope to catch up with you later. Oh dear!' She spots the middle-aged man in front of us who is flinging about the contents of his suitcase like a wilful child. One sandal hits a corpulent woman in a wheelchair, only to be hurled back by her companion, a scrawny woman with a pink tuft of hair that looks as if it has been treated with food dye. Two helpers try to calm the man, who seems to be having some kind of fit, while a third comforts the indignant woman. My sense of having stumbled into a freak show intensifies at the sight of a film crew making a documentary about the airport. No one else shows any concern.

'Never a dull moment, eh Maggie?' Patricia says.

'You took the words right out of my mouth.'

After check-in, we are herded towards the security gates. The long queues make me unusually grateful for Patricia's brazen cajoling of one of the guards to let us join the wheelchairs in Fast Track. 'We're the walking wounded,' she says with a chintzy smile. I tag along, trying to look alert whenever Patricia or Maggie include me in their conversation about the cataracts that Maggie has either just had or is about to have removed.

'Don't Richard, that's disgusting!' I say, grateful that the film crew is no longer present to catch his rigorous nose-picking.

Even the fast track slows to a crawl at the scanning machine, where all but the most infirm are required to step out of their wheelchairs, give up their sticks, and take off their shoes. Much to his delight, Richard finds a large hole over his right big toe, which he accentuates by wriggling it. Patricia shoots me a black look, which she softens on turning to Maggie. 'You mustn't blame Gillian. Richard can be a handful. And she won't let anyone help.' I try to force my features into a suitably harassed but dedicated expression, while concealing the frustration beneath.

We finally reach the departure lounge. 'Shall we try that café over there?' Patricia asks, diverting my gaze from Wetherspoons, as though I were not just a lazy slattern but a chronic alcoholic.

'Fine, I'll grab a table. Do we need an extra chair?' I ask, wondering whether Maggie is to be a permanent fixture.

'Of course, there are four of us,' Patricia says, answering both my questions. 'I suppose it's too much to expect them to come and take our order.'

'I'll do it,' I say brightly. 'What does everyone want?'

'Black coffee for me, please,' Maggie says. 'It'll keep me going till my next fix.'

'I'll have a latte,' Patricia says, lingering over the name with a novice's relish.

'I'll come with you,' Richard says.

'No. You'll be bored. I know!' I say wickedly. 'Why not tell Maggie one of your jokes?'

I slip out of range of Patricia's fury, taking my place in a queue that is already liberally dotted with lime green. Gazing aimlessly across the concourse, I spot Fiona and her parents greeting a pair of priests who have the contrasting physiques of a classic double act: the first, sleek and round; the second, weatherworn and wiry. The large one sweeps Fiona off the ground and kisses her cheek, at which she throws her arms around his neck and tickles it. It is cheering to see a child who displays such affection for a priest. Either she is unusually trusting or else the black clothes and heavy breath that used to terrify me have the opposite effect on her.

The woman ahead of me turns round. 'Excuse me,' she says softly, 'but I couldn't help noticing a fellow Jubilate.' She holds up the tag on her handbag.

'That's right,' I say, grateful for the normalcy of both her voice and greeting.

'I expect you're a regular.'

'Not at all, it's my first trip.'

'Mine too!' She sounds relieved. 'We can make our mistakes together. Martin and I have been to Lourdes with the diocese, but we thought we'd try something smaller. Last year he was put in a room with a lot of older men.' Her voice trails off. 'I'm sorry! Where are my manners? This is Martin.' She draws him round to face me. He is a chubby boy in his late teens, with a long, blank face that looks like a sheep in a biblical painting.

'Hi Martin, I'm Gillian.' I am rewarded by a distended vowel.

'Martin's great but he doesn't say much, do you, love? The strong silent type.' He grins as she rubs his arm. 'Right now he's thinking:

what a pretty lady! She looks kind and a little lost like me. I hope she's going to be my friend.'

'Wow, you're thinking all that, Martin! Well I hope you and your mum are going to be my friends too.'

Mother and son break into smiles, highlighting the family resemblance. We have not yet left the airport, but Patricia's words about Lourdes making me count my blessings are already ringing true.

'Is Martin's condition permanent?'

'Since birth.'

'Always excepting a miracle,' I say lightly.

'Oh no,' she replies with a smile. 'I haven't come here hoping that Martin will be cured, but to find the strength in myself to cope with the fact that he never, ever, ever will be.'

Her smile grows more strained as her eyes fill with tears. 'I think she's ready for you now,' I say gently, as the assistant stares at her with chain-store indifference. Watching her pick up her tray and lead a shuffling Martin back to his seat, I reflect on our respective responsibilities and wonder whether it might not, after all, be easier to care for a son whose disability has extended his dependence, than a husband who was once a free man.

I collect my drinks and carry them back to the table, when I am accosted by the woman who was hit by the flying sandal.

'You're one of us!' she says, her green visor casting a sinister shadow over her face.

'I beg your pardon,' I say, struggling not to tilt the tray as I stoop.

'A Jubilate.'

'Oh yes, hello. I'm Gillian.'

'Brenda. This is my eighth pilgrimage.'

'I'm afraid it's only my first. I'd shake hands but mine are full.'

'And hers are useless,' her companion interjects. 'No better than a man's nipples.'

'This is Linda,' Brenda says unperturbed, pointing to the spindly woman buried beneath layers of shabby, shapeless woollens. 'She's my carer. At least that's what it says on the giro. They should ask for their money back.' She cackles.

'Well I must be on my way before these grow cold. Good talking to you.'

'You with her?' Brenda nods at Patricia.

'She's my mother-in-law.'

'I've been here with her before. Lady Muck!'

'I met a real Lady Muck once, on the ferry, only it was spelt: kke,' Linda says.

'Why do you want to tell her that for? She doesn't want to hear that. Think you're clever, you do!' Brenda looks venomously at Linda before turning back to me. 'I've been watching you. You're magnetic deficient.'

'I beg your pardon?'

'See this!' She nods to Linda, who leans forward and lifts Brenda's arm from under a blanket. A copper bangle hangs from her flaccid wrist. 'It's a life-saver. A miracle-worker. Your own private blood purification bank.'

'It sounds amazing.'

'It helps circulation, disperses nutrients, reduces lactic acid and … what have I left out?'

'Endorphins.'

'That's right: promotes the production of endorphins. Without it, I'd be long gone.'

'Don't tempt me,' Linda says.

'She doesn't mean that.'

'I don't mean that.'

'And it just so happens that I've brought a few with me. You can have first pick.'

'That's very kind, but I really couldn't accept.'

'I'm not giving it away,' she says, affronted. 'I'm a certified agent! I'll take pounds, euros, dollars.'

'Zlotys,' Linda adds.

'Zlotys, why zlotys? I'll zloty you! Come on, my tongue's hanging out.' Linda takes hold of the chair. 'Don't forget – see me at the Acceuil!'

They make their way into the pub and I return to the table.

'I'm sorry if these are cold.'

'I don't like hot milk,' Richard says.

'I meant the coffee, but I was waylaid by two scary women.'

'We saw,' Maggie replies. 'I said to Pattie: "Should we rescue her?" But she said: "No, she'll have to get used to them soon enough."'

'Linda seems an odd sort of carer.'

'She's odd all right,' Maggie says knowingly. 'They've been together forty years. They share a room at the Acceuil like husband and wife. Need I say more?'

'You mean they're lesbians?'

'Sh-sh! Richard!' Patricia says, proving yet again that she does not have the least inkling of what goes on in his mind.

'I don't suppose there's much of that these days,' Maggie says. 'Brenda's got no feelings from the neck down.'

'No normal feelings,' Patricia corrects her.

I stand up, desperate to escape. 'I feel a headache coming on. I'll just pop to Boots for some aspirin.'

'No need,' Maggie says. 'I've a pack in my bag.'

'You wouldn't believe what she fits into that bag,' Patricia says. 'I always say it's like Harrods – everything from a pin to an elephant.'

'Please don't bother,' I insist, as Maggie rummages around ineffectually. 'I could do with an emergency supply. Besides there are a couple of other things I've forgotten.' I try to sound euphemistic. 'I'll only be a couple of minutes. Would you keep an eye on Richard?' I ask Patricia.

'Of course.'

'You know how he likes to wander off in a crowd.'

'Really Gillian!' she replies, in a wounded tone. 'I was keeping an eye on Richard before you were born.'

I walk towards Boots but, once out of sight of the café, veer into Mulberry and browse through the handbags on sale. I pick up an oxblood leather tote when I spot a forlorn-looking girl sifting listlessly through a rail of belts. Her telltale luggage tag encourages me to speak out.

'Snap!'

'What?' she asks nervously. I hold up my own tag. 'Oh, are you one of the organisers?'

'No, just a humble pilgrim. And you?'

'Even humbler. I'm a handmaiden – it's my first pilgrimage.'

'Snap again!'

'I should be at school but they gave me the week off. I've just taken my A levels; the results won't be out till August.'

'A nerve-racking time!'

'This is much worse. I don't know anyone. I've never been away from home before – I mean without my mum and dad.'

'People seem very friendly.'

'I know I won't be able to talk to anyone.'

'You're talking to me.'

'I mean anyone my own age. Not that you're old. I mean not like some of them.'

'Thanks. Though I was expecting a few more young people.'

'They're all coming down by van. They set off two days ago. But I get car-sick – I mean really sick.'

'I can see that might cause problems. But I'm sure once you've met up with them you'll have a wonderful week. I'm enormously impressed that anyone – especially at your age – should give up their time to help.'

'We only had a day's training: how to lift people in wheelchairs and things. Only they weren't real. I mean they were real people, not really in wheelchairs. What if it's different?'

'It will be different, but you'll adapt. I can tell you're a very resourceful person. Now if you'll excuse me, I'd better get back to my husband; he'll be wondering where I am ... actually, he won't, but his mother will. I'll look forward to talking to you again.'

'Me too! You know, I think I'll buy this belt.'

I return to the café where Patricia is talking animatedly to a tall woman with a white pageboy haircut, beaky nose and half-moon spectacles, clasping a clipboard behind her back, together with a good-looking red-haired man, whom I took for one of the camera crew but turns out to be the director. He starts to speak but I cut him short. 'Where's Richard?' I ask Patricia. 'I left him with you.'

'He was here a moment ago.'

'You're always saying you want to help and look what happens. You know you mustn't let him out of your sight.'

As Patricia seeks to exculpate herself and the others offer alternate help and reassurance, two security guards run past and I know instinctively that they are heading for Richard. I follow them down the concourse and into Accessorize, where a quick glance at Richard, pinned between the guards, and the wary woman watching him from a chair, confirms my fears. A small crowd of ghouls stands at the entrance, while two salesgirls fuss over the woman, determined to squeeze every ounce of drama from the incident. Richard catches sight of me and calls my name, straining against his captors, but I am too angry and humiliated to respond. While Patricia and the tall woman, who identifies herself as Louisa Brennan, the pilgrimage director, appeal to the guards, I move to the seated woman.

'Whatever it is my husband's done,' I say, 'I apologise. He has severe brain damage.'

'There you go!' a salesgirl with panda eyes and multicoloured braids says to her colleague, who has a pink poodle tattooed on her arm. 'My auntie's friend was stabbed in Bethnal Green Road. In broad daylight. It's called Care in the Community.'

'The synapses in his brain are impaired.'

'I didn't know,' the woman says. 'You can't tell.'

'We could,' the tattooed girl says. 'Didn't I say, Mandy? Soon as he came inside, I said we gotta keep an eye on him.'

'Then it's a pity you didn't.'

'Excuse me! He's not our only customer.' She gestures round the store. 'See, he's scared everyone else away.'

At that moment, Louisa crosses the floor and I am aware of attention shifting on to us. 'I'm extremely sorry, Madam,' she says. 'Richard's one of the hospital pilgrims we're taking to Lourdes.'

'They ought to lock him up,' the tattooed girl says.

'It was the shock,' the woman says softly. 'He came into the cubicle and wouldn't leave. So I panicked. I'm sorry.'

'No, you shouldn't be,' I say, shamed by her magnanimity.

'And throw away the key,' the girl adds.

'Is there someone we can fetch?' Louisa asks the woman. 'Your husband?'

'No!' she cries, with a vehemence that speaks volumes. 'No,' she says more gently, 'he'd only get worked up. No harm done. Not even the shirt,' she says, inspecting the sleeves.

'You must at least let us offer it to you,' I say. 'A token.'

'No, really. It's not necessary. I understand.'

'I'd like to,' I say, keenly aware that not everyone would be so forgiving. 'Please.'

'Well, if you're sure. Thank you. I'll go and change.' Casting an apprehensive glance at Richard, she retreats into the cubicle. The assistants apart, everyone looks relieved to have the matter so painlessly resolved.

'What time's your flight?' one of the guards asks Louisa.

'Eleven o'clock. We'll be called any minute,' she adds as a further assurance.

With the immediate danger lifted, Patricia feels free to add her pennyworth. 'I knew it was something and nothing,' she says with a smile. 'A silly mix-up.'

I walk over and grab Richard's clammy hand. It is only by a supreme effort that I keep from reminding Patricia that his mind was warped long before his brain was damaged, and that she bears much of the blame. It was her sick subservience to Thomas, not least her connivance at his affairs, that encouraged Richard's relentless womanising. 'In an almost literal sense, he thinks with his penis,' the neuro-psychologist said, explaining the effect of the damaged synapses. 'In a figurative sense,' I wanted to reply, 'that's what he's been doing his entire life.'

No sooner have I taken out my purse than the film director approaches me. 'It's my fault,' he says. 'I'm so sorry. I distracted your mother-in-law with talk of the documentary.'

'Yes, well, she's easily distracted,' I reply, taken aback by his self-regard. 'Maybe one day you people will learn that the whole world doesn't revolve around a camera. Not everyone's burning ambition is to appear on TV!'

I am surprised, but not displeased, that he looks so deflated. Spending his life surrounded by minions and flatterers, he might benefit from meeting someone less easily impressed.

The guards leave the shop. 'I'd put him straight on the plane if I were you, love,' one advises me. 'And take better care next time. The place is full of kiddies!'

Horrified to hear him voice my greatest fear, I tighten my grip on Richard, pay for the shirt and return to the café, deliberately quickening the pace to escape Patricia. Maggie is standing beside our bags looking concerned.

'Where have you been? I slipped out to the you know what, just in case. When I came back, everyone was gone. It's lucky I wasn't any longer. There was a guard sniffing around. Next thing you know, there'd have been a controlled explosion.'

'It's very lucky, Maggie,' I reply, 'thank you. Patricia's on her way. She'll explain. I'm taking Richard straight to the gate. We'll see you there.'

We make our way through the concourse, to wait on the platform for the transit train. As we step inside, Richard says plaintively: 'You said we were going on a plane.'

'We are. This is just so we don't have to walk too far to reach it.'

'I thought you were putting me on the train! I thought you were sending me home instead of on holiday!' He starts to laugh and then, without warning, his voice starts to quaver. 'I've been a naughty boy.'

'You have.'

'I've been a naughty boy.'

'That's easy to say, but it doesn't make it any better.'

'I can't help it. My brain's hurt.'

'I know that. We all know it. But it's no excuse.' I wonder if his remorse is genuine or simply a response to my mood. 'You have to learn to control yourself.'

'You shouldn't shout at me. It's not my fault. My brain's hurt.'

'Don't start crying, please! Look, the train's stopped. Hurry out before the doors shut.'

'Before we get squashed,' he replies with a giggle, his tears already forgotten.

'Oh Richard, what are we going to do with you?'

At the gate, we take the last remaining seats in a row beside an elderly woman in a sleeveless top with skin like a scrunched-up cardigan. She bites into a Danish pastry. 'You know the worst thing to have happened to women in the last twenty years?' she says, smiling. 'The elasticised waistband.'

I sit, with one eye on Richard and the other on the floor, too wound up to read and too wary to risk a glance that might lead to further introductions. Ten minutes later, I look up to find Patricia hovering over me.

'There's nowhere for me.'

'Have mine,' my neighbour says.

'Oh no, Ruth! Really, I couldn't.'

'Don't be silly. You want to be with your family.' I wonder how she knows. 'And I need to walk off some of that cake. See you later.'

'Such a nice woman!' Patricia says. 'The life and soul of the laundry room. Lives in a lodge near Hereford.' She sits down and opens her bag, producing an apple neatly cut into quarters, since she hates to see anyone eating one whole. I take a slice, which is surprisingly crisp. True to form, she makes no mention of Richard's behaviour, having thrust it through the shredder that she calls a memory.

'He's a charming man,' she says between bites.

'Who?' I ask, looking round for another pilgrimage official.

'The director,' she says impatiently. 'Mr O'Something or other. He's worried that you've not signed the release form. If he puts you in the picture – even in the background – and you object, the whole film will be abandoned. Months of work ruined.'

'I doubt it'd come to that.'

'You don't know lawyers! You're the only one who hasn't signed. I was mortified.'

'I had other things to think about. It didn't seem that important.'

'Not to you perhaps. But he wants to feature us specially: you and me and … Richard.' Her voice falters. 'Think what it would mean to the Holy Redeemer!'

'So I'll sign. It's no big deal.' For all Patricia's enthusiasm (which sits strangely beside her objection to seeing 'ordinary people' on TV), I have no wish to spend the week in the shadow of a film crew. Media exposure may be the modern elixir, but it is not a miracle cure.

An announcement across the tannoy that boarding will begin with the wheelchairs sends them racing towards the barrier. 'I don't want to be unkind,' Patricia says sternly, 'but you'd think they were competing in the Paralympics.'

The rotund priest comes over to greet her. 'Ah, the shining star of the dining room, looking lovelier than ever!' He kisses each of her hands in turn.

'Father, really!' she says coyly. 'Not in front of my son and daughter-in-law.'

'Hello, hello! I'm Father Humphrey.'

'Richard and Gillian Patterson,' I say, holding out my hand which, much to my relief, he is content to shake.

'Is it your first time in Lourdes?' he asks Richard, who looks to me for the answer.

'Yes, Father,' I say.

'Well I'm sure it won't be your last. Like Patricia here, you'll soon be hooked.'

'I wouldn't put it quite like that,' she says, wincing.

'Hooked!' he repeats emphatically. 'And you mustn't worry about the flight. You'll be back on solid ground before you know it. The only danger sign is if I start singing "Nearer my God to thee".'

Patricia's fluting laugh alerts me to the joke. 'Such a jolly man,' she says, as he walks away. 'And not just because he's fat.' She nods at the enormous woman being wheeled past by Ruth. 'She's a case in point. Couldn't raise a smile to save her life. Hello Sheila!'

The woman looks up. 'Do I know you?'

'It's Patricia,' she says, pointing to her badge. 'I took you to the baths last year.' Sheila grunts as she is whisked away. 'Never again,' Patricia says with a shudder. 'I try to do my bit, but there are limits. Even with four of us – and one a landscape gardener – I cricked my back.'

'What's wrong with her? Some kind of dropsy?'

'More like some kind of greed. She can't carry her own weight. Like those dinosaurs whose brains were too small for their bodies.'

We are finally called on to the plane where, wheelchairs apart, there is open seating, which leads to problems when several of the older handmaidens vie to sit next to the three priests. One goes so far as to deposit her coat on the empty seat beside Father Humphrey, who gently returns it, explaining that he has saved a place for Father Dave. 'We have to sort out this evening's service,' he says with relief.

Patricia makes for the row directly across the aisle from them. 'You'll think me very silly,' she says, 'but I'll feel happier if there's any turbulence.' Richard grabs the window seat, which leaves me squeezed between them, a discomfort that is not solely physical. Patricia's satisfaction fades when a young couple with a baby sit down behind us.

'Oh no,' she whispers. 'Wouldn't they be better off at the back? He'll be squalling all the way to Tarbes.'

'He seems fairly placid to me.'

'Just wait till his ears pop!'

I lean over to fasten Richard's seatbelt. He squirms as if I were knotting his tie. Patricia stares at the cameraman struggling to fit his equipment in the overhead locker. 'When I was younger, people used to mistake me for Kate O'Mara,' she says pensively.

'You never know – it may happen again. Remember, we're going to Lourdes.'

'Don't be ridiculous, Gillian!' she says sharply. 'We're not going there for me.'

The flight passes without incident. Richard counts the clouds and eats all three of our chocolate muffins, rebuffing my warnings that he will make himself sick with 'That's what the bag's for.' Patricia takes an undue interest in the comings and goings to the loo, chatting to several people as they pass, including Maggie, whose mention of smoke detectors clears up the mystery of her 'filthy habit'. Too restless to tackle my book, I flick through the in-flight magazine, reading previews of summer festivals in places to which I have never been and know now that I will never go.

Shortly before landing, Marjorie walks through the plane, asking hospital pilgrims to stay in their seats while the helpers prepare for duty. 'We won't be on the same coach,' Patricia says. 'Mine will drop me at my hotel, while you'll go straight to the Acceuil. But don't worry, I'll be along as soon as I've unpacked.'

'I expect I'll manage.'

Patricia waits for the crowd to thin before standing and then, with a gesture of helplessness (which is as selective as her memory), asks the man behind to lift down her bag.

'That's very kind,' she says. 'And congratulations on your baby. We were a little worried when we saw you sit down, but we didn't hear a squeak out of him – or her of course – the entire journey.'

'We are most happy that Pyotr has not inconvenienced you,' he replies, with a rasp that goes beyond his accent.

We hospital pilgrims are finally allowed off the plane, trudging and trundling through an airport which, for once, has been designed with the disabled in mind. Any speed that we may have picked up inside the building is lost, however, when we come to load the coaches, which takes over an hour. The ambulant (a word that sounds less formal now we are in France) fill the gaps between the wheelchairs, so that Richard and I find ourselves sitting beside a man of indeterminate age, with a square face, blotchy scalp and caustic BO. He speaks to me, but his voice is so slurred that my only resort is to smile broadly and say: 'And I'm Gillian.' Realising that this is not the right response and seeing no Jubilate official on whom to shift responsibility, I ask if he needs any help.

'Ift … ee … up. Ippin ….'

I have never felt so conscious of consonants as I struggle to decipher his speech. 'He wants you to lift him up – he's slipping,' Richard says, without looking up from his puzzle. I sit, dumbfounded by his comprehension, while the man continues to press me.

'Ift … ee … up!'

'Yes, of course,' I say, wondering how best to gain leverage. With great trepidation, I put my arms around his back and heave him up.

'You're kissing him,' Richard says, and Brenda, watching fiercely from across the aisle, cackles.

'Is that better?' I ask the man.

'Es,' he sputters, with a sweet smile.

Our coach is the first to leave, wending its way through the characterless countryside. 'How often have I been to France?' Richard asks.

'I don't know.'

'You should.'

'You came several times before I met you.'

'You should find them out. You should add them up. Else how will I ever remember?'

A priest at the front of the coach picks up the microphone. 'Good afternoon everyone. To those who've never met me, I'm Father Dave. Along with Father Humphrey and Father Paul, I'm here to guide you through your pilgrimage. And I'm delighted to welcome you all to Lourdes. Hands up those who've been here before.'

Most people, including Richard, raise their hands.

'I can't lift up my hand, can I, Father?' Brenda snarls. 'I'm blooming well paralysed.'

'Yes, of course. I consider myself well and truly rebuked.' He slaps his right hand with his left, sending a deafening clack down the microphone. 'We can always rely on Brenda to keep us on our toes.'

'You're telling me,' Linda says in a stage whisper.

'Well, as those of you who've been before will know, and those who are here for the first time will soon discover, this is a unique place. If only the rest of the world were more like Lourdes, we'd be a lot happier.' I gaze at the sick and disabled people in the coach and admire his certainty. 'Let me tell you a story: a true story; well, all my stories are true, but this one actually happened. A woman came to Lourdes from Paris and wanted to find a mass in French. She looked down the list of services and saw there were masses in Italian, German, Spanish and English, but nothing in French.'

'Swedish!' exclaims the man who disrupted the check-in.

'Yes, Swedish.'

'Danish. Norwegian.'

'Those too, I'm sure.'

'Dutch. Polish.'

'Yes, yes,' Father Dave says, struggling to maintain his composure. 'The point is that there were masses in every language but French. So she went to the information centre and complained: "Shouldn't I be able to hear mass in my own language in my own country?" "But, Madame," the assistant replied, "this isn't France, it's Lourdes."'

His moral is clear and duly acknowledged. As if wary of further interruption, he sets down the microphone and we spend the rest of the mercifully short journey in silence. We arrive at the Acceuil, pulling into a shady courtyard where a dozen youngsters stand expectantly on the steps and a couple sprawl on a ramp. We step off the coach into another round of greetings. A wiry teenager, crackling with untapped energy, asks if I need any help. 'That's fine, thanks,' I say, surprised that he can find no more deserving cases. 'I can look after myself. I'm fit.'

He steps back as if struck. Fearing that I may have insulted him, I give him a smile that seems to increase the offence. To my relief, we are intercepted by Derek.

'We met at the airport,' he says, 'do you remember?'

'Of course,' I reply, wondering if he has misread my notes.

'I've been allotted to you for tonight.' I bite my tongue. 'Are you ready to see your room?'

'Thank you.' I grab Richard and follow Derek into the building.

'Anything you need to feel at home: extra pillows, a plug for your hair rollers, just ask,' he says, as we enter the lift.

'I will ... Stop it, Richard!' I can no longer keep from laughing. 'You're tickling me!'

'I wasn't.'

'Yes, you were.'

'No, I wasn't!' He looks genuinely hurt.

'Well, he's on holiday,' Derek says indulgently. 'A little tickling's allowed.'

'But I wasn't!'

'Is this our floor?' I ask quickly.

'Yes, we came in at the top,' he says, holding the lift doors open. 'It'll all seem confusing at first, but you'll soon get the hang of it.' He leads us through a web of corridors to our room at one corner of an angular building. 'You have one of the very best views,' he says, as if to make up for the decor. 'Come and see!' I follow him to the window which looks out on a small forecourt where scores of empty wheelchairs are lined up like supermarket trolleys. Beyond it a river runs under a stone footbridge, and in the distance a toy-town church spire pokes through a patchwork of green.

'Your luggage will be along shortly. If you'd like any help unpacking, I'll be only – '

'No, that's very kind. We'll be fine.'

'I'd like help unpacking,' Richard says.

'You'll have help.'

'Well then, I'll be off,' Derek says, shifting his weight from foot to foot. 'You're sure there's nothing else you need?'

'Just a wash,' I say, starting to lose patience.

'Yes, right. As soon as you're ready, come along to the dining room. Supper's always informal on the first night.'

He finally leaves and I have the chance to take stock of the room which, in its bleached austerity, feels like a hospital side-ward stripped bare after a recent death. The only colour comes from a bunch of buttercups in a jam-jar on the plain wooden desk. There are two iron-framed beds, one of them attached to a pulley with which Richard immediately starts playing; a small cupboard; an even smaller chest of drawers; and a desk chair that cuts into my back when I sit down. I spring up and, after stopping Richard throttling himself on the pulley, take a look in the bathroom, a simple wet-room with a sloping floor and a shower placed so close to the loo that, for once, I shan't be able to blame the damp seat on Richard.

A woman enters the room, after a cursory knock that alerts me to her profession even before she does so herself. 'Hi there, I'm Susan Gilpin, one of the pilgrimage doctors. And you must be Richard.'

'Yes,' he says defensively.

'That's good. I know you're going to like it here. All the fun things to do. And all the funny people. Why else would I be mad enough to bring a three-month-old baby? And you're Richard's carer?'

'Actually, we're married.'

'Yes, yes.' She is busily reading her file. 'I meant for the purposes of the pilgrimage. And you want to look after his medication yourself?'

'I have done for the last twelve years,' I say, trying to restrain my hostility.

'Quite. Best not to disrupt the routine. As I always say, you carers are the experts, we doctors are just amateurs. But if you need any help, there's always one of us on call. Bye-bye then, Richard. I can see you're in safe hands.'

I doubt that he would agree, since I insist on his having a thorough wash. After my experience in the coach, I am taking no chances. We then make our way to the dining room, to be greeted by an elderly handmaiden with a squirt of antiseptic, which Richard instantly wipes off on his shirt. 'I'm afraid you may find it a little crowded in here tonight, dear,' she says, in a voice redolent of a Cotswold cottage. 'We're sharing with a group of Slovakians, but they'll be gone before breakfast.' Stepping inside, I find her warning inadequate. The concentration of disease and disability in a single room is harrowing. I am sure that by tomorrow I shall be fine, but for now I am glad of the chance to call on Patricia, whose self-absorption relieves her of any such qualms.

'Can I leave Richard with you?' I ask. 'I'm not hungry and I want to press on with the unpacking.'

'Would you like me to bring you some bread and cheese?' she asks, with unexpected concern.

'No, I'm fine, really. Just not hungry. I'll see you at mass.'

I make my escape, catching my breath outside the nurses' station where the young brancardiers are setting out the luggage. I feel an intense desire to be surrounded by my own things – even just clothes and cosmetics – but, inevitably, my case has yet to arrive. While waiting for the next batch, I glance down the corridor where the film crew are shooting an interview with the boy who behaved so oddly outside. At the end, the director strides towards the lift, turning almost as an afterthought to me.

'You're staying here?' he asks.

'With Richard.'

'I thought it was only for hospital pilgrims,' he says, revealing his lack of homework.

'And their carers.'

'You're his carer?'

'So I'm told. I used to be his wife.'

I hurry back to my room, trusting that no one is watching. If I hear the word *carer* once more, I swear I shall scream. Will it be carved on my tombstone? *Sacred to the memory of Richard Patterson and his beloved carer*? When Jonathan Tickell offered his definition of a good wife in his best man's speech, he could have left out the 'cook in the kitchen' and 'maid in the living room', let alone the 'whore in the bedroom' that so offended Patricia. In my case, all that is needed is a carer in the sickroom.

I lie on the bed with my eyes closed, striving to empty my mind, only to be roused a few minutes later by Patricia and Richard who have come to fetch me for mass. We take the lift to the top floor and a small chapel which, in its starkness, might be the spiritual equivalent of the wet-room. We sit beside Maggie and an elderly blind man, whose expectant face makes me feel shallow and ashamed. Before the service begins, Louisa welcomes us to Lourdes and introduces us to various pilgrimage officials. My thoughts wander, and I start to regret having missed supper, when she makes a simple remark that touches my heart: 'What we're doing in Lourdes is God's gift to us. What we do to one another while we're here is our gift to God.' It is clear that, far from leaving everything to God, I must play a part myself. All the prayers, all the candles and all the baths in the world will go for nothing unless I treat my fellow pilgrims with love.

Louisa resumes her seat and we sing the hymn 'Let There Be Love', a favourite of our church youth group. Youth is also the keynote here, since we are accompanied by a scratch quartet of guitars, flute and drums. Patricia whispers that they will have practised in the van on the journey down and, while traces of the autoroute remain in the jolting rhythm, their dedication and enthusiasm make up for any shortcomings. The most affecting contribution, however, comes from Fiona, who stands at the front and conducts us, swinging her tape measure to and fro, more like a windscreen wiper than a baton.

Father Humphrey reads the gospel story of Christ and the paralysed man, elucidating it in his sermon: 'Remember that, however hard it may be for the human mind to fathom, all suffering has a purpose. The Blessed Virgin has cured many people in Lourdes but not St Bernadette herself, who was tormented all her life by asthma. When she was asked why, she replied that it was not for her to question the ways of God. "I'm happier on my bed of affliction," she declared, "than a queen on a throne." She had no more desire to suffer than Our Lord had on His cross, but she knew that it was one of God's gifts. And it is a gift that you, the sick, share with us, the well. You grant us the privilege of your trust, which in turn brings us closer to God. In a world where the old and the frail, the vulnerable and the disabled and the unborn, are too often discarded as surplus to requirements, it is an inestimable joy to discover a different way to live: the Lourdes way. Here we see humanity at its best, where the weak and infirm are treated with love and respect. We may only be here for a few days, but let us make it the pattern for our lifelong pilgrimage. May we be fortified by our fellowship with one another, the love of Our Lady, the message of Holy Scripture and the sacraments of the Church. Amen.'

At the end of the sermon, Father Humphrey shifts into party mode, calling on Father Paul to bless the banner, after which Father Dave restores the solemnity with the Eucharistic prayers. He proclaims the Peace: the moment in the service I always dread, since it wrests me out of my private thoughts and back into the world. It is evident from the start that this is to be far from the usual token greeting. All over the room, people abandon their seats to exchange hugs and kisses. Even Patricia, who I suspect chooses her Sunday pew on the basis of avoiding unwelcome handshakes, enters into the spirit of the occasion. After kissing Richard with an affecting tenderness, she wishes me a 'Peace' of comparable warmth and moves down the row of wheelchairs, which is fast turning into a reception line, with the able-bodied queuing up to embrace the *malades*.

Richard scuttles about and I dismiss the suspicion that he is favouring the women. I am more reserved, sticking to my immediate neighbours, until a sudden impulse thrusts me towards the director. My fear of fawning on him may have led me to be brusque – even rude – in our earlier encounters. This is my chance to make peace as well as to offer it. 'Peace be with you,' I say, holding out my hand, which he takes with a friendly smile. All at once an extraordinary feeling comes over me. I am clasping his hand yet I seem to be floating away. It is as though the peace that I granted him has been extended to me, and I am filled with lightness and light.

VINCENT

Friday June 20

Gillian has left, but her presence is everywhere around me, from the faint indentation on the mattress to the whiff of coupledom on the sheets. Her scent clings to my fingers and, like a pensioner who has shaken hands with the Queen or a teenager with a rock star, I resolve never to wash them again. I am her subject; I am her fan. I leap up and dash to the basin, thrusting my hands under the tap to rid myself of such fatuousness. But her fragrance is a match for Madame BJ's cheap soap.

I rerun my dream, which has remained crystal-clear. I was at home with Celia and Pippa, whose face was bright and vibrant, not the wan, graveyard colour of our recent encounters. In some mysterious way she was both frozen in time and eight years older. Celia asked me to drive Pippa to the mountains. 'How can I?' I replied, 'I have to work.' 'Please,' she begged, 'you know that my licence was revoked after the accident. The air is exhilarating, and she needs a change of scene.' So I drove her up to a ridge, where she clambered about on the rocks while I stayed locked in the car. She pressed her face to the glass but, unlike the squashed features of the African children in the coach, it was fixed in a radiant smile. 'You've brought me as far as you can,' she said. 'Now you must go back and move on.' I know that the words she was speaking were mine, but it makes no difference since it was not Pippa who needed to release me but myself.

I shower, dress and do some desultory packing before going down to the dining room where I find, yet again, that I am the last to arrive. My colleagues look smug, and I wonder whether one of them might have spotted Gillian leaving the hotel. To my joy, I realise that I no longer care. The last remaining traces of the God-stained schoolboy have been laid to rest.

'Good game of charades?' I ask casually.

'Kids!' Jamie says, with a snort.

'Jamie's feeling old,' Jewel says.

'I took off my shirt, grinned like an idiot and knelt at Lorna's feet. But did anyone guess *The Naked Civil Servant*?'

'The closest they got was *Jonah and the Whale!*'

I give him a sympathetic smile and reach for a croissant.

'All ready for home?'

'You bet!' Sophie says. 'Giles flies back from Abu Dhabi at lunchtime. He's picking up the car at Heathrow and driving straight to Stansted. Then we head back west for a weekend in Wiltshire.'

'All right for some!' Jamie says. 'I've promised to help my dad do up the spare room.'

'Never mind,' Jewel says, 'you'll get your reward in Heaven.'

'Oh great!' he says sourly, 'that's just what I need after a week in Lourdes.'

'How about you, Jewel?' I ask.

'Drinks with some mates tonight and a gig at the Brixton Academy tomorrow. Nothing much.'

'Go on, twist the knife in!' Jamie says.

'And you?' Jewel asks me.

I realise, with a start, that I have nothing planned. Even in my wildest dreams I could not expect Gillian to abandon Richard at Stansted and come back to Clapham with me. When Louisa explained how some of the pilgrims had trouble adjusting to everyday life after the intensity and comradeship of Lourdes, I never suspected that I might be one of them and that, far from welcoming an empty weekend to recover, I would feel utterly, terrifyingly alone.

'So what are your overall impressions of Lourdes then, Vincent?' Sophie asks. 'Give us a sneak preview of your commentary.'

'Love,' I say without a moment's hesitation. 'The place may be crass and exploitative; it may play shamelessly on people's credulity, but the pilgrims who come here do so in good faith. Like everywhere else that's been invested with a sense of the sacred, it has an aura. It's that aura that inspires people to keep on coming and, against all the odds, it's inspired me. But it's us – well, them – who've given it that aura: their hopes, their faith, and, above all, their love. It's not something that's been beamed down from on high.'

'You've changed your tune, chief.'

'No, same tune, but I'm no longer playing solo. It sounds quite different when you add another instrument.'

'A fiddle?' Jamie asks with a smirk.

'A Stradivarius. I've found so much love in Lourdes – and I'm not just speaking personally. Take Brenda and Linda – they've been together thirty-seven years.'

'I wish I was a dyke,' Jewel says. 'Yeah yeah, I saw that look, Jamie! And that's one of the reasons. Women are so much more loyal than men.'

'Those two certainly are,' I say. 'A year after they met, Brenda was diagnosed with MS. It spread rapidly and within five years she was in a wheelchair. Linda gave up her job to care for her. For all their bickering, I've never seen such a practical expression of love.'

'So you think that everyone should stick with partners who are incapacitated?' Jewel asks. Sophie and Jamie look nervous.

'Yes,' I reply firmly, 'as long as they do it out of love and not out of duty or guilt.'

After an uncomfortable few minutes, we return to our rooms to finish packing, before bringing our cases down to the foyer where Madame BJ instructs us to pile them under the statue of Bernadette. Given her warnings about gypsies, she seems remarkably sanguine about the security of our unguarded bags, but then her gimlet eye must be a greater safeguard than the sturdiest lock. That said, she announces that she will be away for the rest of the day.

'Every Friday – when the weather is fine – I go climbing with a group of friends. So this is goodbye. It has been a pleasure.'

'Really?'

'Or perhaps I should say *an education* to welcome you. We have 2,000 guests each year at the Bretagne, but I shall remember my pilgrims from the BBC.'

She retreats into her office and we make our final trip to the Domain. Jewel stops to buy a bottle, explaining, as sheepishly as if she were buying dope, that she has promised to take some spring water back to her grandparents. Dissociating myself from Jamie's mockery, I reflect on Gillian and whether she will maintain her resolve once we are back in England. I must find a way to keep her with me both in body and spirit, convincing her that the problems we face are mere practicalities.

'Earth to Vincent!' Jamie says, predictably. 'Are we going straight to the baths?'

'No, the Acceuil. I want to squeeze in a final interview.'

'That wouldn't by any chance be with one Gillian Patterson?'

'No, but you're warm – her mother-in-law. I sounded her out at Stansted and then never got round to it.'

'Are you sure it's a good idea?' Sophie asks warily.

'I've a hunch she'll have some interesting things to say.'

We reach the Acceuil and call the lift, which opens to reveal a group of Jubilates, among them Richard and Nigel.

'We're going to the baths,' Richard says.

'Save a place for us, mate. We'll be along any minute.'

''Old,' Nigel says.

'You'll find it's quite warm in the sun,' Jewel says.

''Old!' he insists.

'Does he need a sweater?' Sophie asks Geoff, who is pushing him.

'No, the water's cold,' Richard says, and Nigel breaks into a smile. 'He's been here before.'

We take the lift to the third floor where the vestibule is already stripped of much of its Jubilate clutter. Brancardiers and hand-maidens are packing up boxes, taking down notices and piling rubbish in green plastic bags. I find Patricia with Maggie in the dining room, wiping down tables and stacking chairs.

'Gillian's not here,' she says icily.

'I know – she's at the baths … I mean I saw a crowd heading that way. Aren't you having one?'

'One thing I've learnt in life, Mr O'Shaughnessy, is that some of us are Marthas and some Marys. Wouldn't you agree?'

'Not necessarily. I believe in choice.'

'That's as may be. But for some it's a luxury and others it's a trap. Now if you'll excuse me, I have a job to do.'

'That's why I'm here. I'd like to film a short interview, if Maggie can spare you.'

'Now? I thought you'd given up on me.'

'Other fish to fry,' Maggie says sourly.

'On the contrary, saving the best till last,' I reply, forcing a smile.

'But I've been clearing up. I look a fright.'

'Not at all. The picture of elegance. Isn't that so?' I turn to Maggie, who gives me a suspicious nod.

'Well, I believe in keeping up standards. Out of respect for the *malades*.'

After a little more cajoling, followed by several minutes at a mirror to 'repair the damage', Patricia is ready. We collect the crew and go down to the non-functioning fountain, which provides the perfect setting.

'Is this all right for you, Jamie?' I ask, as I steer Patricia into position.

'Sure, chief.'

'Will people be able to hear me? There's a lot of background noise.'

'Don't worry. Jewel's going to wire you for sound.'

'Is that safe?'

'Not a real wire,' I assure her. 'Just a microphone in your lapel. There we are. OK for levels?' I ask Jewel, who gives me the thumbs-up. 'Now look at me, Patricia. Not at the camera, at me.'

'Oh dear, there's so much to remember.'

'No, to forget. Starting with the camera and the microphone. Ready?'

'As I'll ever be.'

'Good. Patricia, you've come to Lourdes as a handmaiden several times, I understand.'

'Nine. Not that I'm counting.'

'What drives you to make such a commitment?'

'It's a way of giving back. My life hasn't always been easy, but I still have my health. And that's a great blessing. I've seen someone very dear to me – someone I love very much – struck down by illness, and I haven't always been able ... haven't always been allowed to help. Coming here does a little to make up for that.'

'Thank you,' I say, disconcerted.

'Besides, I believe it's what God wants me to do.'

'Like a calling?'

'Oh nothing so grand. But Our Lord called on us all to visit the sick, feed the hungry and clothe the naked (not that I've had to do much of that!).'

'Do you try to live all your life according to the Church?'

'Of course. Not that I always succeed.' She gives an ingratiating laugh. 'God has given us this extraordinary gift of life. It's up to us to try to live it according to His will.'

Her confidence fuels mine and I press her harder than I had

intended. 'When you were a little girl, did your father ever make you anything? I don't know: a rocking horse or a doll's house?'

'Yes, yes he did.' Her eyes shine. 'He made me a Noah's Ark: the most beautiful one you've ever seen, filled with stalls and coops and hutches. And he bought me a set of miniature animals to put inside. How funny! I haven't thought of it in years.'

'And did he also give you strict instructions on how you should use it? Did he say you could only put the zebras in this stall and the elephants in that? Did he tell you which animals you were allowed to bring out on deck?'

'I see where this is heading.'

'Well did he?'

'No, of course not.'

'No, your father wanted you to enjoy it: to make it your own. Which is what people do when they give presents. So why should God, the supreme present-giver, be any different? Why should His gifts come wrapped in a long list of rules and regulations? I'm talking about the Bible, the most arcane instruction manual of them all.'

'It's easy to argue through stories.'

'But didn't Christ?' She looks shocked. Glimpsing Sophie's uneasy expression, I resolve to change my line of questioning. 'On a different point, I've been surprised – impressed, of course, but also surprised – by how many of the helpers take on tasks, quite menial tasks, that they would never do at home. I once made a film about Armistice Day, and I remember reading notices in *The Times* in which young women whose fiancés had been killed in the trenches offered to marry any maimed or blind or injured officer. And I wonder, with the greatest respect, if there might be an element of that in what people are doing here: getting their hands not just dirty, but as filthy as possible.'

'I'm afraid you've lost me. All I can say is that many of the hospital pilgrims are severely disabled. They need help with their basic functions.'

'I don't dispute that, but what is it that motivates you – you, Patricia – to help them? You said it was giving thanks, but is it gratitude or guilt? Are you trying to humble yourself in penance, not just for being healthy but for being alive: the debt with which all of us – that is all of us who are Catholics – are saddled with at birth and which we can never repay?'

'Not in the least,' she replies fervently. 'That may sound clever, but it isn't true. For a start I've had more than my share of suffering. Do you know what it is to watch your child spend six weeks in a coma?'

'No.' I refuse to trade tragedies with her.

'No, I didn't think so, or you wouldn't see this week as separate from the rest of my life. But I'm not complaining. I count it a privilege to have suffered as I have – it's a sign that God considers me worthy. He knows I'm strong enough to endure it, that my faith will survive.'

'I'm glad to hear it and I hope it brings you comfort, but what right do you have to impose your beliefs on anyone else?'

With a cutthroat gesture Sophie indicates that I should wind up the questions. Patricia misinterprets it, her eyes widening in alarm.

'What am I imposing? I'm simply answering the questions you've asked.' She looks for support to Sophie and Jewel, who remain impassive. 'Impose! I've no idea what you mean?'

'Oh I think you do. You have a daughter-in-law.'

'Is this going out on air?' she asks, so helplessly that even I feel a tinge of compassion.

'No!' Sophie interjects, stepping in front of the camera. 'I think we have more than enough material. Shall we leave it there, Vincent?'

'Sure.' I walk up to Patricia and remove the microphone. 'The interview's over but I'd still be glad of an answer.' I sweep aside Sophie, who is trying to intervene. 'You have a daughter-in-law. What right do you have to impose your beliefs on her?'

'I could ask you the same thing. You want to make her forget – no, to throw out – all her ties and responsibilities.'

'No, I'm trying to remind her of her primary responsibility – her responsibility to herself.'

'She came here on pilgrimage, not for a dirty weekend.'

'Vincent, it's time for us to go to the baths.' Sophie says.

'Just a moment! Please, a moment!' Disturbed by the urgency in my own voice, I turn back to Patricia. 'We only have one life. Even if you believe it extends into eternity, it's still only the one. Doesn't she have the right to love?'

'She has a husband whom she vowed to love and honour.'

'Wasn't that vow mutual? Didn't he break it over and over again with his casual affairs?'

'Lies! Is that what she told you? Well, did she also tell you that she was the one who caused his haemorrhage?'

'What?'

'Yes, that's knocked the stuffing out of you! She threatened to leave him. The stress it caused went straight to his brain.'

'You can't really believe that?'

'Who are you to tell me what I believe?'

'And you've said so to Gillian?'

'Of course not. What do you think I am? But she knows my mind.'

'The guilt must be unbearable.'

'No guilt is unbearable if it's absolved by the Church. But perhaps you realise now that, whatever promises you may have made, you won't be seeing her again once we leave the plane. She's come back to her senses and to her husband and to God.'

'So you really think that Richard was enjoying a relaxing round of golf when the threat of Gillian's departure hit home?'

'Yes, of course. What are you saying?'

'I don't know about anyone else, but I'm going down to the baths,' Sophie says. 'It's almost nine thirty and the women's queue will be half a mile long.'

'Yes, you and Jewel go. Have your baths. Jamie, if you keep a place for me, I'll be along any minute.'

'Are you sure, chief? I can wait here.'

'No, run on down. Then they'll know we're on our way.'

'What about you?' Sophie asks Patricia. 'Would you like me to stay?'

Whether because she fears further public revelations or is convinced that she can refute my charges, she shakes her head. With some hesitancy, Sophie, Jamie and Jewel move away.

'Do you want to sit down?' I ask Patricia. 'There's an empty bench.'

'What? You mean like two old friends out for a stroll? No, thank you. You overestimate your power to wound, Mr O'Shaughnessy. Just say what you wish to say and have done with it.'

'I want you to understand Gillian's position. Richard didn't collapse on the golf course but in bed with one of his secretaries. She was the one who took him to hospital. It was her mother who rang Gillian.'

'Oh really! Were you there?'

'She's tried to keep it from you all these years. She thought you'd been through enough.'

'Whereas you evidently don't?'

'I think you should know the truth. The haemorrhage didn't put an end to his affairs, although *affairs* is too kind a word for visits to local prostitutes.'

'What prostitutes? He's like a little boy. He could never ...' She abruptly changes tack. 'He would never find a way.'

'Some of his old friends arranged it. I don't know if they thought they were doing him a good turn or amusing themselves at his expense.'

'This is vile! It's a slur on someone who can't answer back. Is this how she tries to gain sympathy? Where's the proof?'

'At the doctor's surgery,' I say deliberately.

'What?'

'On one of the visits he contracted herpes, which he passed on to her.' Fearing that Patricia is about to faint, I move to take her arm, but she steadies herself and thrusts me away. Meanwhile we are attracting unwelcome attention from a pair of gardeners.

'But isn't that like AIDS?'

'Don't worry, it's not life-threatening. I had a PA – ' She looks blank. 'An assistant. The doctor assured her she was as safe as the Queen Mother except when she was having an attack.'

'What sort of attack? How will I know?'

'You won't. Gillian thought she was having one this week; it turned out just to be thrush. But it's more than her blood that's infected – it's her self-respect. If she'd moved in the circles I have, she'd know it's no big deal. But she's been left on her own with Richard.'

'She had me.'

'Really?' I try not to sound incredulous.

'I'm not a monster, Mr O'Shaughnessy, whatever you may think.'

'What I think is immaterial. It's what Gillian thinks – and feels – that counts. And that's *ashamed*. It may not be logical – it's certainly not right, but that's how it is. Ashamed in front of you and your Church and all that bloody purity.'

'She should have told me. You can't blame me for something I didn't know.'

'And not just ashamed but inadequate. She saw everything you'd had to put up with in your marriage.'

'She'd no right to say that. It's nobody's business but mine!'

'Precisely. The more she saw you hanging on, making the best of things, the harder it was for her to complain about Richard.'

'But it's not the same. My marriage may not have been perfect, but my husband respected me. Whatever mischief he may have got up to – not that I'm saying he did, you understand – he kept it to himself. He would never bring dirt into the hall, let alone the bedroom.' She begins to weep. 'He always took his boots off at the back door.'

'That's why I'm begging you not to stand in Gillian's way.'

'She's thirty-nine years old,' she says tonelessly. 'She doesn't need permission from me.'

'There are other ways to hold someone back besides locking them in their room. She needs your blessing.'

'I can't do that!'

'Don't begrudge her this chance of happiness!'

'And Richard?'

'She'll never leave him. I might want … but she'll never leave him. Anyway, there are plenty of alternatives. We've not begun to explore them of course, not yet. But look how well he gets on with Nigel. Maybe in the right sort of home?'

'I won't let you shut him away with a lot of hopeless cases.'

'Of course not. Gillian … I … no one would dream of it. But there are homes of all sorts, for all ages. Or else he'll live with Gillian – with us – and have a carer when necessary. What I'm trying to say is that there is a solution. Life doesn't have to be *either … or.*'

'Or right and wrong, I suppose?'

'Oh I believe in right and wrong, just so long as they're not writ in stone.'

'I shan't ever come to Lourdes again.'

'Of course you will. You must. The Jubilate wouldn't be the same without you.'

'I have to go inside. I have to think.' She moves away and turns back. 'I shouldn't thank you for telling me this, but I do.'

She nods and walks slowly towards the Acceuil. I make my way across the bridge, wondering whether my revelations will have any effect. If ever I supposed that my mother was unique in her self-serving servility, Lourdes has disabused me. It beggars belief that, at the start of the twenty-first century, millions of people still cling to the notion that our birthright is sin and suffering. What use is proclaiming that God is dead, when His reach extends so far beyond the grave?

'On your way to the baths?' I look up to see Louisa, who is heading back to the Acceuil.

'That's right. Have you just been?'

'Only on escort duty. Making sure there are no snarl-ups in the women's queue. Don't worry, the men's is always much shorter.'

'I suppose it takes us less time to undress.'

'No, there are fewer of you.'

'Yes, of course.' I feel my knuckles smart.

'We may not have the chance to talk later. As soon as we finish at the Grotto, we're off to the airport. So tell me, have you found the pilgrimage useful? Did you get all you hoped?'

'Far, far more,' I say, with unexpected intensity.

'Yes, I imagine you did.'

'What?'

'Don't look so shocked. Even an old stick like me can put two and two together. A certain person stays out all night, claiming that she was with her mother-in-law.'

'I'm sorry. I hope you don't think I've betrayed your trust.'

'Not mine. Whether you've betrayed anyone else's, I leave to you and your conscience. Just take care, that's all I ask.'

'I thought you'd be horrified.'

'Let me tell you a story: no, not a story, mine.' She glances in the direction of the men's baths. 'Yes, it's quiet – you have the time. Life in the forces can be lonely. Comradeship only goes so far. I used to say I was married to the job (I may even have believed it), but a job can disappoint you as much as a man. Then I met Clive.' I try not to show my surprise. 'He was an academic. A philologist. You wouldn't think we had anything in common – me used to barking out orders, him to studying words – but we did. More than I'd have ever thought possible. We fell in love – we were going to be married. No one in the squadron could credit it. They all made the same assumption as you. It's no use denying it – it's written all over your face … But he was killed in a train crash coming to visit me in High Wycombe (they say it's the safest way to travel). And I soldiered on. I'm sorry – I didn't mean that.' She laughs nervously. 'There again, perhaps I did. At fifty-five, I retired. Back to Chalfont St Giles and my mother. She moved there when my father died. It was a dreadful mistake.'

'Her moving there or your moving in?'

'Both.' We are distracted by a chant that echoes from the Grotto. 'It was as though she'd just been waiting for me in order to give up. Within a few months of my arrival she grew seriously confused, and within a year she'd lost all her marbles. Believe me, nothing in life prepares you for wiping your own mother's bum. I began to drink. I'd never been a stranger to the mess bar but this was something new. Whisky was my tipple, and not just a wee dram. Ten years ago you wouldn't have liked me. Perhaps I should say you'd have liked me even less than you do now.' She waves aside my protests. 'Then one day – a day that on the face of it was no different from any other – I took myself in hand. My mother was dead and I was heading rapidly the same way. I went to AA. I gave myself up to a higher power. In my case that was God. And from that day to this, not a single drop of alcohol has passed my lips. That's the reason I began coming here: not to pray for a miracle but to give thanks for one – the miracle that I'm still alive. A minor miracle, I grant, but one for which I'm profoundly grateful.'

'I think we all are.'

'That's kind of you. Now I've kept you long enough. I have to check on the packing and you have to get to the baths.'

Astounded as ever by the sheer unpredictability of people, I watch as she crosses the bridge. Then, conscious of the time, I stride past the Grotto to the baths, where I find Jamie waiting in a queue which, in its organised chaos, resembles Barnsley Bus Station circa 1970. There is a strict sorting system: hospital pilgrims and their carers in one line; children and their escorts in a second; healthy pilgrims in a third. Each moves at a different pace, although in no discernible order. Priority is given to stretcher cases, priests … and filmmakers, as we discover when, five minutes after showing our permit to an attendant who objects to Jamie's camera, he ushers us inside. A second attendant directs us to one of the small wooden benches in front of a row of blue-and-white curtained cubicles. To my surprise, I find myself next to Lester.

'Jammy bugger!' he says. 'I suppose you waltzed straight in?'

'Fraid so.'

'Some of us have been sitting here the best part of an hour.'

'I wasn't expecting you at all.'

'When in Rome.' He shows no inclination to talk so I look round the shabby vestibule, studying the posters on how to pray. I am about to ask Jamie to pan over them, when an attendant steers Lester and myself into the far left-hand cubicle. He holds Jamie back until I once again produce the permit, which he examines diligently before allowing him in. We join three fellow pilgrims, two stripped to their underpants: a stringy old man with a savage scar across his chest and feet like rock crystal; and a close-cropped young man who might be waiting for an army medical. I have never taken much interest in other men's bodies, either as a source of comparison or fulfilment, but there is enough of the prurient schoolboy in me to gawp at the slack-waisted friar who pulls off his habit, revealing a pair of jazzy boxer shorts and a strikingly protuberant navel. He catches my eye and I quickly stare at the floor. Meanwhile Jamie stands to one side, wreathed in embarrassment, as though he were the one with his pants down.

A hospitaller escorts a young African out of the inner sanctum and summons the friar. I notice that Lester is having trouble unlacing his trainers. 'Would you like any help?'

'Like? No. Need? Yes. Sorry, sorry, thank you. I can't seem to manage this morning. My arms feel as though they've lost a foot overnight. Hey, that's funny. My arms have lost a foot! No, it's not.' I squat and pull off his shoes and socks, leaving his toes looking strangely raw.

The friar returns with a beatific smile that makes me doubly ashamed of my prurience, and the hospitaller leads in the old man.

I gaze at the African who has put on a T-shirt and jeans, the damp patches on his shoulders and back belying all the claims for the miraculous properties of water that dries instantaneously on the skin.

The hospitaller leads out the old man and calls me into a marble-walled chamber with a vaulted grey ceiling and a dangerously slippery floor. An enormous bath stands at the centre, and an image from the *Satyricon* flits irreverently into my mind. Three more hospitallers stand at the ready. Their colleagues must have told them of the filming since they express no surprise at seeing Jamie, camera in hand.

'English?' one asks, in a thick Mediterranean accent. I nod, strangely tongue-tied. A second conducts me to the corner of the room. 'Please take off your shorts and put on this,' he says, in a mild Bostonian twang. He hands me a wringing-wet linen cloth and holds up a towel to protect my modesty. 'Nothing below the waist, please,' he says to Jamie.

'Don't worry,' he replies, 'it's for the BBC.'

With the cloth wrapped loosely around my hips, I approach the bath. I am enough of my mother's son to worry about all the people who have immersed themselves before me. The Friar's skin looked suspiciously sallow. What caused the old man's scar? Has the African been exposed to tropical diseases? I anticipate my commentary as I wonder how many healthy – or relatively healthy – people return from Lourdes sicker than when they arrived, having caught an infection at the baths or a chill from the damp or, simply, taken a tumble on the floor.

I stand on the top step and turn back to Jamie, who has the camera trained on my every move. The American hospitaller takes hold of my arm and asks me to make my intentions. I try to empty my mind, but it is filled with thoughts of Gillian, who has grown so dear to me that I am ready to give up my most cherished precepts, even the one against prayer. After a moment he breaks the silence, saying: 'St Bernadette, pray for us! Holy Mother, pray for us!' before leading me down the steps.

The water is glacial and I feel like a Christmas Day swimmer in the Serpentine. Gripping me tighter than ever, the man directs me to sit down as if on a stool. He draws me back until I am up to my neck in the water. The cold is so intense that I seem to lose all sensation. He then raises me up to face a small plaster statue of the Virgin. I am uncomfortable standing bare-chested in front of her – the *it* has instinctively vanished – until I recall her presence in countless Crucifixions and Pietàs. The man says the Hail Mary and instructs me to the kiss the statue's feet which, whether from courtesy or cowardice, I do without demur. He then guides me up the steps and into the corner, where I unwrap the dripping cloth and clumsily pull on my pants. The first hospitaller escorts me back to the cubicle and calls in the young man, who shows no resentment of my having usurped his place.

'How was it?' Lester asks.

'Teeth-chatteringly cold. But strangely enough, I feel quite warm now.'

'Sometimes you have to live on the edge.'

Looking at him in bemusement, I start to dress. My clothes feel damp but not unpleasant. After a quick goodbye to Lester, I follow Jamie outside to find Sophie and Jewel waiting for us by the river.

'Did you get everything you wanted?' Sophie asks.

'I hope so. You'll have to ask Jamie.'

'Sure, so long as the Great British Public is ready for the sight of the chief in the altogether.'

'The half-together, thank you! We've a quarter of an hour till the Grotto mass. Shall I join you there? There's someone I have to find.'

'If it's the someone I think it is,' Sophie says gently, 'she left the baths with her mother-in-law twenty minutes ago.' My throat constricts as I wonder whether their meeting was planned or if Patricia hurried down here after our talk. With no way of finding out, I suggest that we go straight to the Grotto. The more the film takes shape, the more certain I am that it must stick to the logic of the journey; which makes the final mass the obvious place to end.

At the Grotto, Ken and Derek are setting up for the service. With the help of two Domain officials, they clear the benches of unauthorised pilgrims, arrange the altar and lay out hymn sheets, several of which are immediately scattered by the wind. Shortly afterwards, the Jubilates start to arrive, some in a group from the Acceuil and others in batches from the baths. Ken marshals people to their seats more brusquely than before. I wonder whether his patience has finally snapped or he is simply anxious about time. Even prayer has to defer to Louisa's schedule.

'Toot, toot!' Richard roars down the pavement, pushing Nigel at breakneck speed, an image that risks becoming literal as he swerves to avoid a dwarf with a callipered leg. Geoff, who tears after them, manages to gain control of the wheelchair just as it looks to be heading straight for the river wall. Richard and Nigel rock with uncontrollable laughter. Gillian and Patricia rush towards them but, with neither facing my way, I am left to speculate on their expressions. Geoff wheels Nigel into position beside Brenda, and Gillian threads her arm through Richard's with an intimacy that tortures me. Then, as she leads him to his seat, she turns and fixes me with the most tender, loving and unequivocal smile.

I have passed my A levels; I have been taken on by the BBC; Celia has said 'yes': all in that one smile.

As soon as everyone is settled, Father Paul calls for the Jubilate roll of honour to be brought up to the altar.

'Do you want this, chief?' Jamie asks.

'What? Oh yes, everything.' I struggle to concentrate as four young brancardiers and handmaidens move forward with what looks like an old quilt covered in scraps of paper.

'Are those the names of pilgrims who've died?' I ask Marjorie, who is standing beside us.

'Heavens, no! What a morbid imagination!' she says, nervously fingering her crucifix. 'They're the intentions of all the helpers. We wrote them down during the training day and pinned them on. It's Louisa's idea to help everyone bond. Which it does, of course. Though we may not have time for it next year.'

We sing the hymn, 'Mary Immaculate, Star of the Morning', accompanied by the usual band, although without Fiona, who is too daunted by the crowd to mount the rostrum. Under cover of the prayers, I cast my eye over the assembled ranks of Jubilates, most of whom I shall never see again. I linger on those I chose not to include in the film but whose stories have nonetheless touched me: the teenager whose mental development has stuck at the age of five but whose physical development is normal, leaving her as terrified of her monthly periods as her peers are of pregnancy; the lawyer with breast cancer who has hidden it from her husband for fear of worrying him, pretending that she has spent this week at a conference; the middle-aged man with the tragically unlined face, who shuffles up and down the Domain as though wearing carpet slippers, his every step guided by his eighty year-old father; the woman with cerebral palsy whose sharp mind is obscured by the tortuous process of tapping out her thoughts on her synthesiser, compounded by the robotic male voice in which they are expressed.

Each one of them would have added a different colour to my portrait, but I am confident that none would have changed its shape.

Before the sermon, Father Dave calls on Louisa to deliver the final notices. 'I'm sorry it's not Father Humphrey who's asked me up here because it's the last time I'll have to be obeyed … or even listened to.' She chuckles, to the bewilderment of the bystanders. 'Next year we'll all be in Marjorie's capable hands. So I'd like to take the opportunity to thank everyone who's helped with the running of this year's pilgrimage. You all know who you are and you've all been terrific. I'd also like to thank the hospital pilgrims who've put up with our little foibles – '

'Hear hear!' Brenda interjects.

'Well at least we've one satisfied customer! On a practical note, I'd ask that at the end of mass you proceed straight to the lighting of the pilgrimage candle. That'll be just to my left in one of those strange huts that look like burnt-out railway carriages.' The image startles me. 'Then please make your way as fast as possible back to the Acceuil. Teams A and C to the ward for cleaning duties. Team B with the hospital pilgrims to the top floor to wait for the coaches.'

Louisa steps down and Father Dave preaches a short sermon, which is lost for some in a crackly microphone and for me in contemplation of Gillian's smile. We sing the hymn, 'Sweet Sacrament Divine', during which Father Humphrey consecrates the elements and the brancardiers pass round the collection plates, with Matt and Geoff boldly targeting the onlookers. The offertory gathered, Father Humphrey proclaims the Peace, prompting the entire congregation to break ranks, as though determined to greet everyone with whom they have journeyed over the week. Afraid of tempting fate, I make no attempt to approach Gillian. Instead, I shake Jamie's hand and kiss Jewel and Sophie, before moving on to Derek and Charlotte, Mona and Fleur. Avoiding the crush around the wheelchairs, I head for Lester and Tess. 'Peace be with you,' I say, feeling like an oncologist abandoning them to palliative care.

'Are you getting God, chief?' Jamie whispers, as I return to the crew.

'No, Jamie. Peace. And I have more of it to spread around than I have done in years.'

Everyone resumes his place apart from Nigel, who clasps Richard's hand and refuses to let go. Richard looks alternately perplexed and impatient as he tries to shake off a grip of steely desperation. No one moves to intervene, as though the thought of Nigel's return to life in a geriatric household shames us all. Finally, Gillian walks over to them and, after stroking Nigel's cheek, succeeds in prising them apart. While Richard shows his crushed fingers to Patricia, eliciting surprisingly little sympathy, Gillian crouches beside Nigel and whispers something in his ear which, to judge by his grin, comforts him.

Father Humphrey leads us in prayer. After stressing the link between the manger, or feedbox, in which Mary laid Christ and the altar from which we feed off him, he invites us to do just that, a long-drawn-out process despite the strategically placed assistance of Father Paul and Father Dave. I am amazed to see Gillian standing in line beside Richard and Patricia. Yesterday she was adamant that she could not take communion while in a state of mortal sin, a state that can only have been reinforced by last night. So what has changed? Has she been to confession as well as the baths? Or – it is almost too much to hope – has she refined her sense of sin?

With the walkers returned to their seats and the wheelchairs to their places, we sing the final hymn, 'Dear Mother of our Saviour Christ We Hail Thee, and depart', which is nothing if not to the point. Father Humphrey pronounces the Blessing and we process out of the Grotto, behind the large Jubilate candle with the trademark angel stencilled on the wax, towards what, pace Louisa, looks less like a burnt-out train than a row of kebab stalls. An official directs the two brancardiers who are carrying the candle to place it in a cluster of similar size and varying states of deliquescence. Father Humphrey lifts up Fiona to light it but, despite the priestly wind-shield, the flame repeatedly blows out. So he takes it on himself, succeeding at the fourth attempt.

'May this candle continue our prayers.'

I contemplate lighting a candle for Pippa, a gesture of woeful inad-equacy. Moreover the waste would outrage Celia, who once deeply offended my mother by claiming that Judas was right to condemn Mary Magdalene for pouring oil on Jesus's feet rather than using the money for good works. The thought of my mother prompts me instead to light a candle for her, carefully choosing one of just above average length, balancing her dread of ostentation against my wish that it should last.

'Toot toot! Toot toot!' Richard, back behind the wheelchair, propels Nigel through the crowd, which parts hastily. Linda, however, lingers, with what looks suspiciously like a flirtatious smile.

'You've made a friend for life there, mate,' I say, making him blush.

'Come on you!' Brenda says, twisting her neck a few millimetres towards her companion. 'You'll only encourage him and who knows where it will lead. Filthy beast!' She snorts, prompting Linda to whisk her away. Nigel claps his hands as if the scene had been staged for his benefit, but Richard looks uncharacteristically abashed. I scour the background for Gillian, who is nowhere to be seen.

'A candle, Vincent?' Louisa asks wryly, as I skewer it in place.

'For my mother! It can't do any harm.'

'I told you the spirit of Lourdes would get to you in the end.'

'Some people have managed to remain immune.' I point to the departing Brenda.

'That's up to her … to them,' Louisa says. 'All we can do is present people with it – we can't dictate how they respond. I once saw Clive – my fiancé – give a couple of pounds to a beggar. "He'll only spend it on drink," I said. "What of it?" he replied. "I expect I would if I had his life." You understand what I'm saying?'

'I do.'

'Good. Now we really should head back to the Acceuil, or we may find ourselves missing the plane.'

She moves off and I turn to Richard. 'Have you lost Gillian?'

'No,' he says defensively. 'She's at the river talking to Mother. I expect it's about me.'

Eager to find her, I head first for Jamie, who is standing with Jewel, talking to Lucja, Claire and Martin. 'The coach is picking us up at the hotel, but I have a couple of odds and ends to settle at the Acceuil. Can you grab my case and take it with yours? You know the one – blue with a black band.'

'I should do,' Jamie says. 'I lugged it halfway across Africa.'

'I had food poisoning.'

Jamie winks. I walk through the forest of candles, coming across Maggie, who is talking to an elderly Scottish couple with whom I have barely exchanged one word.

'Maggie, you haven't seen Gillian? Or Patricia,' I add diplomatically.

'Not since the service.'

'If you do, will you tell Gillian I'm looking for her?'

'*If* I do. But I'm about to shoot off.'

'Your filthy habit,' I say lightly.

'Not at all,' she replies, affronted. 'I've promised to take some spring water back for a sick neighbour.'

I reach the final pricket where Tadeusz is holding Pyotr up to the flames. 'See,' he says to me sadly. 'Nothing. I show him the candles and he shows nothing. Not even to close his eyes.' I gaze at the blank face, whose only sign of life is the bubble at the corner of his mouth. 'You should not have lighted the candle,' Tadeusz says, bitter at the betrayal. Then he lays Pyotr tenderly on his shoulder and walks away.

The basilica bells chime noon. In an hour we will be boarding the coach and, in two or three, the plane. I need to know that Gillian has not lost heart: that the intimacy of the bedroom was not washed away at the baths. Images of the service are seared on my brain. All the hope that I took from her smile was dashed when she went up for communion. How can she have welcomed today what she was so adamant about refusing yesterday? Did last night's lovemaking wipe out every notion of sin or, on the contrary, has she confessed and been absolved? Has she chosen the bloodless body of Christ over mine? I stride towards the Acceuil. The time for discretion is over. I shall confront her before the entire pilgrimage if need be. What was it Louisa said about the things that we do to one another in Lourdes being our gift to God? I gave her my love. If she wants to throw it back at me, then let her do so to my face.

'Vincent!' The voice is so vital to my happiness that I need a moment to adjust. 'Vincent!' She crosses the bridge. 'Richard told me I'd find you here.'

'Richard?'

'He said you were lighting a candle.'

'For my mother.'

'Oh, for a moment I thought … never mind! I had to go back and finish packing. I was afraid I'd miss you at the airport. Hospital pilgrims have a separate lounge.'

'I know. We're filming them.'

'Of course. Then I needn't have worried.'

'Did you go to the baths?'

'Yes, it was incredibly moving.'

'So when did you find time to go to confession?'

'I didn't.' She looks at me in surprise.

'But you took communion. What happened to mortal sin?'

'I've seen it in a new light.'

We are no longer in public view but alone in my hotel room. I take her in my arms and kiss her. 'Thank you. Thank you, so much.'

'It's not me you should thank but Patricia.'

'What?'

'Come over here,' she says, slipping out of my grasp but still holding my hand. 'This is the Gave, not the Seine. People are watching.'

'Let them!'

'Please.' She leads me into the square. 'What a day!' she says. 'No, it's scarcely twelve o'clock. What a morning!'

'The morning after the night before?'

'There is that.' She smiles. 'When I got back to the Acceuil, I heard that Richard had been causing trouble and I thought that's it – there's no way I can leave him now.'

'I'm not asking you to,' I say, feeling my heart rip from my chest.

'Please, let me finish! I came to the baths and, in the queue, I met a woman who's been looking after her daughter – a daughter as damaged as Pyotr – for sixteen years.'

'Perhaps she has support? A husband? A lover?'

'No, no husband. No lover. Just love. I realised that my prime – my only – responsibility was to Richard.'

'That's not true!'

'Wait, just wait. I stepped into the bath and I made my intentions. I saw that I was praying for a miracle when one had already happened. You.'

'Yes!' I punch the air. A young boy, walking past with his parents, laughs. Gillian pulls me into the shadow of the colonnade.

'But there are some miracles you have to give up, when you know that they're not meant for you. Like finding a wallet in the street.'

'But even if you don't keep it, you get a reward, don't you? Or is your reward to be in heaven?'

'Are you always going to interrupt? You're worse than Richard.' I fall silent, clinging to the *always* like a drowning man. 'I'd settled everything in my mind, then I came out and met Patricia. She said she needed to talk to me straight away, that it couldn't wait till we were back home. She led me along the riverbank and told me she owed me an apology. "What for?" I asked. "The last eighteen years," she said. "Don't you mean twelve?" I asked. "No," she said, "eighteen." For the first time she seemed to have some inkling of what I'd been through. She said I had the right to some happiness in life. Or else it was like giving me a present and insisting I could only use it her way.'

'She said what?'

'Yes, I know it's strange, a very un-Patricia sort of phrase. I've no idea what got into her. The only thing I can think of is the crystal angel.' I look at her, more baffled than before. 'The one you gave me last night. She saw it and assumed I'd bought it for her. I'm really sorry. But she was so grateful, there was no way I could tell her truth.'

'Don't apologise! If I thought that was all it took, I'd buy her the whole celestial choir.'

'Fool! I promised her I'd never leave Richard. She offered to have him live with her, though, frankly, they wouldn't last a day. I explained that nothing was fixed, but we'd find a way to make it work. In London, in Dorking, in-between. Richard likes you.'

'And against the odds, I like him. We live in an age of step-families. Maybe I could be a step-husband?'

'Be serious!' She laughs. 'Anyway, it's nonsense to worry about the small print. We've only known each other a week. Whatever you think, this place has mysterious powers. Away from it, we may feel quite different.'

'Do you believe that?' I ask. She shakes her head. 'Then why torment yourself?'

'Insurance? You wouldn't, not at first but over time ... you wouldn't resent my commitment to Richard?'

'You're thirty-nine.'

'I know – it's madness. I'm acting like a dizzy schoolgirl!'

'No, I mean, you're only thirty-nine. We might both have to share you with someone else.'

She brushes her hand over her stomach and starts to weep. I clutch her to my chest and wipe her tears with my fingers. 'I never thought I'd be happy again. We will make it work, Gillian. I promise. I can be very resourceful.'

'I don't doubt it!'

'Now we'd better go back to the Acceuil or we'll miss the coach.'

'Sure. No, I almost forgot. You go and I'll meet you there in ten minutes. There's one last thing I have to do.'

'If you think I'm leaving you for a single moment ...'

'You'll make fun of me!'

'Never!'

'All right then – promise you won't say anything.'

'Cross my heart.'

'Remember, you promised.' She drags me across the square towards the statue of the Crowned Virgin.

'Oh no! You can't be serious?'

'You promised! After all, if it hadn't been for Lourdes, we'd never have met.'

I watch as she stands in front of a large rose bed, its railings incongruously strewn with bunches of cut flowers, and bows her head. Meanwhile, Kevin pushes Sheila Clunes in the opposite direction.

'Been Hailing Mary, Sheila?'

'No need. Marjorie Plumley's told me there's already a bed with my name on for next year.'

'I'm happy to hear it. How about you, Kevin?'

———

337

'You taking the piss? I wouldn't come back here if you paid me!'

'May I borrow Kevin a moment, Sheila?' Before she can reply, I grab his arm, leading him further into the square and leaving her temporarily stranded. 'Be honest – it's not all been that terrible, has it?'

'Worse, much, much worse. But I've been a good boy. The Führer's promised to write me a glowing report. Which means they'll let me back in school. From now on I'll keep my head down till I go to college, then I'll make art that will blow all this sky-high.'

'I wish you luck. But you'll find it's remarkably resilient. Believe me, I know.'

'Your trouble is you've gone soft. Ready to give up everything for a sniff of skirt.' He nods towards Gillian.

'Is that so shameful?' I ask, too euphoric to take offence.

'It's pathetic! You're as bad as Matt: you know, the guy I've been hanging out with … at least I did till he met Jenny. He thinks he's found *lurve*. You should have heard the way they carried on when they thought they weren't going to see each other for two whole days. Tragic! I kept them sweating, then told her at the Grotto she could have my place in the van.'

'That's decent of you.'

'No skin off my back. Plus it means I'll be home two days sooner. What I don't get is how none of you have twigged that all this pairing off is a giant con. Love! It's just a myth sold to us by the Church, the media and big business, to keep us enslaved.'

'In which case it's a pretty far-reaching conspiracy.'

'And it's been going on for thousands of years.'

'Kevin! What you doing?' Sheila calls. 'I have a little hole that needs filling.' He winces.

'I better go. They're handing out snacks before the coach.'

'Sure. I'll catch up with you at the airport. But you're wrong about love, Kevin. It's a miracle. At least it's the closest that Lourdes – or anywhere else for that matter – can provide.'

He looks at me with a mixture of despair and disgust and returns to Sheila, straining every muscle to push her towards the bridge. Gillian crosses herself and walks over to me.

'That's me sorted.'

'I hope not.'

'Did you mean what you said before?'

'I'm sorry. I know I promised not to mock.'

'I meant about my – our – maybe having a commitment to someone else?'

'You bet! So long as you promise never to tell her or him or, better still, lots of little thems, where we met.'

'Just checking.' She slips her arm through mine.

'Home?'

'Home!'

Acknowledgements

I owe a particular debt of gratitude to the individuals and organisations with whom I travelled to Lourdes. The Jubilate is a fictitious pilgrimage, but the people I met in the course of my research have inspired me far beyond the pages of this book.

Rupert Christiansen, Marika Cobbold, Emmanuel Cooper, David Horbury, Liz Jensen, James Kent, Bernard Lynch and Ann Pennington gave me valuable help on early drafts of the novel, as did Hilary Sage on the final text.